The Other Hoffmann Sister

Also by Ben Fergusson

The Spring of Kasper Meier

BEN FERGUSSON

The Other Hoffmann Sister

Little, Brown

LITTLE, BROWN

First published in Great Britain in 2017 by Little, Brown

13 5 7 9 10 8 6 4 2

A CIP catalogue record for this book
is available from the British Library.

Hardback ISBN 978-1-4087-0889-7
Trade paperback ISBN 978-1-4087-0890-3

Typeset in Caslon by M Rules
Printed and bound in Great Britain by
Clays Ltd, St Ives plc

Papers used by Little, Brown are from well-managed forests
and other responsible sources.

MIX
Paper from
responsible sources
FSC www.fsc.org   FSC® C104740

Little, Brown
An imprint of
Little, Brown Book Group
Carmelite House
50 Victoria Embankment
London EC4Y 0DZ

An Hachette UK Company
www.hachette.co.uk

www.littlebrown.co.uk

For Tom

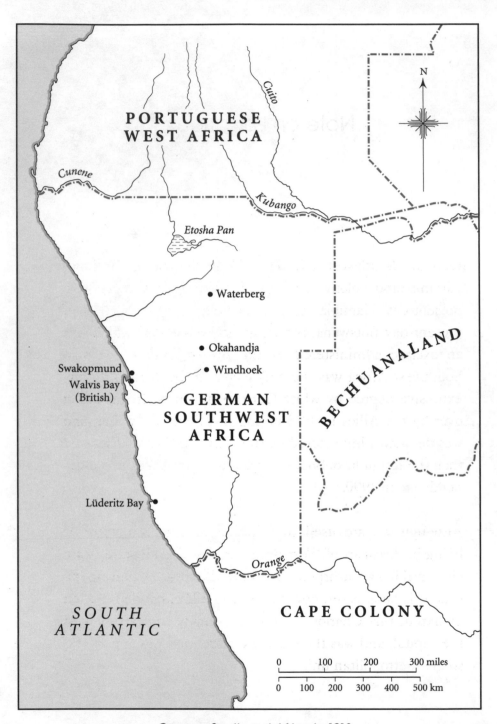

German Southwest Africa in 1918

Note on Locations

German Southwest Africa (1884–1915) was a German-administered colony that broadly shared its borders with present-day Namibia. It also included a small section of present-day Botswana, but excluded Walvis Bay, which was an exclave administered by the British Empire. German Southwest Africa was the only colony to be 'settled' to any extensive degree by white German nationals. It was taken over by the Allies in 1915 during the First World War, and was de facto administered by the Union of South Africa and then the Republic of South Africa until Namibia gained independence in 1990.

Although we are used to thinking of Charlottenburg as being in the heart of West Berlin, it was officially a separate city until it was incorporated into Berlin in 1920. During the time this book is set, however, Berlin had expanded to such an extent that Charlottenburg was already contiguous with the capital, and was therefore understood as being part of a single metropolitan unit.

But oh, the night! oh, bitter-sweet! oh, sweet!
O dark, O moon and stars, O ecstasy
Of darkness! O great mystery of love –
In which absorb'd, loss, anguish, treason's self
Enlarges rapture, – as a pebble dropp'd
In some full wine-cup, over-brims the wine!

Die Nacht aber! Bittersüß! Oh, süß!
Die Dunkelheit aber, der Mond und die Sterne, Oh, die
     Verzückung
der Dunkelheit! Oh, das große Geheimnis der Liebe –
in dem, aufgenommen, Verlust, Qual, Verrat sogar
die Entrückung vergrößern – wie ein Kiesel in den
vollen Weinbecher geworfen, der ihn zum Überlaufen
     bringt.

From *Aurora Leigh,* by Elizabeth Barrett Browning,
German translation by Ingrid Hoffmann

PART ONE

— Arriving —

Okahandja,
German Southwest Africa

— 1902 —

For Ingrid Hoffmann the story of her sister's disappearance began in their first weeks in Southwest Africa, when she and Margarete went hand in hand to the top of the staircase to listen to their parents celebrating with the good Germans of Okahandja. Dusk was descending and candles had been lit in the hallway below. Intermittently insects flamed in them, emitting thick lines of black smoke that travelled high and straight in the still air, dissipating out of sight. The children sat down on the top step, flicking their ears, eyes and noses as flies landed on them – easy gestures that had already become habitual.

Nora, a strict Herero woman, snored behind them. She had fallen asleep in her chair in front of their bedroom door and they had escaped past her in the dark. Below, the house was filled with voices and clinking glasses. Their father said, 'Yes, I'm sure that won't be a problem ...' and their mother was laughing and saying, 'No, I hardly saw myself as a farmer's wife ...' The guests sounded drunk, entertained and happy.

Someone stepped into the hall and the sisters scrambled backwards into the shadows. It was a Schutztruppe soldier, his dress uniform too tight. His face was grey and his dark moustache moist and sagging. He glanced around before undoing his tight belt and removing his jacket. There were large roundels of sweat on his shirt that made the white cotton see-through; Ingrid could see the clumped black hair beneath his armpits. He stood like this for some time, one hand on his hip, the other holding out the jacket like a coat-room attendant, until someone approached from the drawing room and he pretended to be searching it.

'Everything all right?' said the other man. He was bald and his neck and face were burnt claret; his pale crown looked oddly separate, like an egg in a cup.

'Yes,' said the moustachioed man, pulling the jacket back on, 'there was something in it. What with scorpions and the like. Better whip it off, than—'

'There was a scorpion in it?' the bald man said.

'Well, it's not there now.' The moustachioed man did his belt back up over the waist of the jacket and dabbed at his forehead with a handkerchief. 'What do you think of all this lot, then? A bit lavish, isn't it?'

'They've got money,' said the bald man. 'Or they want you to think they do. That wife is hardly aristocratic.'

'They will be soon – by association. The husband's bought all of Baron von Ketz's good land around the wells, the house too. Everything he wouldn't sell to Brandt in eighty-six. They're travelling there tomorrow; taking their daughters with them.'

'That'll be a rude awakening: Baron von Ketz as your neighbour. Imagine! Did you see the boy when they were last in town? Awkward little sop.'

The bald man laughed. 'I did. You know, the Baroness lost eleven children. Eleven! He was the one that survived, if you can believe it.' There was a screened open window on the landing; the cicadas were loud and Ingrid heard a regular duck-like squawk, which their father had been unable to identify as either bird, mammal or amphibian. 'She was a beauty once – the Baroness,' the bald man said. 'And rich. When she arrived here, there was a trail of men after her; that's what old Altersdorf told me. Then she ends up stuck on the veld with von Ketz wasting her money trying to grow mahangu. He's got through her fortune in ten years with his experiments. There's a house back in Germany, Buckow I think, that's falling to pieces.'

Ingrid was beguiled that they were talking about her family, as if the Hoffmanns were important. Her mother really wasn't an aristocrat, so it didn't occur to her to be offended by that. It was very sad about the Baroness and all of her dead children. They used to eat sops in gravy in Germany, but she didn't know what it meant to be one. She didn't understand what the man meant by 'experiments' and pictured the Baron like an apothecary behind a table of glass bottles and India rubber bungs.

'They'll realise their mistake the moment they meet him.'

'They just see the title,' the moustachioed man said. 'Brandt thinks they're Rhenish farming stock. He'd never heard of any Hoffmanns before.'

'Excuse me.'

The men turned to the door that led onto the veranda. There was a silhouette behind the mosquito screen.

'Oi! Get out of here,' one of them said, his mouth jagged. The tone of the hallway had changed and the men's chests were rising and their brows lowering, like dogs.

'I'm here to see a Herr Hoffmann.'

'It's von Ketz's kaffir,' said the moustachioed man. His mouth pursed and he looked at the bald man for support.

'Wait there,' he said to the shadow. 'And get off the bloody veranda.'

The man's form disappeared from behind the screen and, seeing him gone, the soldiers left the hall.

Margarete, whose chickenpox had only abated a few weeks earlier, stroked the itching edge of one of the brown scabs on her knee and said, 'I want to look at him.'

'No,' said Ingrid.

But Margarete was already creeping down the staircase, low like a cat, the dry boards groaning beneath her feet.

'He'll see you inside,' Ingrid said.

'I'll look from the study where it's dark,' said Margarete, and before Ingrid could catch up, she had slipped into the small front room. Ingrid crawled down after her, shaking her foot whenever anything grazed it, in case it was a scorpion, or a cockroach, or a snake.

In the study the shutters were closed. Margarete was holding on to the windowsill, staring through the slats down into the street. Ingrid stared too, her fingers on the sill touching the sharp grains of sand that covered every surface and filled every crack in the house. Standing on the road, his hands folded neatly in front of him, she could see a young black man dressed, disappointingly, in smart German clothes. She had hoped at least for him to be bare-chested, like the Ovambo warrior foil-blocked onto the front of her book.

'I'm tired,' Margarete said, already bored of the game, and dropped her head onto Ingrid's shoulder, so that her long blonde hair tickled Ingrid's bare arms. Ingrid, who

6

was already as tall as her older sister, put her arms beneath Margarete's armpits. Margarete went stiff and Ingrid manoeuvred her towards the door like a puppet, rocking her from side to side. This was the standard conclusion to most adventures instigated by Margarete: agitation, impulsiveness, insolence, laughter, followed by stupor. If they were caught, it ended in screaming and tears. If they weren't, it ended like this – Margarete tired and dead-eyed, sometimes tearful.

Ingrid reached for the door handle, but heard the bald man shout, 'You can wait for him in the study, apparently. Don't you touch anything.'

Margarete came to life and the girls scrambled around the room, their hands touching the dusty desk, the bookcases, trunks and chests, trying to find a hiding place. 'The sofa,' Margarete hissed, and they dropped to the floor and scrambled backwards, their knees scratching on the rug's rough pile. The door opened and the black man walked in, carrying a candle.

'Oh, hello,' he said. 'I didn't realise the room was occupied.' Ingrid saw that the man was very young, that his skin was less dark than the other Africans', and his nose and high cheeks were peppered with black freckles. He was tall like a Herero, but wore German tan breeches and knee-high boots. His jacket was navy rather than soldiers' beige, and was made of cheaper, thinner fabric – a rough cotton that had taken on a sheen with use. And the sleeves were too short, revealing the muscles of his forearms. He filled the room with a different smell than the other men – it was clove oil, which reminded Ingrid of both Christmas Lebkuchen and a tooth abscess her father had had.

Margarete got to her feet and said, 'Yes, well you shouldn't barge into rooms in other people's houses, I suppose.' When the man looked around the room, she said, 'This isn't where we sleep, if that's what you think. Ingrid left something down here, and I had to come with her, because she was scared.'

'I was not,' Ingrid said, standing too.

'Be quiet, Little Fly.' Margarete turned to the man, 'It's none of your business what we were looking for.'

'I see,' said the man and put the candle down on the desk. 'You're in charge here, then?'

Margarete shrugged. 'I suppose I am. I am the oldest.'

'You are older than me?' he said. 'You look very young.'

'I'm thirteen actually, so I'm the oldest white person.'

The man nodded. 'Then use your power for good, and tell a tired man where he might sit to wait for your father?'

He didn't look tired at all and Ingrid wondered whether they should let him sit down. Margarete pointed to the shabbiest piece of furniture in the room: a worn wooden chair, with a seat of shredded wicker. The man sat; the chair creaked.

'Are you a Hottentot?' Ingrid said.

Margarete carefully shifted her heel onto Ingrid's toes and transferred all of her weight onto it. Ingrid squealed and the man laughed. 'No,' he said, 'I am half Herero, half German.'

'Half white?' Ingrid said.

'A Baster,' said Margarete.

The man tipped his head to one side. 'Not quite, Fräulein. A Baster is half African, half Afrikaans. There is not a drop of Afrikaans in me.'

'Do you speak Baster though?' Ingrid said.

'There is no Baster language,' Margarete said. 'You speak

8

Herero and German. You don't have a language of your own if you're half-caste.'

Ingrid frowned. 'Is that true?' she said, turning to the man.

He nodded.

'Do you mind?' she said.

He laughed. 'I've never really thought about it.'

'What's it like to speak another language?' Ingrid said.

The man seemed genuinely perplexed by the question. 'I haven't spent much time thinking about it. In Africa there are many languages, so it is not so very special.'

But Ingrid thought it was special; she thought it was wonderful.

'Do you live in the bush?' Ingrid said.

'Let's go back upstairs,' said Margarete, and grabbed Ingrid's hand.

'Why?' Ingrid said.

'Because Papa's coming.'

'Your sister is probably right,' the man said.

'Have you ever seen a giraffe?' Ingrid said. 'We haven't.'

'Of course,' the man said. 'But don't worry – you have been on the coast until now, and there are no giraffes there.'

Ingrid recalled staring at the dark waves lapping onto the sand at Walvis Bay, hoping to see animals, but seeing only a barren wall of dunes. She had imagined a port like Hamburg – people carrying trays of wares on their heads, bicycles, prams and women in pinafores, the shadows of gulls in the mist, the smell of brown coal, seawater and fried fish, high brick buildings rising from the water like cliffs. But Walvis Bay was like a shimmering smear in the desert, some rocks baked dry, a few British houses, and behind it mile upon mile of sand. They turned the ship's engines off, the mechanical hum was suddenly gone and she heard the sea and the whisper of sand blowing onto the great metal hull.

'Where then?' they heard their father saying. 'Oh, I see.'

'Don't tell him we're here,' Margarete whispered. 'Do you understand?'

The man nodded and put his finger to his lips. The girls scrambled backwards under the sofa.

'Your hair,' Margarete said, and Ingrid scraped it up and held it behind her head, feeling the metal springs of the sofa pushing into the sides of her hand.

'Hans is it?' their father said, coming into the room, small and energetic. He smoothed his sandy hair, frowned and said, 'Or you have a . . . ? Do you have a surname? Of course you do. It's . . . ?'

'Ziegler.'

'Ah, is it? We'll call you Hans, I suppose. That's normal, I imagine.'

'As you wish, Herr Hoffmann.'

'Well, Baron von Ketz was very complimentary, so I hope you don't mind coming over to us. You've been with the von Ketzes for some time, is that right?'

'Over fifteen years. Since I was born, sir.'

'Indeed.' Herr Hoffmann blushed and the scar beneath his right eye, cut in his university fraternity, stood out neat and white. He shifted his weight and said, 'You must know the family very well. I'm sure we'll get on with them. One must with neighbours, and they've already been so generous since we bought the land. Sending you and Nora, for one – letting us have you both. I hope we get along with them.'

Hans seemed unsure of how to respond to this modest concern. He offered a stilted nod and muttered, 'Yes, sir.'

'What are they like, the von Ketzes?' her father said.

Hans stared about the floor blinking. 'They are as they should be,' he said, carefully pushing each word of the odd sentence out.

Her father, finally perceiving the awkwardness of the exchange, cried, 'Good, good,' and rattled the locked drawer of his desk. 'You can write, I hear. German.'

'Yes, sir. And French and English. A little Dutch. Herero of course, and I can understand many of the other native languages.'

'Well, that's excellent – quite excellent. I had hoped to get the girls a tutor, you know, but it seems that Southwest is not a magnet for sensitive intellectuals. Von Ketz wrote to suggest you as a houseboy, and when he mentioned your, well, your accomplishments, that really was for us a . . . That will be useful. If you can give the girls at least a bit of language – the normal ones, I mean – then we'll be a few steps ahead, if they want to return to the city or Europe. One never knows who they'll marry, does one? But I suppose you don't have children.'

'No sir.'

'You speak German well – very well. But you're half German, aren't you?' and before Hans could answer, their father added, 'Yes, best not to talk about that with the girls – black and white makes most sense, doesn't it?'

'Yes, sir,' Hans said.

'Ingrid will badger you mercilessly, I'm afraid. She intends to learn everything and used to drive Nanny mad. Margarete needs to be strong-armed into reading a word of German, let alone anything foreign, so you must do the best you can with her, but don't expect any miracles.'

In the dark of the sofa, Ingrid reddened at this insult –
besides, she had had no nanny to annoy in the first place, so
that was also a lie. She moved forward to defend herself, but
Margarete grabbed a fistful of her black hair, and her father
said, 'The farm – what's it like?'

'It's hot most of the year, sir. It's the veld and it's very
empty. But it has a beauty of its own, you might say.'

Their father laughed. '"A beauty of its own." Ha! Listen
to you! You're a veritable Schiller, the way you talk. How
funny. I thought you lot would all be leather skirts and
bones through the nose, but listen to you! "A beauty of its
own." Wonderful stuff. That is good. Well, tomorrow morning then. Until then.'

And he was gone.

Ingrid stuck her head out and said, 'Will we see giraffes
on our way to the farm?'

'Maybe,' Hans said.

'I'm sure we'll see some when we all live in the bush
together.'

Hans smiled and her sister pulled her out from under the
sofa, through the door and back upstairs.

*

The journey to the farm was by bullock wagon. Ingrid and
Margarete sat in the wagon waiting in the red dusk, brushing flies from their faces with their grubby hands. The
commissioner's daughter had given Margarete a horse-tail
whip for the flies, but she flicked it with too much alacrity,
striking Ingrid in the face while she was trying to read,
making her scream. Their mother wrested the whip out
of Margarete's hands and threw it back onto the commissioner's veranda, where his daughter, embarrassed, picked

it up and took it back into the house. Margarete cried for a few minutes, then sat in silence, the dirty rivulets of tears dry on her face.

The bullock wagon was a biblical-looking transportation, a tubular white canopy on a wooden frame, pulled by sixteen oxen, led at the front by a Herero boy, and whipped from the wagon seat by an Afrikaner. He wore a wide Schutztruppe-style hat, the brim pinned up at one side, which, along with his stone-coloured shirt and trousers, was covered in salty tide marks, showing the outer limits of his sweating. Ingrid was embarrassed by her father, who wore a similar outfit, but crisp and pristine, as if he had dressed up as the driver for a parlour game. In the hot purple shade of the white canvas, she kept her eyes on the back of the driver's head, where his hair stuck to his red neck in sweaty spikes, and intermittently she sniffed the stinging sharpness of his body odour mixed with the dung of the oxen, that she thrilled at seeing pat-patting from under their lifted tails.

In the heat of summer, it was decided they should travel at night where the roads were good enough, and rest during the hottest part of the day, but there was already a problem. On his journey in, Hans had been stopped near Osana, on the banks of the Swakop, and two traders posing as officials had made a show of checking his papers, then confiscated his horse. Unarmed and outnumbered, Hans had completed the journey on foot. It had therefore been assumed that he would travel in the second of the two wagons that Ingrid's father had procured, but the supplies Herr Hoffmann had bought in Okahandja were stacked too high to allow extra passengers.

Their parents stood on the street arguing. Her mother dominated the scene with a height that she had bequeathed to Ingrid, and a constant motion, which Margarete had inherited. In her early middle age, though, Frau Hoffmann had lost Margarete's moth-like fragility; she was equine, long and powerful, always on the verge of being dangerously startled, her fingers permanently striking her broad chest, signalling the relentless onset of indigestion. Herr Hoffmann listened shaking his head with exasperation, small and – next to the other sun-wrinkled settlers – incredibly boyish-looking, with a thick mop of blond hair. Beside his wife, it was enough to inspire glances and titters, this Amazon and her David, but they were practised in entering rooms chin up, unimpeachable.

Ingrid was thirsty and asked for water. Her mother, still on the street, held up her hand to silence her, saying to their father, 'Are we to sit the girls on the kaffirs' laps?'

Hans and Nora stood away from the road. Hans, very still, carried only a small satchel slung across his chest; Ingrid marvelled at his neatness, after the journey from the von Ketzes' farm, thinking of their own trunks piled up behind her. Nora was almost as tall as him, her eyes were slender like his, but her mouth was smaller, fixed in a disapproving pout. She wore a bright red headscarf and was wrapped in a blue cotton shawl, giving her a look, Ingrid thought, of the French Revolutionaries in her copy of *Les Misérables*.

Both Hans and Nora were impassive, staring blankly at the cattle. Later, she would learn that she was meant to see the blacks as furniture, to believe that they were no more concerned about the family's talk than the snakes beneath the floorboards, but for now she was mortified and ashamed of her mother for talking about people as if they weren't there.

After several return trips to the commissioner's house, and cries of 'this God-forsaken desert' and 'follow you round the damn world for your filthy money,' their parents quietly climbed into the wagon, their mother sitting between the girls, their father opposite.

Herr Hoffmann patted his leg and whistled and, astonishingly, with a scrabble of claws, a dog, honey- and black-patched, jumped into the wagon. Its ears lay flat to its head above its large brown eyes and it moved forward with vast supplication, wagging its tail in wide swings that distorted its body. The girls, open-mouthed and hushed, said, 'Is it ours?'

'Yes,' said Herr Hoffmann.

'It's a working dog, girls,' their mother said. 'You aren't to make it a pet.'

They reached out their hands to touch its fur, watching their mother to see if she would disapprove. She nodded wearily and the girls stroked the animal and it whimpered with delight.

'What's it called?'

'She's called Pina,' their father said. 'After her owner's daughter. Died of typhus, poor thing. And the owner.'

'Johannes!'

'Oh Hedwig,' he said. 'You mustn't be so soft.'

The driver lifted his hand, the plaited leather whip arched upwards impossibly high against the purple sky then bowed and cracked, causing the animals to low and shuffle and the wagon to jerk forward. Pina, in an ecstasy of petting, laid her head on the wooden floor and let out a sharp whine of joy.

The town dissipated, as did the sun, dropping away not in a slow blue haze, but a dazzling burst of red, striated with thin purple cloud. Tired, but kept awake by the strange sounds of the veld and their mother's stiff body, the girls stared out of the wagon until the blackness afforded a few grey shapes, lit by the carpet of stars overhead.

'Are there lions?' Ingrid said.

'No idea,' her father said. 'Hans, what do you say?'

Her mother tensed in the dark and muttered, 'Be an example.'

Ingrid shifted on the wooden seat to catch a glimpse of Hans, but only heard his voice the other side of the canvas answer, 'There may be lions – they often come at night. You would hear lions.'

'Are there more flies where we are going than in Okahandja?' Ingrid said.

'The same amount of flies,' Hans said.

'Are there locusts?' Ingrid said.

'Yes, there are sometimes locusts. The Damara drive them into fires and eat them.'

The girls squealed and their father laughed.

'Have you ever eaten locusts?' Ingrid said, the volume of her voice dying under the weight of her mother's glaring eyes, the whites of which had emerged from the darkness.

'No, Fräulein Ingrid,' Hans said. 'I am not a Damara.'

Her mother reached over slowly, as if she was going to brush something off Ingrid's dress, but instead pinched her leg hard, producing a burning, bruising pain of such intensity that Ingrid threw herself into her father's lap and sobbed into the new cotton of his trousers, which were stiff and smelt of vinegar.

*

Eventually Ingrid was lifted onto the sacks of provisions and laid next to her sister. As she was moved she murmured in protest, calling for Pina. It was her mother who picked her

16

up, kissing her, but Ingrid refused to look at her, her leg still aching. She hoped that they would bathe the next day, if they had already arrived, and she could let her mother see the bruise that she could feel forming like blackened lips. Their mother became sorrowful if her pinches bruised them, and if they pretended to be scared of her and didn't let her touch the bruises it made her cry.

Ingrid lay down on the sacks, which were itchy where the sacking found bare patches of skin at her neck, and between her long socks and the hem of her petticoat. The wagon shifted. The smell of hessian was strong and her sister's hair crept across the sacks and found its way into her mouth. She wanted to dream about the languages that Hans was going to teach her. She imagined herself at a dance, someone offending Margarete in English or French, and her turning and saying perfectly, idiomatically, '*Well, that's rather rum, and you'd better shut up.*' The aggressors would look at her askance, the dancers would stop, astounded by her skill. She tried to hold on to the joy of this feeling, but found herself, in the heat, sunk into the sacks, attacked by sleep – it washed over her in dark waves, pulling her down in jerks so strong that they woke her back up again, until she startled herself awake and found the wagon silent and full of sleep, but for the clatter of the wheels and the groaning of the cattle.

Ingrid crept down from the sacks and over her father's outstretched leg and sat on the floor of the wagon. She held her arm out in the dark and Pina came to her and licked her forearm and elbow, then settled down in the semicircle made by her legs and torso.

'Hans?' Ingrid said quietly, her fingers exploring Pina's fur.

There was a pause, and then he said, 'Yes, Fräulein Ingrid.'

'Are you going to walk all night?'

'I'll walk as long as we travel.'

'Aren't you tired?'

'We'll sleep tomorrow, Fräulein,' he said.

She liked the wise depth of his voice.

'Aren't you thirsty?' she said.

'I'll drink in the morning.'

The driver muttered something in Afrikaans, but Ingrid couldn't understand what he'd said.

'Why do you keep breathing like that?'

'Like what?' Hans said.

'Little gasps. Like you're afraid.'

Nora said, 'Best let Herr Ziegler rest, Fräulein Ingrid. Best get some rest yourself.'

Ingrid frowned. How could Hans get any rest, when he was walking? But she didn't ask any more questions and lay down on the bare wood of the wagon, holding the dog. She could see the stars and the cooler night air touched her face and she fell asleep.

*

Ingrid woke to the sound of a river and the splash of hooves. They wouldn't cross a river in the dark, would they? she thought as the wheels of the wagon broke into the water and she felt the freshness of spray in the air. How would Hans get across? But she was already drifting back to sleep, rocked by the jerking wagon.

The heat woke her. She could hear cicadas and the hard clatter of shoes on the floor of the wagon, which rocked as people climbed out. She rolled onto her back and saw her sister sitting up on the sacks, looking disoriented. Pina stretched on her forelegs and yawned, letting out a high whine like an iron gate.

'Are we there?' Ingrid said.

Margarete squinted at the wagon's bright opening. 'I don't think so.'

They were on a great plain of grass, pale yellow and green, shifting dry in the hot morning wind, dotted with flat acacia trees, like cloud islands floating over smears of silvery thorn.

'Where's Mama and Papa?' Ingrid said.

Margarete climbed down from the sacks and draped herself over the dog. Stale-breathed, she whispered, 'They're going to the toilet, I suppose.'

Ingrid smiled. 'But there aren't any toilets here.' The girls giggled.

Margarete's laughter faded.

'What is it?' Ingrid said, recognising the forced smile that had presaged many sad events in Germany: Margarete pulling over a cabinet that contained their mother's good dinnerware; her scratching the horses' eyes out on the painted chest in the hallway; and the night she had disappeared into the steep woods above Cochem when she was ten, returning grubby and bewildered the next day when they were sure she was dead.

'I'm just tired, Little Fly,' Margarete said, and let go of the dog, climbing down from the wagon, jerking her head away from the oxen's flicking tails. Ingrid followed and then Pina, who squatted, creating a curling trail of urine, a black worm in the amber earth. They stared over the veld, that became more and more bare as it reached a mountain of crumbling red stone and dark green scrub, at the bottom of which was a house.

'Is that the farm?' Ingrid said, afraid of the bare little building.

'No, no,' Hans said.

The girls turned. He was standing by one of the wagon's wheels with a tin cup in his hand and a spoon. The sweat on his forehead reflected the sun as a large white spot above his left eye. He smiled.

'Who lives there then?' Ingrid said.

'Baron and Baroness von Ketz and their son.'

'Oh,' said Ingrid, and at the mention of aristocratic names, they turned back to the house, shielding their eyes. There was a shallow creek snaking past the front of the land, with what looked like a wooden bridge as a crossing, bleached almost white. But the house itself was drab – small and wooden, broken black shingles on the roof, glistening with spots of melted tar. There was nothing around it at all – no trees, just a few outhouses made of brick stacked open to let the wind through. It was nothing like the immense white villa of verandas and balconies that Ingrid had modelled in her imagination on the grandest buildings in Okahandja.

'Baron and Baroness von Ketz live there?' Margarete said.

Hans nodded. He was spooning water onto the wagon wheels.

'What are you doing?' Ingrid said.

'You shouldn't talk to him any more, Little Fly,' Margarete said. 'They'll be back soon.'

Ingrid watched him drip the water onto the silvery wood, staining it black.

'It's for the wheels,' Hans said. 'To stop them cracking. Wagons should be kept in the shade, but there's no shade here.'

'What if we need to drink it?' Margarete said, leaning on the great wheel, so that Hans had to stop his work.

'We are only two hours away now,' Hans said, standing back, holding the spoon out ready to start again when Margarete moved away. 'There will be fresh water at the farmhouse. There is a well. Your father has bought very shrewdly.'

'I'm not sure it's right to talk about what our father does or doesn't buy,' Margarete said. 'I'm not sure it's your business to comment on it at all.'

Hans face died as it had in Okahandja when their mother was swearing. It was as if his soul had temporarily left his body. He didn't seem offended, he didn't seem anything; he seemed not to be present at all.

Ingrid pointed to the von Ketzes' farm. 'What about their bit of the farm? Was that good to buy?'

They heard a stifled cackle and turned. It was from Nora, hidden from view on the shaded side of the wagon.

'Baron von Ketz bought all of this land,' Hans said, alive again. 'But your father bought most of it from him, except this corner where their plot is.'

'Is the bit we bought better?' Ingrid said.

'Ingrid, we shouldn't talk about being better,' said Margarete. 'It's vulgar.'

'It is better situated,' Hans said. 'There are wells with clean water. Herero, sometimes Nama, sometimes Damara when it is very dry, will come a long way for the wells there. They have never been owned, the wells.'

'How silly,' Ingrid said. 'Why didn't anyone buy them before?'

Hans shrugged. 'Now someone has.'

Margarete pulled at Ingrid's hand and said. 'Let's go. This isn't important. We shouldn't be asking about other people's money.'

'It is important if they're going to be our friends.'

'They're not going to be our friends. They're aristocrats and Papa's a farmer.'

'But there's no one else to be friends with here!' Ingrid said.

'You'll learn the hierarchy when you get some proper schooling. The Kaiser, aristocracy, merchants, farmers, peasants and then the kaffirs,' Margarete said. 'And then dogs, I suppose.' She picked up Pina and climbed into the wagon with her and dropped down with such force that the metal suspension creaked.

Ingrid turned back to Hans and whispered, 'Don't mind Margarete – she gets gloomy sometimes and says cruel things. But we'll be friends, won't we?'

'Of course, Fräulein Ingrid.'

'There won't be any girls to play with, I suppose,' she said sadly.

'That's probably right,' Hans said.

'What's "girls" in French?' she said.

'*Filles*,' said Hans.

'Teach me something to remember in French,' Ingrid said.

'You had better wait in the wagon with your sister, Fräulein Ingrid.'

'Just teach me one line,' she persisted. 'Something I can learn by the time I get to our farm. Something just to repeat.'

He squinted over at the von Ketzes' farmhouse. 'I can't think of anything appropriate.'

'You're thinking of something though,' she said. 'I can tell.'

He smiled. His face was perfect: the features fine, the jaw smooth, the nose sprayed with black freckles, the hair trim, the ears small; perfect except for a scar, a smooth rivulet the same colour as the rest of his skin that ran from his eyebrow almost to his hairline. '*Comme je descendais des Fleuves impassibles,*' he said, '*Je ne me sentis plus guidé par les haleurs.*'

The sound of it thrilled her and she mouthed it as he said it, then tried to repeat it, saying, '*Commje desendey floves impossible, jenemesent . . .*' and then she was lost.

Hans laughed. 'That's very impressive. You are very good at remembering.'

She flushed red, but defended herself, saying, 'But you just said it.'

He chuckled. 'Try again,' he said. '*Comme je descendais des Fleuves impassibles.*'

'*Commeje desendey floves impossible.*'

'*Je ne me sentis plus guidé par les haleurs.*'

'*Jeneme sonti ploo giday parles aler.*'

'Can you remember it all?'

'*Commejedesendey flovesimpossible jenemesontiploogiday parlesaler.*'

'Well, there you are,' Hans said. 'We will teach you in no time.'

Ingrid wanted to stare at his face and speak French until she was told to stop, but, afraid of her parents, she moved away from him and drew shapes in the dust with the toe of her boot, biting her lip to keep from smiling, and repeating in her head, over and over, '*Commejedesendeyflovesimpossible-jenemesontiploogidayparlesaler.*'

*

When her parents returned, she was at the wagon's steps, and her mother lifted her in. The wagon moved off. Ingrid knew they must be close to the farm, because her mother set about combing their hair and washing their faces roughly with water from a leather flask that had been warmed in the sun.

'The farm,' Hans announced, and they saw in the distance a house more impressive than the von Ketzes'. It was a long building of large ochre stones divided by thick white mortar, crouching low on the veld, topped with a great metal roof, painted red. The size of the roof and the brightness of the sun on it made the house beneath look as if it were cowering in the shadows, like a turtle beneath its shell. Around the house the thorn had been cleared and the yard was marked out by a low wooden fence with a single rung. There was otherwise nothing to signal what was veld and what was garden; the fenced land was barren except for a row of high, red-barked gum trees that hid one end of the building.

In the shade of the gum trees were two men on horses. As the wagon neared, the men resolved into two very different figures. The older man wore the boots, beige breeches and jacket common to Germans in Southwest Africa. His skin was livid red and his small black eyes were shaded by a wide-brimmed hat. He sat on his horse, holding the reins in one hand, the other in a fist resting on his side. He looked like the sculptures of famous men on horseback that Ingrid had seen in Hamburg.

The other man was barely a man at all – a long thin boy in a shirt and brown trousers, his hat covering a compact head, tanned brown, but with a few red spots around his mouth, and rings of them about his neck where he had shaved. His sleeves were rolled up and the hair on his coffee-coloured arms was bright blond. He sat up straight in his saddle like a boy in a village parade. As the cattle in front of the wagon turned, coming to a halt in a tangle of cracking whip and animal groans, the horses shifted nervously. The boy jerked on his horse until it was still again, the older man moved fluidly above his like a gyroscope.

The Hoffmanns climbed down from the wagon and the men dismounted and tied their horses to one of the trees. The older man came forward and shook Herr Hoffmann's hand. 'You're here,' the man said. Ingrid could hear the cattle snorting and the high echoing whistle of a bird of prey in the blue sky. She stared at the man's face; despite the youthful darkness of his hair and stubble, his scarlet skin was striated with deep folds and wrinkles and his teeth were yellow and worn down, like a sheep's.

'Baron von Ketz,' Herr Hoffmann said brightly. 'You are too kind to wait for us here. You have been too kind already.'

Ingrid had imagined a Baron to be a slim feminine sort of person, with a silk waistcoat, medals and lambchops. She had a weary sense that all of her fantasies were going to be frustrated in Southwest.

'Someone had to be here,' the Baron said, and offered his hand to Frau Hoffmann.

'You've really been too kind,' she said.

'Emil! Introduce yourself!' the Baron said. 'My boy has had little company – he's become rude.'

The boy moved forward and took Herr Hoffmann's hand. 'It's nice to meet you,' he said, and offered his hand quickly to Frau Hoffmann. Unlike his father, he continued on to Margarete and then Ingrid, who took his hand, and felt the dry, alien warmth of it. No one had ever shaken her hand before, and she held on to it for too long.

'We won't keep you,' the Baron said, 'but I didn't want to leave the house with the servants in charge. You must get the better of them immediately; it's not like at home.' He looked over at Hans and shouted, 'Where's your horse, boy?'

'It was confiscated, Herr Baron,' Hans said. 'At the last river crossing.'

The Baron strode towards Hans with his fist raised and Ingrid flinched, but he drove it into the wood of the wagon, causing it to heave on its suspension. 'Jesus Christ, boy!'

'Herr Baron, the girls,' her mother said, laughing the last words to take the sting out of the criticism.

The Baron flicked away the comment and Ingrid saw that his knuckles were bleeding.

'Traders?'

'Yes, sir.'

'Damn it!' he said. He absently rubbed his knuckles against his pale trousers, back and forth, making six soft brown lines that crossed like a Chinese character.

'You need water?' he said to Hans.

'No sir, I've drunk.'

The Baron turned to Herr Hoffmann. 'It's all there for you. We've moved everything we need. You saw the new house on the way in, so you know where we are. I need Hans right away. I will still need him from time to time – I hope that was clear. You'll see he's invaluable. There's Herero up on our land – blacks will drive their cattle across your land willy-nilly if you don't put a stop to it. You'll see soon enough. You don't need him right away?' This last question was spoken as a statement.

'No,' Herr Hoffmann said.

'Good,' said the Baron. 'It's all there, in the house. Be careful of the snakes, especially in the water tank, and don't open up the windows tonight, unless you've got mosquito nets – you'll be eaten alive. Anything big enough to do you any harm, shoot it – kaffirs too.' He pointed to the horses tied up beneath the gum trees and said to Hans, 'Take Gernot. Emil will walk back.'

The Hoffmanns looked over the shimmering heat of the veld. 'How long is the walk?' Frau Hoffmann said, touching her neck with her index and middle finger.

'Not more than three hours. Quicker if there are lions out,' the Baron said, and laughed, turning to the Hoffmanns to signal that this was a joke. They mumbled a little muted laughter, except for Margarete, who said, 'I'm tired, Mama.'

'Perhaps Emil could stay with us until you're back?' Frau Hoffmann said.

'I won't come again tonight and he'll need to get back before dark – the Baroness shouldn't be left alone. It's a nasty corner we've been left with. Don't worry about him – the more they're in the sun, the hardier they get. Same for your girls.'

Frau Hoffmann's eyes wandered nervously over Ingrid's face and then her sister's.

'Come on, boy,' the Baron said, and mounted his horse.

'Until tonight,' Hans said, and followed the Baron, jogging towards the horse and mounting it in one graceful hop. He tugged at the reins but they wouldn't come free.

'Come and fix this bloody knot!' the Baron shouted. Emil ran over to the horse and struggled with the knot he had made. They heard his nails picking at it, then Hans saying, 'It'll come now.' He tugged it free with one jerk, pulling the reins into his hands, and galloped away with the Baron. How beautifully Hans rides, Ingrid thought.

Emil stood beneath the tree shielding his eyes. Ingrid

wondered if he was going to walk away without taking his leave, but Herr Hoffmann said, 'Do stay for a few minutes, or drink some water.'

Emil turned. He was frowning.

'Or show us the house. At least that. Until some of the heat's out of the day,' her mother said.

Emil nodded and took off his hat. His blond hair was stuck to his head as if someone had poured a pitcher of water over him.

The stone walls of the house were half a metre thick and the dark hallway beyond was pleasantly cool. The Hoffmanns followed him in and, holding his hat by the brim like a beggar, Emil said, 'This is the hall.' His voice had started weak, but he had spoken louder with each word, until 'hall' echoed over the white-painted walls. Behind them they heard voices, and Nora and a tall African they hadn't seen before carried their cases through the door and into the house. There were finger marks on the walls and the floor was covered in so much dust that it lifted into the air like smoke when they walked.

Ingrid's mother looked at the floor, then at Nora and the African and said, 'Who's that? Should I follow?'

'That's Wilhelm,' said Emil, 'and Nora. You can get rid of anyone you don't want, I suppose, but we haven't made any changes to the help.'

The tour took them through the cool low rooms and all the while new Africans appeared with boxes, until Frau Hoffmann became so agitated that she left to direct proceedings. Margarete, Ingrid and Herr Hoffmann were shown room after room, all cool with white cave-like walls and reddish wooden floors. In each room, a few items had been left behind by the von Ketzes, but were often unidentifiable in the ankle-high dust haze that they kicked up wherever they went.

The kitchen, where they had been left a large wooden table, was also filthy. On the table was a milk pail, the rim caked in a yellow crust and the lumpy liquid inside filled with swimming insects. 'I suppose you can keep all this,' Emil said. Ingrid looked out of the window, touching the sill; it crumbled beneath her fingers and she realised that what she had taken to be black wood was a beard of dead flies.

Emil showed them through to the large drawing room at the back of the house, while Ingrid rubbed her fingers on her dress, nauseated by the memory of the flies' dry crackle. Leading off from this room was a corridor and at the end Ingrid spied a small room, very different from the others. It was furnished with a chair and a camp bed, and on the camp bed was a neatly folded bed-sheet, on top of that a dark black book. The floor was so scrubbed and the room so clean, that it looked like a *trompe l'œil* painted onto the wall. 'Whose room is that?' Ingrid said.

'That's where Nora sleeps,' Emil said.

They heard a crash and the sound of breaking furniture. Their father ran back to the hall, calling their mother: 'Hedwig!' Margarete, Ingrid and Emil stood alone looking out over a few shrubs and a square of dug earth in the back garden. In the centre was a bush of cabbagey-looking leaves, surprisingly tender, with pale yellow flowers the size of saucers. 'It's a hibiscus,' Emil said. 'Mother likes to garden. She tried to remove most of the flowers to the new place, but they haven't taken. I don't know why she left that.'

Ingrid thought that he was sad about the garden. She thought the spots on his face and neck looked painful. 'Was this your house, then?' It occurred to her that she shouldn't speak to him so directly, but he had shaken her hand, after all.

'Yes,' said Emil.

'I didn't realise we were having your old one,' she said. 'Is that what you're sad about?'

'I'm not sad,' Emil said.

'It's just a house,' said Margarete. 'One shouldn't get sentimental about a house.'

'That's easy for you to say – you haven't lost yours,' said Emil.

'You didn't lose yours either,' said Margarete, kicking at the wall. 'Look, it's still here.'

This made Ingrid laugh, and it echoed in the bare room.

'That's rather cruel, I'd say,' Emil said. 'Especially for a little girl.'

Ingrid stopped laughing and felt hot with shame. But Margarete said, 'I'm not a little girl; I'm thirteen. And anyway, it's just a joke. You mustn't take it personally. No wonder you're so miserable.' She skipped out of the room. Ingrid stared at the patch of wall where her sister had kicked it. Emil said he had to leave.

Ingrid and her parents gathered beneath the line of gum trees. He pulled his hat on and, without meeting their eyes, said, 'It was nice to meet you Herr Hoffmann, Frau Hoffmann,' and turned to Ingrid and added, 'Fräuleins.' His boots crunched on the stony ground, and they watched him, head down, make his way up the path they had come down in the wagon.

'Doesn't he need water?' Frau Hoffmann said.

'I'm sure he knows what he's doing, Hedwig,' said their father.

Luisenhof Farm,
German Southwest Africa

— 1903 —

Ingrid had tried to plait her own hair, but she could feel that it had taken off at an odd angle, the black tail hanging beneath her armpit. She went onto the veranda where Nora was twisting her sister's hair into two fine ropes that circled her crown. She was joining it at the nape of her neck to hold the rest of her hair back, which had been brushed straight and golden down to her hips.

'I thought she'd have something more natural,' said Frau Hoffmann, uncertainly. 'That's certainly the fashion back home.'

'It will fill with dust, Frau Hoffmann,' Nora said. 'The wind will blow it into a nest – it's too fine.'

Ingrid held out her hand, touched her sister's hair and said, 'Can I go next?'

'Nora can do your hair another time, when you're visiting the von Ketzes,' said Frau Hoffmann.

'Am I not visiting the von Ketzes?' said Ingrid. 'Why am I not?'

Her mother moved her out of the way and knelt by

Margarete's side to pin a brooch on her – a glittering blue sprig of enamel forget-me-nots with yellow quartzes in their centres. 'Where's my brooch?' said Ingrid, her plaits abandoned and tears running down her face. 'Margarete?' she said.

'Oh Little Fly,' said Margarete. 'I'm just going to keep the Baroness company.'

'Why does she want your company?'

'She only has men there. We'll talk about women's things, I suppose.'

'You'll learn to behave in society,' Frau Hoffman said.

'What about me? What about me in society?'

'I'll learn to be more like a lady. You have your French and English with Hans, so it's right that I should learn something too. You'll go soon enough, when you're more grown up, like me. And I'll tell you all about it when I'm back.'

Margarete stood. She was wearing a new dress that Ingrid hadn't seen before. It was white and, instead of stopping at her bare knees, it dropped down to her stockinged calves. She reached out her hands for Ingrid and Ingrid took them both. Her mother pulled at the shoulders of Margarete's dress and Nora, with a pin and needle held between her lips, began to repair the hem at the back. 'Your dress is very pretty,' said Ingrid, between shuddering breaths, as her tears dried.

'Mummy brought it especially for the visit.'

Ingrid looked to her mother for confirmation of this betrayal, but Frau Hoffmann didn't comment. She dipped a handkerchief into a ewer on the card table and carefully worked at Margarete's face, extracting the dirt she had missed in her morning wash.

Hans came onto the veranda from the house, his hair damp and combed.

'Is everyone going?' Ingrid said.

'I'm going on a horse,' Margarete said. 'Hans will ride over with me until I've learned to ride on my own.'

This was the final injustice. Ingrid pulled her hands out of her sister's and fled inside, where she threw herself weeping onto her bed. No one came for her, so when her tears had dried for the second time she stayed in her room and read two chapters of *The Swiss Family Robinson* in the hope that her absence might be felt more keenly.

Eventually Pina found her, and licked her bare ankle. She pulled it away and the dog left the room. Ingrid got up and followed her to the veranda. Hans was there and Pina dropped to the floor at his feet. He had laid four rifles out across the wooden boards and was cleaning a fifth with a soft cloth and oil from a tin bottle that Ingrid didn't like the smell of.

'Did you not go?' she said hopefully.

'I've been and come back, Fräulein Ingrid,' he said.

'Did you leave her there?'

'Yes,' he said and looked away from her as if the criticism pricked.

She bit her lip, to stop herself from crying again, because her head already hurt from it. 'Will she be there all day?'

'Not all day,' he said, and the concern in his voice tallied with her own sadness, so she felt he had understood.

Her parents were always preoccupied with the farm, so Ingrid spent the day distracting herself with Pina, exploring the thorn bushes beyond the garden and a young baobab tree that Nora had told her to look at, if she was bored. It was like a tree in a child's drawing with stubby branches up high, covered in dark green leaves. She didn't think it was so very interesting, except for its barrel chest, which she gripped and pressed her ear against, wondering if the sound of flowing liquid was the sap of the tree or the blood in her own head.

Beyond the gum trees, an African boy she didn't know was chasing a wild cow. Outside the fence, she often saw Africans with goats and cows, usually Herero, their presence regulated and approved by her father in consort with Hans, engaged in some system of mutual benefit that Ingrid didn't understand. Sometimes a little group was allowed inside the fence to start a fire beneath the gum trees and would cook up stews of meat and bones; the smell would reach her even if she was still in bed. Her mother forbade her from talking to the Africans they didn't know, so she would sit staring at them with her chin on the veranda's balustrade. If she was lucky, they wore tribal dress, the women with iron coils on their legs and leather headdresses, with little ears that stuck up like a fox's. But often they just wore German clothes like Nora, Hans and the farmworkers, and Ingrid would quickly tire of them and go and throw stones at the nest of red wasps in the nearest thorn bushes, until they were angry enough to force her back inside.

The boy brought the wild cow down and milked it into a beaten metal bucket. Ingrid heard hooves and watched Hans and her father ride out into the veld. She sat beneath the gum trees and read her book to the end. Then she went and found Nora, who was mopping the floors, now done twice daily. She watched her cycle through the housework she had once seen her mother doing, along with the few chores that were her and her sister's duties in Germany. This was a good thing, she supposed, but only compounded the tedium.

She went and found her mother, who had retired to her

bed, because the heat and the necessity of drinking most of their milk sour gave her stomach cramps. 'This climate is very harsh,' she said, not opening her eyes. 'It is hard to come to it as an adult.'

Finally, when the shadow of the house had stretched over the veranda, almost to the gum trees, Ingrid saw three horses, and realised that Hans was coming back with Margarete. The wait for them to reach the house was unbearable.

But when Margarete descended the horse, she didn't look at Ingrid. She seemed exhausted, and her hair had lost its morning sheen. The dry wind had blown it coarse where it was loose, just as Nora had predicted. Ingrid followed Margarete to their room, but Margarete said, 'Can I be alone for a little while,' in a very adult-sounding voice, and so Ingrid sat on the floor in the corridor and waited for her.

Margarete didn't tell Ingrid about the journey when she emerged in her normal clothes. She didn't eat the buttered corn they were given at dinner, and when Ingrid settled beneath her mosquito net and read aloud from *Heidi* Margarete said that she was tired and didn't want to listen.

'But I can't go to sleep without reading,' Ingrid said.

'Read to yourself.'

'But then you'll miss a bit and you won't know what's happened.'

'I don't care,' Margarete said. 'You've read it to me about a hundred times. And anyway, it's a book for children.'

Ingrid cried silently, burying her face in the crook of her arm. Pina barked outside and their mosquito coil crackled in the dark.

*

Margarete's visits to the von Ketzes' continued through what Nora called the wet season. Ingrid had imagined the soft rain of her early childhood spotting the windows and the earth greening beneath a sky of broken clouds. This rain was sporadic though, and often spilled from the belly of great dark clouds that whipped the dust up in the yard and then emptied themselves onto the house, dashing at the roof like a million pebbles. The sparse grasses and shrubs on their plain darkened after these showers, but the air remained hot and dry.

For Ingrid, it was in that season that Margarete changed, when her sister mounted her horse every Wednesday next to Hans and made her way to the von Ketzes' farm without her. It was the first time that any important experience hadn't been shared between them, and when she returned to Ingrid, Margarete seemed unable to recall anything but the most mundane details about what she did there at the von Ketzes' all day.

Ingrid felt their worlds separating in other ways too. Margarete didn't like to bathe at the same time as her any more, and turned away from Ingrid when she dressed. She gave up the shared passions of their childhood – cutting paper stars, stroking each other's arms, dolls, rice pudding – every week rejecting something new. She continued to draw, but did it alone with chalk on a rough piece of blue granite that their father had brought back from the fields. Ingrid sat behind her, watching her sketch hills, rivers and churches. When she asked her if it was meant to be Cochem, Margarete answered, 'I don't know.'

There were spells in which Margarete was full of energy and keen to please Ingrid, making her recite the English and French she had learned with Hans, showing her how to push down her cuticles, telling her secrets about how miserable the von Ketzes' house was. But these were followed, often immediately, by a terrible gloom. Sometimes Margarete would be cold and silent, would tell Ingrid to stop badgering her. Other times she would just cry.

They had always been different. Margarete was funnier and quicker, but easily bored and temperamental. To Ingrid, therefore, her behaviour was an extension of these differences, and she wondered if this was what womanhood brought: a firming up of one's intrinsic temperament. But Margarete also started saying things that Ingrid didn't understand at all. When they were doing their sewing on the veranda, she laid her frame aside and said, 'Why, I could go to sleep now and never wake up again. Don't you sometimes wish so too? Just to lie somewhere cool and never open your eyes again?'

'I suppose,' Ingrid said.

Once, when she was showing Ingrid how to saddle the horse, she stopped, holding the saddle in her arms like a tired washerwoman, and said, 'Wasn't it all better before the rain came?'

Ingrid squinted at the cloudless sky and said, 'Perhaps it was.'

One night, Ingrid lay awake listening to her sister's sleepless turning and sighing until dawn broke. In the morning Margarete's eyes were grey and sunken. It was a Sunday and Margarete argued with Nora about washing her face and wouldn't come to breakfast on time. Herr Hoffmann's early mornings and Nora's management of all the tasks relating to the house and the children meant that Sunday breakfast was one of the few meals that Ingrid ate with all of her family, an island in the general loneliness of her weekly routine. She was thus all the more disappointed not to have entered the room holding her sister's hand.

Breakfast was eaten early, because of the heat, and always consisted of sago followed by bread rolls, which Nora baked before they were up. Their mother had it organised in such a way that, when they walked into the bare dining room, the food had been set out and left, as if it had emerged of its own accord, and to Ingrid this added a festive magic to the occasion. But not this morning, because Margarete wasn't there.

With no church to go to, a fuss was made of grace, which was longer and more idiosyncratic than the usual meal-time prayer, with special mention made of the Kaiser who had been shot in Bremen, but escaped with his life. Frau Hoffmann unfurled her hands and gripped her husband's arm for a second, then served him from the coffee pot. Ingrid was given cocoa; Margarete's cup remained empty.

'Tell us about your French, Ingrid dear. Say something French,' her mother said.

Ingrid swallowed a slimy mouthful of unsweetened sago with difficulty – she was eating around the spot of jam, which she was saving until last.

'What would you like me to say?' she said.

'You're always gabbing about something with Hans out there,' Frau Hoffmann said. 'He teaches you poetry, doesn't he?'

Ingrid nodded.

'Let us hear something, then,' Herr Hoffmann said.

Ingrid rolled her eyes to the ceiling to think, then repeated from her last lesson:

> *'Et voici que parmi l'effroi d'un long éclair*
> *Sa pâle blouse a l'air, au vent froid qui l'emporte,*
> *D'un linceul, et sa bouche est béante, de sorte*
> *Qu'il semble hurler sous les morsures du ver.'*

Frau Hoffman took her husband's hand and they smiled at Ingrid.

'Well, isn't that impressive?' said her mother.

Ingrid blushed, because it was just something she had learned off by heart, which wasn't very difficult. She took another mouthful of sago.

'What does it mean?' said Frau Hoffmann, pulling a roll apart, a jangle of poppy seeds spraying her plate.

Ingrid said, falteringly, 'It's something like, "And there in the terror of the endless lightning, his pale ... blouse, I suppose, is ... it becomes a shroud in the cold wind, and his mouth is so ... wide open that it seems to scream at the gnawing of the worms."'

Her mother and father were silent. The split roll was held uneaten between her mother's fingers. 'The gnawing of worms?' she said.

'I'll have a word with Hans,' said her father.

'I don't even know what it means, really,' said Ingrid, which was a lie, because she thought of the images the poems made constantly, seeing Pierrot screaming in a pit, beset by maggots.

'Why is everyone so quiet?' Margarete said, finally stalking into the room.

She sat down at her place and her mother pulled her bowl away. 'You're not to have a thing,' she said, 'wandering in here like the Queen of the Netherlands.'

Margarete grabbed the edge of the bowl and pulled it back towards her.

'How dare you!' her mother said.

'Let go of that!' said her father and, with the hint of a smile, Margarete released the bowl and it shot back and sprayed her mother with sago. The clot of jam slid down the gluey whiteness over her shirt and neck and dropped from her breast to her lap.

In one movement her mother swept the bowl from the table and clapped Margarete about the face with an open hand. Margarete ran screaming from the room pursued by her mother and then Ingrid, who appealed hopelessly for Margarete to quieten and her mother to show mercy. Frau Hoffmann struck out wildly and wrestled Margarete into their bedroom. She ordered Nora to keep her there. Ingrid watched as Margarete lunged for the door, screaming terrible things at Nora and at her mother. Nora seemed unconcerned about her spiteful tongue, but Ingrid was stunned. Nora took Margarete by the arm and walked her back to her bed, where Margarete retreated, scratching and hissing at her like a cat.

Ingrid found her mother; she was weeping in her room.

'What's wrong with Margarete?' Ingrid asked.

'She's having a turn,' Frau Hoffmann said. 'Girls have them at her age. It's normal. Don't badger.'

Nora set up a reeded wooden chair outside the shut bedroom door and sat humming hymns and, using a nail, carving small gourds that she retrieved from the pocket of her skirt.

Ingrid stood ashen, a metre removed from her.

'Will she get better?' Ingrid said.

'She is wilful,' Nora said.

Ingrid stayed by the door. She watched Nora attack the blackened skin of the gourds to reveal the orange below, creating patterned bands across which elephants, giraffes and zebras walked in single file, like the dancing animals Ingrid had seen in the spinning cylinders at the fair in Koblenz.

Nora finally looked up at her and said, 'Are you going to wait there the whole day, Fräulein Ingrid?'

'I just wanted to make sure Margarete was all right.'

Nora blew the black dust off the gourd she had been working on and handed it to Ingrid. 'You can hold it if you like. While I work on the next one.'

Ingrid took the little gourd. She rubbed the scratched surface and some of the black and amber dust came off on her fingers. 'What do you do with them?' she asked.

'Sell them,' Nora said.

'To whom?'

'A man comes to the farm every month and collects them.'

'Is it a very old tradition?' said Ingrid.

Nora laughed. 'No, my dear. This is not tradition. It is just something for the Germans – they like to buy things, but they don't want to buy anything that is truly Herero. What would they do with it? So we make them these things.'

Ingrid was disappointed and her interest in the little gourd waned. She looked up the corridor at the window there. In this new climate she was never sure if she should be outside or not. Hans and Nora spent as much time in the stone coolness of the house as possible, but it seemed strange to always be inside. In Germany they were only inside if it rained.

She looked at Nora's hands and wanted to reach out and touch them, but was afraid to. She said, 'Margarete gets very angry sometimes, and then very sad. But she always comes right again.'

'She's flighty,' Nora said. 'She's been spoilt.'

'We weren't spoilt in Germany – not at all.'

'Hmm,' Nora said, laying the gourd and nail in the bright filings on her lap and retucking her head scarf.

Ingrid squinted at the window again.

'Should I go and play outside?' she said.

Nora said nothing. She only ever answered questions if she had an answer to give, otherwise she remained silent.

*

That night, Ingrid had to sleep on a cot in her parents' room. She woke the next morning to screams. She ran out of the front door and saw the veranda floor chalked with drawings of fish, hundreds of them, some long and eel-like, others fat like carps, weaving between weeds. Frau Hoffmann was hitting Margarete, who cowered beneath her howling.

'It'll wash off,' Ingrid said, tearfully.

'Yes, and you'll do it,' Frau Hoffmann said, and slapped Ingrid about the back of her head so hard that she fell to her knees.

With Margarete back in her room, Ingrid scrubbed at the wood with a bucket of water and a hard brush. It released a dusty fungal smell, like German summer roads after rain, but undercut with something foreign and resinous. When half of the beautiful fish had been eradicated, Nora joined her. She did not acknowledge Ingrid, but started at the other end with her own brush. When there was just one fish left they were kneeling side by side. They looked at it, their hands on their knees, and Nora said, 'She can certainly draw fish,' then dashed it in half with one stroke.

Margarete became more vicious. She said poisonous things to Nora and Frau Hoffmann, and her mother's rage only fed her own. When Ingrid tried to talk to her, she said, 'Get away, Little Fly, get away,' and shooed her out.

One night Margarete crept out of bed and took the lamp from the bedside table. Ingrid, drunk with sleep, heard her moving and climbed out from under her own mosquito net. She found Margarete in the long drawing room that looked over the hibiscus in the back garden.

'Come back, Margarete,' she said, and tried to put her arms under Margarete's armpits and steer her back to bed. But at her touch, Margarete ran for the window, smashing it with a blow from her hand. It shattered and the insects that had been clamouring at the glass seethed around the lamp and she dropped it, setting the oil and her dress on fire. Ingrid screamed and stamped at the flames, burning her foot. Hans ran in in his night things and covered them and the fire in a thick blanket, filling the air with the smell of oil and burnt wool.

When Hans removed the blanket, Margarete was small underneath it like a chick in a nest. He lifted her up and took her back to bed, where Nora dressed her burns and the cut on her hand. Her mother fussed until dawn about what could be done to keep Margarete from killing herself and her family with her, but her concerns were unfounded as Margarete's rage abated and she closed her eyes for two weeks.

Only Ingrid knew that she wasn't always asleep. She would talk to her then, not asking her to open her eyes, just describing the day to her, until her mother or Nora rapped on the door and she fell silent.

*

Ingrid read *Heidi* to Margarete, wrapped in her muteness. On the second day, Nora came and sat at the end of Ingrid's bed as she read, and once she had finished Nora took out

43

a small Bible and read from Genesis, up to chapter five, intoning a dizzying list of men, hundreds of years old. Nora returned on the third day and again waited patiently for Heidi to finish her next adventure, then read while Ingrid listened. Over the weeks, Ingrid cycled through the few children's novels she had, and Nora made her way implacably through the Bible.

In the day though, Ingrid was alone again. She wandered the dusty yard, and sat up in the gum trees looking out over the veld, wondering how far she would get if she set foot on the path and kept on walking.

Ingrid went into her parents' room and touched the neat shirts and skirts kept in the open steamer trunks. She took the top off her mother's perfume bottle, sniffed at it, then pretended to dab it on her wrists and neck, as her mother did. 'I'm dog-tired,' she said to her imaginary husband. 'We can't let the servants speak to you that way, dear. It's not to be endured.'

She looked at herself in her mother's mirror. It was impossible to judge her own face, except to say that her hair was black, where Margarete's was wavy and blonde; that her features were altogether longer, especially her nose, which she pushed at with her fingertips, pleading for it to stop growing. She was at an age where everything was growing, and the cramps she sometimes got in her legs felt like her bones were being prised apart. There was no delicacy in those bones and she knew it.

She read all of her books over again and badgered her mother to order more from Windhoek. Her mother dropped her sewing on the veranda, and retired to her bedroom with indigestion.

Ingrid, left on the balcony, touched the half-embroidered

44

bird on her mother's circular frame. She ran her fingers over the needles and pins in her cushion and saw on the floor a pin with a particularly fat head, made of orange glass with slivers of royal blue spiralled into it. Ingrid picked it up and turned it in the light. Then she put it in her pocket. She wandered about the house stroking the secreted object. Experimentally, she visited Nora and her sister, whose eyes were still shut; no one noticed that she was touching something illicit.

She heard hooves and ran to the front of the house, where her father and Hans had dismounted and were tying their horses to the gum tree. Her father's clothes were creased and dusty and his neck and face burnt dark red. He kissed her on the crown of her head as he passed into the house, calling for Frau Hoffmann. He smelt of sweat and soil. Hans lingered between the horses and the house, so Ingrid went to him holding her stolen pin, but even he only nodded to acknowledge her. He had no idea what she had done.

'Were you at the wells?' she asked him, knowing little else about the land that they lived on.

'No, we were dealing with tribal issues,' Hans said.

'Issues?' she said.

'We were talking to some Herero elders.'

She imagined the elders as very old wrinkled men and women, with stretched lips and earlobes.

'What was it about?'

Hans smiled. 'You should ask your father about the farm work.'

She wanted to say something to Hans that would bind them together. She felt in her chest such a longing for it. 'What will we learn this week?' she tried.

45

'I haven't thought.'

'Are there Herero poets?'

Hans laughed. 'No, Fräulein Ingrid. Not in the way you understand poetry.'

She flushed red and said, 'Well, then I suppose it's just Negro jabber anyway,' and ran back to the safety of the farmhouse.

In the drawing room Ingrid kicked the wall, where her sister had kicked it that first day. She kicked it again and again, until a little plaster came away, dusting the floor white. She decided that she would be cold with Hans at their next lesson and she took the pin from her pocket and stroked the glass top.

It had never occurred to her to steal anything, but the stolen pin, this single transgression, loosed something in her. Whenever she was left alone she would feel a wave akin to desire and would look about her for something to pilfer: a leather button, a playing card, a ring. When she laid her hand on it, there was a fearful thrill, but this was followed at once by shame and sadness, and when she placed the objects in a hollow in the crook of the gum tree, she couldn't bear to look at the small hoard she had gathered. But the stealing went on unabated and only stopped with Margarete's first tentative steps out of bed.

*

Ingrid's French and English lessons took place one afternoon a week and were for her a singular joy. To her delight, what her mother called Margarete's 'convalescence' freed Hans for a second weekly session, when he would normally have been riding with her to the von Ketzes'.

They sat under the gum trees, Ingrid on a square of calico

to keep her dress clean, Hans on the ground. She had split a long blade of grass in three and was plaiting it, the end looped around her big toe, grubby with red earth. Pina lay between them asleep.

'*Je ne regarderai ni l'or du soir qui tombe,*' Hans said. '*Répétez s'il vous plaît.*'

'*Je ne regarder . . .,*' she said. '*Je ne regarder . . .*'

'*Rai,*' he said, '*Je ne regarde*rai, which is?'

'Future,' she said abruptly, because he knew she knew.

'Yes, go on.'

She closed her eyes, her fingers stopped plaiting, and she said, '*Je ne regarderai ni l'or du soir qui tombé.*'

'*Tombe,* it's not past participle here.'

'*Tombe,*' she repeated.

'Now translate,' Hans said.

'I'm never going to look at the falling evening gold?' She looked at him for approval, rubbing the sharp edge of the grass with her thumb, but she was tired and knew that the effort was poor and would be rejected.

'Again,' he said.

She took a deep breath. 'I will never look upon the descending gold of the evening.'

'Yes,' Hans said, frustrated. 'But you don't have to pick a more pretentious word. "Falling" is fine, but your construction was poor in your first attempt and it's not "never" but "neither". "I will neither look upon the falling gold of the evening," is fine,' he said.

He paused to think of another line.

'Is Emil von Ketz a good person?' Ingrid said.

Hans looked baffled. 'What do you mean? What's he done?'

'Oh, nothing. He doesn't do anything. I just wondered if

it was planned that he was going to marry Margarete one day. I thought that maybe that was why she had to go to the von Ketzes' so often. So I wondered if he was a good person. Whether he would be able to look after her.'

Hans looked worried. 'I don't know that anything like that has been agreed,' he said.

Ingrid nodded. 'Have you always lived with the von Ketzes?'

'Fräulein Ingrid, we should continue our lesson.'

'*Why do you speak French?*' she said, switching to French. '*Why do you speak German like a white person?*'

He screwed his eyes up and looked over at the faint path that led across the veld to the low mountain range and the von Ketzes' house. '*I'm half German. I grew up with the von Ketzes – I have always worked for them. French and English I learned from the various missionaries that have come through over the years and left books with me. One, Father Hopkins, still brings me poetry when he comes.*'

'*How old are you?*'

'*Sixteen.*'

'*Who's your mother, then?*'

'*Nora.*'

'*Oh,*' said Ingrid. She looked back down at the grass around her toe. Her skin was white where it pinched her. '*You must know the von Ketzes very well.*'

'*We work for them. Like we work for you.*'

'*Does that . . . ? Does that . . . ?*' She couldn't get at the subtlety in French, so she finished in German: 'Does that mean you don't know somebody? If you work for them, you can't ever know them?'

Nora called for Hans, meaning that their hour was over.

'We'll continue next week,' Hans said.

'OK,' said Ingrid. She unhooked the grass plait and wrapped it around her hand. She flicked her calico square in the air, and Pina jumped up; they had brought nothing else out with them, no books or paper, and walked towards the house, the sun on their backs a great weight.

'Can women write poetry?' Ingrid said.

'Of course,' said Hans.

'Why don't we learn any poetry by women?'

Hans thought about this. 'There aren't any famous women poets – it's more of a hobby for women.'

'Oh,' said Ingrid, disappointed, because over the past year she had begun to see herself as a great poet, but when she considered this she was indeed dressed as a man in her imagination, wearing white buttoned breeches, a cravat and a frock coat.

Wanting to talk on as much as she could before he was pressed into service again, Ingrid asked, 'Will you always live with us?'

Hans looked at her thoughtfully, then said, 'What if your father wishes to return to Germany?'

'Wouldn't you come with us?'

He laughed. 'There are no black faces in Germany.'

'Would you miss it, do you think?'

'Miss what?'

'Southwest.'

He looked towards the house. He was sweating; it glistened in his hair. She wanted him to say that he would miss the Hoffmanns, miss her, but instead he said, 'You know, we never read German poetry in our lessons, and this reminds me of a German poem.'

'A German poem?' she repeated.

'Yes,' he said. 'Listen.'

'A spruce stands solitary
in the North on a bleak elevation;
it sleeps; encircled in a white sheet
of ice and snow.

'It dreams of a palm
that, distant in the Orient,
suffers solitary and silent
on the blazing precipice.'

It seemed rather obvious to her, but she said, 'Lovely.' He lifted his hand in farewell and left around the side of the house.

*

Margarete began to sit up when her sister came to read to her, and soon she was able to walk out to the veranda, where she sat quietly listening to Ingrid's chatter. Her stone and chalk were returned to her and she drew elaborately popu-lated islands, encircled by monster-filled seas. She would describe each building in detail, telling Ingrid who lived there and what they did, who they were friends with and who they didn't speak to.

Ingrid thought about Nora as Hans's mother, about how different she looked from him. The secret gave her plea-sure, and she sat on the wooden slats at Margarete's feet and decided not to tell her. She looked at her sister's bare dusty toes, at the golden hair that had newly sprouted on them, and said, 'Would you marry Emil, do you think? If he asked you?'

The sound of chalk on stone stopped. 'It's probably what Mama and Papa want, I suppose.'

'Perhaps,' said Ingrid.

*

Then a storm came, like a test. It rumbled deeply and
the slim leaves of the acacia trees stood out bright green
against the blackening sky. Ingrid had never seen anything
like it, and stood on the veranda holding her sister's hand
as the cloud rolled towards them over the wide veld. From
its mouth fired webs of lightning, disconnected from the
deep roars that came from all sides. As its breath picked up
sand and leaves and shook their skirts, Nora called from the
house, saying, 'You must come in now.'

They sat together in the drawing room, watching the
hibiscus bush swaying in increasingly desperate throes.
The room darkened and then the rain came. On the tin
roof, it sounded apocalyptic, a lion's roar bearing down on
them from above. Only Hans and Nora were still, Hans
lost in thought, staring out of the window, Nora mend-
ing one of Herr Hoffmann's shirts. The rain knifed the
hibiscus, flinging the green leaves and yellow flowers into
the air like confetti. A few wet petals stuck to the shaking
windows.

The Hoffmanns, though, were not watching the storm.
They were watching Margarete, who sat calmly on the floor
beside Ingrid. She blinked and bit at her nails, and when
the storm lifted and the whole veld outside was transformed
from amber to a deep liver brown, she said, 'Ingrid, come
and play islands in the guest room. I'm bored listening to
the rain.'

They went to the empty guest room and threw hand-
kerchiefs down on the polished floor and hopped from one
to the other. Sometimes the distance was too far, and the
cotton skidded on the varnish, causing Ingrid to fall hard

51

on her behind, but never causing tears, because she was so happy to be playing. Only Pina whimpered and cried, jumping up at them and scratching the cotton of their dresses. Rain dripped from the roof, Frau Hoffmann went to sleep on the veranda, Nora filled the shade of the house with the dull knock of the laundry stone hitting the wet linen of their underclothes and Ingrid was happy.

*

Margarete's serenity during the storm led to her reintegration into the life of the house, and once she would let Nora dress her and brush her hair again, Emil was invited to visit. He came to play the piano that had been left because the von Ketzes' house was too hot for it and the Baron hated the sound of it. Emil was asked to teach Margarete, and they sat together on the stool working their way through Schubert, the only sheet music that Emil owned. When they played together in the hot afternoons, the household would stop and listen, often for the whole hour, Ingrid on the veranda, her mother in her room and Nora in the kitchen turning the butter churn. When they were done, Margarete would join Ingrid, sitting behind her and plaiting her hair as she read, and Emil would make his way from room to room, saying goodbye to everyone, before mounting his horse and riding back home.

Each week, Frau Hoffmann entreated Emil to stay, each time with a new inducement: some music from the gramophone, a game of cards, even a reading from the Bible. Each time he shook his head, no, and Frau Hoffmann and the girls would stand and watch him struggling beneath the gum tree with the reins of the horse. Ingrid watched her sister as he rode away. Her face was tired and impassive.

It was food that finally convinced Emil to stay. Frau Hoffmann said, 'I have baked something – Bundt cake.'

He blinked – his eyelashes were bleached bone-white. 'Thank you, Frau Hoffmann,' he said.

They sat, Emil, Frau Hoffmann and the girls, at a little table set up in the shade at the back of the house, near where the hibiscus had bloomed. They had coffee. Emil ate one mouthful of the cake and said, 'This is very good. Where did you get your flour from?'

'Herr Hoffmann was in Okahandja last week – we've been spoilt for treats.'

'I'm terribly jealous,' Emil said.

Ingrid and Margarete looked at each other. This was more than he had said to them since they had arrived.

'Have more,' Frau Hoffmann said, delighted.

'Oh, I can't,' he said, and smiled.

Frau Hoffmann laughed and forced another slice onto his plate. 'Herr Hoffmann can't bear cake,' she lied, 'So you must finish it. Everything dries to dust so quickly in this climate.'

He ate, blinking nervously, then looked up at the house and said, 'You must have had a time in the storm. It makes a racket on that roof.'

'It chopped that hibiscus to pieces,' Ingrid said.

Emil looked at the dried root where the plant had been and laughed. His whole face changed, all mouth, fine small teeth and a deep bass chuckle. Frau Hoffmann and the girls burst into laughter too. 'Poor hibiscus,' he said, and this seemed very funny.

For a few weeks Emil was transformed and the cake routine held, always on the table at the back of the house and always accompanied with laughter. Even Margarete looked forward to the visits, waiting on the veranda and staring at the wide horizon for the trembling form of Emil on his horse.

Then Herr Hoffmann announced that Margarete was well enough to visit the von Ketzes again, saying she had been much missed. Margarete burst into tears and ran about the farm screaming. Her father looked dismayed, but Ingrid's mother got hold of her, and after an hour of muttering, haggling, tears and chirruping cries, it was decided that, since it was almost Christmas, the visits could wait until the new year, and for the first visit a party of them would go: Hans, Herr Hoffmann, Margarete and Ingrid herself.

Luisenhof Farm,
German Southwest Africa

— 1904 —

The vineyards in Germany had been too steep for horses, and so the girls had never learnt to ride. When Margarete was taken to the von Ketzes', she was led as normal by Hans, but Ingrid had to ride with her father. Margarete rode side-saddle for the first time, though the saddle wasn't made for it, and for the two-hour journey across the veld she grunted and wheezed as she tried to stay on top. Ingrid clung to her father's back and looked away from Hans and Margarete, over the veld. She had been thrilled by the idea of escaping the confines of the farmhouse, but the landscape changed little, except for a few giant termite mounds and, halfway through the journey, a great flat acacia tree with black men hanging by their necks from one of its limbs.

'Are they Hereros?' Ingrid asked.

She felt the muscles in her father's back move as he turned.

'Good God, Ingrid, look away,' he said, and she looked the other way, at Hans, also looking now, and Margarete, whose position on the saddle meant that she couldn't turn away.

Her father shifted uncomfortably and the sweat on his back dried the moment she lifted her head.

'They're criminals,' her father said at last.

'What did they do?'

'Well,' he said. 'They'll have stolen from Baron von Ketz, I should think. We're on his land now.'

'Is that what he told you?'

'No,' her father said.

Then with a thump, like dropped laundry, Margarete slipped off the saddle.

'Margarete!' Ingrid cried, but her sister stood up and said, 'It's OK, Little Fly, I'm OK.'

But when she tried to pull herself back onto the horse, she squealed in pain.

Hans dismounted and inspected her foot. 'It's just a sprain,' he said.

'Take her on your horse,' Herr Hoffmann said. 'Otherwise we'll never get there.'

As they neared the mountain, the wooden house came into view, the unpainted posts holding up the veranda still raw and bright. It was all smaller and bleaker than Ingrid remembered, and the four open windows and the door covered in black mosquito screens gave the façade the look of a gawping, dead-eyed head.

The Baron was waiting alone in the bright sun. He shouted something as they came close. Her father raised his hand to his ear to show that he hadn't heard, but Hans stopped and dismounted and lifted Margarete onto the ground.

The Baron shouted again: 'You don't let a kaffir ride your daughter on his horse, Hoffmann. Christ, man!'

Her father's arm dropped. He also dismounted and lifted

Ingrid down. She ran to Margarete, and together they walked towards the farmhouse, hidden behind their father, Margarete limping.

'The Baroness is unwell,' the Baron said as they followed him into the house. The air was stale and hot and smelled strongly of wood, tar, sour sweat and alcohol. The floor was covered with the same thick layer of dust that had filled the Hoffmanns' farmhouse when they arrived, and it stung Ingrid's throat. The Baron went to a small table in a pantry covered in greasy bottles and glasses. He knocked into it, causing a bottle to topple over and a glass to ring. She looked for Hans for a signal as to how to behave, but he wasn't there – he had stopped at the veranda and was waiting outside.

'A drink,' the Baron said. He filled one glass with Korn and handed it to Herr Hoffmann.

The liquid in the tipped bottle pat-a-patted onto the floor.

'Go and find Emil,' Herr Hoffmann said to Ingrid and Margarete.

'He's in the other room – the other one can go upstairs. There are toys,' the Baron said.

'Can Ingrid come with me?' Margarete said.

'Your sister can play upstairs,' the Baron said.

Margarete looked crestfallen and led Ingrid into the only other room on the ground floor of the house – a dark drawing room with a large German dresser in very dark wood, filled with dusty crockery, and five stuffed armchairs, placed too closely together. In one sat Emil, looking stiff and nervous. 'Hello,' he said.

Margarete turned to Ingrid. 'Stay,' she said.

But Ingrid couldn't bear the idea of the Baron scolding her and she retreated to the staircase without looking her sister in the eye. It creaked as she went up, and she felt like a trespasser. She heard her father's low voice and Baron von Ketz's booming justifications: about the way he farmed, how his fortune would rebuild the family estate in a way his feckless elder brother hadn't, the way he had buried two daughters and a son beneath the hot red earth, the way he treated his blacks.

A bedroom door was open. She stopped and looked through the crack. Baroness von Ketz must have decorated it and she wondered where in the house the Baroness was. Silent in a chair in another dark room, perhaps. It looked like a woman's bedroom and disturbed Ingrid in this house filled with raw boards, a carpet of tarred canvas and stinking of drink and men's bodies. There were some pretty curtains at the window and one of the twin beds was covered in a neat, quilted satin counterpane, the colour of dusty violets. She touched the satin with the tips of her fingers – it was the softest thing she had ever felt and she couldn't bear that it was here, in this house, that she had to leave it and wait until they came back to touch it again, if they ever came back.

Beneath the pillow on one side of the bed she saw the corner of something lilac, which she tugged at, revealing a beautiful handmade nightdress case, made of silk and embroidered with a bird, like the *Reichsadler*, rising up out of a fire. She tried to imagine her mother holding it in her large hands, and in that moment she hated her and wished that they could have a new mother, who powdered her face, wore scent during the day and didn't sweat through her dresses. Someone thin and docile, like the Baroness must be, someone airy and pretty.

She heard something scuttle across the floor and looked at

the open door. Baron von Ketz laughed loudly in the kitchen below. She looked at the von Ketzes' wedding picture on the bedside table and saw that Baron von Ketz had once been handsome and that Baroness von Ketz, in a dark dress and holding a long bouquet of flowers, had been beautiful, but for her bad teeth.

There was a scraping of chairs and Ingrid dashed from the room, aware that she was still holding the nightdress case in her hands and that she couldn't return it. She ran through an open door, where there was a narrow bed and a few grubby tin toys that she knelt in front of, as if in prayer.

The footsteps came closer and she shoved the case into the top of her dress, straightening it out so that it lay flat against her chest.

'Margarete?'

She turned. It was the Baroness, dark and small, like a widow in a picture book, wrapped in a lacy shawl as if she had been sleeping. Ingrid was too afraid to correct her and stayed kneeling on the bare floor, trapping the pyjama case against her body with her elbows. The rims of the Baroness's eyes, like her lips, were loose, pink and watery; her lips were thick at the sides, as if the flesh that should have been in her mouth had prolapsed, and she wetted them constantly with nervous touches of her tongue, as if checking that they were still there.

'I have a terrible headache,' the Baroness said. She sat on the narrow bed in the room; it barely sank under her scant weight. She stared out at the bright floor of the veld beyond the insect screen at the window. Ingrid, in a panic, was struck by the thought that the Baroness had been watching her the whole time and that this interview was her tortuous punishment, before she demanded the silky bag back.

'How old are you now?' the Baroness said.

'Almost thirteen,' said Ingrid.

'Do you ever think about marriage?' the Baroness said, without looking at her.

'One thinks about it,' Ingrid said, thinking that that was the adult thing to say.

'I thought about marriage a lot as a girl,' she said. 'Do you ever recall how you imagined something would be?' Without turning from the window, she pulled at her shawl, tightening it as if she was cold. 'I do. I recall what I thought marriage would be like. I see it as clearly as if it really happened. The man – a tall Junker with a sword. But I also feel completely the shape of the marriage, which was like . . . ' She paused to locate the right words. 'It was like an intense union, not like those crushes one has with other girls at school.' She looked Ingrid in the eye now. 'Of course, you were never sent away to school, you poor thing. You were just carried off to this ghastly place.' She touched a bracelet of linked silver acacia leaves at her wrist, stroked it sentimentally with her middle finger. 'Well, we all have our burden. Marry well, that's the crux of it. For yourself.'

Ingrid heard heavier footsteps. She didn't move. Her knees hurt. Her father looked into the room uncertainly, staring at Ingrid in drunken confusion, at the toys in front of her and then at the window. He didn't seem to see the Baroness, who stayed perfectly still. 'You tidy this up, Ingrid, and come with me,' he said. 'I'll wait outside.'

Ingrid stood and went to the door. 'Ingrid!' came the Baroness's voice, suddenly sharp.

Ingrid turned to her. 'It is Ingrid, isn't it?' she said.

'Yes,' said Ingrid.

'Why on earth didn't you say?'

60

'I don't know,' Ingrid said. 'I was scared.' She ran down the stairs and out to Hans, her sister and her father, who were all already in the saddle.

Herr Hoffmann reached down and wrenched her up by the arms. He whipped the reins and they set off at a trot. She saw Baron von Ketz standing near the creek with his gun, too far away for her to read his expression. She had overheard her mother saying that he had buried his children up at the creek, and imagined that he had laid their bodies in the water there and watched them float away downstream. She had been afraid of waterholes ever since, terrified that the dead von Ketz children would appear again, imagining their eyes still intact, staring out at her beneath the surface of the water. But also imagining, whenever the sun was high, how wonderful it would be to live one's life floating in the cool water of a stream.

As they moved further and further away from the von Ketzes' house she gripped her father's back and felt her heart beat against the stolen silk pressed at her chest. She waited for the crack of gunshot and the shock of her body being torn from the horse. But all she heard was the rattle of the dry yellow grass, quivering in the wind like the spines of a startled animal.

She turned to her sister, who was back on her horse, side-saddle. But on the return journey she was facing away from her. Her hair was ruffled and her dress creased, as if she were at the end of a very long journey. Her little fists gripped the reins so tightly that her fingers were white.

Ingrid tried to make out the hanging Hereros in the dying light. She wondered what it would be like to be hanged by the neck. She wondered, exhausted, hot and thirsty, whether there might not be some relief in it; the rope burning at the neck, yes, and the shame, but perhaps a falling to sleep, a darkness.

*

Margarete found the nightdress case beneath Ingrid's pillow the next morning.

'I made it,' Ingrid said.

'You did not,' said Margarete.

'I did make it – I made it for you.'

Margarete's mouth fell open. 'You did not,' she whispered with breathless excitement.

Ingrid, sad to let it go, but thrilled by the victory, shrugged and pretended to be cross that she'd discovered it.

'What's that on the front?' Margarete said reverentially.

'It's a bird.'

'What kind of bird?'

'A phoenix,' she said – it was in a story that Hans had told her, but she couldn't remember what the story was.

'What's a phoenix?'

'We saw one on the way here – in Okahandja.'

'Oh yes?' her sister said doubtfully.

'It's meant to be for your birthday,' she told Margarete, 'a surprise. You'll have to wait until then to use it.'

Margarete suddenly lost interest in it and it dropped to the floor as she passed it back to her. 'What do you talk to Emil about when you're over there?' Ingrid said, picking up the case and brushing the dust off it.

'Oh, nothing interesting.'

'I saw the Baroness. She thought I was you.'

'Did she?' Margarete said, unsurprised.

'It's odd isn't it? Because you've been over there so often.'

'She's never there when I go. She's always hiding

somewhere. She has stomach problems, or . . . headaches, I think.'

'So you just talk to Emil?'

'And Hans on the way over.' She offered Ingrid an exhausted smile. 'It's better when you come.'

She left Ingrid in the room, and Ingrid felt very alone. But the loneliest evening came a few weeks later, when Ingrid clung to the posts of the veranda and looked out at the empty veld. 'Come inside, dear,' Frau Hoffmann said. Ingrid turned to her mother. Her skin was milky white, despite the red blotches that suggested the heat in her cheeks and on her neck.

'Can I wait for Margarete to come back from the von Ketzes'?' Ingrid asked.

'She's staying tonight,' Frau Hoffmann said. 'The Baron came to pick her up personally.'

'Why is she staying the night?' Ingrid said, imagining Margarete in the dusty room and on the narrow bed the Baroness had sat on.

'It is a house visit,' Frau Hoffmann said. 'It's what people like the von Ketzes do. And people like us.'

'Oh,' said Ingrid, thinking about the evening without Margarete stretching on in front of her. 'Can Papa buy some more books in Windhoek?' she asked, foreseeing that this was to be the start of a new routine and that she was always to be alone.

'Perhaps,' her mother said. 'Now come inside.'

*

Ingrid lay beneath the mosquito net, tied up above her in a giant knot. Using her pillow to prop herself up, she read her worn copy of *Heidi*, slowing as she neared her favourite moment – Clara's father and grandmother returning to see their daughter walking towards them, her wheelchair in pieces at the bottom of the mountain. There was a soft knock at the door. Nora came in with clean night things and the mosquito coil.

'You will be eaten, child,' Nora said, shoving the window by Ingrid's head shut and slapping at the mosquitoes dancing about Ingrid's candle. She used the same candle to light the mosquito coil and its incense-like smoke rose up to the ceiling. Ingrid slipped off the bed and held up her arms, so that Nora could pull off her dress by the sleeves. She put on her nightdress, and Nora started to brush her hair. Ingrid closed her book and put it on the nightstand, by the candle.

'Are we not to hear *Heidi*?' Nora said, who had started to make Ingrid summarise the plot to date, before her nightly reading.

'Margarete will be cross.'

'Why?'

'Because she'll miss the part we're on.'

Nora stopped brushing and pulled Ingrid round. 'Where is she?' Nora was holding on to Ingrid's arm too tightly and it hurt. She grimaced and Nora released her.

'At the von Ketzes'. It's a house visit.'

She turned Ingrid back round and finished her hair in three violent strokes.

'You can still read to me from the Bible,' Ingrid said.

Nora manoeuvred Ingrid into bed and unwound the mosquito net. She tucked it in roughly beneath Ingrid's mattress and left the room, pulling the door shut. In the close heat of the bedroom, Ingrid turned her face to the wall and cried. She drifted off in between her shuddering breaths until, finally, she was asleep.

*

Ingrid woke feeling as though someone had shouted her name. She pushed herself up on her elbows and listened to the low crackle of the mosquito coil. Anxious at being so suddenly awake, she got up, untucked her net and went to the window. Everything was silent and – looking at the vast bush through the glass and the distant mountain range, purple in the dawn – she felt as if she was completely alone, as if there was nothing and no one between the farm, Okahandja, the edge of the desert and the sea.

She walked down the corridor to her parents' room, where she stared through the crack in the door. Their beds were empty. She went to the front of the house and unbolted the door to the veranda. 'Pina!' she called, afraid to shout loudly into so thick a silence. She waited for the dog's excited paws on the dust of their yard, but heard nothing. Sometimes she doesn't come, Ingrid thought. If she'd seen a genet or a scrub hare she might have chased it all the way to the wells – sometimes their father found her there dehydrated and had to put her over his horse and ride her home.

The sun was higher and she felt the heat of it where her foot poked out past the shade of the tin roof. Was it Sunday? Because there was no Nora and no Hans, who were always awake before the family were. She thought about the dryness of Hans's hands, his smell – of cloves, sandalwood and sweat – that clung to her clothes when he carried her from the veranda if she fell asleep there. She should have been able to hear the quiet industry of the farm labourers too, hidden by the thorn bushes and gum trees. But all she could hear were the larks in the acacia trees and the sound of dust being picked up by the breeze, turned and dropped again, like soft rain.

It must be a celebration, some sort of tribal feast day, and she imagined, hopefully, them dressed in feathers, dancing around a campfire. She went round to the back of the house to the small shelter by the monkeybread tree – a makeshift frame with a tarpaulin to shade it from the sun, where the farmworkers were allowed to take their break if they were working near the house. They rarely stood in the shade of the shelter though, preferring to stand beneath the tree; the women waited for them there with their food in pots or wrapped secretively in clean rags. The shelter was empty.

She sat on the narrow seat – a plank of wood bleached silver. There were greasy marks, from food or the farm-workers' sweating bodies. When they had arrived, just after Christmas, Margarete had asked their father how they could work in the sun all day. 'They are more physical than us,' he said. To Margarete it had seemed to mean something very terrible, something that made her afraid to be near them, especially the men; Ingrid had only pretended to understand her fear.

Ingrid left the shelter and stood on the top of a large wedge-shaped rock that the sisters had named 'the Load-stone'. It was a name that they'd read in one of their mother's books but had forgotten the significance of. They used it for games, when Margarete still played with her – either to sleep on like lions or as a sacred place for coronations and executions. She stuck her tongue into the dry iron-tasting cracks at the corners of her mouth and squinted out at the horizon. A black flock of birds flew over the hills, but were so far away they made no noise. The heat burned it all away, the colour, the sounds, the smells.

She heard movement in the house. Perhaps Nora was there after all. Perhaps the celebration was only in the morning. She tried to imagine Nora stripped to the waist and Hans naked, feathers through their noses and red earth on their skin.

When she looked away from the hills, down at the wide thorn bush in front of the Loadstone, its dark shadows turned a flashing blue. There was a strip of cloth, white and tattered, caught on the thorns. As the vision of hills faded, she saw that the bush contained a dark shape, like ink, that clung to the branches. She hopped down from the rock and a soft puff of dust bloomed out around her. The thorn bush was wet, the tips of its long spikes black. At the end of one the blackness had gathered into a droplet and she held her hand up to it and touched it and it bloomed across her finger, filling the lines of her skin with bright red blood.

'Ingrid!' her mother called. She ran round the house, but by the time she got to the veranda, the door was shut.

She found her mother in the kitchen. The table was covered in jars, tins and bowls, all opened up and ordered regimentally. At the other end sat her father with his forearms on the table, his fists closed tight and his wrists turned up, as if he were waiting to be manacled. Behind him stood Emil von Ketz, even though it wasn't his piano day.

'Hello Ingrid,' Emil said. He looked sad, as if she was about to be punished and he knew how terrible the punishment was going to be.

'Hello Emil,' she replied, rubbing the blood on her finger into the back of her hand to hide it, wondering if they had whipped Hans or Nora so hard that they had bled. Her eyes stung at the thought of it.

'You should . . .' her mother was unusually hesitant. She took a tin of milk powder off the now sparse shelves, flicked open the lid and made a note on a torn sheet of paper. She put her hand on her hip and, without looking Ingrid in the eyes, said, 'You should say Baron von Ketz now.'

Emil and her father looked at her.

'Johannes, that's right now. That's what's right.' And, as if in reply to a counter-argument that hadn't been voiced, 'We have to hold onto that now.'

Ingrid blinked. She understood what this meant – that Baron von Ketz was dead – and the news seemed very great and she was frightened. Was that where the blacks were? Burying him? Would there be a funeral? Would they have to sing? Would she have to see his body?

'What's that all over you?' said her mother.

Ingrid looked down at her nightdress – it was speckled with blood, already dried brown. 'I was outside.'

Her mother placed the tin of powdered milk on the table.

'What's happening?' Ingrid said.

Her mother turned back to the shelves. 'We're going on a trip. To Okahandja.'

Ingrid licked the hard edge of one of her emerging molars and felt suspicious of her mother's pacifying tone. She recalled little from Okahandja, except the house they had stayed in that first week, what a shock the heat was and how badly she'd slept, with flies constantly at her mouth and nose; and Hans of course, silhouetted behind the insect screen.

'Where's Nora?' she asked, holding on to the doorframe, the foot of one leg pressed against the calf of the other. She wanted to say 'Where's Hans?', but was afraid they might guess that she intended to run off with him the moment she was old enough to have a baby; that he was going to lead her across the veld and then the desert, into Bechuanaland and then into one of those big British cities in Rhodesia, where she could use the English and French she was learning with him and he could pretend to be her houseboy until they could get married and have a baby. She hadn't yet revealed her plan to him and now they were going to Okahandja – for how long she didn't know – and what if she had missed her chance?

Her father looked up. He was tired and dirty. He smiled comfortingly. 'Ingrid my dear, we have been abandoned.'

'What do you mean?'

'He means they've all disappeared – they all have.'

'Why?'

Emil von Ketz looked at them nervously.

'We don't need them anyhow,' her mother said. 'We're setting off today – the Baron will help us.'

Emil tried to mimic her father's comforting smile, but his lips stretched into a painful grimace.

'Where's Margarete?'

'In the drawing room,' her father said. 'She's fine.'

'Why shouldn't she be fine?' said Ingrid.

'Don't badger her,' said her mother.

'I can't find Pina,' said Ingrid. 'Did they take Pina too?'

'No,' her father said softly. 'She'll have chased a hare down to the wells.'

Ingrid thought about Pina and the blood on the bush, then she thought about Hans and Nora and her eyes stung again. Some of the labourers might go, she supposed – the proper Hereros who went to tribal meetings and talked to each other in clicking song – but Hans and Nora would not really be gone. She looked at her parents and felt that they were expecting her to say something, so she said, 'Are we not having breakfast then?'

'In Germany, you'd be whipped for that mouth of yours,'

her mother said with measured disgust. 'And you keep quiet, you hear – Baroness von Ketz is asleep in the guest room. She is *not* to be disturbed.'

Ingrid spun on her foot and walked heavily to the drawing room. In the corridor she heard a light crack. The Baroness stood in the doorway of the guest room looking at her. She was shaking and her mouth was ajar and her staring eyes were two white discs, red-ringed and perfectly round. She'd gone mad; her expression was one of joyful awe. 'They got him,' she said.

Her mother appeared behind her and snapped 'Ingrid,' projecting her into the drawing room and slamming the door shut.

Margarete was sitting in the hard little wingback chair pretending she hadn't been listening. Her body had distorted strangely over the last year and her legs jutted out from the chair, incongruously long and awkward, the knees smeared with grey bruises, the calves covered with a light blonde hair, struck through with bright red slashes from thorns and splintered wood.

'What happened?' Ingrid said. 'Is the Baron dead?'

'Yes,' said Margarete.

'Did you see it?'

Margarete shook her head vehemently.

'Emil and the Baroness are here,' Ingrid said. 'There's blood on the thorn bush. And Hans and Nora are gone. I can't find Pina.'

'Hans didn't disappear with the others. He's with the Baron. He's sorting him out, then he's going to meet us in Okahandja.'

Ingrid's body slumped with relief. 'It'll all be all right then,' she said, taking Margarete's icy hand. 'At least we'll have Hans.'

Margarete smiled, but it was all lip, so that Ingrid knew that something terrible was coming. 'What is it?' she said, crestfallen.

'Nothing,' said Margarete.

Ingrid put her hand on the soft down of her sister's arm. 'Come on Margarete,' she said, stroking her. 'Don't be gloomy. They've all gone and Mama's in a terrible state. You can't be gloomy too. You always think it's terrible and it's only what comes after that's terrible.'

But Margarete was already stiff and Ingrid knew it had taken hold of her. She stared at her legs, pushed tightly together, as if they'd been bound.

'I'll get Mama,' said Ingrid, her voice shaking despite herself.

Margarete grabbed her by the arm, her fingers painfully pinching her skin. 'Don't leave me.' Margarete's eyes were large and green and protruded from her face a little too far, this morning even more than usual.

There was a crash of feet outside the door, followed by their mother's muffled call.

'What are they doing now?' Margarete said, but it was a sad, searching question that wasn't meant to be answered.

'I suppose the Baroness is very upset about the Baron.'

Ingrid looked at Margarete. They had both hated him, because he was a big, cruel drunk, and their father was strange and weak when he was with him. But the thought that he might have succumbed to whatever threat was hanging over the house was terrible. Because if he could disappear, so could anyone.

'Play baby with me,' Margarete said.

They never played baby any more, and when they did Ingrid hated it, because she was younger and so she should be the baby. But she wanted to ignore her parents' raised voices and the sound of furniture being moved in other rooms, and if they didn't play it, what else could they do?

Margarete went back to the chair and shifted down in it, making a pretence of looking more wan and unwell than she already did.

'Are we going to play it here?'

'Well, we can't play it in our room now, can we?' said Margarete sadly. 'They put the Baroness in there.'

Ingrid tucked her sister into the chair, while humming a lullaby. She felt, for the first time, as if she was acting rather than playing, as if her actions were the result of deceit rather than imagination, and she was embarrassed by her false gestures. But her sister didn't seem to notice; she just stared at the photograph of the Kaiser on the wall that their father had tacked up above the piano, so that Emil von Ketz thought they were decent when he came and played.

Ingrid brushed her sister's hair away from her face and said, 'Go to sleep baby.'

They heard a door slam and Ingrid and Margarete jumped. A flock of larks took off whistling and both girls ran to the window. They squinted out at the land behind the monkeybread tree, at the grey thorn, the rocks and the orange mountain beyond. But there was no trace of anyone coming for them. There was no trace of anyone at all.

*

The girls were woken by their father. The cicadas rattled and a scops owl chirruped cautiously in the night. The single candle held in his hand turned the smoke from the mosquito coil from blue to orange and picked out the pale angled shadows of their mosquito nets. Ingrid watched Margarete sit up beneath her own veil and rub at her dry eyes. She stroked the netting as their father talked.

'It's time for us to go,' he said. 'Just for a while, so we can't take much. You must only take what is most precious.'

Ingrid looked at the black sky behind the mesh of the window.

'Have they come for us?' Ingrid said.

'No,' said her father. 'We can go. You're safe. We're all safe.'

Their mother walked out with them and their footsteps were very loud on the dust. Outside the air was cool and the cicadas were shrill. There was no wind and the stars and crescent moon were bright enough that they could make out the curve of the wagon's canopy and the dark mountains in the distance.

A match was struck and they saw Emil's face, glowing orange, fading, and then a lamp warming and the light of it spreading over Emil at the head of the wagon, over the oxen and then over the bushes. She thought she saw feet there, but they were gone, and then she heard the barest traces of movement: the creak of a branch settling, a thorn cracking off, the butt of a rifle rested on the ground.

Silently, her mother pushed them forward. Emil climbed up to the driver's seat. The girls were lifted up and found the wide space under the canopy almost empty, except for two chests and a sack, pushed between them, not even tied up at the top, and Baroness von Ketz a thin silent body in one corner.

Frau Hoffmann sat against one side of the wagon and Ingrid and Margarete gripped her. Their father came out of the house, moving swiftly, holding something. It was a long gun, a rifle, and in the dark a figure came forward and their father stopped dead. The way he moved, sideways towards the wagon, circling the shape in the dark, made Ingrid think for a moment that it was a lion that could smell their fear in the blackness. One never turns one's back on lions, Hans had told them.

Her father shouted, 'Get moving!' He was scrambling up into the wagon. Their mother pulled him, but his trousers were caught, and he was swearing and saying, 'Go, Emil, go!' He threw the rifle clattering onto the wooden floor and the whip cracked. The cattle groaned, the rope groaned, the wooden axles groaned, and the wagon moved forward. 'Get me up! Get me up!' their father squealed in a high voice, and Ingrid thought with horror that he was crying. Behind him the figure didn't move. It stood still as the wagon picked up speed, as their father finally fell in with a strange cry and a rip of cloth and curled up with their mother on top of him, whispering maternally to him in the dark.

The wagon shuddered as the path became rougher. Their father calmed and sat with his back against the canvas walls breathing in shuddering gasps, clutching the rifle to him. Their mother found her way back to them and pulled them in to her.

'What about Pina?' Margarete said.

'Oh, she can't come, darling ones,' said their mother. 'She'll be safe here.'

'We have to go back!' said Margarete.

'Pina!' said Ingrid and they cried, a slow mournful wail for their lost friend.

Through her tears, Ingrid watched the path behind winding away. There were shapes in the bushes and Ingrid thought they were trees and then Hereros and then trees again. Sometimes a tree's crown was revealed, sometimes the shadow shifted and moved away back into the bush, and once white eyes blinked and the shadows moved onto the path behind them and remained there shrinking as the wagon moved on.

Her mother gasped, and Ingrid felt her breast shake. From behind the house a pale cloud of smoke had gathered, rolling upwards. Flames burst from the door and seconds later the high peal of broken glass reached them. Fire licked out of the windows and the doors and, veld-dry, the house ignited with a soft dry woof. They started at the sight of it, and then once more at the sound. Margarete's hand found Ingrid's. In the dark her mother put her hands over Ingrid's face, but only one eye was covered, and she watched the flames rise into the sky, three times the height of the house. She saw figures gathering around the house, but they were too far away to hear now. They were just sparkling orange bodies in the night.

*

They stopped near some low mountains and Emil got down from his seat. Their parents had fallen asleep across each other, their mother in their father's lap, their father lying across her back, his hand outstretched, twitching. The Baroness remained a hard mound in the corner. But the cessation of the wagon's rocking and the lowing of the oxen didn't wake them.

The sun rose yellow from behind the hills and the veld was filled with purple light. The dirt of the road and the rocks of the hills glowed red in response. The black spots of acacia turned a dark forest-green and were as hard and still as stone.

Emil appeared at the back of the wagon. His face was

tired and dirty and his shirt was soaked in sweat despite the cold of the morning.

'There are wild currants here,' he said. 'Do you want to pick some? Are you hungry?'

The sisters shook their heads.

Emil nodded and they listened to him walking into the bush to relieve himself. Ingrid looked at Margarete, whose eyes were tired and wide with fear.

'Don't worry, Little Fly,' Margarete said. 'We'll go home to Germany now.' But instead of embracing her, Margarete fell into Ingrid's lap and wept wildly. Ingrid leant back on the cloth wall of the wagon and stroked her sister's hair. She listened to her muffled sobs and to Emil's footsteps returning and wondered if it had been Nora out there in the dark by the house. Or was it her in the bushes or on the road? It was like she had been washed out to sea, into something far too vast to be found again. But Hans was coming back to them. She must take consolation in that, she supposed.

PART TWO

— Returning —

Lüderitz Bay,
German Southwest Africa

— 1906 —

Ingrid sat on the chair in the hallway in her good dress. She had got ready for the dance early, and when the postman arrived she stood and waited for him to dole out the letters and telegrams to Frau Wille, who ran the best of Lüderitz Bay's three guesthouses. Frau Wille sorted the letters and abruptly handed the Hoffmanns' to Ingrid without a word; she found this daily routine tiresome. Ingrid's fingers walked over the edge of each envelope and found only one with handwriting she didn't recognise, and which therefore might contain news of Hans.

The door to the street opened. The bell above it clattered and a breath of hot wind met the stale air of the hallway.

'Waiting for good news?'

Ingrid looked up to find a young priest kicking the dust off his boots against the doorstep. He removed his black Lutheran beret and, despite his youth, she saw that he was already bald, with a strip of close-cropped black hair circling his head and pooling in a single dot, like an inky thumbprint, above the glossy skin of his forehead.

'Schäfer,' he said and offered her his hand.

She shook it and said, 'Ingrid Hoffmann.'

'Your letter – are you waiting for good news?'

It had been so long since they had lived anywhere near a church that she had no idea how she should speak to a priest, especially one younger than her parents. He is a man of God, she thought, so she stared at the starched white bands at his neck and said, 'It's our houseboy Hans, from our old farm. We had to flee in the Herero Uprising, and he was meant to meet us in Okahandja, but never came. I'm afraid they killed him or he was captured. Now we're in Lüderitz, because we're taking the ship back to Germany – if he doesn't find us now, he may never.'

Schäfer shut the door and used his cap to brush off the dust that clung to his gown. 'You're one of those Hoffmanns, then?' he said. He smiled and frowned at the same time, which gave him a look of friendly concern. His eyes were startlingly blue.

'Are we infamous, Father?'

'No, no,' he laughed. 'I didn't mean to sound flippant. I had heard about your troubles in the Uprising. Frau Wille had mentioned it. Tell me about your houseboy.'

Ingrid clutched the correspondence protectively to her breast and said, 'That is all I can tell you. We left him over two years ago now, so there's not much hope, I know.'

'Was he Herero?'

'No. Well, half. Half-caste.'

'Half white?'

'Yes,' she said. 'He taught me French and English.'

'He sounds like a veritable polymath.'

'No, not a polymath. But he was our friend.'

Frau Wille poked her head out of the breakfast room and

80

said, 'Private conversations should be held in private rooms.' And then seeing the priest, added, 'If you don't mind me saying, Father.'

'No, indeed. Quite right, Frau Wille.'

'I have to get back to my room anyway, Father,' said Ingrid. 'We have a dance.'

The priest seemed saddened by this and Ingrid felt a pang of guilt. She ran up the stairs to their rooms and, already sweating, handed the packet to her father, who was sitting in the little drawing room completing his correspondence on the escritoire. Without comment, he sliced open the envelope with the strange handwriting, glanced at the contents and said, 'It's about the railroad land.'

Disappointed, Ingrid went to her room and threw herself down on her bed. Minna, the guesthouse maid, was doing Margarete's hair. Ingrid caught Margarete's eyes in the mirror and waited for her to say something.

'Don't plait it too tight, Minna,' she said. 'I'll get a headache.'

'No news about Hans,' Ingrid said.

'He abandoned us, Ingrid!' Margarete snapped.

'He might have been killed.'

'He ran off with the other Hereros. You can't trust them since the Uprising – even half-castes. Ask Minna.'

Minna, who was Ovambo, flicked a bunch of Margarete's golden hair up and put a hairpin in her mouth, thus silencing herself.

'I don't know why you're being so touchy about it,' Ingrid said. 'He told Papa he'd find us. Papa doesn't think he ran off with the others.'

'I'm not being touchy,' Margarete said. 'And anyway, Papa's sentimental. Mama always says so.'

'What do I always say?' said Frau Hoffmann, entering the room, filling it with the smell of Voilette de Madame.

'That Papa's sentimental,' said Ingrid sitting up on the bed.

Frau Hoffmann lifted Ingrid's chin and said, 'The boy's dead, Ingrid dear. It's sweet of you to hope, but you're also an irritation to Frau Wille, and she's already at me about the ungodly hours your father's keeping with his work.'

'Well, we're leaving soon and then he'll never find us, so I suppose you'll be happy then.'

'Don't be dramatic, Ingrid,' her mother said and clapped her hands. 'Up, up Margarete. Minna's done quite enough to ruin that beautiful hair of yours. Let's be on our way.'

Margarete stood and Ingrid roused herself. Their mother shooed them down the stairs and onto the street. They had returned to Okahandja, and stayed for a year at the commissioner's house, where Ingrid had been thrilled by the shelves of books, but terrified by their mother's reports of the Uprising. 'We've been terribly lucky' was repeated again and again like an invocation, whenever their father read from the newspaper about another atrocity perpetrated by the Herero or Nama in their bid to slaughter the Germans. Once the route was deemed safe, they made their way to Lüderitz Bay, where they took rooms at Frau Wille's guesthouse and waited for their father to tie up his interests, so that they could sail back to Germany.

Ingrid felt their time on the farm had brought about a change in her mother; she had, in the words of the commissioner's wife, taken on airs. This Ingrid had overheard in Okahandja. Her father seemed older and more commanding. Margarete had calmed, though she still had bad days when she couldn't leave her room and a few nights when Ingrid had woken to hear her weeping. She would climb into

Margarete's bed and hold her. She would wipe at her face and say, 'It's all right, Little Fly. It's nothing. I'm all cried out. Go back to sleep.'

As they made their way across the street, Ingrid felt that only she had stayed the same.

The sun was dropping and their shadows elongated before them on the yellow road. The telegraph wires snapped and the telegraph poles filled the air with the smell of warm creosote. Sand was swirled by the breeze in eddies that rattled drily across the ground before sweeping up to settle on the sill of a window or against the wheel of a cart, so that the cart seemed to sink down into the ground, into the granite beneath the town.

'I can barely walk in this heat,' Margarete said, 'let alone dance.'

'You needn't dance,' her mother said. 'You're just there to make up numbers.'

'I won't dance,' said Ingrid, recalling the sharp dungy smell of the sweat-stained Germans that loafed about the streets and on the verandas of Lüderitz, imagining them pulling her close to them, the stink of their stiff shirts.

'You're both far too young to go to a dance as it is,' their mother said, as they approached the clubhouse and heard the drunken sweep of a waltz, the instruments slightly out of tune. 'But there's barely a young woman in the town and your father promised Frau Biedersheim. Just sit about and look decorative.'

'We can't talk to anyone?' Ingrid said.

'You can talk to Baron von Ketz – he should have arrived today.'

'Why is he always following us around?' Margarete said. 'We can't even leave the country without him.'

'You think this sort of talk makes you sound clever, Margarete, but it only makes you sound stupid, my dear. Dull people complain like that, so that others believe them to have an edge of some kind. You have no edge; you're seventeen. You have only your youth, and that's fleeting, and a place in the world that your father has struggled to claim for you.'

Herr Lüd's loud greeting at the door cut off any response and the girls dutifully followed their mother into the terrible closeness of the room. The white of their dresses, which reflected a little of the heat of the sun, did them no good in the dingy light of the dance hall. The sun that had turned the lace curtains golden quickly died and the oil lamps lit the room a browny orange. Their mother hurried the girls to the back of the room, laughing and sharing snippets of conversation with the elder women of Lüderitz, their faces tanned and creased like packing paper.

The girls were placed at a trestle table where sprigs of desert edelweiss and yellow mouse-whiskers wilted in the heat, dropping their leaves onto the white tablecloth. Their mother left them the moment they had sat, returning to the clique at the door.

'Dear Frau Hoffmann, why didn't you leave from Swakopmund or Walvis Bay? What a hellish goodbye to Southwest,' one of the women said to their mother.

'Herr Hoffmann had something important to do in Lüderitz. It was imperative, apparently.'

'Is he diamonds, like my Michael?'

'No, land.'

'Diamonds is where the money is of course – land is so insecure, though I'm sure Herr Hoffmann has learnt that the hard way,' the woman said, carrying their mother away.

A few groups of men were gathered in distant corners. Their mother joined a circle around a woman severe and important enough to collect a clutch of younger hangers-on around the wicker seat that had been brought in especially for her.

'Who's she?' Ingrid asked.

'I don't know,' Margarete said, taking her sister's hand and stroking her cheek with it.

'Are you all right?' Ingrid said, searching Margarete's face for signs of strain.

'Oh yes, yes,' Margarete said throwing herself back in her chair. Sweat gathered at her hairline and she scratched the side of her little nose with her middle finger.

'You look very pretty,' Ingrid said.

Margarete looked at her seriously. 'You never think of yourself, do you, Little Fly?'

'What do you mean?'

'You're always watching me, worrying about me. Or worrying about Mama and Papa. Worrying about Hans. Worrying how best to react to things. But what about you?' She touched the ruched collar of Ingrid's dress. 'No one worries about Little Fly, because she's so good and so easy. Because she's no trouble at all.'

'I'm not good,' Ingrid said.

Margarete laughed. Her hand slipped from Ingrid's shoulder and she turned back to the room, taking a long, hot, exhausted breath.

'When do you think Emil will arrive?' Ingrid said. 'Do you think he's changed much?'

'Why should he have changed?'

'The war against the Hereros.'

'I can't imagine eighteen months of shooting at the natives will have made much of him.'

'Will you marry him the moment we get back, do you think?'

'He hasn't asked me.'

'You can't think he won't.'

'No, I suppose I can't think that,' Margarete said. 'But I'm sure he'll wait until I'm eighteen.' She was staring at the few other young women in the room; the three youngest stood bunched together nervously and must have been barely older than Margarete. Two sat: lipless blonde-haired twins in matching dresses. The third stood: a girl they knew to be called Fräulein Hannig, with a boss eye and poor teeth. They also knew that they were meant to be kind to her, because her parents had died and she had no relations left in Germany that might take her back. This girl made Ingrid feel afraid; she was so alone and cut loose from the world.

Margarete said, 'No one's going to marry that poor girl, are they? Perhaps she's terribly clever. If no one marries her, she may as well put an end to it.'

'She'll become very pious I suppose,' Ingrid said. 'I met a missionary today in Frau Wille's guesthouse – Father Schäfer. He's just the sort who'll take her.'

Margarete laughed. 'And she can die of malaria in Damaraland to the sound of the natives singing German hymns. Lucky thing.'

Ingrid laughed. At that moment Fräulein Hannig caught her eye and Margarete gripped Ingrid's hand.

'You little fool – she's going to talk to us now.'

'Why should it matter if she talks to us?' Ingrid said, trying to make herself feel better about giving in to her sister's acid tongue, but she was also filled with dismay when the girl whispered something to the twins and made her way over to them. They stood and shook hands.

'You're the Hoffmanns.'

'Yes, it's Fräulein Hannig, I believe,' Margarete said.

'Yes,' she said, in a low voice that was softened by the extent of her front teeth, which protruded from her mouth, giving her a slight lisp. 'Sit, sit,' she said. 'This heat's unbearable.' They did as they were told and Fräulein Hannig said, 'You won't be with us for much longer, I hear.'

'No,' said Margarete. 'We're back to Germany, thank God.'

'We'd like to have stayed longer,' Ingrid said, embarrassed, though Fräulein Hannig showed no signs of embarrassment.

'Southwest is a hard place for young women,' she said, looking out over the dance floor, frowning as if she were searching for someone. 'You were caught up in the Uprising, I believe.'

'Barely,' said Margarete.

Fräulein Hannig threw her a confounded look beneath which the sarcastic purse of Margarete's lips collapsed; she sniffed and picked at the lace doily beneath the flower vase. Fräulein Hannig said to Ingrid, 'Wasn't the old Baron von Ketz killed? You were neighbours?'

'That's right,' Ingrid said. 'But we didn't know what had happened until later. Everyone was just gone and we had to leave.'

'What an awful state of affairs,' she said, without any sense of conviction. 'And they all just left? The Negroes, I mean.'

'Yes, they all left,' Ingrid said. 'But since then we've heard such awful stories about people attacked. None of that happened to us.'

'They did burn our house down,' Margarete said in a bored tone, as if it barely mattered.

'Ghastly for your parents I'm sure. One accommodates so much change when one's young, doesn't one? One is so in the moment that one takes it all on one's shoulders immediately and lets it all roll off again when it's over.'

Ingrid didn't think this was true at all. She often lay awake, wondering which of the dark shapes had been Nora, wondering if she had joined the Herero or been taken by them. 'Joined, of course,' her sister had said, but still Ingrid thought about her. And Hans. When they walked the streets of Okahandja and then Lüderitz, when they entered a store, she wondered if she would see the back of a smart beige coat and he would turn, his face fixed in brief shock. Then he would smile and hold out his hand to her.

Fräulein Hannig stared out at the room. No, she wouldn't be a missionary's wife. She would become a missionary herself. Ingrid felt that Fräulein Hannig was on the edge of some great discovery. She saw her as a small resolute figure, wind and red sand cracking on the white cotton that covered her head and her body, travelling through the desert alone to save souls, with complete conviction about the task ahead. She felt jealous of her. I will never have conviction, she thought sadly. I will never blindly be able to believe in anything.

Fräulein Hannig's gaze shifted to the door and Ingrid looked up to see Emil von Ketz. He was shaved except for a neat moustache, the blond a little darker than that on his head, and the spots around his mouth were gone. He was wearing the military uniform of the Schutztruppe and since they had last seen him he had fought at Waterberg. Standing up straight in his uniform, he seemed to have aged ten years. He took off his hat and she saw that he'd cut his hair short. He brushed his fingers through it in an adult gesture she didn't recognise: a movement, like his posture and the way he had shaped his moustache, that he must have learnt from other men his age, having been deprived of young male company for so long on the farm.

'Who's that?' Fräulein Hannig said.

'That's the Baron von Ketz,' said Margarete with a studiously casual tone. To Ingrid's delight he spotted them and waved.

He was caught by their mother as he passed, but he brushed her off with a friendly word of greeting and found Ingrid and Margarete at the back of the room. He kissed their hands one after the other and gave Fräulein Hannig only the briefest greeting.

'The Fräuleins Hoffmann! How have you been?'

'Gosh, you look well,' Ingrid said.

Von Ketz smiled.

'I'm ready for Germany,' said Margarete, placing her hand on his shoulder and leaving it there too long. Fräulein Hannig kept glancing at it, like a cat at a flash of light cast from a pocket watch.

'You are to return home with the Hoffmanns, I hear,' Fräulein Hannig said.

Von Ketz sat down, Margarete's hand fell away, and he dropped his hat into his lap, resting his arm on the table and flicking a few of the fallen petals onto the floor. 'That's right,' he said.

'Word has it that you've been a very brave volunteer.'

'Word has it, eh?' said von Ketz.

Margarete and Ingrid stared at him.

'Look, you've surprised the Hoffmanns, Fräulein Hannig. They only know me as an indolent youth who plays the piano.'

Margarete and Ingrid laughed, Margarete ending with an unnecessarily elaborate cackle, touching the bare skin of her neck above her breasts.

'It's no laughing matter,' Fräulein Hannig said. 'I suppose it helps to make light of it, but our German civilisation here was at risk of being wiped out. It was you, Herr Baron, and your comrades that drove Samuel Maharero and his Negro traitors back.'

Von Ketz's smile faded and he said, 'Quite right, Fräulein Hannig. It's good of you to say.'

She dipped her head, content with this concession. Her fingernail tapped at the table, then stopped. 'I was very sad to hear about your father.'

Ingrid's stomach tensed, but von Ketz nodded, not looking at her, and said, 'Yes. Well, thank you, that's kind,' and then said to Ingrid, 'Aren't you going to dance, Fräulein Ingrid?'

Ingrid smiled. 'I'm not allowed to dance.'

'Why on earth not?'

'Mother won't allow it,' said Margarete. 'She's too young.'

'How are we to get you a husband if you aren't allowed to dance?'

Margarete rolled her eyes, but Ingrid laughed brightly.

'Baron von Ketz,' Fräulein Hannig said. 'Have you met the Britz twins? I'm sure they would be happy to take a turn.'

Von Ketz opened his mouth to answer, but stopped himself. Ingrid waited. She felt her heart beating and was afraid that it might be heard, because it meant nothing to her if von Ketz danced with the Britz twins. She just didn't want to be left alone, bored – that was all she was afraid of. She felt a pain in her cheek, which was only relieved by Margarete saying, 'Oh, do go and dance, Herr Baron. We'll survive your absence.'

Von Ketz nodded and they watched him weave through the chairs with Fräulein Hannig, who did not say goodbye.

'What a ghastly girl,' Margarete said, flapping at herself with the paper programme discarded on the table.

'It's nice that Emil came.'

'Oh Ingrid, he's such a fool.'

'He is not,' she said.

'Germany will be full of chaps and you'll see what a bore he is and what a trap Mama and Papa have set for me.'

The twins and then Fräulein Hannig danced with von Ketz. A number of married couples joined and at one point eight couples were spinning at the same time. There was a sense of relief that the dance had been a success. Ingrid watched von Ketz; sometimes he caught her eye. Mostly he turned and turned and the sweat beaded on his forehead and his neck flushed red. Once or twice she saw him saying something to one of the older girls, and felt possessive; he was theirs, the Hoffmanns'. He had come because they were there.

Ingrid's mother appeared by her side and picked up her hand. She kissed it and placed it against her cheek. 'You always have such lovely cool hands, Ingrid,' she said.

'They're large,' said Ingrid, thinking how soft the down on her mother's face was. 'And they sweat.'

Her mother kissed Ingrid's hand again and held it to her chest. The back of her fingers touched Ingrid's cheek.

'Don't you think you should let Margarete dance with Emil?' Ingrid said.

'The Baron has no interest in the Britz twins.'

'They're quite pretty.'

'You don't need to worry about these sort of things, Ingrid. Your father and I have taken care of it all. Where is she?'

'Margarete?' said Ingrid. She saw that her chair was empty. 'Oh,' she said, 'I don't know.'

'Is something the matter?' It was von Ketz, who had rushed over as if there were a crisis, but her mother had not cried out. She was still holding Ingrid's hand and looked at von Ketz with undisguised surprise.

'Margarete's gone,' Ingrid said.

'She's not gone,' said her mother. 'She's wandered out somewhere. Why always this drama, Ingrid?'

'I'll go and find her,' Ingrid said.

'Let me go,' said von Ketz. 'Just outside to check.'

'Oh, that would be kind,' her mother said, then placed Ingrid's hand back in her lap and whispered to her, 'I'll look in the WC. Don't you dare leave.'

She watched von Ketz disappear through the door and then her mother move slowly out of the back of the building, smiling and nodding as she went. When she was out of sight, Ingrid slipped out past the stern woman on the wicker chair and onto the dark street.

Ingrid's dress was damp with sweat and she felt a blissful flutter of wind on her forehead and at her neck. She saw von Ketz disappear down Bismarckstraße and followed him, avoiding the questioning gaze of a group of drunk diamond-traders at the inn on the square and a gaggle of African children opposite in the doorway of the laundry.

Emil passed Moltkestraße without turning, perhaps

because it was unlit and black, and people moved in the dark there. But Ingrid stopped. Eyes looked at her, children and drunks. She saw behind them, looking out to the jetty at the sea front, the forget-me-not blue of Margarete's dress, lit by the gaslight at the quay.

'Fräulein Ingrid!'

It was von Ketz, who had turned and seen her, but she dived into the darkness, passed the people there, smelling the sweat and the alcohol, hearing a dog bark and then whine, tripping on something metal and landing in the soft sand that covered the street, picking herself up as a cold sweat broke across her back, afraid that von Ketz would get to her before she got to her sister.

'Margarete!' she called out.

Margarete turned. Her face was white. Ingrid grabbed her shoulder and stared into Hafenstraße. At first she couldn't make out what was happening in the copper-coloured gaslight. There were wagons and mules and white men with whips. Out of the wagons came groans and the shrill jangle of chains. A door was opened – the sharp crack of a metal catch and wood clattering. She smelt faeces and the sweat of the sick, she smelt vomit and blood, and saw a group of figures, black men, being led by the neck onto the street. From another wagon came the voice of a woman calling. She heard children crying.

'That's what we've done to him,' Margarete said. 'I can't bury it. I try so hard.'

'Who?' said Ingrid. 'Bury what?'

'Hans,' said Margarete.

'Hans isn't there, Margarete.'

'He's somewhere like this.'

'You said he'd run away,' said Ingrid, afraid.

'Because I can't bear to think about it.'

'I thought you didn't care about him.'

Margarete looked at the wagons. 'I care if he's there like them. Of course I care.'

'Get away from there,' said von Ketz, dodging in front of them with his arms held out as if he could cover up what they were seeing.

'Who are they?' said Ingrid. Margarete turned at the sound of von Ketz's voice and buried her face in Ingrid's neck.

'Get away from there,' said von Ketz, pulling Ingrid's arm.

'Oh, Emil!' she said, forgetting his title, 'Who are they? What's happening to them?'

'They're Herero and Nama of course. We captured them when we were putting down the Uprising. They're prisoners of war.'

'Where are they going?'

'Shark Island. To the camp.'

'Margarete was worried that Hans was there.'

'Hans?' said von Ketz. 'What do you mean? Why would Hans be there?'

'You see,' Ingrid said. 'You're not to worry about it, Margarete.'

They heard a whip hit flesh then a weary cry. Sand-filled wind crackled against the walls around them and the black sea slapped the granite of the harbour rocks. Ingrid pulled Margarete away, back into the darkness, back to the street. Von Ketz gripped her shoulder; she put her hand up and touched his fingers, where the skin was rough and dry around the fingernails.

'Get away from us!' Margarete said.

Ingrid felt von Ketz stiffen.

'Oh, Margarete, the Baron's helping.'

'I didn't put them there,' von Ketz said. 'They're prisoners – they put themselves there.'

Margarete shivered where Ingrid gripped her waist. The world was terrible, Ingrid thought, and perhaps Margarete was the only person who felt it honestly.

*

Ingrid felt hot and dizzy in the cabin, as the ship, still at anchor, gently rose and fell in the harbour waters. She held on to the bedpost and watched the doctor press the black horn of his stethoscope to Margarete's heart. The doctor looked up at Frau Hoffmann and nodded, a signal that she should leave with Ingrid, so that he could give Herr Hoffmann his diagnosis. Ingrid felt her mother pull her; she held on to the wood of the bed frame for a second, no more, to protest at her removal.

Her mother put her hand on her back and navigated her down the corridor. She reached out and let her hand stroke the wood panelling until her mother gently placed her hand back by her side.

'What's wrong with her?' Ingrid asked. 'Will you tell me, when you know?' Since the quay, Margarete had been pale and silent, unable even to hold clear soup in her mouth or swallow water without her jaw being held shut for her.

Her mother gripped her arm, pulling it as if she was arresting her. Ingrid looked at her face, but it wasn't angry. 'There is nothing wrong with her body, Ingrid. You understand that, don't you?'

The corridor smelt of polished wood, tobacco and face powder. At Frau Hoffmann's neck a mother-of-pearl dragonfly had settled near her collar. It watched her with its garnet eyes.

'Yes,' Ingrid said. 'I do understand that.'

*

From the top deck of the ship, Ingrid stared at Shark Island, at the dirty ochre rock of the peninsula and the low buildings there, that shimmered like fuzzy silver strips from where they were anchored. She felt light as if she was at the edge of something, unsure whether she would lift into the air or tumble into the darkness.

She looked down from the top deck at the hats of the passengers below. The Hoffmanns had all travelled together in two second-class carriages when they had come to Southwest, she was sure they had, though her mother said that she was misremembering. Now she had her own cabin with a porthole beside her narrow bed, a dressing table and a small stuffed chair. She had never had a room to herself and that would change her further; she barely knew who would walk down the gangplank into Europe inhabiting her body.

She heard footsteps on the wood that she knew to be von Ketz's. It was a man approaching too consciously to be a casual acquaintance and without the tight, confident urgency of her father.

She saw his hands appear on the railings. She could smell the soap on them – the violet soap that she had in her own cabin.

'Is the Baroness comfortable?' Ingrid asked.

'Yes,' he said. Distantly she could hear the hush of the sea breaking on the rock of the port. 'I talked to the governor's son about the Negroes.'

'Oh yes?' said Ingrid.

'They are prisoners from Keetmanshoop. It's six hundred kilometres from the farm – it's not possible that your sister saw Hans in that crowd. They're just Herero left over from the Uprising.'

'She didn't say she'd seen him.'

'Why was she so upset then?'

'She thought something similar might have happened to him, I think. It was selfish of me not to realise she'd been worrying about him too. And she's right – it is possible he could have run away and fought in the Uprising, so it's not unimaginable he might have been put into a camp. What did they do?'

'The Herero?'

'No,' Ingrid said, 'those specific Herero.'

'They all rose up – all the Herero. They're dangerous. They're prisoners.'

'I thought the war was over.'

'War's never really over,' he said. 'Not until they're all gone.'

'Gone?' she said, but he didn't respond.

Ingrid felt her body shifting and the floor beneath them shuddered. The wind carried black smoke then grey over their heads and towards the island. From this distance she couldn't make out individual people, only sensed a mass of bodies. She thought of Hans there among them, a thick iron chain round his neck, Nora, naked and manacled, her face still held up against the sun like a shield. She felt a pressure in her throat and realised too late that it was tears and she buried her face in her arm and turned away from von Ketz.

'Germany's really home,' he said. 'If you think about it.'

'Yes, it's hard to leave,' she said. 'That's what it is.'

97

She heard a long sorrowful moan. It was the boat. She touched the metal of the railing, felt the warm buzz of the ship and, realising it wouldn't stop until they reached Europe, wondered if it would be that that drove her mad.

Windscheidstraße 53, Charlottenburg

— 1908 —

In an apartment in the front building of Windscheidstraße 53, Ingrid and Margarete stepped up to each doorway cautiously and peered into each room. Margarete gripped Ingrid's hand, relieved to be away from the clamour of people on the streets, the cliffs of apartment blocks and the constant noise, of men and machines, rising and falling, over and over again. The tumult made Ingrid dizzy and nauseous. Her only peace had been the train from Hamburg, when they had had their own cabin and she was able to open the window and get the wind on her face.

'What's this going to be?' Ingrid said, her voice echoing off the hard shiny floors and bare walls.

'Well,' said her mother, reaching up to clunk open the hidden catch of the high double doors and pushing them open, 'this will be the drawing room.'

They walked in. The room was empty. There were three huge windows in a row, with double frames. The sun shone through them, making the dust glow and the panes translucent. Ingrid scratched at the dry scab of an old mosquito bite on her arm and her eye followed the edge of the room up to a white stucco ceiling where a band of vines snaked to the centre and bloomed into an intricate floral mound. A shining copper wire for an electrical light hung down from its middle. There was a constant coolness coming from the walls. She shivered.

'What's the smell?' Margarete said. 'It's like dirt.'

'That's the fresh plaster,' her mother said. 'We're the first in and I think it's wonderful. Quite wonderful.'

'If it's new, why are the windows so filthy?' Margarete asked.

'The windows will be cleaned,' said her mother, in her most teacherly voice.

Margarete looked at the room suspiciously and sniffed again at the sour smell.

'And then over here,' Frau Hoffmann said, her boots cracking on the rugless parquet, 'is what we call the in-between room, here in Berlin, which is where we receive guests.'

'Ha!' Margarete said, clinging even closer to Ingrid, the blonde hairs on her bare tanned arms standing on end.

'Yes, guests, Margarete. You girls are society age and you need to meet people,' her mother said, clicking at a hard light switch that turned nothing on. 'I wanted to show you the electric light,' she said, 'but I suppose the wires all still need joining up.'

'We don't know anyone.'

'We have friends, dear. Baroness von Ketz will be here soon.'

'And Emil,' said Margarete.

'The Baron,' her mother said.

Margarete rolled her eyes.

'This is why we need guests, girls. I can't be here to correct you all the time. You've been babbling with no one but
your parents and kaffirs for six years or more and I don't
even know if it was right to keep you there so long. But
we're here now. You'll like Madame Durant – you'll get on
well there, especially you, Ingrid. She'll drum some manners
into you, which will be a relief.'

'Am I a lost cause?' Margarete said.

'Margarete, dear, I thought we'd left all that in Africa.
Let's make a new start, eh?' she said, touching Margarete's
chin. Margarete had begun to improve in Las Palmas and
by the time they reached Lisbon she was on deck and
joined them in the city to walk through the steep streets of
Mouraria, up to the São Jorge Castle. Her mother liked to
talk of the 'recovery', but the phrase made Ingrid nervous.
She touched the new bracelets and necklaces her mother
had bought them in Brittany, counting the links like a
rosary, hoping to ward off the return of her sister's hysteria.

Ingrid put her head on Margarete's shoulder. Her feet
ached and she felt that if she concentrated too hard on the
sensation of her toes squeezed together in her new boots
she would go mad herself. 'Can I take my boots off?' she
pleaded.

'You certainly can't,' said Frau Hoffmann, tapping involuntarily at her chest. 'You don't walk about barefoot in
Germany, my dear.' She stared into the empty in-between
room, stretching herself with her fists pushed into her back,
and said, 'We shouldn't have let you girls run so wild for so
long. There'll be some adjusting to do, that's for certain.
Your father's too soft on you.'

The stretch ending, and her body retracting, she walked
into the in-between room and pulled open the inner doors

to the balcony and then the outer. A rush of spring air rolled in.

'Thank God we aren't in Berlin proper. Breathe it in girls,' she said, wafting the air at her face. 'This is what you pay for in Charlottenburg.' She stepped out onto the balcony. 'Come and look. Stop dawdling. You're clinging to each other like a pair of little matchstick girls. Let her go, Margarete,' she said and separated them.

'Come,' their mother said. 'Come.'

Ingrid had stared up at all the balconies as the cab drove them from Berlin Zoo station. She had loved them as a child in Cochem, but now puzzled at how they stayed on the buildings at all. She imagined how it would feel as it went from under you, how much of the crashing and falling you would feel as it crumbled, before it folded up and crushed you.

She stepped gingerly out, touched the edge and peered over. Margarete hovered at the door, then committed, gripping the balustrade and leaning over too far into the street. 'The tram's loud isn't it?'

'The tram?' her mother said, leaning too, looking pale and harried. 'What tram? I can't hear the tram.'

'Can you hear the tram, Ingrid?' her sister said.

'A little,' said Ingrid.

'Oh,' her mother said. 'A tinkle, a bell, barely a racket. Dear God, Margarete, how everything is the worst with you. The absolute worst.' She put her hand on Margarete's forehead, but it was flapped away. 'Are you all right, dear?'

'We've travelled halfway around the world and I'm hungry and I want to sleep,' Margarete said.

'Is there no room for joy here?' Frau Hoffmann said, her eyes disbelieving. 'We've left Africa, survived the Uprising, thanks to your father, and we're in this beautiful apartment – again thanks to your father – and all you can do is complain about trams and sulk about like two monkeys freezing in a zoo. Is this not wonderful?' she said, again cupping the air and bringing it up to her face.

'I suppose Papa must have done very well out of Africa,' Margarete said.

Her mother struck her across the face.

Margarete stared at her. Her face was chalk. Ingrid saw a red hand mark, clearly outlined, forming beneath the soft bloom of her face.

'How dare you be so crass. You'll never understand what your father's done for you, and you mock it.'

Margarete ran from the room into the darkest unexplored part of the apartment.

*

For Ingrid, the first weeks in Berlin were a blooming of life, after the emptiness of Africa and the constrictions of the ship that had carried them home. She fell in love with the weight of the buildings, the plaster faces and cornucopias on the pastel façades, the brick of churches, the stone of civic buildings, that changed from bright grey to river brown at the merest touch of rain. She loved how green the oases of parks were, how subtle the smells of nature in the city, of slippery autumn leaves, of warm bark and fountain spray. And the people. She sat in the Englischer Garten and watched men and women, soldiers, tradesmen, beggars, drunks, nannies with children, and could barely think with the din of German that filled the neat gravelled paths.

Margarete, at first afraid of their excursions into the city, armed herself against the urban clamour with disdain, holding her face away from the beggars, using her allowance to pay for cabs rather than taking the tram or train, and never going out, when she might stay in. When Margarete's nerves kept her at home, Ingrid was always sad and afraid, but also troubled by her pleasure at the resulting freedom given her to visit the Royal Library, the history exhibitions in the Zeughaus, and wander through the columns and galleries of the Museum Island.

The blind of Margarete's contempt was also drawn against all new acquaintances, including the girls of Madame Durant's academy. Margarete was briefly courteous to Madame herself, but the thin Parisian with steel-grey hair and an unvarying string of pearls encircling the plain pleats of her blouse was not to be won over by charm. Margarete's lack of interest in the simplest fundaments of the French language saw the loss of her briefly held place at the front of the little classroom on Karl-August-Platz, along with her attempt at maintaining any semblance of interest in the subjects taught.

Of the twelve other pupils, Margarete showed a particular dislike of Hannah Mandelbaum, a small dark-haired girl and the only student more naturally accomplished than Ingrid. But Margarete's frequent absences meant that Ingrid and Hannah easily fell in together. When Margarete was gone, they talked in French by the samovar in the morning and walked together after lessons to Hannah's train station, their hands in the pockets of their woollen coats as Hannah regaled Ingrid with gossip about the other pupils and lurid fictions about Madame Durant's imagined private life.

Without it being discussed, Hannah understood that when Margarete was in attendance they had to behave as if they had never met one another. Only once did Hannah run and catch up with Ingrid and Margarete at the end of lessons.

'I saw her, I saw her!' Hannah said, grabbing Ingrid's arm, making a chain of the three girls.

'What on earth are you talking about?' Margarete said, her lip drawn up beneath her nose.

'Madame Durant,' said Hannah. 'She was walking past the Hohenzollern Museum with her beau. A great big moustachioed chap – looked like an Italian baritone.'

Ingrid, feeling the enthusiasm of Hannah's grip on one arm and the iron tightening of her sister's on the other, said nothing in reply. Hannah smiled and looked ahead at the little turrets of the Goethe-Haus. They walked on in uncomfortable silence, but Hannah did not let go until they had reached Grolmannstraße, where she said, 'Goodbye you two,' and kissed Ingrid on the cheek.

'Filthy little yid,' Margarete muttered, as Hannah headed up to Knie Station and Ingrid brushed her face where her friend had kissed her.

'What's a yid?' said Ingrid.

'She's a Jew, you fool.'

In Southwest Africa, Ingrid had not met any Jews, nor had any cause to consider whether they were good or bad. 'She's very clever,' Ingrid said.

'They all are,' said Margarete.

*

Margarete couldn't avoid visitors to the house though, and hid away with Ingrid in the drawing room when their father received business associates and their mother's acquaintances gathered from church or the Union of German Colonial Women. That morning, hearing the bell, the girls had retreated. Margarete took her drawing things to the card table and Ingrid made her way to the red velvet sofa without taking her eyes off the book she was reading. But their mother called them back. Through the closed double doors they heard, 'Girls! Girls!' Margarete looked up doubtfully, but Ingrid encouraged her to abandon her sketching and they found their mother standing with Emil von Ketz and a short little man with soft blond hair so thin they could see the shine of his scalp beneath.

'The Baron is here with his friend, Herr Horvath,' Frau Hoffmann said. 'He's a painter. You can talk to him about your drawings, Margarete.'

There followed an awkward half-hour of coffee and cake, with Horvath, who was Hungarian, telling a story about an exhibition in Budapest in bad Austrian-accented German that they struggled to understand. Von Ketz smiled at his friend encouragingly, but seemed generally mortified, and their mother peppered the story with laughter, as if every new sentence brought another wonderful joke.

'There's a plan afoot to go to the zoo. They've got a tribal display on,' Frau Hoffman said. 'They've got some Herero and Nama, Fräulein von Torgelow told me – like a little piece of Southwest.'

Ingrid watched von Ketz's blank face and Horvath's pained smile and saw that their mother had planned the whole thing.

The tribal display was in the exhibition halls at Berlin's Zoological Gardens, past the elephant enclosure. Ingrid walked towards it with Horvath, behind Margarete and von Ketz, who stared at the crocuses emerging from the black soil of the planted borders and listened to the mixed squawks of exotic birds. The Baron held his hands behind his back, tipping his head down, so that the brim of his straw boater revealed red spots on his neck where his hair had been newly cropped.

Margarete walked beside him in silence, her hands in a muff, though it was warm enough for the rest of the party to leave their furs at home. Margarete's head was turned away from von Ketz and the brim of her own boater obscured her face, but Ingrid could see from the angle of her head that she was staring at nothing, not the flowers, nor the animals.

'Apples!' said Horvath, pointing to a woman and a child offering an elephant a slice from a little plate on a stand, covered in browning chopped fruit and tiny flies.

The elephant was standing at the wide bars of its enclosure reaching out for a slice which the giggling child was holding a few centimetres away from the full reach of its trunk. The elephant's trunk grasped desperately, shuddering with sensation. Annoyed at the boy, Ingrid picked up a great handful of apple slices and leaned in with them. The boy fell silent and his mother tutted as the elephant grabbed a trunk-full and gently placed it in its mouth, losing a slice on the way.

'I should make an apology,' Horvath said. 'My German is bad. And you do not speak Hungarian.'

'No,' said Ingrid, as the trunk came back and the edges of the elephant's hairy snout brushed her gloved hand. 'French?' she offered.

'*Oh yes!*' said Horvath in French. '*Thank the Lord – I was hacking my German to pieces. Terribly embarrassing. Does your sister also speak French?*'

'*Not very much,*' said Ingrid.

Horvath nodded. '*Might I ask, is she quite well today? She's been very silent.*'

'*She's well*,' Ingrid said vaguely, throwing the last of the apples into the enclosure. She searched in her pockets for a handkerchief to wipe the residue of apple and elephant from her glove. Horvath gave her his and she thanked him. The elephant flapped its scarred ears and slowly bent its head towards the concrete floor where the last apple slice had fallen.

'*Come on*,' she said, thinking about the drawing room, the stove and her book at home. '*Let's catch up with the others. We should go and see the tribal display, since we came for it.*'

Beneath the curving roof and brass chandeliers, hung with scarlet tassels, the exhibition hall smelt strongly of hay and bodies and was filled with a cacophony of drumming, shouting and singing. A signposted route led them in front of enclosures with low barriers, behind which whole African villages had been constructed, with huts made of mud, wood and grasses, with only the shape of the roofs distinguishing one tribe from another. The barrier of each enclosure contained a hand-painted sign: Maasai, Ethiopian, Himba, Bedouin, Chaga. Around the huts stood Africans, men, women and children, in traditional clothes. They sat in front of unlit fires, stirring cooking pots filled with cold water. Some shivered in the unheated hall. Others played drums, let out warbling cries, danced. The Maasai men jumped into the air, their ankles cinched together; the Bedouin women shook hips clothed in gauzy fabric and hung with tiny bells; the Tigrayan women wore long white dresses and swayed about barefoot to music plucked by the men on rough wooden harps.

There were no Hereros. Southwest Africa was represented by a small group of Himba, their skin and hair covered in terracotta-coloured mud.

'*Is this what it was like in Southwest?*' Horvath said.

'*No, not really,*' said Ingrid. '*In fact, not at all. We weren't up north, where the Himba come from.*' A German woman gave one of the Himba boys a banana. The child looked at it dubiously until his mother came and thanked the woman and took the banana off him, concealing it in a pocket hidden beneath her leather skirt. '*Though I can't imagine it's much like this there either.*'

In nearly all of the enclosures there was a group, usually of women, engaged in a culturally appropriate commercial enterprise: basket-weaving, carving, doll-making, all of which could be bought. The women received the money, taking it behind the huts and through a black curtain.

'Would you like anything?' von Ketz said to Margarete, as if they were in the Kaufhaus des Westens.

'Of course not,' she said. 'I can't breathe in here.' She ran from them, out of the building.

They emerged from the stale air and relative dimness of the exhibition halls, and found Margarete on a bench in the bright light of the early Berlin spring. 'I can't bear anything African,' she said to Ingrid, who took her hand. It was shaking.

'We'll go home,' said Ingrid.

'Please,' Margarete said.

They left through the oriental confusion of the Elephant Gate, Horvath and von Ketz walking together in silence. Horvath hailed a cab.

'Thank you for taking us,' Ingrid said to von Ketz.

'That's OK,' he said. 'Did you enjoy it?'

'Not really,' Ingrid said. 'Did you?'

'I suppose not,' he said.

Ingrid and Margarete watched them climb into the cab

and disappear down Budapesterstraße. Ingrid wondered if she should speak to von Ketz less familiarly.

They walked home. Margarete stopped at a few shop windows to look at gloves, but was otherwise silent. 'You're very quiet whenever von Ketz is around,' Ingrid said.

'I can't think of anything new to say to him.'

'And how was it?' Frau Hoffmann said, when they returned.

'Awful,' Margarete said and went to her room.

'Wasn't Herr Horvath charming? Very creative. His father's something terribly important in Decebren.'

'I think it's pronounced Debrecen,' Ingrid said. 'Am I meant to marry him?'

'Good Lord, Ingrid! You only went to the zoo with him.'

'Which you arranged.'

'Cut that tone, my girl,' Frau Hoffmann said, unpicking a stump-work rose. 'There's no conspiracy to have you married off.'

'I didn't understand a word of his German,' said Ingrid. 'We had to speak French – it was terribly embarrassing.'

'You are such savage critics,' said their mother, screwing up her face and rubbing at her chest. 'Good God, this heartburn! Ann-Kathrin's coffee is killing me. It's like molten lead.'

Windscheidstraße 53, Charlottenburg

— 1909 —

The following winter, Baron von Ketz came to Windscheid-straße for dinner, but without his Hungarian friend. The Von Ketzes were staying with Baroness von Torgelow in Potsdam, while their house in Buckow was opened up. The Baroness von Torgelow sent her apologies, but her daughter, Fräulein Liese, came. She was pretty, with an oval face, auburn hair and pale freckled skin. Ingrid had spied her from the in-between room. She was taking off her shawl and handing it to Ann-Kathrin, the new maid, and Ingrid had a shiver of excitement at the thought that Fräulein von Torgelow might become a friend, imagining her laugh, clean and handsome, clattering through their apartment. But when they stood to greet her, she came with the studied walk of a middle-aged woman.

She smiled when Ingrid gave her her hand. The simple silver cross around her neck, which Ingrid had at a distance found elegant, looked pious, and Ingrid was suffused with disappointment at the loss of a friend so briefly made.

Fräulein von Torgelow had brought a poet called Gottlieb, who didn't fit Ingrid's idea of a poet at all. Balding and overweight, he had arrived wearing a smart grey hat and carrying a cane, and over his white shirt he wore a white waistcoat. Everything else was as beautifully matched: the navy of his tie with the navy of his jacket, even the brown of his thinning hair and Tsar Nicholas beard was strikingly like the ash of his cane and leather of his shoes. His lips were pink, as if he were wearing rouge, and he talked with a lilting Württemberger accent that sounded childlike to Ingrid. She mourned the romantic long-haired vagabond she had imagined when her mother had said the word 'poet'.

Von Ketz arrived next with his mother. The Baroness seemed as bird-like and weakened by the noise of Berlin as she had done by the heat of Southwest. But, seeing von Ketz through the eyes of Fräulein von Torgelow, his height, his dark tan and the violent blond streaks in his now-pomaded hair, he looked strong and exotic and she felt a pang of jealousy when Fräulein von Torgelow laughed at a whispered joke he made.

Herr Hoffmann greeted the von Ketzes and then removed the Baron to the study.

'What is he doing with him, do you think?' Ingrid whispered to Margarete.

'Drawing up the details of the marriage contract, I suppose. Everything itemised.'

The sisters watched them come out a few minutes later, von Ketz looking worried. 'The conditions must be terrible,' Ingrid said.

Margarete laughed for the first time in months and said, 'I want twenty children, and a motor car, and to keep pigs. The man's realised what trouble I am.'

'Oh, I don't imagine he'll ever quite realise.'

Margarete laughed again.

Ann-Kathrin brought out Sekt, which the Baroness refused, because it gave her painful hiccups. Ingrid was struck by how strange it was to find her family and the von Ketzes here, these immigrants. She felt as if they were paper dolls in a children's book, removed carelessly from one setting to another. Fräulein von Torgelow and Gottlieb fitted, but the Hoffmanns and the von Ketzes seemed to be badly playing parts, and she was afraid that their guests might find them out.

Gottlieb knocked a candlestick to the floor, and Margarete caught it. There was a gasp of concern as a gobbet of wax hit her skirt, but then she raised the candle in the air triumphantly and the assembled guests cheered and clapped. She did a faux curtsy and even the Baroness von Ketz smiled. Though Margarete did not like sparkling wine, she drank her whole glass of Sekt and bullied Ann-Kathrin into filling another while her parents were trying to elicit some polite conversation out of the Baroness.

Ingrid joined them. 'This piece of plaster,' her mother was saying, pointing to a corner of painted stucco on the ceiling, 'has never dried. And then Hilde Warschauer, who I know is a great friend of yours, said that it might be a leak from the plumbing in the apartments above. Italians, would you believe? With all that room and no children ...'

The Baroness turned her head slowly and blinked at the thin brown stain in the corner of the room that Frau Hoffmann had pointed to. The Baroness's skin was so pallid, Ingrid thought, that she must never have been outside in Southwest. She remembered her sitting on the narrow bed and wondered if she had just wandered from room to room for all those years in that stifling heat with that awful husband. It must have been purgatory.

'It's probably faeces,' the Baroness said.

Ingrid's mother was silenced. Her father let out a surprised 'Huh.'

Ingrid watched her mother's face. Her lips were working, trying to form what might be the appropriate response, but failing and failing again. The Baroness turned to Ingrid and said, 'Dear, what are you going to do about marriage? I worry about you particularly – you must be terribly careful.'

Ingrid flushed and her mother said, 'Ingrid's just eighteen, and—'

'One feels so much pressure so soon,' the Baroness went on, as if Frau Hoffmann wasn't there, 'and I think you must consider your options carefully. You must marry of course, but consider where it might take you, or not take you.' She looked again at the brown stain on the ceiling. 'I will look out for you as much as I am able, but ... ' The sense of the sentence left her and she was quiet again.

Margarete squawked. She had been cornered by Gottlieb, who was telling her anecdotes, making her laugh wildly as he wagged his finger at her, her beautiful mouth stretched open, baring her fine teeth. Ingrid moved away from the Baroness's wet stare to rescue Margarete, but before she was even close, Margarete said, 'Oh Ingrid, he's telling me the dirtiest jokes – go and tell Mother,' and shooed her away. Ingrid wasn't sure if she really meant her to tell their mother or not, so stood dumbly by von Ketz and Fräulein von Torgelow as the latter explained the plot of *Ein Walzertraum* and then described it as silly, though judging by her description, Ingrid thought, she couldn't have seen it.

Unable to break into the conversation, she looked over at her parents and was relieved to find them smiling at her sister, happy that the guests were being entertained. She had saved the party, Ingrid supposed, and felt a flush of envy, wishing that she could be bright and entertaining, but knowing that she would only embarrass herself if she tried.

When they were called for dinner, her mother caught her by the arm and whispered, 'Well done for humouring the Baroness, darling one. The poor woman's gone gaga.'

At dinner Ingrid was placed opposite Gottlieb and between her mother and father. Panicked by the profusion of cutlery, she watched Baroness von Ketz, waiting for her to pick up the correct item, but she just sat and dabbed at her mouth and neck with a small square of embroidered silk. Fräulein von Torgelow picked up the round spoon, barely glancing down to select it and Ingrid did the same. Margarete, seated opposite von Ketz, was slumped in her chair drinking the soup with her dessert spoon, saying, 'The Baron here used to come and play the piano at our farm. He was a silent one back then, weren't you Herr Baron?' and she laughed again.

Von Ketz smiled nervously and Frau Hoffmann tried to fix Margarete's gaze, but Gottlieb laughed loudly enough to encourage her teasing, and she went on. 'He was not a natural talent; I think we can agree on that. It was nearly two hours on horseback farm to farm, wasn't it Herr Baron? And just for the piano! Poor thing – sent over to the Hoffmanns' every week in that terrible heat.'

'I enjoyed it very much,' von Ketz said, his hand on the table in a fist. 'I wanted to come.'

'His father didn't want him to go at all. It was a terrible

inconvenience,' the Baroness said, taking a first sip of soup and swallowing it down with a shudder, like medicine. 'What a shame to discover it came to naught, when one thinks of all of those lost days on the farm, all the things that needed doing. Thank God your father's dead and can't hear it,' she said. 'I thank God for his death. We all do.'

No one spoke. They listened to Ann-Kathrin stacking plates.

'Oh gosh,' Margarete said, laughing to herself. 'I didn't mean to get you into trouble, old thing.' She took another gulp of soup, dribbling some onto her chin, and catching it with the heel of her palm. 'Some of the natives killed him. Did you hear about it?' she said to Gottlieb and Fräulein von Torgelow, her mouth still full. 'It was the Uprising. They clubbed him to death, poor soul. We were all there, except Mama and Ingrid. The sound of it! Makes one shudder. Of course von Trotha wiped them all out after that – I suppose we're meant to be grateful for that.'

Ingrid looked at her mother. She was scarlet. Von Ketz stared at his plate, but the Baroness seemed uninterested and continued to eat.

'It must be a remarkable place, Southwest,' Gottlieb said.

Ingrid looked around to see who should answer and her mother's intense glare and tight-lipped smile suggested it was her. She put her spoon down and said, 'Not really.'

Her mother pushed out a light ersatz laugh, Margarete a loud cackle.

'No,' said Ingrid, flushing, trying to recover the comment before her mother chimed in. 'I just mean, it isn't very remarkable if you know it. Nothing is remarkable if you're used to it, and we were quite young when we went.'

'It is funny to think of you all out in the Namib desert,'

Fräulein von Torgelow said. 'You must have been terrified of the niggers?'

Margarete laughed again. Her mother made dagger eyes at her and she made a show of stifling her laughter with a napkin.

Fräulein von Torgelow blushed, but her expression of wry disdain laid the embarrassment squarely on the Hoffmanns' side.

'They were very good to us, really,' Ingrid said.

Her mother clucked and Ingrid corrected herself. 'Hans, our houseboy, and Nora. And the farmworkers, though they did disappear during the Uprising.'

Now Fräulein von Torgelow laughed, a high tinkle like breaking glass.

Ingrid said, 'I mean, we don't know what happened to Hans, but . . . '

'Oh, don't be mean to poor old Ingrid,' Margarete cried from the other end of the table. 'Hans was the perfect ally in Southwest. Taught her French and English and I don't know what. She was terribly in love with him, weren't you, Little Fly?'

Ingrid stared at her sister, incensed.

'Do forgive me, dear Fräulein Ingrid. I'm sorry,' Fräulein von Torgelow said, but didn't seem sorry at all. 'What a darling thing to say, though. It's so innocent, my dear – and you must remain so as long as you can manage in this city. Don't let us embarrass you.'

'Yes, Hans was a good chap,' von Ketz dropped in.

Ingrid smiled at him gratefully and Fräulein von Torgelow's smile faded. 'I'm sure they were a hoot,' she said, making eyes at Gottlieb.

He said, 'Where do you think they are then? Your Hans and Nora?'

'They just disappeared,' her mother said, in a tone that made it clear that it would be the last word on the subject. 'And we left.'

'Well, it must have been quite a contrast to Berlin,' Fräulein von Torgelow offered.

'Indeed,' her mother said.

'But I thought I detected an accent,' Gottlieb said. 'I would have placed you further West, Frau Hoffmann.'

Margarete and Ingrid's father stopped eating and looked up at her. 'Oh,' she said, 'Where are you from, Herr Gottlieb?'

'Lübeck.'

'Traders one and all, eh?' said her father.

'Indeed, and where—?' Gottlieb said, but her mother ran on over him.

'Johannes, did we visit Lübeck? Is it the one with the wonderful old town hall, like a gingerbread house?'

'The town hall is beautiful,' Gottlieb said.

'No, you're thinking of Breslau, Hedwig,' Herr Hoffmann said, and turned to Gottlieb. 'I say, you must do us a bit of poetry later. Ingrid would be particularly pleased. She translates poems for fun.'

Sweat broke out across Ingrid's back and she wished her father silent.

'What are you translating?' Gottlieb asked.

'It's only practice.'

'Do your Donne,' her father said, finishing off his soup with a few enthusiastic scrapes.

Ingrid looked at him pleadingly, but his expression of warm encouragement didn't change. He had decided what she would do and his pleasant smile would remain painted on his face until she gave in. She looked at her mother, who shook salt onto her hand and then rubbed her palms together, sprinkling it over her bowl. She looked up at Ingrid and blinked, meaning that Ingrid should quickly give in to her father's wishes and rescue the dinner for everyone.

Ingrid turned to Gottlieb. 'I'm sure you wouldn't want to hear it. It's very juvenile. I don't have a poetic touch – I translated it for fun.'

Fräulein von Torgelow giggled.

'Don't be so modest,' Gottlieb said, but weakly, so that she knew he was ashamed for her.

'*No one is an island in themselves, every person*—'

'Stand up!'

Ingrid looked at her father.

'Stand up, Ingrid. Do a thing properly, if you're going to do it.'

Ingrid pushed back her chair. She heard her sister put down her knife. The pendulum of the wall clock cracked back and forth. A candle spat.

'*—is a piece of the—*'

'No, start again,' her father said. 'From the beginning, dear.'

She thought she might cry and her cheeks burnt. She hoped she would faint mid-verse and then he would be sorry.

'No one is an island in themselves, every person is a piece of the continent, a piece of the mainland. If a slab is washed into the sea, Europe becomes less, just as if it were a headland or estate of your friend's or your own. Every person's death is my loss, because I'm a part of humanity. And so ask never to know for whom the hour strikes; it strikes for you yourself.'

119

Her mother let out a murmur of appreciation. Her father said, 'See, not so bad.'

She sat down abruptly without looking at Fräulein von Torgelow or Gottlieb. After a pause, Gottlieb said, 'Yes, very nice Fräulein Hoffmann. If I might give you a few pointers, as something of an expert, you might say. "Slab" here is not quite right, I think. The English is more like "clod", something smaller that heightens the pathos, if you see what I mean. And you've gone for a clock striking here, whereas in the original it's a bell, I believe, which has much more power because one imagines it ringing away on some hill in Greece, doesn't one? In the background, reminding you of your mortality. Do you see? That's the point of the piece – one's mortality.'

'Yes, I—'

'And you've rather neutralised the gender, whereas in the English it is quite specifically talking to a man.'

'But it's addressed to all of humanity. It was just the turn of phrase when it was written,' Ingrid said.

'I'm sure the word "person" existed when Donne wrote it,' Gottlieb said, laughing, and Fräulein von Torgelow joined in with her glassy tinkle. 'But he chose not to use it. You must think why. You must respect his choices. Even if he was a reformed Papist,' he said, and the gathered guests laughed, the Hoffmanns and von Ketzes joining in less enthusiastically. 'The woman translator will always respond emotionally of course, which is her talent, but she lacks classical learning. Do you speak Latin, Fräulein Ingrid? Or Greek? Have you read Homer, Virgil, Ovid? Why should you have? So this sentimentality is completely natural and you mustn't take such criticism to heart.'

Ingrid had read all of those poets in Voß's translations, but supposed that admitting so would invite further derision. Instead she stared down at her bowl. The remains of the soup had dried to the sides.

'Well, I thought it was rather moving,' von Ketz said.

'I think it's a marvel anyone can speak another language at all,' said her mother.

'Oh, it was a joy, Ingrid,' she heard Margarete say distantly. 'Cheer up, old thing!'

*

After the meal, and needing to go to the toilet, Ingrid excused herself, desperate to be alone for a few minutes. As she left the room she heard her mother's creak and knew that, if she turned, she would see in her eyes that this was not the done thing. Was she meant to hold it throughout the whole evening? The idea of her mother loudly relieving herself after five hours of eating and drinking made her smile at least.

To cool herself, and because the contraption was still a wonder to her, she went through the back of the apartment, past the servants washing the dishes in the kitchen, and to the back stairs, to one of the flushing water closets. There she rolled up her skirts and petticoat and untied the string of her knickerbockers. She sat and rested her head on her hands. She wished they would all go away. She wished that she would return to the dining room to find her family there alone and Margarete in one of her loving moods. She pushed her hands against the cold tiles of the wall and then pushed them against her face.

As she went back into the apartment, she was suddenly faced with von Ketz. He was standing at the open door.

'Oh, Baron von Ketz! Is something wrong?' Ingrid said.

'I needed some air,' he said. 'I got rather lost.'

'It's hardly a labyrinth,' Ingrid said, doubtfully.

He smiled, but it faded. His brow furrowed and he looked down at his hands. She could hear chatter from the kitchen and the cook laughing. There was a hollow metallic knock at the foot of the staircase and the echo rattled up towards them. He looked so sad that she wanted to embrace him and tell him he would settle, they would all settle, in time.

'I liked your poem.'

'Oh don't,' she said.

'It was lovely.'

'We should go in,' said Ingrid.

'I can't bear these sorts of things. Can you?'

'I don't mind so much. One just feels very out of touch with how it all works.'

He didn't move and Ingrid wondered if it would be improper to barge past him, especially since he was the Baron now. 'What did Papa talk to you about in his study? You looked very affected?'

'You don't miss a thing, do you?' said von Ketz.

'Sorry,' she said. 'You needn't tell me, if you don't want to.'

He looked about the wall beside them as if he was inspecting the paintwork. 'It was a letter from Africa. Brought up some things.'

'Emotional things?'

'Yes,' he said.

Ingrid felt awkward. 'That's OK,' she said. 'You know, Mama wants you to talk to Margarete, not moon around here with me.'

He was probably well aware, but she hoped the revelation might drive him back to the party.

'I think she's drunk,' von Ketz said.

Ingrid nodded. 'She gets this way – she'll be herself tomorrow, tonight even.'

'Why?'

'I don't know – she's always been like that.'

'No, I mean why does your mother want me to talk to Margarete?'

'Because you're going to marry her, I suppose.'

'That's true enough,' he said, laughing.

'You don't sound very enthused.'

'It's never been in question, that's all,' he said.

'Has it not?'

His frown deepened. 'No.'

'But you could say no.'

He laughed again.

'You should be glad to have her,' Ingrid said, unsure of what his laughter implied. She touched the banisters. The new gloss paint was cold. She could still smell the linseed oil in it. 'She's a good person. She's very pretty.'

'Yes,' he said. 'There are lots of pretty girls in Berlin, aren't there?'

'What's that supposed to mean?' Ingrid said, feeling that he was talking about her, and seeing a fantasy of herself, children, a title, a house at the lake. But then he'd said it with such venom that she couldn't possibly hope that he was talking about her. But if he had gripped her now, pulled her to him, his hands filled with the silk of her skirts, his hair between her fingers—

'I didn't mean it like that,' he said. 'I only mean that it's strange being presented with all these hopeful women, when all you've known is your parents and farmworkers and the Hoffmanns, and it's already been decided anyway ... '

'*You* must decide, Herr Baron,' she said. 'We can't be ruled by duty.'

'What should we be ruled by, then?' he said.

'I'd hardly say your father was ruled by duty.'

'Don't talk about my father.'

'I'm sorry.' She shivered; there was a draught on the staircase. 'It was rude of me.'

'I just don't want to think about it,' he said. He touched his head where his top hat had left a ridge in the oiled blond hair. 'Say, why did she call you Little Fly?'

'She always calls me that.'

'Why?'

'Because I seem harmless, but really I won't leave anything alone. If she's being nice she says I'm tenacious, if not, that I'm obstinate. I'm not sure it's true, but that's what she says.' They heard scraping chairs. 'Please let me get back,' she said.

'Of course,' he said, standing aside. But as she passed, he caught her by the arm. She could smell the wine on his breath and she thought he was going to kiss her. 'You know, we all owe your sister. It is duty, but we must do everything we can for her.'

'Of course,' Ingrid said, not understanding at all, and fleeing the stairwell.

*

That night Ingrid lay shivering under her blankets. She often lay awake, used to sleeping in the dry, black silence of the sandveld. The noises that broke the night's quiet there – the shrill twitter of insects, the groan of a nocturnal mammal, even a great electrical storm battering the tin roof – were comforting sounds that, once registered, were driven away by sleep. But here, the sound of coal being emptied into the courtyard, the echo of doors opening and closing, the rattle of tram and train, the shouts of men in the street selling newspapers, bread rolls, matchsticks and fish, the smell of coal dust, factory smoke, wet wool, all woke her, disconcerted her and kept her awake, turning and turning to try and find a way to make her body comfortable beneath the weight of bedding and damp air.

She thought about Emil von Ketz. She thought, half-thinking, half-dreaming, of him in Africa, his visits to the farm, his salt-marked riding trousers and sweat-grey neckerchiefs. She thought about him climbing into bed beside her and holding her, his lips at her neck, his long fingers creeping down the cotton of her nightdress, and the thought made her anxious and light. Perhaps they could be one of those intellectual childless couples. She pictured them in a drawing room, books in hand, at a private view perusing modern pictures, in a bazaar in North Africa selecting rugs and *objets d'art*.

There was a tap at the door. 'Who is it?' she whispered.

'It's Margarete.'

'Go away – I'm sleeping,' Ingrid said.

Her sister slipped in and before the snap of the door's latch had dissipated she was under Ingrid's sheets.

'Get out!' Ingrid hissed, kicking at her, but Margarete gripped her from behind.

'Be quiet!' Margarete said. 'You'll wake up Mama.'

Ingrid pulled up her legs, so that they weren't touching Margarete's, and closed her eyes tightly.

'I can't sleep any more. Africa's ruined me. It's so cold here.'

Ingrid didn't answer. She willed herself to sleep, but knew

she was hours away from it. She could hear in the silence Margarete trying to think of something to say that would make her talk. She landed on, 'Ann-Kathrin ripped the nightdress case you made me in Southwest.'

Ingrid didn't open her eyes, but felt mortified, imagining the gossamer threads of the torn grey silk.

Margarete shifted grumpily, surprised at Ingrid's resolve. 'Is Mama terribly angry with me?' she said, pinching at Ingrid's sides.

Ingrid fired back her elbows. Margarete let out a muted yelp and then gripped her sister around the arms, like a wrestler, kissing her neck. 'Don't be like that, Little Fly, it's only jokes. You're not in trouble – you saved dinner with your lovely poem.'

'No I didn't,' said Ingrid, inflamed with shame at the memory. And then, as pride doused the heat of it, whispered, 'Did Mama say so?'

'No, but that fat poet was about to out us as proles.'

'What do you mean?' Ingrid said. Her sister's fingers had loosened and she was intertwining them with her own.

'The stuff about Mama's accent.'

'What about it?'

'You know, Mama and Papa were nothing before Africa.'

'You mean our farm on the Rhine?' Ingrid said, seeing the faded snatches of steep hills and vineyards, apple trees and snow.

'It was in ruins when Papa inherited it. He built it all up, bought more land around it, then more again, until he had enough to get us to Southwest. Then Papa fixed it all for us in Africa.'

Ingrid didn't answer. She was trying to remember something specific about the farm before they left, but saw only raindrops caught on the gable of the roof and a pig in a yard, the gloss of its nose leaving strings of slime on the grey wood of its enclosure and bright vegetable peel in the dirt around its trotters.

'You were talking to him a lot,' Margarete whispered.

'Who? Von Ketz?' Ingrid said. 'Only because you wouldn't.'

'I don't mind if you want to marry him. I certainly don't.'

Ingrid turned over. She looked at her sister's eyes, black in the dark. 'Why don't you want to marry him?'

'Oh, you know. He's just Emil. It's hard to believe that in the whole German Empire the man I'm meant to marry is the lump from the next-door farm in Africa.'

Ingrid laughed. 'The only marital prospect in a hundred kilometres.'

Margarete snorted loudly. They heard the creak of a floorboard and put their hands over their mouths. They stayed completely still until the apartment was silent again.

'What if he asks?' Ingrid whispered.

Margarete shrugged. 'I suppose I'll say yes, and then ...'

'What?'

'Oh God!' she said, throwing her head down on the pillow. 'I don't think I could stand it in the country with the Baroness. Von Ketz one could endure, but everything that goes with it ...'

'Wouldn't you like to be a Baroness?'

'I suppose,' Margarete said. 'I wish I could be something interesting like you.'

'I'm going to get married too. Just to some ghastly old academic,' she said, the image feeling cold and grey: a man, a rug across the lap and a small, ineffective stove. 'Or that Hungarian midget, if Mama has her way.'

Margarete laughed. 'But you'll translate poetry. And read books.'

'Those are hobbies. Not life.'

'I suppose not,' Margarete said. 'And you don't speak Latin, dear, nor Greek.'

Ingrid giggled.

Margarete, sounding sleepy, said, 'But you'd be able to stand it in the country. You can stand everything. You know you can.'

'You stood Africa too, despite everything.' She looked at the grey shape of Margarete's face in the dark. 'Von Ketz said we all owe you for Africa.'

'Did he?' Margarete said. Her eyes were closed and Ingrid couldn't read her tone.

'What did he mean, do you think?'

'I don't know,' she said, pressing her face into the pillow.

'What did you use to talk about when you were alone with him over there? At the von Ketzes' house in Africa, I mean.'

Margarete was very still. 'We weren't left alone. I'm not sure I've passed more than a few words with him on our own.'

'But what about when I went over with you? And all those afternoons at the piano?'

Margarete yawned. 'Let's leave all that in Africa, Little Fly,' she said, and her head fell to the side and her cold feet found Ingrid's warm calves. 'I can't think about it now.'

Ingrid turned away from her sister and closed her eyes. She pushed the image of von Ketz away and thought instead of her usual bed partner, an imaginary Hans Ziegler, who ached to hold her through the night, unable to sleep if he wasn't touching her. She pretended that he knocked on the door, a gentle tap, and locked it in some way that would mean her parents could never open it and climbed into bed behind her. She felt the muscle of his arm against her arm. She felt him fold his leg over and then between hers, so that his bare flesh touched her flesh. And he slept there – because there was no other way he could sleep – until the early morning, when he would slip out, disappearing before she had woken.

*

A week later, Ingrid received a letter from von Ketz. It read:

Dear Fräulein Hoffmann,

It was a pleasure to see you at Windscheidstraße. It is all so strange here, that it was something of a life raft to see the Hoffmanns all standing together as you always have done. I hope it is not out of turn to say that I hope that you and your sister see how rare it is to be a family as you are a family. What a joy siblings must be.

Mother is glad to be back in Buckow, but her nerves are in a bad way. She always hated the veld and the heat in Southwest, the natives too. She was pleased about the Uprising. She said she had been waiting for it from the beginning. But she is not so adaptable as all that and, although she would not admit it, she is always cold and she finds to her great chagrin that, in this climate, she has rheumatism.

One gains much from living somewhere quite different – that was certainly Papa's thinking. But I wonder now, back in Prussia, whether leaving one's country makes one forever homeless, forever a wanderer. It is certainly a pleasure to hear so much German spoken, to be so unafraid of the world, of the landscape. And yet it is as if my body, my spirit, has been readjusted clumsily, like a badly repaired machine. The first rainy night here woke me and the dark day that followed filled me with such despair; I cannot describe it sensibly. Do you also find it so? It would be a comfort to know.

I hope you don't mind me writing. My thoughts here are weak and dull and I wouldn't burden your sister with them. You have always watched and listened, Fräulein Ingrid, and this, I'm sure, will always be of value to you. It is a mark of your good character.

I reread this letter and wonder if the whole thing is out of turn, but Africa has ruined me and I have no idea what is decent any more. I'm sure this will change – my mother wills it and the house, which is collapsing, and the estate, which is a mess, must now be dealt with. Perhaps this will make me a hardy Prussian after all and the patter of rain on ceramic tile will soon fill me with joy and lull me to sleep.

Write to me about how the Hoffmanns are getting on, and I will remain your ever-dutiful servant,
Baron von Ketz

The letter made Ingrid feel feverish. Because, although she could imagine his voice reading the words, they were at odds with how she liked to understand him: as a cipher, a vague representation of their collective future. If Margarete was to marry him, she didn't want him to be complex, to be warm. She wanted him to be a puppet, so that she could board the train back to Charlottenburg, glad to leave them to their noisy children.

She slipped the letter into the book she was reading and

sat with her father in the study, reading a French novel, asking him for the translation of particular words. He never knew. Looking up from his own correspondence, his smile would dissipate and he would say, 'Doesn't it mean "antici-pate"?' And then he would shake his head and say, 'It's your mother who's the linguist.' Ingrid would look the word up, happy with this exchange and the break in the silence of the room.

It took her mother a matter of hours to find von Ketz's letter. She came into the study and spotted the millimetre of paper protruding from the pages of Ingrid's book and with-out a word of warning she knocked the book to the floor. The spine thudded and the letter spun out.

'What's this?' her mother said.

'It's a letter.'

Her mother picked it up and scanned it.

'From Baron von Ketz.'

'Why are you saying it like that? I didn't make him write it. Look, the spine's cracked,' said Ingrid, picking up her book. 'You can't just destroy my things and read through my letters.'

'While we're in this house, they're your father's things. Everything is. Why are you writing to him?'

'I didn't write to him.'

'Johannes!' her mother said, and gave him the letter.

Ingrid looked over at her father and said, 'Why is everyone allowed to read my letter? It's mine.'

Her father glanced over it. He looked up over his spec-tacles at his wife. 'It's hardly indecent, Hedwig dear. Nice to know the boy feels something.'

'Johannes!' her mother cried.

'Opportunities, my dearest one,' he said, handing the

letter back to Ingrid. 'I hope you aren't expecting to marry him,' he said, looking at her seriously.

'I don't want to marry him at all!' Ingrid cried. 'I didn't even write to him.'

'That's just as well,' her father said. 'We'll line up a brain for you, my dear. No fear.'

'What have you been up to, Little Fly?' It was Margarete at the door. Her face was red and her eyes were wet.

'Nothing,' Ingrid said. 'I didn't write to him. He wrote to me.'

'Well, it seems as if we have some work to do, Johannes,' her mother said, taking the letter back off Ingrid. She gripped it to her chest. 'God, where are my salts? Ann-Kathrin!'

'Work?' Ingrid said.

'What have you done?' Margarete shouted.

The ferocity of it stunned them all. She was shaking and her tears dripped audibly onto the floor.

'I haven't done anything,' Ingrid said. She wanted to say too that Margarete didn't even want to marry Baron von Ketz, but knew it would only inflame her. 'Margarete – I didn't write to him.'

'Why are you all always trying to ruin everything for me?' Margarete shouted. She held a shaking finger up to her father and said, 'Ingrid and her dirty letters. And you taking him off to your room to show him your nasty letter from Africa. I saw it. I saw what they wrote to you.'

'What letter?' Ingrid said. 'What was in the letter about Africa?'

'This is as much your fault, young lady,' Frau Hoffmann said to Margarete. 'Do you think the Baron would be writing your sister letters if you had taken the trouble to be civil to him at dinner?'

'I was civil!'

'For God's sake, don't scream, girl!' her father said.

'You sat there flirting with anyone that would give you the time of day and it was disgusting,' Frau Hoffmann said. Margarete tried to respond, but her mother shouted over her. 'Margarete! Now that von Ketz is a Baron it's incumbent upon you to act like a Baroness.'

'But I'm not a Baroness.'

'You will be, if you behave more appropriately.'

Margarete laughed loudly, tears still streaking her face.

'Yes, everything's a joke, dear. A joke until it turns into some appalling drama. It disgusts me the way you force out your laughter. It's disgusting.'

Margarete caught Ingrid's eye. There *was* something appalling about Margarete's laugh, the way she pushed it up like that, low and rattling, through her tears.

'Then I won't marry Emil,' Margarete said. 'If none of you think I'm good enough. If Ingrid wants him.'

Their father, without looking up from the newspaper, said, 'She's teasing you, Hedwig. You mustn't rise to it.'

'Oh, don't come the innocent with me. You would be the Baroness von Ketz. You would have everything that that status brings.'

'What does it bring?'

Her mother blinked. 'Its own reward.'

Margarete laughed again and Ingrid winced.

'Oh, that's amusing, is it?' her mother said. 'And if you don't marry the Baron, who might you marry?'

'No one.'

'And stay with us for the rest of your life? No thank you.'

'I try my best to please you all,' Margarete screamed, 'but you still hate me for it. If I'm too quiet you hate me for it, if I'm too loud I'm disgusting.'

'Mama didn't mean you were disgusting,' Ingrid said.

'She just said it!'

'Margarete, the servants!' her mother said.

Margarete's neck dropped and her shoulders rose like a cat. 'I don't care about the bloody servants,' she said.

Her father dropped the paper. Her mother's arms went limp.

'Margarete,' Ingrid muttered, 'What's the matter?'

'Johannes, say something!' Frau Hoffmann said.

Margarete ran from the room, her feet thumping on the parquet, shaking the whole apartment. Her mother ran after her. Ingrid and her father shared a look.

'What did she mean about the letter from Africa?'

'You'll only hear bad things if you go snooping about for scraps,' her father said.

'It wasn't about Hans, was it?'

'No,' he said. 'Let's not talk about Hans any more. It's been years – the man isn't going to turn up now. You really don't let anything drop, do you, dearest? Anyway, that whole affair made me miserable. There was nothing to be done about it when we were there, and there's certainly nothing we can do about it from Berlin. We remember his goodness, then forget him.'

Shaken by Margarete's outburst, Ingrid sighed and went back to her book, fingering the place where the spine had been dented in. Herr Hoffmann picked up the *Kreuzzeitung* and flapped the sheets a few times to get the pages to stay upright.

Ingrid tried to act for her father as if she had been

unaffected by the exchange, but she felt tearful and her face and ears were burning. The idea of Margarete descending into another depression filled her with dread.

The air in the room changed, a coolness that folded the newspaper into itself. Ingrid heard a flutter of material, like a sail cracking in the wind. She heard raised voices through an open window, then window frames banging together and a scream. It was her mother, screaming for them.

They ran out of the room, into the in-between room, to the balcony, where the windows were open. Her mother was there and below, crumpled on the cobbles, was Margarete, her arms and legs bent at strange angles, the street filled with the low clunk and crack of windows being opened and a hundred thrilled and horrified gasps.

PART THREE

— Loving —

Haus am See,
near Buckow, Brandenburg

— June 1914 —

Although Frau Hoffmann was upset about the numerous fractures in Margarete's leg, they did at least represent a physical ailment that called for both healing and rehabilitation, and thus an excuse for Margarete's long sojourns in the spas of Wiesbaden, Bad Homburg and Franzensbad. Even a few years after what the Hoffmanns had come to refer to as 'the fall', Margarete's limp was pronounced enough to explain away extended absences, whether in Berlin or abroad, and the ongoing postponement of her marriage to Baron von Ketz.

The Baron visited Berlin weekly, telling the gathered Hoffmanns about the repairs being made to the von Ketzes' country house, but, as in Africa, Margarete was often absent, and when not she stared at the heavy clawed feet of the drawing-room chairs, looking exhausted and wan. A brief stretch of good health led to an official engagement in 1913, but this was again followed by crisis and convalescence.

Ingrid noticed the first portents of a change that Christmas. Margarete opened her gift from Ingrid – a ream of paper, six red Murano glass pens and a bottle of black Pelikan ink – and she cried. Not hysterical tears, but soft sentimental tears, and she picked up Ingrid's hand and kissed her fingers.

Margarete appeared at breakfast looking well rested, and she concentrated when Ingrid read her a poem she had translated, asking her about her choice of words and noting the lines she liked. When von Ketz made his weekly visit, she did not have to be summoned; she was already waiting in the drawing room, the sun illuminating the pale down on her pinking cheeks, a look of content contemplation on her face. She was even pleasant to Hannah when she came to pick up Ingrid before a Camille Saint-Saëns recital, finding them putting their coats on in the hall and saying, 'It's sweet that you indulge her French follies, dear Hannah.'

Hannah looked as shocked as if one of the paintings had spoken. Recovering herself, she said, 'It is me who is indulged – I'm an incurable Francophile.'

'You will always look after her,' Margarete said, and Ingrid, who was buttoning up her sable, couldn't tell if it was a demand or an observation.

Then one morning, after Herr Hoffmann had read aloud from the *Allgemeine* about the explosion at the Zeche Minister Achenbach mine, Margarete asked what, in his opinion, might be done to improve mine safety. After she had endured her father's surprise at the question and listened to his considered answer, she agreed to his summary of the problem and added, 'Do you think he'd marry me this summer?'

'The Baron?' Ingrid said, looking up from her book.

Her sister smiled and said, 'Who else, you silly thing?'

'Of course,' Frau Hoffmann said, wet-eyed, her voice shaking.

*

The von Ketzes' country house was near Buckow, a pretty town on a large lake that had become a resort when the Prussian Eastern Railway arrived at Müncheberg. During the von Ketzes' absence in Africa, a small branch line had been built down to the town itself, and they returned to find Buckow transformed into a haven for jaded Berliners in search of the gentle air recommended by Friedrich Wilhelm IV's doctor sixty years earlier; a recommendation repeated a thousand times on signs, in pamphlets and on painted boards hung across the town.

The von Ketz house was a long walk or a short ride in the Droschke past Oberbarnim. Sitting in a hollow in a steep wood with its back to the high road, the house overlooked its own lake that, smooth and rippling, reflected the dark and light of the sky and its wooded enclosure. The house had been rebuilt by von Ketz's great-grandfather at the height of historicist zeal, modelled on a small French chateau, with a steep gabled roof covered in tiles and round, lipped windows. Its Prussian origins were evident only in the walls, which were not stone, but stone-coloured render, and a long balcony that ran across the front of the building, between the two protruding wings.

On the evening of the long-awaited von Ketz wedding, Ingrid sat on one of the window seats in a large bedroom listening to the guests crowding below, drowsy with wine and chatter. A firework went up. It shot awkwardly from the jetty, juddered over the lake and exploded above the tree line – a burst of green sparks mirrored in the black water.

There was an eruption of male shouts from the water's edge and the voice of Astrid, a young cousin of von Ketz's, exclaiming 'Oh, the boys!' in a tone crippling in its leaden self-awareness. Ingrid, at the window, put her hand to her throat and wished the girl gone.

Margarete rushed over, limping on her bad leg as if she had a stone in her shoe. She gripped both sides of the window frame and leant out slightly too far. Ingrid pinched the skirt of her sister's wedding dress, as if that might stop her from falling.

'Was it a rocket?' Margarete said. 'Where did it come from?'

'Well, you haven't let them play any of their games,' Ingrid said.

'Who likes wedding games?' Margarete said. 'I said no wedding games.'

'Of course everyone hates wedding games, but you still have to play them.'

Margarete scrutinised the edge of the lake, her irises indigo in the twilight.

Ingrid looked at her sister, a bride. It was lovely, the way she had threaded flowers into her hair – little roses, jasmine and honeysuckle that tumbled over her ears in loose swags pinned away from her thin neck. Would von Ketz tear them out of her hair with his fingers? Would she pick them out at the dressing table as he sat in bed, nervous, waiting? She looked at the large bed in Margarete and von Ketz's new room – they would share it tonight. The thought made her afraid. She mustn't become the hysteric now that Margarete was better, she told herself, and touched her sister's cheek. 'You've done it all so well.'

Margarete dropped down to the window ledge beside her.

'Don't be a bore, Little Fly, it's been a horror.'

'It has not!' Ingrid said. 'It's been wonderful. I've never witnessed a more restrained Polterabend: a few local widows dropping some crockery beneath your window. A sweet ceremony and Father Ingelmann—'

'Who forgot Emil's middle names!'

'Well, that's a story. You have to have a few anecdotes from your wedding.'

'Perhaps,' Margarete said. 'Anyway, I don't care about any of that. It doesn't upset me, not really.'

It was undoubtedly just the experience of years past, but, despite Margarete's apparent contentment, Ingrid couldn't escape the feeling that there was something nervous in her rising up; that it was going to reach its apex tonight, before she crumbled again.

'Stop looking so worried!' Margarete cried, breaking into laughter. 'Just don't leave me with these aristocrats,' she said, with affected melodrama.

Ingrid smiled.

Margarete put Ingrid's hand into her lap and stroked her palm as if she were going to read her fortune. She turned back to the lake, blinked and shook her head as if someone had blown dust into her face.

'Margarete,' Ingrid said. 'You're well. You've been so well.'

'Oh, I know,' said Margarete. 'It's not that. It's nothing. You must stop worrying about me.'

'I always worry.'

'I know you do. But you don't have to now. I'm married and everything's working itself out as it should.'

There was a warbling cry. Ingrid looked down onto the meadow where three Ovambo men and two women were packing up their bowls and canes, while their German manager stamped out the last embers of a small fire lit for their performance.

'What did you think of the African surprise?' Ingrid said, laughing. 'What was the Baroness thinking?'

Her sister smiled and looked at the little group. 'It's rather silly, isn't it? Thoughtful, I suppose.'

'Is it?' said Ingrid. 'I met a lot of Ovambo in Southwest, nearly all of them at church in Lüderitz Bay. I don't remember drums. You know, I'm sure I recognise them from that native exhibition Mother made us go to at the zoo.'

'I'm sure you're right,' Margarete said. 'There can't be that many places in Berlin to find an African tribe for a wedding. Anyway, Emil's cousins enjoyed it.'

As if to challenge Ingrid's disapproval, one of the Ovambo men rattled his fingers against the skins of his drums one last time, to sporadic clapping from the guests. Ingrid watched them leave the little meadow and mount the drive up to the main road above the house.

'Are they not staying?' Ingrid said. Her fingers found the little white gold bracelet on Margarete's wrist – a chain link with narrow leaves, fashioned to look like a sprig of acacia, covering the pale scars that fretted the soft skin up to the elbow. She wanted to tell Margarete that she was good enough, that they were all good enough, but their mother called, 'Ingrid!', apparently embarrassed to shout for the bride.

'I've barely had any time with you,' Margarete said.

'We've had a bit of time,' said Ingrid. 'And there'll be lots more – it's barely half an hour from Berlin, once you're on the train.'

Their mother called again. She was in the house.

'Shall we go down?'

Margarete jumped up and said, 'Come on, Little Fly.' She grabbed Ingrid's hand and swung her around, pretending to waltz, until she stumbled on her bad knee and knocked Ingrid back into the washstand.

'Careful Margarete!'

'Don't be such a bore, darling,' Margarete said, aping the clipped voice of her new mother-in-law.

'But life is such a bore!' Ingrid parroted, playing along.

'Let's find the beast!' Margarete said, and pulled Ingrid out of the room.

'Mother, we're coming!' Ingrid shouted, and the girls laughed as they ran to the staircase, Ingrid grabbing at her skirt so as not to trip over it, holding in her stomach where the whalebone pinched her flesh, worrying that the small heel of her shoes would slip and turn her ankle.

The landing was dark and the sisters descended the curved stairs to the large hallway, squinting in the light of the candles, emerging thick on candelabras and sconces, reflected by the great gilt mirror on the wall opposite. The room was filled with the smell of jasmine that grew abundantly around the door to the house and, in the twilight, shed its beautiful sickly scent.

'Such luxury,' Ingrid announced in a grand voice, continuing the joke. But Margarete gripped her sister's arm and whispered, 'These are almost all the candles in the whole house. Emil's mother moons around in a funk the moment the guests are out of sight spitting on her fingers and pinching each one out.'

'It sounds like a very thrifty approach. You shan't want for candles.'

'Well, Papa is paying for the candles.'

Frau Hoffmann stood at the bottom of the staircase, holding out an arm as if to help them into a boat.

'Come and find me later,' Margarete whispered. Ingrid put her arm around her waist and squeezed her, feeling her hipbone beneath her fingers.

When they got to the bottom, Margarete gave their mother her hand, but she pushed her on and grabbed Ingrid. 'Leave your sister to the guests and her husband, darling one,' she said, speaking so close to her face that Ingrid could smell the sour Sekt. 'Ingrid, that Hungarian friend of von Ketz's is trying to speak German to Tante Anna. Didn't you speak French to him when he visited us in Berlin? Margarete, Gottlieb is looking for you. You must do the rounds – that's important.' Their mother shooed Margarete towards the door. 'Find him, please darling. I can't bear another searching question from him, and you know how close he is to the von Ketzes, especially your husband – and doesn't that sound wonderful? Doesn't that sound marvellous? Your husband.'

Margarete limped down the steps, landed on the grass and moved out onto the dark sea-green of the twilit lawn, towards the low marquee by the lake, strung with white electric bulbs. They lit her neck, the top of her small back and sharp shoulder blades, her fragile hands.

'Herr Gottlieb,' she said distantly.

'You mustn't bully her, Mama,' Ingrid said as they followed her out. 'We mustn't strain her.'

'Don't be insolent, Ingrid,' Frau Hoffmann said. 'This is her day – you'll have yours and God knows you'll be the centre of attention then.'

Ingrid freed herself from her mother's grip and ran down the steps into the garden.

The elder Baroness, shaky and twig-like, had joined Margarete. She was wearing a black velvet dress with shadowy gaps at her sleeves and at her neckline. Her fingers were constantly touching her stomacher as if it might come loose. Without looking up at Margarete, she rattled out a series of concerned phrases, tapping out her points with a raised finger, staring at the ground with her protruding eyes. She would be filling her up with unnecessary concern, thought Ingrid, about the house she would inherit and their forester, who was a drunk, and the beaver in the lake that was destroying the trees. Margarete looked about her nervously, and Ingrid was afraid. She wanted to join them, despite her mother's protestations, but her father caught her, calling, 'Ingrid, I've made some wonderful new friends.'

Ingrid's father was lying across a cane recliner that he had procured for himself from the outhouse that morning and convinced one of the servants to repair. A group of young officers and their wives had drawn up chairs and built a circle around him. There he lay, his small frame and un-oiled hair making him appear too youthful for the wrinkled mask and gloves of his face and hands.

'This is my youngest, Ingrid,' he said with drunken joviality, holding out his hand to her. He took hers, wrapping it in his short dry fingers, and skipped through the names of the strangers.

'Ingrid is the liberal – the thinker. Translates. Translates poetry,' He turned to the group and said behind his hand in a loud stage whisper, 'She has Jewish friends. What's that sweet little Jewess called, Ingrid?'

'Hannah,' Ingrid said.

'Yes, she's charming and only you could have dug her out.

They read English and French, the both of them – what a pair of traitors, if this war comes, but jolly clever traitors. All jolly clever. She goes to galleries and the like. Reads like a Trojan. She's going to marry some important professor I think, like that cuckold in that fat Russian book, eh?' He knew perfectly well what the book was called. 'Yes, that's Ingrid's sort. Handsome in his way, hair thinning at the front, little pince-nez that leave red pinch marks permanently on his nose and very high collars. That's the sort, isn't it Ingrid?' he said laughing, 'And I'm always right. When she was a little girl, who did I say Margarete would marry?'

'A German soldier.'

'A German soldier! And they always thought I meant she was going to run away with one, no doubt, and had all sorts of romantic fantasies, but of course Papa knew what he was talking about.'

'Am I allowed to escape before you start reminiscing about Africa?' Ingrid said.

The group laughed and her father laughed and said, 'That professor will tame her for sure. He won't understand her jokes, but what books they'll read! What conversations they'll have! And then one grandchild, I suspect – a son. Tall, pale and terribly curious, like my Ingrid, eh?'

'Yes, Papa,' Ingrid said.

He released her hand as he roared with laughter and then told a story about Ingrid and Margarete getting lost in the bush in Southwest.

Ingrid had lost sight of her sister and was afraid that no one else would see the panic welling up in her, because in Margarete the internal welling up was an external damping down, an electric stillness that sparked with hysteria.

Ingrid passed a cousin of von Ketz's crouching down on the lawn by her son, who dipped a long waxed taper into a paper lantern, almost as big as he was. The flame disappeared into the translucent body, dimmed and then the white paper tube glowed, suddenly bright, and lit up the smiling faces of the mother and child.

Ingrid was struck that Margarete would become a mother. She had thought often of the marriage bed in her sister's new room and her sister navigating the practicalities of running a house, but she had not imagined her kneeling down on a summer lawn cradling her child. Ingrid heard her mother address one of von Ketz's aunts and then her loud laughter jarring in the fragrant air. The cousin looked up, frowned and stroked her child's head in maternal concern.

*

In the hallway, the hired waiters were passing with dishes for the dinner table. Ingrid counted three trembling aspics in fluted mounds, piped with white mousse, and wished that the wedding had been in Berlin with table service and closed doors, so that she could have kept an eye on Margarete the whole night. Here by the lake it was all so open and the von Ketzes' country house so large that she could disappear anywhere.

An indoor toilet flushed near the kitchens and Ingrid's fear gripped her like a spasm – a sense that the wedding had already been too much for Margarete, that if she didn't stay by her side, she would be found in some dark room moaning, that she would start her marriage with one of her turns.

It wasn't her job to stop them now, was her futile argument to herself, because she knew it would be awful, worse than anything.

She saw Renate, the maid, backing around the corner, pulling the end of a trolley.

'Renate, have you seen my sister?'

'The young Baroness came inside a few minutes ago, miss. She was talking to Fräulein von Torgelow in the hall.'

'Did she go upstairs to her room?'

'Not that I saw, miss.'

Ingrid pushed through the nearest door and found herself in the smoking room, the lamps unlit. She leant her bare back against the painted wood of the door to cool it and touched the diamonds at her neck, fingered the warm stones, and thought how wealthy she must look in her elegant sleeveless dress. Her parents hung it all off her and she exhibited it like a mannequin, to make up for her long nose, her mannish hands and off-putting chatter.

In the darkness she could make out the high glazed bookshelves on three sides, the knobbly scrolls and knots of heavy furniture and the top curve of a great old globe with the countries all peeling away, as if it had been left out in the rain. Behind it, the tall windows were framed with the silhouettes of ivy leaves growing up the front wall of the house. She would have to let go of her sister, if not in this moment, then certainly tomorrow when she would board a train and return to Berlin, to sit alone in that drawing room, staring at the blue wallpaper with her book in her lap, while her sister's life spooled out without her.

She closed her eyes and listened to the house. If she could accept the loss, it would free her. Renate laughed and there was laughter in the garden. A door closed and the knock boomed through the corridors above her. There was the crackle of something burning.

She opened her eyes and started. Adjusted to the darkness, she saw the figure of a man in the corner of the room, a tall shape near the stone mantelpiece, with a flush of blond hair, holding a pipe with a glowing bowl. She smelt the tobacco where before she had smelt only dust and polish.

'I'm sorry,' she said, standing up straight. 'I didn't see you. I didn't see that anyone was there.'

'It's all right,' the voice said.

'Who is it?'

'It's me. Emil.'

Yes, she saw now. She could make out the bright flashes of waistcoat buttons and his long fingers around the bowl of the pipe.

Ingrid supposed she should leave. She moved over to the window so that she could see him and rubbed her arms, which felt cool and exposed. 'We haven't seen you much at the party,' she said.

'Oh?' said the Baron. One side of his face was lit grey by the last of the evening light. Ingrid looked out at the sky – there was a beautiful blue crack above the tree line, surrounded by pink and yellow cloud, the colours of soap advertisements. She felt a pressure at her throat as if she were going to cry, but she wouldn't cry.

'Your necklace is very lovely,' he said.

'Yes,' said Ingrid, disappointed by the compliment. 'The house looks very lovely too, all spritzed up.'

'You'll visit often, I hope.'

'Yes,' she said, 'I suppose we must.' She was afraid that he didn't understand it was a joke. But no, he laughed, and then looked thoughtfully down at the pipe in his hand. 'Was this how you imagined it all? Probably rather strange,' she said, trying to give him permission to feel the way he appeared to be feeling.

He looked up at her and frowned; he seemed offended. She could smell the sweat from his navy-blue dress uniform. She looked at the parallel lines of red piping and silver buttons and thought that he was still that same boy from Africa, sad about his lot, happy eating cake by the wreckage of the yellow hibiscus. 'Imagined being married?' he said.

'Yes,' said Ingrid. 'I suppose.'

He shrugged and seemed to genuinely consider the question. 'I don't suppose I ever did imagine it.'

'You never imagined your wedding day? I feel it's all we've been thinking about since we arrived at the farm in Southwest.'

'Really?' he said. 'I suppose it was always written in the stars.' He smiled. 'It's been a funny old journey, hasn't it? But here we are in a house by the lake getting married, as if we were like anyone else.' It was like he was talking about her. 'Do you think about getting married?'

'What girl doesn't?' she said automatically, but the words sounded coquettish and ugly in her mouth. She looked down at the varnished floor, then up at the window frame, and touched the window's cold metal catch. She tried to imagine her wedding day, but saw instead her childhood fantasy: herself and Hans crossing the border into South Africa, the gold of their wedding rings mute in the blackness of the night. If she tried to imagine a wedding here in Germany, she was just a woman, some woman quite different from herself, standing in a churchyard. A blurry, faceless daub and no groom there at all. 'But I suppose,' she said, flicking the catch, so that it rang like a low plucked string, 'I suppose I don't particularly have a picture of it.'

'You'd rather not marry?'

She shook her head, 'No, it's not that. I just don't have a picture of it.'

She imagined she was Margarete standing in front of her husband, awaiting the wedding night, awaiting life. What a shock it gave her. Because it would happen to her too, she supposed. Von Ketz seemed to notice the change in her face, so she threw out: 'There haven't been any speeches. Won't there be a speech?'

'God, I hope not.'

He was smiling at her still, quite charmingly.

'Do you love her?' she said.

The smile died. 'That's a very bold question.'

She tried to imagine her sister next to him, holding his hand. She tried to imagine them making love, his moustache brushing her wide lips, his mouth at her delicate neck.

'What is it?'

'What?' she said.

'You're looking at me in a queer way.'

She shrugged. 'Oh nothing. I'm always daydreaming.'

He had a handsome brow and a square compact head. Yes, she could find him handsome. His brow, his soft nose, his hands – one could knit something together for oneself – a good, handsome German, tall and too thin, but a good solid brow, a Teutonic angularity.

'Do you ever think about Africa?' von Ketz said.

'Often,' said Ingrid. 'I think a lot about the day we left; that strange morning when I thought everyone was gone. You know, if I wake up very early now, I still wait in bed until I hear someone else moving. I'm so afraid of finding everyone gone. You?'

'I think about it all the time,' von Ketz said.

'I suppose you don't want to talk about it, because of what happened to your father?'

He didn't acknowledge this, just blinked, the pipe back between his lips.

It was the memory of his father that loomed large. Emil was a nervous presence at the edge of things – the sound of the piano being practised in a distant room. But the old Baron came to her in sensual gobbets: the black stubble on his scaly red skin; the sharp smell of his sweat-stained shirts; his flat black thumbnails; the rasp of his voice as he shouted at his son, shouted at his wife, shouted at Ingrid's father; the sound of his hand as it sharply met Hans's head.

'I say,' von Ketz said, 'there's Horvath. The zoo, remember?' She turned and saw Christian, another cousin of von Ketz's, talking to the little Hungarian, who had grown more stocky since she had seen him last. His hair had receded to a strip around his ears and the back of his head, and what remained was shabby and unkempt. His hands were in his pockets and he was rocking on his heels and laughing like a boy.

'Of course I remember him,' she said. 'I'm sure he was thrilled to be able to enjoy a bit of African culture again tonight.'

'You mean the little Ovambo show?' von Ketz said. 'Yes, that was odd, wasn't it?'

'It was odd,' said Ingrid. She remembered the Himba boy from the zoo staring at the banana, remembered the cut apples that the elephant dropped on the concrete floor. 'Mama said I should go and speak to Horvath. I suppose she still has it in mind that I might marry him.'

Von Ketz laughed nervously.

'Mama's not very subtle about these things, but sweet you're going along with it.'

'He'll be a cheaper proposition than me: the Horvaths are very wealthy,' von Ketz said, affecting an effete voice, and twisting his pipe round with mock sensuality.

He held this pose waiting for Ingrid to laugh. But she said, 'What's that meant to mean? Proposition?'

His pose collapsed back into itself, his frown returned and his body locked again. 'It was crass, of course. Sorry. I thought we were joking around. I've always been terrible at getting the right tone.'

'You don't have to make it sound as if you've been bought off,' Ingrid said.

'He's a good chap, is all, and you'd do him good. You'd do each other good, I'm sure. He's a painter, I know, but his father's something important in Debrecen and he barely ever sees him. He's got means. That's what I mean. If that's the sort of thing you're worried about.'

Ingrid was suffused with disappointment – not about Horvath, but about the conversation she was having with von Ketz. Perhaps he really would suit Margarete – someone who, like their father, saw the world in terms of gains and trade-offs.

They both looked at Horvath. His chin was held high as he told Christian an amusing story, pointing in the air and dancing on the spot as Christian laughed. Despite his short-ness, Horvath's trousers were too tight at the groin and his jacket too small at the shoulders, as if he had grown out of them, making him look all the more adolescent.

She felt an emptiness like hunger, imagining her life with this stranger. She supposed this was how one felt when one thought about one's life rolling on – children perhaps, a house somewhere. She felt mortally tired.

The room filled with bright white light. Ingrid covered her eyes.

'Good God, these electric lights are an abomination,' von Ketz said, closing his.

'Sorry, sir.' It was Riemann's voice, an old servant who had sustained the house in hibernation when the von Ketzes were in Africa. He had very short-cropped red and grey hair and his forehead was speckled with dark liver spots. For the wedding he wore his most formal attire: a long double-breasted navy jacket, with breeches, long black socks and buckled shoes. He flicked the light back off again and was transformed into a tall silhouette of a butler in the doorway. 'If I may sir, we've had a call on the telephone for you.'

'A call?' von Ketz said. 'We've hardly had the thing for a month. Who on earth is calling now?'

'He said he was from the Wiesdorf house. Something to do with one of the servants. He said it was a sensitive matter.'

'Sensitive?'

'Where's the Wiesdorf house?' said Ingrid.

'Up the road,' said von Ketz, 'but it's a bother to go up there now. Is this some sort of wedding game?'

'I could put him off, sir,' said Riemann.

'But he said it was urgent?'

'Yes sir.'

'I'm sorry, Fräulein Ingrid. I'll have to deal with this,' von Ketz said, shaking his head.

'I have to look for Margarete anyway,' Ingrid said.

'Yes, yes, go and find her – she'll be here all by herself soon – you should make the most of it.'

Was this meant cruelly? She followed him out, past Riemann, and watched him climb the stairs to his study.

*

She searched for Margarete in the garden, but didn't find her. The air was warm and she knew she was being bitten – the mosquitoes danced black-speckled in front of the bulbs on the marquee. Fräulein von Torgelow greeted her warmly and drunkenly and said, 'Are there going to be more fireworks?'

'I don't know,' Ingrid said, turning to a group of the Baron's friends, in military dress, who were at some game, laughing nervously, heating a spoon over a candle. She glanced through the door of the summer house where the forester's wife was swaying and carefully ladling the last of the fruit out of the punch bowl. The estate workers were meant to have left after the Sekt, but she couldn't bear to betray her to von Ketz's mother. 'Your sister looks so beautiful,' the forester's wife said.

'Yes,' said Ingrid. 'Thank you.'

A child screamed and she turned to see one of the paper lamps in flames, a ring of liquid fire undulating up a blackened wire frame, disappearing almost instantly in a few spinning embers that danced up high into the dusk where the stars glimmered.

'Margarete!' she called over the guests, but no one answered. She looked up at her and von Ketz's bedroom and saw Margarete pass the window, the dim grey form of her slim arm.

Suffused with relief, she ran back into the house. At the top of the stairs, Renate was passing with a set of keys in her hand bound together on a brass ring. Ingrid stopped her and said, 'Renate, can you bring me and my sister a bottle of Fachingen water and two glasses.'

'Yes, miss. But I have to go to the linen closet first and fetch fresh towels. They went missing from the Baron and Baroness's room.'

'Missing?' Ingrid said.

'Yes, miss. Quite odd. I'll bring them now, then go down for the water. Unless the water is more urgent?'

'No, it's not urgent. Thank you Renate.'

Ingrid walked the corridor to Margarete and von Ketz's bedroom and opened the door. There were no lights on and the dying evening light had turned the room into a collection of grey shapes.

'Miss, the towels,' said Renate behind her. 'Shall I . . .'

She stopped as the shapes on the bed resolved into Margarete, small, white and naked, trapped beneath a dark mass, a body, dressed in dark fabric, except for a line of red piping and a line of silver buttons and a man's bared buttocks contracting and arching rhythmically like a retching animal.

Ingrid pulled the door closed, seeing Margarete's face turned towards her, her eyes black and pleading in the dark. Ingrid pushed Renate, saying, 'Get away from here!' Renate fell backwards, the towels tumbling from her arms. A little blue scalloped soap rolled like a pebble across the floor and knocked into the skirting board. Ingrid picked up the soap and offered it to Renate, but the maid scrambled to her feet, scraping up the towels, and ran down the corridor with them gripped to her chest like a swaddled child, the keys jangling in her pocket.

*

Ingrid walked onto the lawn. She felt the pulse of heart in her chest so strongly that she was afraid it would be visible on the bare skin of her neck. She looked about for her mother, but what could she tell her? Instead she would have to find a quiet place, a corner where she wouldn't be found. She would hide herself in the woods.

She crossed the meadow, forcing a smile every time her name was called. She felt like she had been attacked, like she was covered in filth and knew that she could never get it off. As she passed the summer house, she heard a crackle of branches and, turning, saw a flash of white in a large bay bush.

'*Why Fräulein Hoffmann,*' came a voice in French. It was Herr Horvath, holding a Sekt glass in his hand, stumbling out backwards. Had he been urinating?

'*Herr Horvath?*' she said in French, as her mother had instructed.

'*You haven't forgotten me, then,*' he said, and fell forward, having to touch her shoulder to steady himself. '*Oh, I am sorry,*' he said, and tried to take a sip of Sekt from the empty glass. The brash electric light from the marquee caught the softness of the thin hair on his head, which moved in an imperceptible breeze, like the fine tentacles of a sea creature.

'*I was going to get some air.*' She smiled and wondered what the quickest way to get rid of him was.

'*Of course you must be tired. Have you been very involved in planning the day?*' he said.

'*Not very.*'

'*You've been busy with your work, I imagine.*'

'*My work?*'

'*I heard you wrote books,*' Horvath said.

Ingrid flushed. '*Who told you that?*'

'*Von Ketz. Or was it poetry?*'

'*No,*' she said, thinking of the worked-over pile of translated poems, bound with grubby pink ribbon, hidden in the deepest side of her writing slope.

'*I thought you wanted to write books of poetry – he said something of the sort.*'

For a moment, like the guttering of a candle, she saw herself saying, 'Yes, that's right. I'm a translator.' She imagined herself reciting a line of de Musset and Horvath being astonished by her skill. '*I just do a little translating as a hobby,*' she said.

'*Are you staying here at the house? Lovely place, isn't it, what with the lake? Though I couldn't sleep – it sounded like they were smashing up the dinner service outside my window.*'

'*They were – that is, they were smashing porcelain outside Margarete's window. Usually there's a party to go with it, but Margarete didn't want one. It's a Prussian custom.*' Her name brought back her black eyes in the dark and von Ketz's buttocks and she thought she might cry.

'*For what?*'

A bell rang to announce the buffet. '*Shards bring luck!*' Ingrid said.

'*What's that?*'

Horvath was sweet, she supposed, but she needed to get away from him. And she certainly couldn't marry him; she wouldn't have him working away on top of her like a dog. '*Shards bring luck,*' she said again. '*That's what you say. But, I don't know . . . It's just one of those things you do.*'

'*Is that the dinner bell?*' Horvath said. '*You look pale – it is hot. We should eat.*'

'*I'm not hungry, just tired,*' she said. '*I should find my mother.*' But he took her by the arm and led her back inside, into the music room, where the food was laid out on narrow trestle tables in front of the dark panelled walls, painted with gold coats of arms and family inscriptions. The centrepiece was a tiered stand containing Klemmkuchen rounded into cones and filled with cream and cherries. The abundance of the feast seemed vulgar, like piles of coins in a Swiss safe.

Ingrid saw how shining the parquet was, sanded and varnished and flush as glass. She looked at the large windows and saw how finger-smooth the putty around their edges was, how white the grouting between the tiles of the ornate Gründerzeit stove, which reached floor to ceiling behind the buffet table, each dividing line crisp and regular. We have paid for it all, she thought. All of this for a title and for Margarete to be bred like an animal. It knocked her about the head, waking her up, sobering her up completely. The smell of the cream and sugar, mixed with the smoky fragrance of the cured meats and the sweaty shine of the aspic jelly, filled her nose, and it sickened her.

'Fräulein Ingrid.' There was a hand on her shoulder and she turned to find von Ketz, neat and smiling as if nothing had happened. 'You should eat something,' he said, touching her arm with his bare hand.

'Please don't touch me,' she said, nauseated.

'Ingrid?' he said, frowning. Had Margarete not told him that she'd seen them in the bedroom? Did he not know that she had seen him on her sister?

'I have to get some air,' she said.

'*Let's eat something,*' said Horvath.

'*No,*' she said, and pulled away from von Ketz, fleeing into the hallway and back out to the garden. She snatched her skirts up in her sweating fists and heard the guests' voices dissipate and felt the darkness deepen as she crossed the meadow and entered the woods. She followed the path at the edge of the lake, half-running. The air was cool on her bare neck; she touched it and was abruptly stopped. Her skirt was snagged on a thorn.

The water of the lake lapped against the black roots of the trees and the wind shook the leaves and rattled the branches above her. She tugged at the silk, stretched out beside her, a pale glowing sail in the dark. She heard a few vibrato notes from the party and her sister's voice calling for her. She pulled the skirt hard and heard a high tear that made her wince, but she stumbled on, not daring to look down or back.

Halfway around the lake, at the furthest point from the house, she found a little bay, filled with the smell of fresh water and rotting wood. She sat on a log, listening intently, terrified that she had been followed. She looked at the lake, a flat black mirror reflecting the lights of the house and the marquee.

No one came. She wondered if her feeling of horror would subside and she would be able to go back to the party, to embrace her sister, to say goodbye to the guests. But it all felt so soiled. She was surprised at her own tenacity, listening to the water's lapping and the fading chatter of the guests, feeling the sting of insect bites up and down her arms, on her ankles, her neck, on her face.

She waited for the guests to go and then for Margarete or her mother to call for her, but no one called and no one came.

When the house was finally dark she made her way back through the woods. It was harder with no light from the party, but the fear the dark induced, the itching heat of the insect bites and the thorns that caught her skin helped her exorcise a little of the terror she felt at what she had seen.

The house was black except for a light at a high window, beneath the gables, where the attics were. Perhaps that was where Riemann or Renate slept, she thought.

She crept up to the front door – it was unlocked – and climbed the stairs, using the banister and then the dado rail on the landing to lead her to her room. She undressed in the dark and brushed her hair and lay on top of the sheets, her skin still burning with bites and scratches. She closed her eyes and listened to the knocks and creaks of the great house and, despairing of ever looking her sister in the eye again, fell asleep.

*

She was woken by Frau Hoffmann. 'Ingrid, it's Mama,' she said.

Ingrid rolled over. Her mother looked exhausted.

'Are you all right?' Ingrid said, pushing herself up onto her elbows.

'It's Margarete.'

Ingrid was flushed with shame. How could Margarete have told their mother what she had done?

'She's gone.'

'Gone where?' Ingrid said.

'The lake.'

'The lake?'

'The lake, Ingrid. She's drowned herself in the lake.'

*

Ingrid chastised herself for everything she might have done in Buckow and hadn't. Her mother told her to dress, but didn't return and Ingrid sat alone at the window of her room in numb silence, rolling a desiccated woodlouse beneath her finger on the white-painted sill.

'Fräulein Ingrid.'

She had left the door open for her mother, but it was Riemann who stood there, the sockets of his eyes deep with sleeplessness. In his Brandenburg dialect, he narrated the events of the evening to her; the first and last time she would hear in any detail what had happened, though there was little detail to speak of. The party had ended, Margarete had gone with von Ketz to their room. She was agitated, von Ketz had said, but he could not understand what was wrong with her.

I understand, thought Ingrid, seeing her sister's pleading eyes beneath the great length of him.

The Baron had awoken at four to find Margarete gone. He summoned Riemann and they had searched the house and the garden in the hope of finding her without having to disturb the Hoffmanns. They had found her night things halfway around the lake by a little bay that she liked and had swum from a number of times. Ingrid wondered if it was the same place she had sat, selfishly removed from her family and her sister, when they needed her.

'Where is she now?' Ingrid said. 'Can I see her?'

'The body hasn't been found.'

'How is that possible?'

'She had cut the rope from the boat at the jetty, miss. She probably used it to tie something to her, to weigh herself down. We found the boat afloat on the wrong side of the lake.'

164

'Then you'll drain it.'

'The lake cannot be drained, miss. The lakes here are fed by the river – it all runs underground, and if she isn't caught up in the weeds she might be drawn away, anyhow. A fisherman went under the ice in Schweriner See when I was a boy and was taken out at Königs Wusterhausen two summers later.'

'What a terrible story, Riemann. I wish you hadn't told me it,' Ingrid said.

Riemann looked down at the tips of his boots.

Ingrid crushed the woodlouse; it disintegrated into shell, legs and dust. 'Do you sleep in the attic?' she asked.

'The attic, miss?'

'I saw a light up there when I came in last night.'

'No, miss, but a lamp might have been left up there, with so many things needing to be cleared away again after the wedding.'

Ingrid thought about her sister in her nightdress, a rock lashed to her waist, the feeling of being pulled underground, the muted sounds reverberating in the water. 'If there's no body, how do we know she didn't just run away?'

'She left the Baron a note.'

'I want to see the note,' Ingrid said.

*

A policeman stood in the smoking room by the great globe writing in a pocket-sized book. His helmet lay on the table by him, the note on blue paper beside it.

'This is the young woman's sister, sir,' Riemann said. 'She asked if she might see the note.'

The officer studied Ingrid, as if her appearance might influence his consent. 'I don't see why not,' he said.

165

He stood and held out the sheet to her. It was small and the von Ketz crest was stamped in black at the top. In a purplish ink was written: 'It has all been too much. I am sorry. Margarete.'

'She wouldn't have written this. She would have mentioned Mama and Papa. She would have mentioned me.'

'Is it not her handwriting?' said the young policeman.

She looked at the note again and said, 'No, it is her handwriting. It just doesn't make sense.'

'These things never do.'

She looked at his face. In the direct summer sunlight she could make out a straight line razored in the down on his cheeks until her vision blurred with tears.

Baroness von Torgelow sent her motorcar for the Hoffmanns to be driven back to Charlottenburg, so that they didn't have to meet any returning wedding guests on the train journey back to the city. No one spoke until they passed Genshagen, when Ingrid shouted out, 'Why didn't anyone come and find me? If I'd come back, I might have seen something.' But over the noise of the motor engine and the wind battering their ears through the windows, her parents didn't seem to hear her.

She should have gone to the attic, she should have gone back to the little bay, she should have studied the note, she should have talked to von Ketz, looked into his eyes to see if he was telling the truth. She didn't do any of these things, though, because, like her sister after her own attacks of hysteria, she was stupefied in the face of all-consuming emotion. In this at least she felt close to Margarete, felt that she finally understood the feeling that had driven her so many times to lie dead-eyed in bed, unable to get up. Sometimes she had a notion that her despair was Margarete's despair, released from her body in death, inhabiting her own like a ghost. She felt separated from the world and the physicality of it became ridiculous to her. Train carriages, outdoor shoes, appointed mealtimes, lessons, spoons, bathing, days of the week, buttons; it was all so laughably meaningless.

But Ingrid wasn't Margarete. She tried to hold on to the completeness of her despair, but it kept eluding her. Though she felt that permanent stupefying pain was the only appropriate response to her loss, after a few weeks there were seconds, even minutes when she wasn't thinking about Margarete, and it left her riddled with guilt. Her daydreaming made it hard; she found herself thinking about the wedding, von Ketz, then Horvath, thinking about painting, then galleries and for a while she was gone. She berated herself for these lapses, as if not holding on to Margarete's memory for the briefest moment might lead her to forgetting her altogether; forgetting her when she had already abandoned her to hide in the woods and, in doing so, lost her for ever.

The daydreaming worsened, particularly during her walks. Her appetite returned and she found herself stopped at bakery windows, queuing unthinkingly for confectionery, nuts and salted pretzels.

Idly picking up a novel, she would lose herself for twenty pages at a time, then emerge, as if from sleep, and throw the book to the floor, furious at herself.

When Hannah called, having read about the tragedy in the newspaper, Ingrid realised, as she embraced her, that she had missed her. And when Hannah described someone treading on the lanyard of her brother's sailor suit on the omnibus, causing him to fall off the bottom step, Ingrid laughed. Realising immediately the betrayal of it, she burst into tears.

Ingrid's loss also distorted her conception of the wider world. It wasn't that the crisis in the Balkans had passed her by, rather the assassination of Archduke Franz Ferdinand was refracted through her own tragedy, and the increasing inevitability of war seemed to her an appropriate and expected outcome to the darkness that existed in every corner of her life.

Even as the daily intensity of the pain waned, grief washed over her according to a mysterious waxing and waning of its own. It caught her in the dark of the picture house, as she jumped off a tram, during breakfast, an hour into reading the newspaper. Apparently ungoverned by her other emotions, it forced her in tears to her knees at will and without warning.

In quieter moments, the details of the wedding night haunted her, and when her questions about it silenced her father and drove her mother from the room she fantasised about returning to Buckow to try and get the answers for herself.

Then, the day after Germany declared war on Russia, Ingrid saw an envelope on the letter tray with the old Baroness's name and the von Ketzes' address on the back.

'Has the Baroness written?' Ingrid asked at dinner.

'She has,' her father said.

'Is it Margarete?'

'No,' he said.

Her mother stared out of the window. The summer sun made her grey eyes very pale.

'Is Emil well?' Ingrid said.

'The Baron is preparing for war,' said her father.

'It'll be a relief for him to go, I imagine,' her mother said.

'Is that why she wrote?' Ingrid said.

'There will be a reception at Buckow for those men going,' said her father.

'Will we go to the reception?' Ingrid asked.

'We will not,' said her mother.

Ingrid did not put much thought into the rights or wrongs of travelling to Buckow alone and without permission. She simply realised that once von Ketz went to war, she might never find out what had really happened to her sister.

Haus am See,
near Buckow, Brandenburg

— August 1914 —

The train passed the racecourse at Hoppegarten, but the grass was dry and moss-yellow and the course was empty of horses. Ingrid fell back in her seat as the heavy heat billowed through the open window of the carriage, scented with steam and burning coal. Would all the horses be taken for the war? she wondered.

She looked through the compartment door into the corridor. A man stopped to light his pipe and looked up, smiling in response to his friend's call. They are all so horribly cheerful, Ingrid thought, imagining this same man, beard sticky with blood, beating a French soldier to death with a rock. She saw the bloodied face of a Herero warrior, flies already swarming joyfully in his wet tears, and thought that of course it would be all guns in France; they wouldn't use rocks at all.

She wondered whether her parents had found her note yet. She had left it in her room, so that they would only find it when they started looking for her. Her mother's reaction she could judge – affected disbelief, dramatic fury – but since Margarete had gone she found her father's moods harder to guess. He had

170

withdrawn in the months since Margarete had disappeared and everything Ingrid said to him was an invitation to connect. He always responded politely, but rarely with joy.

Ingrid took a carriage from the station to the church at Oberbarnim. She heard the laughing crowd as they neared and the horse slowed to a walk. She couldn't see von Ketz anywhere in the crowd, nor his mother, and was worried that she'd misread the invitation or that it had been rescinded, when Father Ingelmann found her and said, 'Fräulein Hoffmann! I'd understood that the family wasn't able to make it.'

'I am here to represent us,' Ingrid said, a phrase that she had planned for this moment, but, deployed, sounded dry, like a political statement. The priest guided her to the front pew. He's taking me to our old seats, Ingrid thought, where we sat to watch Margarete getting married.

'We have been praying for your sister,' Ingelmann said.

'Thank you, Herr Pfarrer,' she said.

'Did your father get my latest letter about Father Schäfer's Negro, do you know?' said the priest, laying a large hand on her shoulder. 'I never heard back and I was worried it had lost its way. I should have asked at your sister's wedding but what with the—'

'Father Schäfer's Negro?'

'I should talk to him about it in person,' Father Ingelmann said. 'And perhaps your father wrote directly to Father Schäfer – I'm sure that's it. It's just that Schäfer wrote to me a month or two ago saying he hadn't had news, but I know how slow these ships are, and I'm sure with this war things are in a terrible muddle down in Southwest. You'll be going to the von Ketzes' after the service, I hope. There is so much to talk about,' and he turned to engage the next huddle of parishioners.

171

'Father Schäfer?' she said, recalling the man from the guesthouse in Lüderitz Bay, but Ingelmann was already deep in conversation with another parishioner, so she took her seat and looked crossly about the church. Had the missionary found Hans and they were keeping it from her? She took off her gloves and bit the knuckle of her index finger. He had probably been found dead, and they didn't want to tell her after what had happened to Margarete – that was just the sort of thing her parents would do.

She looked at the window by the altar, where the polished edge of a trapped brown pebble was visible. She recalled it perfectly. She had stared at it throughout her sister's wedding ceremony, wondering if it could be plucked out. She had thought that returning would reveal some trace of her sister, would move her spiritually, but the only thing she recalled clearly from that service was the little brown stone.

Baron von Ketz arrived late. Father Ingelmann stood at the pulpit and the parishioners' chattering was silenced. Von Ketz made no apology. She tried to catch his eye, but he was too fast, acknowledging the row with a nod that might have been intended for any of them.

He was dressed in Prussian military grey and sat at the end of her pew, at the very front where von Ketzes had always sat in the red-stone church in Oberbarnim. He crossed his legs; Ingrid could see his foot sticking out behind someone's skirt. As Father Ingelmann talked, she traced the brown cracks in his leather boot. Was it a sign of good breeding that his boots were old and battered? Or was it in poor taste? She didn't know, so she looked back at Father Ingelmann and then her eyes and thoughts wandered to the stone lintel and the polished brown stone.

*

Ingrid left the church searching the crowd for von Ketz, who had left first. The church bell was rung with such zealous alacrity that she could hear the wood of the headstock thumping dully against the stay. The men in the church had held themselves upright with self-conscious pride as the vicar read from Ecclesiastes: '*A time to rend, and a time to sew; a time to keep silence, and a time to speak; A time to love, and a time to hate; a time of war, and a time of peace.*'

Many of the women had shed a tear, but it was only Frau Heller, a corpulent civil servant's wife with eight children, five of them boys, who had really cried. She was known for her nerves, and her shuddering sobs had made everyone in the church uncomfortable. She had collapsed on the steps as she left and the worshippers stepped over her limp, outstretched legs to join the excited crowds on the green.

Ingrid caught Father Ingelmann and said, 'A lovely service – we were very moved in our row.'

'You're very kind, Fräulein Hoffmann. It is a strange and powerful time to be a man of God.'

'Indeed,' she said. 'I do worry about Father Schäfer in Lüderitz Bay, you know. Did Papa say we knew him? A charming man and so dedicated to the natives.'

'I do not know the strength of the connection, Fräulein. But you are right – one must have a deep faith to combat the innate sloth of the Negro.'

'I didn't read the letter, but Papa implied there was mention of Hans, our houseboy in Southwest.'

'I don't remember a Hans,' he said. A tall woman in a dark-green hat was tugging at his gown. 'It was so long ago,

173

Fräulein – eight years or more. You must ask your father or Baron von Ketz.'

'Why von Ketz?' she said, but he turned to the tall woman and gently took leave of Ingrid with a pat on the shoulder.

Ingrid crossed the grass of the churchyard towards the carriages. 'The atmosphere in Berlin must be exhilarating,' a verger said as she reached the street.

'Well, they're queuing up to go, if that's what you mean,' she answered.

He nodded enthusiastically and said again, 'It must be exhilarating.'

She pushed past a group of boys bayoneting each other with sticks and was caught by the older Baroness von Ketz who, without surprise at her attendance or preliminary greeting, said, 'Riemann is too old to go to the Front! Can you imagine?' Ingrid had not considered how old Riemann was, but assumed in his late fifties at the very least. She offered Baroness von Ketz a few comforting words about how there would be others to take his place. The Baroness's grip tightened and Ingrid looked at the blue of her bulbous downcast eyes and the papery translucence of her skin. She knew every detail of the terrible things shared between their families, and yet Ingrid couldn't fathom what the woman thought about anything. Was this aristocracy, she wondered, this inscrutability?

'Fräulein Hoffmann, *Bonjour*!' The greeting was so out of place that Ingrid didn't at first think it was for her. Then Leo Horvath's sweet grin, his black eyes and thin blond hair appeared in front of her.

'Herr Horvath,' Ingrid said, 'I had no idea. I thought ... I thought you would be in Budapest, perhaps. Or was it Vienna?' She remembered that they had spoken French at the wedding, recalled his accent, and understood his greeting.

'Budapest – beautiful,' the Baroness said, her head shaking as if the city were to be destroyed in the coming conflict.

'Yes, I'll be travelling back,' Horvath said. 'What with Germany joining in and England and France now, no doubt, it's all going to grow and grow and we shall all be swallowed up in it.'

'Must you enlist?'

'I must,' he said, without joy.

He was a painter, she remembered, and snatched up the newly recalled knowledge, saying, 'Will you go as a war artist?'

The Baroness hooted.

He smiled. 'No, a dull old soldier.'

'I always imagined that all artists were pacifists.'

'Pacifists,' cried the Baroness. 'There are no pacifists in Buckow, my dear.'

'You have a romantic notion that all artists are principled and courageous enough to act on those principles. I'm sorry to disappoint you,' Horvath said, and seemed genuinely so. 'It's wonderful to see you in Buckow again,' he added, and only his eyes gave her any sense of the sadness, the appropriate sadness that she felt was due her. 'Ride with me.'

She felt inclined to say no, but the sight of Baroness von Ketz's face falling, her mouth opening to protest, made her respond, 'Yes, why not. It's not far.'

He helped her up into the barouche and she noticed how firm his hand was and how strong his arm, despite his shortness. 'He makes you feel safe somehow,' she would tell Hannah, when she got back to Berlin.

Horvath sat down opposite her and called, 'Ride on! Let's

not wait,' with such warm authority that the carriage jerked away immediately, despite there being two seats free.

'Your German's perfectly serviceable, you know,' said Ingrid.

Horvath laughed. 'Who said it wasn't?'

'Mother did. And it wasn't wonderful when we first met in Berlin. That's why I talked to you in French last time.'

'I thought that was sophistication.'

She smiled at this, despite herself.

One of the village lads ran alongside the open carriage and called out, 'Miss,' handing her a rose. She looked after him as he ran back to join a line of them off to enlist, his embarrassment overcome by their barely restrained jubilation and goading cheers. Ingrid laughed, smelt the flower, which had the lightest raspberry scent and, when they were clear of the village, let it drop onto the road, where it burst into soft pink petals. Horvath, who was facing backwards, watched the flower fall and his eyes followed its remains for some metres.

Ingrid, embarrassed, said, 'Are your lot this jubilant about the war?'

'My lot?' he said.

'Your countrymen.'

'Oh,' he said, 'them. Stoic, I'd say, in Hungary at least. My brother's thrilled by it all, but he's been playing soldier since he was a child and is desperate for a good fight.'

'Is he in the army?'

'I'm sure he is by now – he'll jump in feet first.'

The dust that the horses were raising from the road caught in Ingrid's nose and she wrinkled it up to stop herself sneezing. 'The assassination seemed so ghastly a month ago,' she said. 'But now it feels like it was inevitable. I suppose all wars feel like that.'

Horvath didn't answer. He folded his arms and considered what she had said, making her wish she had said something braver and more intelligent. She stared out over the fields, rolling waves of barley and wheat, high and ready for the coming harvest. Would there be enough men to scythe it all? Would the old men do it? Would the women do it and the children? Perhaps it would be left to rot and when they came back victorious in winter they would stare at it all with happy, foolish guilt.

'It's always romantic, isn't it? Wind in barley,' Leo said. 'When the line of the wave rolls across the field like that and you feel like you're in a ship on the sea.'

The warm wind buffeted Ingrid's ears and she held the great brim of her hat, seeing the tips of the ostrich feathers on top dancing over the black lip. 'Very poetic,' she said and then, because it had sounded cutting, added, 'Lovely.'

'You're a poet aren't you?' He was smiling – he didn't seem injured at all.

No,' she said, happy that he'd remembered. 'I translate poems.'

'But you must want to write them too, no? Isn't that the logical next step?'

'Is it?' she said. 'I don't think so. Translation isn't like writing.'

'But it is writing.'

'Only in the sense that painting a wall is the same as painting a picture.'

'Well, I don't see that,' said Horvath, squinting into the sun. 'A translation of a poem is a poem – if it's done well, you couldn't tell it was a translation. To be a good translator you have to be a good writer. You don't need to be a good painter to paint a wall.'

'You need to be able to make the edges straight.'

Horvath laughed. 'I hope you could tell the difference between a painting of mine and a white wall.'

'I'm not talking about the finished thing – and maybe I'm oversimplifying – but I mean the process. You're not being inspired, you're uncovering something at first, like freeing a fossil from a rock. And then it becomes like an instrument that you're tuning. You change a word, and then you pluck the string and it sounds flat. Then you change it back, add something, take something out, and then you pluck it again. And eventually you have the whole thing singing. If it goes well. It's like a beautiful game. Like chess – the engaged concentration, I mean.'

Horvath smiled at her the way that men used to smile at her sister. She had watched them, across rooms, on the other side of naves and train carriages, watching Margarete, smiling unconsciously, drinking her in. Ingrid dropped her head and the top of Horvath's face disappeared beneath the brim of her hat. He took control of his mouth, which he fixed into a serious, straight line, and said, 'Do you play chess?'

'No,' she said. 'Do you?'

'No. Not well. Perhaps you're not confident enough.'

'To play chess?'

'No, to write your own poems. To write about what you really feel.'

'No, that's not it.'

The brief high of the conversation had subsided and she felt disappointed and confused. She should ask him about his paintings, she thought, but wasn't sure what to say that wouldn't sound trite. He changed the subject himself, saying, 'It is difficult, I imagine, coming back to Buckow. Is it the first time, since . . . ?'

178

She fixed her eyes on the short trees by the roadside, the smooth roll of the pale green fields, the blueish forests in the distance. Was this what France looked like? She imagined the scene filled with men screaming and hacking at each other, piles of them dying among the barley. The fields that were waiting for them must be this beautiful, this quiet.

'Yes,' Ingrid said, 'I wasn't too keen on the idea, but mother wants to hold the connection, I suppose. It was barely two months ago that Margarete ...' Her voice broke on her name and she dabbed her eyes with a handkerchief. 'It's not easy to talk about.'

'Of course,' Horvath said. 'But it's quite right that you're here. They're still married, so you're still family.'

'What do you mean?'

Horvath seemed surprised at her question and cocked his head. 'Well, your sister went missing and wasn't ... They didn't find her, did they? Unless she's officially declared ... Unless the court says she's passed away. Even if that is the most likely scenario.'

'Scenario' – what a horrible word to use. She looked at his short hairy fingers, the fat of his neck bulging out above his high collar, above his gold tie-pin and scarlet tie, caught the smell of his lemony cologne. 'Doesn't the marriage have to be consummated?' she said drily.

Horvath blushed and said, 'As I understand it, legally speaking, your sister is still the Baroness von Ketz.'

Her face flushed in response, recalling Margarete beneath von Ketz. Had Renate told him? Or von Ketz? Had he boasted to him of the conquest of a woman marked for death, perhaps driven to death by what he'd done to her?

They turned at the crossroads and the barouche made its

way through the wood that enclosed the house. The road deteriorated and the carriage shuddered. 'You don't think she's still alive, do you?' Ingrid said, shouting over the carriage's rattling.

Horvath frowned. 'No. I wondered about them not finding the body, but—'

'Riemann told me all the lakes are connected. That she might have been dragged away underground.'

'If he says that's possible ... '

'Where else would she be?'

He eyed her with concern, unsure of how he should proceed. She saw that he was gripping the folds of the carriage's collapsed oilskin hood, massaging the thick leathery crease. He followed the course of her stare and removed his hand, placing it calmly on his lap. Horvath turned to the woods and said, 'You know, Fräulein Hoffmann, I'm speaking out of turn. Picking up loose threads from overheard conversations. It's wrong of me. I was asking how you felt. How you feel about returning to Buckow.'

'Don't worry about me,' Ingrid said. 'Might she really have run away? Do you think it's possible?'

'No,' said Horvath. 'I feel terrible if I've put that idea into your head. Emil said she was upset that night and of course she left the note. I even think Riemann's boy, Otto, heard someone go into the water.'

'No one told me that.'

'Sometimes Emil talks of her as if she's not dead, but it's only because he likes the idea that she might have escaped and be living a happy life in some far-flung corner of Europe.'

'Why would he want that?'

They passed into the woods, and the cold shade flicked

over the driver and Horvath, then plunged over her. 'Then his wife wouldn't be dead,' Horvath said.

'But you said that *you* wondered about them not finding her body.'

'Did I?' he said, as they turned sharply onto the sloping drive down to the house and the lake. 'Then I've misrepresented myself. No, I meant that of course one's mind wanders when one can't bear the reality and hopes for simpler and better solutions. At the same time, when I think it all through, and think about her medical history – because I believe it's no secret that her nerves were not as strong as your own – then, if I am to talk plainly, the taking of her own life is the most likely scenario.' As the house came into view they heard the scraping bangs of folding tables being put up. '"After all, it is easier to die than to endure a harrowing life with fortitude",' he said.

'Are you quoting Goethe at me?' said Ingrid.

Horvath looked embarrassed. 'It's hard to know what to say,' he said, with such gentle honesty that Ingrid found herself touching her eyes again with her gloves, pretending that the dust had irritated them.

*

The marquee from the wedding had been dragged out and the tables and chairs unfolded, though the Baroness had frowned when the tablecloths were brought out, and Renate had slowed, turned and run back inside with them.

The punch bowl was set up in the marquee, with bottle after bottle of the cheapest Blauer Portugieser in the cellar glugged over sugar and some hastily shredded garden herbs to make a makeshift Maibowle.

Ingrid tried to find von Ketz, but he was absent from the

celebrations, and the Baroness, without looking her in the eye, said, 'Will you help serve the punch, Ingrid?'

If she couldn't talk to von Ketz, Ingrid wanted to go into the house and find her way into the attic room where she had seen the light at the wedding or to the spot where Margarete entered the lake. She tried to think of an excuse that would release her from duty. But a horn from the road announced an open-topped motorcar that curved down the driveway. Sitting in the back seat, Ingrid saw her mother, a new straw boater perched on her head, and her father shouting out a joke to Riemann, who had set out from the house to meet them.

'Of course,' Ingrid said to the Baroness. 'Is there a spare apron?'

The recruits came up with their cups and steins from home and Ingrid ladled the punch into them, the chopped mint and lemon balm floating on the surface like cut grass in a pond. She listened to her mother skilfully explaining to Horvath invented reasons for sending Ingrid ahead.

Her mother made a beeline for Ingrid, greeting the Baroness and saying, 'You must let me take over. You look so exhausted.'

The Baroness, whose strength had waned after five minutes, accepted this offer stoically and wandered into the house, as her mother tied the apron on and said, 'Ingrid,' encapsulating in the articulation of her name all of the rage that would erupt the moment she could be decently got alone.

Frau Hoffmann went at the work with gusto, sharing a joke with each of the recruits as they came up. Ingrid felt her mother's taut presence at her side, but also saw that Emil von Ketz had finally found his way onto the lawn. Why did no one else blame him for Margarete's disappearance? Because of her nerves, she supposed, and von Ketz's character, which was solid but sensitive. Because he did everything that was asked of him, with no joy, it was true, but certainly without complaint.

Ingrid thought of him in Southwest, his short brow wrinkled, the stolid sorrow of his mouth, his hands clenched into fists, enduring. And now he would go to war and lead lesser men into battle. He would be killed, but it wouldn't be a pistol shot to the head as he was carrying three men across the field to safety. It would be something tragic but bathetic: his boot sucked into the mud and a stray shell, a grenade knocked from a comrade's hand, a field gun leaping backwards and striking him, an amputated leg, a gangrenous cut, a fever and a cold November night.

She heard dogs barking in the woods. The sun was waning and the blue sky was darkening. Von Ketz was talking to the forester's wife, a cordial blonde woman, whose small pretty features were fading beneath heavy cheeks and the smooth curve of flesh between her chin and the collar of her blouse. Von Ketz was talking with controlled gravity, explaining something with his index finger outstretched. The forester's wife touched her face and looked full of sorrow. He put away his commanding finger and listened.

Perhaps he wasn't enough for Margarete. Perhaps it was Margarete who took him to their room, ripped her dress, clawed at him like an animal, and he had found her terrifying and bestial and, understanding fully the monotony of her future, Margarete had drowned herself in the lake. Would she have been capable of that? Ingrid wondered. Yes, she would. She certainly would have been capable.

Von Ketz finally looked over at her. He smiled and she nodded.

'Are you going to bayonet a Tommy for me?' her mother shouted at the forester's son, who was barely twenty.

'Mother!' Ingrid said.

'Ten on my first day,' the forester's son said, and her mother filled his glass with punch, which spilled onto his hand. He flicked it and put his mouth to the sweet spot where the punch had hit.

'You've turned quite the zealot,' Ingrid said.

'Oh Ingrid, why must you always be the ghost at the feast? They're going to fight. For us. Or do we also have to heap your moral judgement and disdain on them too?'

Otto, Riemann's son and the youngest servant, joined the queue. As he arrived in front of her, Ingrid said, 'I'm not sure you're even old enough to drink, let alone fight.'

'I'm eighteen, Fräulein Hoffmann,' he said to her, with a grin. 'You can check with my recruiting officer.'

'Oh, Otto,' she said, 'There'll be plenty of fights when you're really eighteen.'

'Ingrid,' her mother said, 'Don't harry the boy. You're a good lad.' She filled his cup with punch from her own ladle. 'Don't let this traitor dissuade you from doing your duty.' She cackled and gave Ingrid a sideways shove, so that her ladle dropped clattering to the table.

The Maibowle ran out and Renate hauled the empty punch bowl back into the house as the young men's parents arrived with greasy bottles of homemade fruit wine and schnapps. To keep her mother at bay, Ingrid engaged Frau Ingelmann, the vicar's wife, in an intense conversation about the church and war, until she saw von Ketz run up the steps into the house.

Ingrid took off her apron and followed him.

'Ingrid!' her mother called, but she didn't look back.

She found the hallway dark and empty. She peered down the corridor and saw the Baroness anxiously directing the setting of the breakfast table for the next morning. The smoking room was empty too, so she went upstairs, but there was no one on the landing.

Hearing her mother calling her name downstairs, she walked as quietly as she could down the corridor of the eastern side of the house, hoping to find the way up to the attic. She put her ear to each door and then opened it, but found only two empty guest rooms and a linen press. She opened the door of what had been von Ketz's room. It had been closed up and sheets lay over the furniture. At least he can't bear to be in there thinking of her, she thought.

She went to the other end of the corridor and through a glazed door into the servants' end of the house. Here the floor was unpolished and the air smelt strongly of antiseptic tar soap and damp. She resumed her listening and opening, but found only bare servants' rooms, with little framed photographs, pinned-up prints and newspaper cuttings and windowsills filled with sentimental objects to differentiate them from one another. As she put her fingers on the handle of the last door, she heard crying.

She pulled away at once, but a voice said, 'Come in.'

She opened the door and found Renate in the dark, sitting on her bed. She raised her small head and the dusk's scant blue light made her scraped blonde hair look like a white cap. She gave Ingrid a tight smile and her wonky incisors protruded from her mouth. 'Are you looking for somebody, miss?'

'Just wandering,' she lied. 'Is everything all right?'

'Of course, miss. It's only this war coming and the boys are all going off, even little Otto.'

'Is he old enough to go? Perhaps we could speak to his recruiting officer.'

'Oh no, miss,' Renate said, standing, sniffing and brushing down her apron. 'We are very proud of them, Otto too. It was silly of me and I'm sorry you caught me.'

'I was looking for the attic,' Ingrid admitted, feeling somehow that this confession made her invasion into the girl's grief less improper.

'What on earth for, miss?' Renate said, coming out and closing her bedroom door.

Ingrid followed her back into the gaslight of the main upstairs corridor. 'A whim.'

'Right you are, miss,' Renate said, confused. 'It's through the study,' she said, pointing to a nearby door. 'You'll need to get the key from the Baron or the Baroness, otherwise Riemann has them for the whole house.'

'Thank you,' Ingrid said, despairing of ever reaching the attic.

'You can rest in your old room, if you're tired, miss. Frau Hoffmann mentioned that you would be staying the night, so I've made your bed up there. Riemann brought up the luggage, but left it in your parents' room.'

'Thank you, Renate.'

'I think your mother's been calling for you, miss.'

'Yes,' Ingrid said and motioned to the French windows by the staircase. 'I might take a moment on the balcony.'

'Should I tell her you'll be down shortly?'

'Do that,' Ingrid said.

She walked out onto the long balcony that stretched across

the house and looked down on the boys, lit by a few hurricane lamps, the candle flames flicked by summer moths trapped inside. She saw von Ketz leaning against a tree, her father patting him on the shoulder and muttering at the ground. She would have to go down again now, but was overcome with fatigue and a desire to lie down on the reclining chair beside her, pull her legs up and sleep. How wonderful it would be to wake up in the early morning as the birds were singing, not moving until the sun on her face was too bright and hot to resist.

Some of the lads had gone to the jetty and she heard them drunkenly singing '*O Deutschland hoch in Ehren*', the broken melody snatched up by the wind that stirred the trees, brushing the leaves on their branches together, an always oncoming hush.

Ingrid hummed the melody and rocked, embracing herself. She saw von Ketz touch her father's arm warmly and then break away and head back towards the house.

She made her way down the staircase and into the dark corridor. She stopped at the smoking-room door, and thought about Margarete in the black water of the lake, her arms borne up and her hair teased out in soft fronds.

She felt a hand on her waist, the brush of leather soles on the runner. She felt someone's lips on her neck. She breathed in sharply and turned, her back to the shut door, and the hand came up to her breast. The thumb pushed at her nipple and she opened her eyes and saw Otto, his drunken eyes wet in the dark.

'No,' she said, and pushed his hand away.

He stumbled backwards and hit the wall, then slid down it, covering his face with his hands.

'What do you think you're doing?' she said.

187

'I thought ...' he said, 'I thought it might be the only time I kissed a girl. It might be my only chance.'

'For God's sake,' Ingrid said. 'You stupid little boy.'

She grabbed her breast, hot with shame, and marched down the corridor, to the sound of the boy's black sobs in the dark.

*

Baroness von Ketz had cleared the estate women from in front of the house and Ingrid could no longer avoid her mother, who guided her into the house to join the Baroness. They were offered kümmel or cognac by Riemann, which both Ingrid and her mother presumed to be a trick, demurring until the Baroness chose cognac, saying, 'We may as well finish off the good stuff, before the enemy cuts off the supplies.'

The three women sipped at their drinks in silence. Ingrid, finding it unbearable, searched for a topic, but found nothing that her mother would have deemed acceptable.

'I often think,' the Baroness said, staring through the hall, out of the front doors, 'that it must be cold for her in the lake, even in summer.'

Ingrid looked at her mother. Expressionless, Frau Hoffmann drank her cognac and placed it back on the drinks tray.

The Baroness finished her own drink, made some vague patriotic comments about the boys and ordered the lamps in the sitting room to be put out. The evening was at an end.

Ingrid made her way up the stairs and to her room. Her mother followed her closely all the way like an executioner. When they were finally alone her mother said, 'Can you imagine the upset you've caused today?'

Ingrid took in a great lungful of air and said, 'You wouldn't have let me come if I had asked. You won't talk about her, or what happened. I needed to come and try and make sense of it.'

'Make sense of it? You think this sort of behaviour makes sense of it?'

'Don't scold me like a child,' Ingrid said. 'I left you a note.'

'Yes, Ingrid, you left us a note on your bed. We couldn't find you and we found a note on your bed. Can you imagine what we thought had happened?'

Ingrid went cold. She hadn't imagined at all.

'We thought you'd gone. Your father thought you'd killed yourself. We were wild – I almost couldn't bear to open it. And it turned out to be childish nonsense.'

'I'm sorry,' Ingrid said, tearfully. 'I didn't think.'

'Clearly,' her mother said.

'I thought there would be something here to make sense of what happened.'

'Nothing will make sense of it, Ingrid. Nothing.'

Ingrid stared out of the window over the lake. It was a flat black sheet, flecked with undulating silver stripes. She could hear her father's laughter among the men below in the meadow.

'And what an extraordinary thing for the Baroness to say,' Frau Hoffmann said.

She didn't move, keeping Ingrid's bed between herself and the window. She's staying away from the lake, Ingrid felt. She wondered if her mother had looked at it at all since they'd been there.

'How long did they search for her?' Ingrid said.

'A long time, of course,' her mother said.

Ingrid imagined her sister walking down a dirt road in a

bedraggled dress, her eyes wild, saw the lace of her petticoat peeping out beneath a man's greatcoat as she stepped onto a train.

'Why didn't you come and find me on the wedding night?'

'We knew you'd run away and hidden in the woods – Riemann saw you go.'

'I could have done something,' Ingrid said, embarrassed. 'Why didn't anyone try to help her?'

'You think we didn't try to help her? After everything we did?'

'Perhaps it wasn't enough,' said Ingrid.

'You ungrateful little girl,' her mother said. She went to the door and, with her hand on the handle, looked Ingrid straight in the eye. 'We should have had you marry him. You would have been able to stand it. She was always too weak.'

'Stand what? Being married to someone she didn't love for the good of the family?'

Her mother stiffened. Her eyes darkened. 'Do you remember the vineyards in Cochem?' she said.

Ingrid shrugged.

'Do you remember them?'

Ingrid recalled only impressions: the greenness of the valley, the lime-coloured vine leaves above her head as she ran up the steep slopes with her sister. She remembered wasps crawling over squashed grape skins, the cooing of pigeons and the sound of hunting – shots echoing from the woods. The house was less clear, but she remembered its whiteness, a crack in a wall above a lead pipe, peeling paint, bottle-green, on a window frame. A dusty sprig of lavender hung upside down above a black iron range and the smell and sound of potatoes in bubbling water.

'Do you remember an old woman?'

'Wilhelmine,' Ingrid said, proud that she had caught her mother out.

'That was your grandmother. Your father's mother.'

Ingrid frowned. 'Is she still alive?'

'Our grandmother? Not if God has any mercy.'

'Why didn't she come to Africa?'

'She was hard,' her mother said, unlocking a memory for Ingrid: her mother being berated by the elderly woman, who hit her across the face with a wooden spoon. 'Your father had something better in mind for his girls.' Ingrid saw the white light in her mother's eyes growing and shimmering and knew that she was crying. 'It was a hovel,' she said, the tears not affecting the strength of her voice. 'We were born poor.'

The disgust in her mother's voice made Ingrid shudder. 'Did Wilhelmine lose the money?'

Her mother laughed. 'There was never any money, Ingrid. Your father made the money by building up the vineyard and the farmland, then selling it. Your grandmother was furious. But your father had met Baron von Ketz by then and saw an opportunity that most men wouldn't have been brave enough to take. He sold everything we had and took us to Africa where the money from the farm made us rich. You can't comprehend what he's done to give you the freedoms you take for granted.'

'The freedom to have your marriage arranged for you?' Ingrid said. 'I call that oppression.'

'You think that's oppression? Poverty's oppression. Breaking your back every day to try and drag yourself out of the poverty you were born into – that's oppression. Money, a title – that's freedom, my girl.'

Ingrid tried to imagine her father in ragged trousers,

climbing up between the vines with his sack tied around his waist, his fingers calloused at the tips.

'What about when Papa was a student at Heidelberg?'

Her mother laughed. 'Your father never went to university.'

'He has a scar,' Ingrid said, pushing on as if it were an argument she might win. 'From the Burschenschaften fraternity, from fencing.'

'He cut it himself. With a bread knife. For you, Ingrid. For all of us.'

'So I should be grateful that Margarete's dead?'

'You think I don't think about her? You think I need you to tell me to feel sorry that my daughter is gone? Why do you think we didn't have you marry him?'

'Margarete was the pretty one.'

'But you were the prodigy. With your father's money and a Baroness for a sister, you have everything, Ingrid, even now. You were always better than any of us. Your sister needed that title to make something of herself, but for you it was a gift, it still is. Unimpeded admission to a world I couldn't have dreamed of entering as a girl. You think you'd speak French and English, you think you'd have your little Jewish friend if you were poor?'

'Well, I don't want it. A dead sister isn't worth it.'

'You know, we all enjoy your reading and your wit, your acid charm, but when I look at you, you know what I still see? The same selfish little girl you always were.'

She turned the handle and left the room, shutting the door softly behind her.

Ingrid slumped onto the chair by the dressing table. She unclipped her leather jewellery roll and took out the orange and blue glass pin that she had stolen from her mother in Southwest Africa. She stroked the glass along her bottom lip

192

and shuddered at the thought of her father drawing a blunt bread knife across his cheek. Did her mother watch him do it?

Ingrid turned her lamp down and unfastened her dress, letting it fall away into a pile. Then, aware of how tight her girdle was, she attacked it, clawing at the hooks and eyes that kept re-catching, until she pulled at it so hard that a few hooks sprang from it and tinkled off surfaces invisible in the half-light. She peeled off her long stockings, ripping one, and threw them to the floor until, finally, she was naked.

She pressed at the painful red impressions left by the girdle in her skin, beneath her breasts and on her sides. How ridiculous this all is, she thought. Perhaps she would never wear another stitch of clothing again.

She sat on a small leather armchair, which felt thrilling against her naked skin. She stroked the arms of the chair, stared down at the dark hairs on her arms, with a misery like a stone between her stomach and her heart.

A breeze had shifted some of the heat of the evening and pushed the heavy curtains in the bedroom forward, making them bow out, and then roll open, revealing the sky turned indigo, before they fell shut again. In these moments she could make out the high relief on the tiles of the coal stove surround, catching the light in elegant curves and lines. She could make out the second bed in the room, in which Margarete had slept before her wedding day.

Ingrid heard a bird calling, a singular, fowl-like cry, like a shrill call for help.

The curtains whipped. She could hear the water of the lake, lapping, lapping, lapping. She could hear the breeze in the branches and a lone woman's voice like Margarete's, singing a military song.

*

The strange bird called again. Ingrid was spinning forward, breathless, and stuck out a foot to reconnect with the earth, hitting it flat on the floor. She had pulled the shawl over herself – she kicked it away now, and sat up in the chair, awake, her heart beating in her throat, her mouth dry.

There was a carafe of water by her bed. She went to it and drank it down, her fingertips on the cold marble of the washstand. She worried that someone had filled it while she was asleep. Had she covered herself completely with the shawl? It didn't matter.

She parted the curtains. Dawn was coming. The meadow outside was empty. She washed her face at the ewer and basin and put on a fresh blouse and the skirt she had worn the day they arrived, pinned up her hair loosely, and left the room, aware that at this hour her outfit would not have to be checked by her mother.

She gently tried the study door in the empty corridor in the hope that someone might have carelessly left it open, affording her access to the attic. It was locked, so she abandoned the house. There was already a little grey light in the sky. The air was cool and smelt both fresh and sour, of water, long dewy grass, earth and vegetation about to go over. A huge shrub with red spikes and thick succulent leaves had toppled over onto the frost-splintered steps, where it met the meadow. The dew on its browning flesh beaded like sweat and she felt as though she was leaving an Indian bungalow, the misty coolness a precursor to the white burning heat of the day.

She felt waves of relief, almost of being safe in the world, but somehow, in the fresh beauty of the morning, she could not ground herself completely and the anxiety in her

194

stomach would not lift. She wanted so much to be in the moment, to feel the garden fully, to feel the lifting of danger fully, but it wouldn't come – she had to traverse it delicately, always higher up, looking down.

The lawn was bare except for two long trestle tables, their dirty wooden tops and chipped metal legs uncovered. The lake lay beyond, a thin layer of mist about it like a pillowy stream of cloud.

The bird called again. It echoed, but it was close.

She walked to the jetty. Her shoes clattered beautifully clear on the weathered wood of the steps. Shocked and afraid, but also glad, she found von Ketz there. He looked up at her, biting his pipe, and their meeting felt inevitable.

'Hello,' he said.

'Good morning,' she said.

He had his hand in his pocket and he turned back to the lake.

She stood next to him.

'You're up early.'

'Yes,' she said. 'Have you been to bed?'

He shook his head.

The bird called – a plaintive double caw.

She had wanted to lead the conversation quickly to Margarete, but the otherworldliness of the morning had already lifted the barriers around them and it was von Ketz who said, 'It must be strange to be here again. You must miss her very much.'

'Of course,' she said. 'I wanted to talk to you yesterday. But I felt you were avoiding me.'

'Perhaps,' he said. A breeze, very light, moved the strings of weeping willow around them, and a few yellow leaves fell onto the surface of the water.

'Should I not talk about her?' Ingrid said.

'You can talk.'

She watched the willow leaves turning on the water, sticking together and moving beneath the jetty on the soft ripples of the lake.

'Riemann said she was already gone when you woke up,' Ingrid said.

'That's right.'

'That she was agitated.'

'Yes,' he said.

'What about?'

'I don't know. You know how Margarete was. One never knew for sure.'

'Did she say anything about me?'

'Not to me,' von Ketz said. He must have noticed her stiffening, because he added, 'She didn't ask me for anything. She just seemed . . . troubled.'

'What do you think happened, then?'

With the pipe still at his lips, his sigh made the tobacco in the bowl glow orange and then fade. It wasn't sadness, it was tiredness. They were all so tired of it.

'In the lake I suppose,' he said. 'I like to imagine her escaping through the woods though. I like that idea. A hood over her head on a boat. Her staring nervously through a train window.'

'And then?' Ingrid said.

'Oh, I don't know; Paris, Vienna, London.'

'Do you think?'

'No,' he said. 'I suspect she ended up in a lake, even if it wasn't this one.'

She felt sick. 'Why do you say that?'

'Because of the note. Because she had been ill.' He took

his pipe out of his mouth. 'She went missing before. She tried to ... hurt herself. Before, in Africa. In Berlin.'

'No,' Ingrid said automatically, looking at the ivory stem of the pipe, wet with his saliva.

'I'm very sorry about all this, you know.'

'Why should you be sorry?' Ingrid said.

'Everyone thinks it's hardest on you.'

'That doesn't make sense.' She reached out to steady herself, but there was no barrier on the jetty, nothing to stop her toppling into the water. 'She was your wife, however briefly.'

'You have the biggest heart, though.'

'Don't try and make me cry,' Ingrid said, her voice wavering. 'Please.'

'She's gone, Ingrid,' he said.

'No,' she said, pushing at the edges of her eyes to stop the tears.

'There have been so many years of struggle and unhappiness and maybe now there's a chance, for you at least, to get on with your life. The rest of us are so encumbered.'

'What do you mean?' Ingrid said.

'I can't put it better, I'm afraid. Other than to say many people want you to be happy.'

She looked at the pinkness of his lips, the broken cuticles of his fingernails, the sweet shabbiness of him, and thought about doing something terrible: hitting him; pushing him into the water; kissing him. She imagined his mouth on her neck and the sound of the pipe hitting the wood of the jetty. She imagined him pushing her back against the willow, the trailing branches catching in her hair, the rough bark marking her skin through her shirt, bright green stains on the white cotton. She could have survived that.

'You chatted to Horvath yesterday,' he said.

'Is he meant to be my future?'

'Not if you don't want him. There'll be no forcing anyone any more.'

'Any more?'

'I'm trying to talk openly with you, Ingrid, as openly as I can, and I feel you're trying to trip me up at every turn.'

'But you're talking in riddles!'

He looked away at the other side of the lake. Ingrid saw, between the trees, the peacock. It was staring over at her, two specks of dawn in its shining black eyes. The bird lifted its head, jerking it upright, then to the side. Looking past Ingrid, it called out, its crop pulsing, its cry replying from the woods around them.

'Do you know anything about a letter to Papa from a Father Schäfer in Southwest? Something about a Negro?' Ingrid said.

Von Ketz looked at her and sighed. 'Aren't these things better left alone? Sometimes when people keep things from you, Ingrid, they really are trying to protect you. You must understand.'

'But how can I understand if I'm always in the dark?'

Von Ketz dragged on his pipe thoughtfully. 'Your father mentioned something about it at that dinner with Fräulein von Torgelow and that terrible fat poet.'

'That was five years ago!'

Von Ketz shrugged. 'What of it?'

'Did he say something about Hans?'

'Yes, he thought he'd found him.'

'He found him?' she said. She saw the sweat darkening the cotton of Hans's shirt where it stuck to his back, her running to touch the shirt on the washing line and finding it dried stiff by the arid air of the veld. She thought of their constant call and repeat in foreign tongues beneath the gum trees and the hundreds of lines he'd given her caught in her ear like prayers: *Listen! you hear the grating roar of pebbles which the waves draw back, and fling at their return, up the high strand, begin, and cease, and then begin again.* 'Where is he?'

'Schäfer was a charlatan. Your father wrote to him and nothing came of it. It wasn't Hans at all – just some Negro who could speak French.'

It was cold. She folded her arms.

'You weren't fond of Hans, were you?'

'I was, actually,' she said.

Von Ketz laughed. A chuckle, then a rolling guffaw. He laughed so loudly that it bounced off the water and cackled back to them.

Ingrid waited for the sound to die. 'He was a better man than most,' Ingrid said.

'Yes, yes,' said von Ketz. 'He was a paladin, our Hans.' Her anger apparent, he added, 'Ingrid, you are too good. Hans was a perfectly decent chap, good on the farm, jolly bright for a half-caste, really very bright. But he was also just another kaffir who ran away. That's what they do. You mustn't assign your own feelings to them and expect them to stick.'

She dropped her head and touched the pins in her hair and recalled Hans reading by the light of a candle in his little room at the end of the corridor, his fingers pressed into his forehead.

Von Ketz scrutinised her face. 'Listen,' he said, 'your sister ... Whatever happened to her, she wanted to do it. That's the point, you see. Lake or train or lover – she left us and she knew what she was doing.'

Ingrid offered him a yielding nod. He patted her arm. 'I have to do a few estate chores. Will you go back inside? Go and try and rest, even if you can't sleep. The forester sets traps at night and the woods aren't safe, even if you stick to the path.'

'Of course,' Ingrid said.

She listened to him walking up the wooden steps, then away into the woods. She left the jetty and walked in the opposite direction, along the shore of the lake, screened from the path by the thin trunks of beech trees that had taken root beneath the shallow water. She was tired, but felt a pride in being awake so early, a sense that she had tricked the day, that this time had been stolen from it. The peacock called again.

She felt an urge, rising in her like panic, to get round to the spot where they said that Margarete had gone into the lake. She crossed the grass and entered the wooded part of the path which, even in the grey dawn, was cooler than the open meadow. She sensed how it trapped the air, feeding it with its cool damp breath. The ground below was filled with the sound of creatures scurrying under dry leaves and the water with the pop of surfacing fish.

Only when she was halfway to the spot did she question von Ketz's warning about the dangers of the woods. Were there really strangers there, poachers, who might kill her to keep from being discovered, or animal traps; traps that would have been forced open by someone's shaking arms, the spring ringing; traps that would crack shut like gunshot and crush her bones?

There was a second path. To her left, leading away from the lake. She slowed and stopped at the opening. The mud and leaves on the earth had been trodden into a silver line leading away from the trail. She followed this line and her heart beat hard.

The path, a dusky tunnel of pollen-dusted leaves, led her to a clearing and a small cottage, built in red brick. The shutters were open; she could see through the front windows, right through the back of the house to the trees behind. She went to the downstairs window and stared through the squares of glass. The floors were scrubbed boards, bare but for a short striped runner beside a varnished wardrobe that was too large for the room. By the window where she stood was a little round card table covered in a white embroidered square of cotton, with two hard-looking chairs. She was filled with a painful desire to live in a house this simple, in a clearing in the wood, a spinster.

She tried the door – it was open. The room smelt of coffee, wood fires and old oak. She looked up at the boards of the upper floor; through the gaps she could see the light of the upstairs rooms.

'Hello?' she called, afraid that she wasn't alone. There was no answer. She waited, listening for the merest creak, but none came.

The downstairs room was divided by a staircase running down the middle. On the right-hand side was a little stove and two oval-backed armchairs covered in stained yellow silk. On the arm of one, someone had left a book: a French novel called *La Porte Étroite*. She flicked through the pages – someone had made notes.

She put the book down. On a windowsill behind the sofa someone had collected up old horse chestnuts and arranged them by size. She picked one up and saw that on the pale brown circle of each was a skilfully carved face, so that the whole conker looked like a monkey's head. All of the conkers had been carved this way. The one she held showed wrinkled smiling lips and closed eyes. Did

201

Horvath paint monkeys? she wondered. She slipped it into her pocket and moved the remaining horse chestnuts to cover her theft.

She looked back at the little kitchen. On the table she saw a tin-plate percolator, a little beaten one with a fat belly. Horrified, she saw a thin wisp of steam slithering out of the spout and that two empty cups, pretty porcelain cups decorated with sprigs of peonies, were waiting, empty and ready to be filled. Her eyes jumped around the room for a face, but she found none. She looked at the staircase, at the gaps in the floorboards, and stumbled backwards, hot and confused, and ran back down the path to the lake.

She would swim. That was why she had come out so early in the morning, she could tell her mother. That was why she had come the wrong way and wandered around Horvath's cottage like a thief. She could swim out and be in the water and understand the calmness of her sister before the wedding, a final connection that would string everything together. When she returned to the house, her hair wet, her mother would say, 'Where on earth have you been?' and she would say, impetuously, 'In the lake,' and her mother would chastise her and rush her up to her room, but secretly she would see that she was wild and free and later, days later, they would be sitting in the apartment in Windscheidstraße and her mother would put down her sewing and say, 'Swimming!' and shake her head, and they would laugh and refuse to tell her father about their private joke.

She came to the spot where she had waited in the dark on the night of the wedding. The path was black and loamy. She looked at the gap in the trees, the little beach of soft brown silt. The sky was brighter and there were flecks of blue on the still water. She searched for clues, but saw only a pleasant spot from which to climb into the water for someone who knew the lake well.

She took off her blouse and skirt and laid them on the trunk of a fallen tree, then her skirt. She took off her boots and her stockings, then her petticoats and finally her drawers. She was naked.

She stepped forward onto the silt, which was beautifully soft, and touched the edge of the water with her toes. It was cold and clear. A small shoal of bronze fish startled and fled. She walked in up to her ankles. The cold of the lake dissipated and she only felt the water where it lapped up onto the dry skin of her legs and wet the fine hairs there.

She looked over the lake, at the jetty in front of the house. The high beeches covered most of the windows and she understood, with a great sense of submission, that it didn't matter if she was seen, that she was just a body, that there was no danger in her bare neck, her white arms, her breasts, her tuft of black hair, her bared ankles; there was no danger in any of it, and she waded forward, and the silt mixed with sharp sticks, then abruptly gave way and she dropped in deep, flattening her body against the shock of the cold, letting her head go under and then emerging, swimming forward, listening to the water, her strokes, the slow movement of the trees around her. Had Margarete dropped down at this point? Would her toes brush the tips of her outstretched fingers? Or had she kept walking as the stone bound to her waist pulled her under, letting the current pull her away underground?

She stopped moving forward and trod water. She was in the middle of the lake. She saw the boat at the jetty that

Margarete had cut the rope from; it had been retied and the new rope was bright and clean. The water was smooth and smelt elementally of life, of leaves and minerals, of earth and air.

She listened for the peacock, expecting its call to break the stillness, but it didn't cry. Instead, she heard a muffled sound at the end of the lake and she saw von Ketz and Horvath. Von Ketz was bending and Horvath was reaching up and holding his face as if he was trying to remove something from his eye. He was stroking away von Ketz's tears with his thumbs, he was muttering to his friend, very close to his face, so close that it looked as if they were kissing.

Horvath saw her. Their faces turned into pink circles with round black dots. She turned away from them and remembered Margarete in the water and began to cry. The sound of her own shuddering breath sounded very close. She dropped below the surface of the water, the sound and light closed in on her, her tears dissipated and she cried out, releasing a blast of bubbles that poured over her face and fizzed through her hair like soda.

She came up and gasped. Horvath and von Ketz were gone. A pigeon sang, cu-coo-coo cu-coo-coo. She heard her mother.

She looked at the jetty; her mother was running down the steps, still in her night things, wrapped in a red Chinese robe.

Her voice, distant, said, 'Help! Help!' and then she froze, her eyes fixed on Ingrid. She has seen my nakedness, Ingrid thought, and, hearing the door to the house open and voices, she let her body drop in the water, so that her open mouth was at the water's surface.

'Get back!' her mother was crying, and her father, who

had also appeared now, gave her a single shocked look, before racing up the steps and shouting for people to keep away. Her mother took off the robe and held it out like a screen and shouted, 'Come here at once,' her voice desperate. 'Ingrid! At once!'

Her mother disappeared behind the great square of silk, revealing the full extent of the design, a monstrous Chinese dragon, royal blue against a scarlet background. Its claws were bared and its crazed eyes stared out at her as it flapped flag-like in the breeze, following Ingrid's progress as she tipped forward and swam slowly back to shore.

*

In the train Ingrid said that she felt dizzy, so as not to be talked to, though her mother hadn't uttered a word to her since they had swiftly packed and left the house, leaving her father to offer the official goodbye and try and explain his daughter's behaviour, 'without further stoking our reputation as a family of ridiculous hysterics'.

Her mother made a great fuss of finding her salts, stopping at intervals to grip her chest and to say to no one, 'It's eating me up today.' When she eventually settled she ordered tea and Ingrid watched the liquid seesaw back and forth in her untouched cup, the steam misting an oval above it on the glass of the train window.

'I hope you're satisfied now,' were her mother's first words directed at her.

'No,' said Ingrid. 'I'll never be.'

'I believe you,' her mother said. 'But you're to leave it now.'

Ingrid shielded her face with her hand and stared out of the window. At every station into Berlin, she looked up and saw queues of men waiting to sign up. She thought about the journey to the von Ketzes' farm and the bodies strung from the acacia tree. She thought of the little red house. She thought of Horvath and von Ketz touching each other's faces. She thought of Hans. She thought of her sister in the lake, her wrists thin like branches.

PART FOUR

— Revisiting —

Windscheidstraße 53, Charlottenburg

— November 1918 —

'There's five of them now.'

Ingrid pushed a pin through her hat and caught her breath as it scratched her scalp.

Her mother turned sharply, her hand at the open curtain, revealing the black sky and dim apartment buildings opposite. Misreading her daughter's reaction, she tried to hold back a smile of triumph. 'For God's sake, Ingrid, there's a group of them now,' she said.

'I'm only going to meet Hannah. A friend of hers has read some of my translations.'

'And is that worth dying for? A few English poems?'

Her mother's eyes were large, the irises grey, ringed with crescents of dark, freckled skin. The smile faded and she looked at Ingrid's feet. She was preparing herself for disappointment, rising to her full height, her chest out, so that she looked tall, heavy and unimpeachable. Unimpeachable save for the chronic look of distant melancholy in her grey eyes. Ingrid could have embraced her, but her mother would have clung on desperately for just a second, before pushing Ingrid away as if she were being smothered.

Ingrid went to the window, her fingers still trying to place the pin, and looked down at the group of young men lingering in the dirty green light of the tobacconist. Her mother's posture softened and she placed a dry, heavy hand on Ingrid's shoulder. The men were dressed in brown wool and wore soft caps, two wearing ill-fitting demob suits, the trousers too short on one, the sleeves too long on the other. They were better fed than their friends, who pulled their jackets around them to stave off the cold and didn't let their pipes and cigarettes wander far from their lips.

'They're shooting people in the streets, Ingrid.'

'They're not shooting anyone, certainly not in Charlottenburg,' said Ingrid. 'And I'm only going to Kantstraße – I'll be back by ten.'

'I've taken your ration stamps – they're locked in my bureau.'

'Why would you do that?'

'Because otherwise you'll be doling them out like a tram conductor the moment you're out of the door.'

'Fine, keep them.'

'And what about the influenza?' her mother said. 'It's tearing through the city. One of the von Hagendorfs' boys – Karl-Heinz – succumbed on Friday.'

'He'd been gassed in Cambrai, Mother.'

'Oh, well then we shan't give him a passing thought,' Frau Hoffmann said.

Ingrid left the room and called for Ann-Kathrin, who brought her her coat. 'How much has she drunk?'

'Oh, it's not one of those nights,' Ann-Kathrin said jovially, smoothing down the fabric at Ingrid's shoulders with two rough pats.

Ingrid opened the front door.

'Your father wants us to move to Buckow!' her mother shouted from the drawing room. Ingrid looked down at her gloved fingers on the door handle. She could feel the sharp cold air of the staircase ahead of her and was loath to turn back into the stale fug of lamp oil and coal, the lingering scent of Riesling and coffee, and the fish, cold on her mother's dinner tray. She heard Ann-Kathrin retreating into the back rooms of the apartment.

Ingrid closed the door and went back to the drawing room. She found her mother in her armchair, staring into her empty wine glass. A sliver of zander and a few salt potatoes lay untouched beside her, the sauce a congealed puddle. Her mother raised her chin, hopeful of a criticism that she could rail against. When it didn't come, she said, 'Ingrid, call Ann-Kathrin,' as if Ingrid had just arrived home. 'I need a *digestif.*'

'Why would Papa want us to stay with the von Ketzes?'

'Your father!' her mother exclaimed. 'Why should I understand anything he does? He's incomprehensible. He doesn't tell me a thing.'

'How can we go back to Buckow again after Margarete?' Ingrid said, feeling breathless in the warm room beneath her outdoor clothes.

'You went back willingly enough before the war,' said Frau Hoffmann.

'And that was a great success.'

'Because you behaved awfully.'

'Because of Margarete.'

Her mother's body slumped. 'This has nothing to do with her,' she said.

'Buckow has everything to do with her.'

Her mother rested her face on her fist and said distractedly, 'It's got nothing to do with that.' She picked up some needlework. 'Look, it's all rot,' she said, picking and then tearing at the canvas backing, fraying it beneath her nails. She threw the frame down onto the rug. 'I bought that canvas last week and it's coming to pieces. They're celebrating that they've kept the shops open, but everything they sell is rot.'

'In the north and east they're starving,' Ingrid said.

'What am I supposed to do about that?' said her mother. 'They're not scrabbling in the dirt for embroidery fabric. And it's tight for us all. We can't just flatten society, so that we're all starving – what purpose will that serve, other than pleasing the Tommies?' She stared out of the window, at the reflection of the table lamp in the glass. 'I don't fancy Buckow any more than you do, but we can't stay in Berlin at the moment, with all this fighting. Not people like us.'

'Who are people like us?'

'People with connections.'

'What connections?'

'Don't be glib, Ingrid. Your sister was a Baroness.'

'For half a day and then she killed herself.'

'No,' said her mother, massaging her chest to show that her heartburn was building. 'I won't hear that sort of talk. I won't.'

'But—'

Her mother shouted over her, 'Your father wants to go to the country to protect us and where else are we going to go, Ingrid? Back to Africa? The von Ketzes are the only family we have here.'

'I thought you didn't want to go.'

'I have concerns; naturally I have concerns, but perhaps

it's for the best. Lord, I don't know. Tell Ann-Kathrin to bring me a glass of Fachingen water – my stomach is in knots. What will happen to us if we stay here? Shootings in the streets. The servants are going to cut our throats in our sleep.'

'She can hear you,' Ingrid mouthed, nodding to the back rooms.

'I had a letter from Hilda von Seelow – their garden boy complained to the chief of police, because her son Albert caught him smuggling out hazelnuts. Pockets full.'

'Why did he call the chief of police?'

'Because Albert beat him! That's illegal now! The boy is nineteen. That's what your precious Chancellor Ebert has done with his revolution.'

'It's about time.'

'Yes, thanks to your glorious generation. How grateful we should all be the Kaiser's fled to Holland. You've got your vote and one of our war heroes is in jail.'

Ann-Kathrin came into the room and quietly delivered a glass of water to the side table by Frau Hoffmann, removed the dinner plate and left. The water sparkled.

'Is Albert in jail?' Ingrid asked.

'He can't even beat his own servant – are you listening to me? What do you think is going to happen to all of us here, when these men start seeping down from the north and east? And that ham-headed socialist Ebert is in the Reichstag! Am I allowed to beat them when they're in here robbing me, when they're cutting my throat?' Her mother picked up the glass and took two gulps. She grabbed her stomach and screwed up her face.

'So that's it then?' Ingrid said.

Her mother threw up a hand. 'That's it! Yes, that's it!

Just your mother murdered by communists in her own bed. That's it. Go celebrate your successes with your Jewish friends. At least when they're running me through I'll know you were happy about it all.'

Ingrid, realising that she had allowed her mother to say everything she wanted, left the room and tried to leave the apartment again. But her father was shouting her name.

She went to the study door. Her father was sitting with a book in his lap and his pipe smoking in his hand. He smiled at her warmly, drunkenly. The war had diminished him further. Before he had gone to the recruitment office, there had been loud rows, followed by a solemn lunch at the Adlon, her mother crying in front of an untouched plate of Klopse. But he hadn't been allowed to sign up, because of his age and short-sightedness. He returned serious, chastened, and it was never mentioned again, save for vague murmurs about 'your brave father's disappointment'. The armistice had knocked out the last of his clinging youth. The grey of his hair had imperceptibly taken over the blond, and the bags of his eyes were fat little ropes looped beneath the flat grey skin of his eye sockets. His elfin compactness remained, but in certain movements betrayed frailness. His raised hand shifted side to side for just long enough for one to notice that the movement wasn't a mollifying gesture, wasn't in fact voluntary.

He held the book up to her. 'It's falling to bits.'

'The book?' Ingrid said.

'The newspapers too. Have you noticed? It all yellows so quickly and then falls apart. I've lost five pages in the last hour.' He pointed to a pile of leaves on his side table. 'I don't know what they're making it from. It's all gone to pot. This is what a world with the shutters down looks like, my darling one, and I'm sorry you have to see it.'

214

'Is that all you wanted?' Ingrid said.

'What news from the ministry?'

'Today was the last day.'

'Ah!' her father said. 'Well, we knew that was coming, didn't we? One door closes, and another opens, eh?'

She saw the high room at the Reich Foreign Office, heard the shouts in the street and the U-Bahn train passing on a section of raised track. All of the girls had gathered as Herr Rabe explained that the language services were being severely cut and that they were only keeping seven girls. They read out the names and the girls came forward, betraying their pride in the effort with which they held their neutral masks. One or two of the chosen fixed their eyes on her friend Hannah, who was known to be the best and fastest translator, but whose name had not been called.

Ingrid went back to her desk and looked at the letter she was working on. 'Shall I finish this off?' she said to Herr Rabe, but he shook his head, no. She touched the paper, followed the handwritten French words with her fingers and thought how much she would miss them. To be paid to translate had been a very fine thing.

As she left the building with the others who had been let go, she looked about at the crowds of factory workers and demobbed soldiers in the street. Across Wilhelmstraße, beneath the arches of the Reich Ministry of Justice, another crowd of tired-looking men and women descended the grand stone steps. But she had her poems, her own pile of papers that represented useful work, that meant something, at least it did if she didn't think too hard about it.

'I assume that squawking was your mother telling you about Buckow.'

'I'm not going back to Buckow,' Ingrid said.

'Yes, I thought you wouldn't be keen, but do consider it. I've written to Baron von Ketz and he's been very generous. He is still family, you know. It would only be until things in Berlin calm down. It might be a month or two, but it could be just a few weeks.'

'And Margarete?'

Her father's smile wavered for a second. 'Ingrid, my love, consider it,' her father said gently. 'We've been back since—'

'Has everyone forgotten what happened?'

They stared at each other. She knew that her father was expecting that she would give in once she had made her protests. 'Why are you even in touch with von Ketz?' she said.

'He's my son-in-law. Whether Margarete threw herself into the lake or not, she still did it as the Baroness von Ketz.'

Ingrid had no idea how to address the vanity of this statement, how to counter her father's petty pride even in the face of Margarete gone. Her father barked, 'This is to our advantage, Ingrid.' But his tone mellowed instantly. 'That relationship, which I have maintained at what emotional cost I don't know, has now borne fruit and we have somewhere to go in the midst of a revolution. That's why I'm in touch with Baron von Ketz. That's how the world works.'

'How one works the world.'

'To our advantage.'

'At what cost?'

'At what cost? Ingrid, we've paid. We're all paid up. Financially, emotionally. Are we to get nothing from them? Dear, we are owed.'

She pushed herself away from the door, left the apartment and ran down the first flight, mouthing the cutting retorts to both her parents' protestations that had failed her seconds earlier.

'Ingrid!'

Ingrid stopped and looked up from the landing to the apartment door. It was ajar and she could see her mother, her face high in the gap, her grey eyes watery.

'Be careful, darling,' she whimpered and appeared suddenly very drunk.

'Yes, Mama.'

'Keep to the main streets.'

'I will, Mama.'

Her mother swayed, then Ingrid saw her father's hand on her forearm. 'Come on old girl,' he said. 'Let's leave her to it, eh?' Her mother's eyes shifted from Ingrid to the floor and then to Herr Hoffmann's face. He kissed her on the cheek and she submitted, letting herself be led back into the apartment, her father smiling but not looking at Ingrid as he shut the door.

※

On Windscheidstraße, it was cold. The snow hadn't fallen, but she could smell it coming – a mineral bite that burnt at her lips and the edges of her nostrils. The buildings around her were silent and the street lamps – only every third lit now – created pools of dusky gaslight, laced between rivers of darkness that she plunged into, the cobbles disappearing beneath her feet, the buildings around her becoming looming black cliffs. In the doorways men moved invisibly, muttering and shuffling around the glow of pipes and cigarettes, skipping orange dots in the blackness. A bucket was dropped in a courtyard and she heard a clock strike the hour. She waited for the lilting beat of the distant factory bells, but the factories were still. Only one bell rang out, like a village church remembering the dead.

'Miss!'

She half turned. She heard thin leather pat-patting on the cold cobbles. She trotted forward, her heart quickening. She longed to be in the comforting circle of the distant lamplight.

'Miss!' came the voice again; it was near her shoulder and she recoiled, her boot jerking into a hole, filled with sand and grit. She yelped and the man grabbed her.

'Get off me!'

She was released and, getting her balance, saw the tallest of the young men from the group outside the apartment, his cap pulled low, one hand in his pockets, the other still held out towards her. In the grey light, she saw only the pale mask of his smiling face and the rolling cloud of his breath.

'Meier, miss,' he said, touching his chest. 'Are you all right?'

'What do you want?'

The man held his hand out flat to calm her as if he was trying to catch a stray dog. 'We've just been demobbed, miss.'

'What of it?'

'We've come back to nothing. Kleidmann's arm's broken. In five places. I'm half blind,' he said, and she saw that one eye was covered with a grubby dressing. 'I haven't eaten anything hot since the hospital train – that was two weeks ago.'

'Yes,' she said, aware of her sweaty fist squeezing the fabric of her skirt, of her legs bent low like a wrestler, of her face so tight that her head was aching, of the sweat slick in her armpits, on her back. She managed to move, to brush down her coat as she stepped out of the hole in the road, to walk on like someone who wasn't afraid and say, 'I'm very sorry about all of that, of course.'

She could see Kantstraße up ahead and heard the clattering of the tram, a squeal and a shaking thunder as it passed a junction.

He touched the shoulder of her coat. 'Miss, we've—'

'I said don't touch me!'

He pulled his hand away from her and held it high in the air. 'Miss, anything you might have would—'

'But I don't have anything,' she said and, close to the main road, she felt able to stop and look at him. In the brighter light near the street corner, she saw that his face was very young and that he was smiling hopefully, not sneering. She looked down at the floor, at the grey wool of her skirt and the tarnished sheen of its brass buttons that, under his solitary glare, looked like a mute row of coins.

'I won't give you anything,' she said. He was smiling weakly, with resignation. 'Can't you go to the demob office? Don't you get a better pension, because of your eye?'

The man shrugged. 'You're meant to be able to, but there's no money to give out.'

'Why do you all go then?' Ingrid said, thinking of the queue snaking down the street

'Because it's heated.'

'Oh,' she said. They stood together a few seconds more, then he nodded and left her.

*

Even as far out as Charlottenburg, the tram was full of demobbed soldiers and listless unemployed workers, and as people clambered on and off she was shifted along to a seat in the middle of the car, unable to get off easily, but trying not to think about that imminent struggle. She was glad that the seat beside her was filled by another woman, but then she felt a leg jerking involuntarily against her own and she wondered if the woman was mad.

Ingrid turned away from her and watched the streets stream past. The suburbs around Berlin looked exactly as they had always looked – grand and bare in these newer quarters, where the trees, planted only a decade or two earlier, had barely grown above the first-floor windows. But the war had cast a sense of stasis across everything, and the towering plaster façades belonged to another age.

As the tram moved further east, the number of hand-painted signs pasted to doors proliferated, invitations to the returning masses to take rooms, divide them up, occupy them. And those same masses increased in number – idle clusters of men standing in groups, sitting in doorways, leaning against the walls of temporary recruitment offices, queuing to become Freikorps – militias that represented a bellicose refuge for the war's rejected.

She thought about the pages of poetry she had given to Hannah after so much badgering; she thought about the cream leaves and felt ashamed at her vanity. She longed for the moment when the meeting was over and the publisher, Necker-Weiß, would hand them back and she could secrete them in the deep pocket of her coat and not speak of them again.

'Stop touching me.'

Ingrid leant her head against the wood of the tram wall and put her gloved finger on the cold brass around the window frame. She could smell the bitterness of the metal and it made her melancholy.

'Stop touching me.'

Ingrid realised the voice came from the woman beside her. She half turned, afraid to engage her in conversation.

'You're touching me,' the woman said.

Ingrid looked at her. She was wearing too much make-up and smelt strongly of musk covering something sweet, unwashed and human.

'Pardon?' Ingrid said.

'You keep touching my arm. I don't like it.'

'No,' said Ingrid, but when she looked down she saw that her fingers were in the fur of the woman's coat and she recalled now, like some long-forgotten memory, the feeling of the hairs beneath her fingertips.

'Oh dear, I am sorry,' she said, and folded her hands together in her lap. She turned away to the window again and smiled involuntarily at the thought of sitting there stroking the window frame and the woman's sleeve like some idiot, deaf to the poor girl's protestations. She would tell Hannah and it would make her laugh.

In the reflection of the dark glass Ingrid saw that the woman was looking her up and down. 'You don't have a few pfennigs, I suppose? A ration stamp you don't need?'

'No,' Ingrid said, without turning. 'They're all at home.'

The tram turned onto Savigny Platz and she put her hand up and held the cord for the bell in preparation for her stop and to signal to the woman that she would need to get by. The tram shook and trembled as it turned off Kantstraße and she rocked from side to side and thought about her sister, emerging from the house in Buckow. Not in her wedding dress – that was later – but in a simple white shirt and black skirt. She had looked so smart and grown up, and tears had welled up in Ingrid's eyes, but her sister had grabbed her like she always grabbed her – a crazed enveloping hug filled with kisses, and said, 'There you are, come to save me again. It's been awful without you.' And then holding her at arm's length, affected a clipped voice and said, 'It's been such a bore!' and Ingrid aped her, crying, 'Has it been a terrible bore?' Later that same night, though, she had woken to find Margarete in the second bed in the room she'd been given, curled up and crying, saying, 'Don't mind me. Just let me sleep here a bit. Just until morning.'

*

Ingrid had arranged to meet Hannah at the Romisches Café and waited for her under a striped awning next door. The café building was grand and ugly, an awkward Romanesque fantasy of a façade wrapped around the head of a narrow block where two streets converged, steaming towards the Kaiser-Wilhelm-Memorial-Kirche like the prow of a ship. Nearby a short young man whose eyebrows joined in the middle shouted, '*Red Flag*! *Red Flag*! Liebknecht declares socialist republic from the palace.' The newspaper was new to Ingrid and, knowing that Hannah was usually late, she gave the boy his ten pfennigs and received in return eight thin pages printed in Gothic script. The repetition of the newspaper's title in the headline was almost comical: 'Berlin Under the Red Flag: Police Headquarters Stormed – 650 Prisoners Freed – Red Flag at the Palace'.

She heard her name called and looked up to see Hannah running across the street. Her friend pressed her cold cheek to Ingrid's and said, 'Darling, you've found the organ of the revolution all by yourself. Reading outside the Romisches Café like a perfect little socialist. You know that's the first edition – have you read the Rosa Luxemburg piece?'

'I haven't read a word. He was just selling it – I didn't know how long you'd be. Are we really now a "free socialist republic"?' she said, reading from the cover.

'Well, that is the Spartacists' newspaper, so they haven't made much of Scheidemann declaring Germany a republic for the Social Democrats at the Reichstag down the road. And of course the Social Democrats have the army on their side.'

'But isn't Scheidemann a socialist as well?'

'Not a proper one,' said Hannah, taking Ingrid's arm and leading her towards the door of the café. 'I've got you for the whole evening, haven't I?'

'What do you mean? I thought we were just meeting this publishing chap. I can't be home too late.'

Hannah frowned. 'You said I had you for the whole evening.'

'You do, but I—'

'Well, that's wonderful,' Hannah said, joyful again. 'I have an errand to run. You're going to come with me to meet some people after we're done with Necker-Weiß. You'll be an expert on socialists and Spartacists and Bolsheviks by the end of the night, I promise.'

'What people?' Ingrid said. 'I really can't be late.'

'Oh, you're a sweet thing, Ingrid Hoffmann,' Hannah said and pinched her friend's cheek.

The café was stuffed full of tiny round tables between a few straggling parlour palms, all doused in the smell of tobacco, sweat, alcohol and hair oil. The warm chatter of the room hit them and Hannah shouted over the noise, 'Can you see them? There'll be a little group.'

'I thought we were just meeting your friend the publisher about my poems.'

'Well, Necker-Weiß isn't a friend like you're a friend. He has his own clique, and he goes everywhere with them. There'll be Bach, I should think.'

'Is he a publisher too?'

'No. He was a civil servant before the war. But connected to the palace, which of course means he's on shaky ground now the Kaiser's absconded. The Chancellor is using the old civil servants for the moment, but all these workers' councils are trying to turf them out. He finds himself terribly amusing, I'm afraid. Just ignore him. And Rosenbaum will be there. He's more a friend of Bach's. Had quite a time at the Front; you'll see what I mean. He's a queer. That's the extent of Necker-Weiß's circle. They're an all right bunch.'

'What's a queer?' Ingrid said.

'Has sex with chaps,' said Hannah.

'Oh,' said Ingrid, thinking of Horvath wiping away von Ketz's tears at the edge of the lake in Buckow. 'Exclusively?'

'That's the idea,' said Hannah.

Was that why Margarete had killed herself? Because von Ketz was a pervert and was in love with Horvath? Perhaps it was that simple.

Hannah undid her coat, revealing a striped shirt and loose bow tie that matched the darkness of her poker-straight hair and her eyebrows and the mole at the edge of her lip.

'This is very chic,' Ingrid said.

'I thought it was rather conservative. It's black!'

'In mourning?'

'For my evening,' Hannah said.

The main room of the café was crowded with babbling Berliners pushed up against giant arching mirrors. The tables flowed out of this room into a conservatory, where the glass walls and ceiling made the patrons' voices shatteringly loud. 'They'll be in there,' Hannah shouted. 'In the fishbowl.'

'Under the glass?'

'Here they say, "Are you swimming or are you not swimming?"'

'And we're swimming if we're in the fishbowl?'

'That's right,' Hannah said, waving until a hand in the crowd jumped up in response.

Hannah surged forward and Ingrid followed, keeping her eyes on the neat seam down the back of Hannah's coat. 'It was decided months ago,' said a man. Another, 'He'll be back – it's all he knows. You know, his son ... ' She watched the patterns of the tiles closing and opening beneath her feet, and the chair legs and the shoes of the men and women around her. 'He's the real power behind it, Liebknecht. They'll name a street after her, but only when she's dead ... ' A small dog on a lead barked and was yanked back between someone's legs with a yelp. 'I just wish we knew. I can't bear the waiting – poverty, fine, war, fine – but the waiting ... ' Hannah pulled out a chair. 'It's a victory for the people of Germany – that's who. Ebert be blown – we don't need another—'

'Boys! This is Ingrid Hoffmann,' Hannah said, and there was a squawk of scraped-back chairs.

'Fräulein Hoffmann, yes,' said a Scandinavian-looking man with a large blond moustache and a Bavarian accent. 'Necker-Weiß,' he said, giving her his hand. 'Nice to meet you at last.' What did he think of the translations? She tried to read his green eyes, so that she could break away from him, so that she could stagger back through the crowd to the door telling him to burn them.

'This is Rosenbaum,' Hannah said, indicating a small dark

man, clean-shaven and so quiet that she missed what he said and asked him to repeat himself.

'Pleased to meet you.'

'Bach,' said another man, fat and older, arriving before they had sat down and drying his hands on his trousers before offering one up. 'Ah yes, the translator. Fräulein Mandelbaum has told us so much about you,' he said. 'Please sit.' He was so naturally red-faced that the skin around his lips and eyebrows looked yellow in contrast.

Both Bach and Necker-Weiß signalled to an elderly waiter with high grey gums, who took an order for schnapps and a coffee.

'Coffee!' Hannah said to Ingrid. 'You need something stronger to keep the cold out.'

'For God's sake, Hannah, let me drink what I want,' said Ingrid in mock-frustration.

The men laughed. Even Rosenbaum smiled and stuck his neck out, but sharply, and she wondered if he had developed a nervous tic at the Front. She saw him huddled in a barbed-wire-covered trench, his white face contracted into a mask of numb terror.

'Terrible nag, isn't she?' Bach said.

'There's no coffee today, madam,' the waiter said, and then, as if she might not have realised, added, 'The supply is still very poor. It's very touch-and-go, because nothing's coming in at all.'

'Of course,' Ingrid said. 'Then schnapps for me as well. Williamsbirne, if you have it.'

'There's barely anything left to order – I don't know how they're keeping it open,' said Bach as the waiter darted away, fishlike, between the tables. 'The bulk of them aren't even here yet – most of the boys at the Front aren't due back until December. Imagine that? As if it wasn't bad enough already.'

Rosenbaum stared at Necker-Weiß's hand on the table, and Ingrid wondered if he was a queer too. Perhaps that's what being in the fishbowl really meant.

'These poems then,' said Necker-Weiß.

'Yes,' said Ingrid, and congratulated herself for the calm, flat tone of the response.

'They're very good of course.'

'Thank you,' she said, feeling the muscles of her stomach release a little, seeing Hannah's smile in the corner of her eye.

'But in book terms, you'll know yourself that they're not publishable.'

'Yes—'

She was going to add, 'of course', but Hannah cried, 'Not publishable! Good Lord, Necker-Weiß, dear – don't be a boob. They're remarkable.'

Necker-Weiß laughed off Hannah's comment with a perfunctory chuckle and said, 'Women's literature is always going to be a struggle, and then there's the odd chap in there. This George Eliot, for instance.'

'It's a woman,' Ingrid said. 'It's a pen-name.'

'Well, that's a bit of a trick, isn't it?' He looked down at some notes he'd made. By George Eliot's name he wrote 'not a man!!!' The exclamation marks seemed excessive.

'The poem wasn't published in her lifetime,' she said. 'Even in English. And none of these poems have been published in German at all.'

'Yes, yes. They're good. I thought the Eliot one was very good, but it's about England, woman or not. Of course that's the main problem, really. Thematically. Well, the women are a problem too, but really it's that they're nearly all English.'

'There's French. Du Bellay,' Hannah said. 'That's terribly old. That's ancient.'

'Mercœur,' Ingrid blurted, stung by her high, panicked tone.

'Yes, of course, but French isn't any better, is it?'

Bach laughed and shook his head. 'French isn't better!'

'It's not about the quality of the translations,' Necker-Weiß said.

'Did you read all of them?' Ingrid said. 'Because . . . '

Necker-Weiß snorted. 'Of course I read them all, Fräulein Hoffmann. But history's not on your side, I'm afraid. I can't publish poems called "In a London Drawing Room". Who wants to read about that now?'

'But it's not about nationalism,' Ingrid said. 'That's the whole point. It's about homes and intimacy and friendship. It's about small things, but things that matter.' She was making it all sound so twee. 'It's the opposite of what people are reading about now, which is why I put them together as a collection.' She was hot and couldn't swallow. 'Can you give the manuscript to me? Can you give it back?'

Necker-Weiß's body loosened at the obvious weight of her disappointment and he said, 'It's not the translations, Fräulein Hoffmann, as I said. It's just the poems themselves. Have you got anything else? Anything more suitable? You're very talented.'

They listened to the clinking chatter of the room.

'What about something Swiss?' Bach said. 'Nice and neutral. What about Keller? He's a poet, isn't he?'

'He writes in German,' Ingrid said, without looking at him.

228

Someone's ugly guffaw built and built at a distant table, rising in bursts, until it broke into fervent coughing. 'No,' she heard someone saying, as if to a child. 'No, no, no.'

'Can I just have the manuscript back?' she said.

'I've passed it on – as I said, the translations are very good, and—'

'To whom?' Ingrid said, looking up, enduring the patronising sympathy of Necker-Weiß's pale stare.

'A friend. Frau von Galen.'

'Von Galen?' said Hannah. 'Oh Ingrid, she publishes too.'

'What does she publish?' Ingrid said.

'She hasn't published anything for a while,' Necker-Weiß said.

Ingrid felt the black pall of disappointment pulled over her again. She would stay beneath it now; hope was too painful.

'I want the manuscript back,' she said. 'I can go and pick it up from her.'

'Ingrid, do let her read it. She's a real publisher.'

Necker-Weiß flinched at this attack, but kept his eyes on Ingrid.

'No,' said Ingrid; the sense of these strangers watching her humiliation was unbearable. 'Give me her address.'

Necker-Weiß wrote it on the back of his visiting card with a silver propelling pencil. He passed it to her. 'It's not for me, as I said, but I'd let her read it if I were you.'

She looked down at the address, at the strong uprights in his capitals, at the smooth grey lead on the card. She tried to make sense of the address, but couldn't take it in.

Ingrid stood and the men stood too. 'Will you excuse me,' she said.

'I'm sorry, Fräulein Hoffmann, if you—'

'It's fine,' she muttered and listened to Bach's grand sympathetic sigh as she walked away.

*

In the bathroom Ingrid looked at her face in the mirror. Her eyes were dark and her skin grey. She looked hungry. The last of the good weather had died, the war was lost and the country was falling to pieces. And she was crying in a bathroom, because somebody didn't want to publish some poems she'd translated. She thought about the house at Buckow, about Margarete, and she cried again. She listened to the worried mutters of the women milling about behind her and tried to think about elemental emotionless things – water, paper, soap, silver – until she was able to dry her eyes.

She pushed back through the café. From a distance, she saw Rosenbaum's neck twitch again. Yes, he must have fought. He should have been an academic, a cheerful little lecturer in a provincial university, a convenient marriage with a small mousey wife, dandruff, walking holidays in the Märkische Schweiz. And now he's ruined.

As she neared the table, she heard Hannah's conspiratorial voice intoning, '... came back from German Southwest Africa – well, I suppose it's called something else now. "British Southwest Africa". Then her sister disappeared.'

'Disappeared?'

'At her wedding. They never found the body.'

'How gothic!'

Bach looked up nervously and Hannah leant back in her chair again. The table was silent. Ingrid sat down and took a sip of her fruit brandy. It didn't matter that Hannah had betrayed her, she supposed. It was only a small betrayal. She opened her mouth to say something, though she had nothing to say, and was saved by the sound of chairs scraping back near the door and raised voices. They turned to see a man, pink from running, picking through the crowd and finding friends, who he whispered to, causing them to leap to their feet and race out through the door.

'Ho ho,' said Bach. 'Something's afoot.'

A waiter went and spoke to the man, then broke away, heading to the back of the café. Necker-Weiß stood as he came close and caught him by the arm. 'What's going on?' he said.

'There are crowds all down Unter den Linden. They've released the rest of the political prisoners. Everyone's free.'

'Come on,' said Hannah, standing. 'We've got some of our own friends to meet.'

Hannah knocked back her drink.

Necker-Weiß stood as well. 'I'll take you back home.'

'No,' Hannah said, 'We'll survive it. Look Ingrid, you haven't touched your schnapps,' and she picked up Ingrid's glass and drank it down in one. The men laughed awkwardly. 'That'll steel me to fight off the militias,' she said, slamming the glass back down on the table.

'OK,' muttered Ingrid, pulling at Hannah's sleeve. 'But quick. Let's get away before we're chaperoned.'

They nodded their goodbyes and set off through the sea of chairs, tables and barking customers. Ingrid watched the room breaking up, men pulling on their coats and falling into the street. But she was thinking of Africa, of von Ketz playing the piano. She was thinking of the church in Oberbarnim, following her sister after the wedding service, following the congregation out at the start of the war, her sister gone. She imagined her sister running along the path at the other side of the lake between the trees and was with her, panting and sweating, holding up her skirts and running. And all the time her hand rested against the pocket of her coat, wishing that Necker-Weiß had given her her poems back, wishing that they were in her possession now.

'We'll get a cab,' Hannah said, and held her hand out. After a second, the grey index finger of her dog-skin glove shot out and, as if this were the decisive signal, a cab drew up in a clatter of hooves and steaming hide. 'Sedanstraße, please,' Hannah said.

'Not many travelling down that way,' the driver said.

'Then you'll have the roads all to yourself,' said Hannah, and opened the door to guide Ingrid in.

'Where's Sedanstraße? I should get home,' Ingrid said, as she bumped her head on the plush of the cab's ceiling and fell onto one of the stiffly upholstered seats.

'Oh, don't make me go alone, Ingrid. I have to drop something off for Mama – it's important, it's for the cause. And you'll meet some wonderful people, I promise. It'll cheer you up. You're not to argue. After I failed with Necker-Weiß, I've got to be of some use to you. I'm terribly sorry about your poems. We will get them published.'

'It's doesn't matter, especially at the moment,' Ingrid said. 'But I've had quite enough of meeting people. I really would rather sleep and forget all about the book. Besides, I can't be home too late – mother thinks we're just having coffee.'

'Ingrid,' Hannah said, taking her hand and coming so close that Ingrid could smell the alcohol on her breath. 'You are an artist and you're going to have a life filled with incident. The world is coming apart and re-forming around us and we must be part of it. It's vital. It's absolutely vital.'

'Where on earth are we going?'

'I want you to meet some people, that's all. I'll have you back in Windscheidstraße well before midnight.'

'What do you have to drop off? Are we going to your apartment first?'

'Lord no! Trude's got the Blitz catarrh, poor thing. And my brother's still enthroned in the glory of the son returned from war – he's impossible. He arrived at the Front a month before it ended and spent two weeks on wiring duty before they started packing up. I doubt he got his boots muddy, but the stories he comes up with. No, no, we're going to Schöneberg.'

'South?'

'Down south, my dear,' Hannah said, patting Ingrid's knee, and breaking into song, 'Down south and far away.'

The journey made Ingrid more uncomfortable with each passing minute. She squinted into the black streets. Sporadic dim lamps lit groups of men huddled in the cold, so still they might have been waxworks, and the air was filled with the smell of brown coal and frozen dung. Ingrid wanted to be home in bed.

'What are you delivering? Why couldn't you post it?'

'It's just some scraps of paper. Some information that Mama has gathered up and it's urgent – it's needed tonight. Things are moving so fast.'

'Are we going to meet political people?'

'The most!' said Hannah.

Ingrid bit the knuckle of her index finger. 'I really can't talk to anyone about politics. I can't even talk sense about some poems that I wrote.'

'Do you know what you'd say if you were a man?' said Hannah. 'You'd say, "What a lot of rot that Necker-Weiß talked about those poems. What a fool he is."'

Ingrid considered this. 'It doesn't change the fact that I can barely follow what's going on since the war ended.'

'No one can,' said Hannah. 'That's got nothing to do with your inability to understand politics. You are political, because you exist in society and you want to form it. You know what you think right and what not right, and the rest you wish to inform yourself about. Other people voice their opinions with more confidence, of course, but those are the ones you must trust least.'

Ingrid recalled her parents' assurances about Buckow, and wondered if they were ever to be trusted. 'I can see why the war was futile and that things must change,' she said. 'But aren't you scared it's all going to come apart at the seams?'

'That's why we have to be involved in forming it, Ingrid. That's why we fought for the vote. Do you know Clara Zetkin? *Die Gleichheit* – it's a magazine.'

'No.'

'Brilliant. Quite brilliant. I'll bring you a copy. She's very good on our need to be involved. The war is where the system leads, the system we had. Our aristocracy has been leading us to war after war for the last ten thousand years. Finally people understand it can't go on.'

'Is that where we're going? To see Clara Zetkin?'

'She may be there, but no, I'm taking you to see the second edition of the rag you just bought.'

'The *Red Flag*?'

'That's right. Mama's very close with all the important socialists. She's very committed to fighting Chancellor Ebert, as are we all.'

'But isn't the Chancellor a socialist?'

'Barely. Ebert's to the right of his own SPD and voted to stay in the war. What's worse he's now courting the

Freikorps militias to bolster his cause. The Spartacists, who you're going to meet, publish the *Red Flag*. They refused to vote for more war bonds and for that they were thrown into jail.'

'But what if they ask me about the USPD? Or the Revolutionary Stewards? One reads all these names in the papers, but it's impossible to make any sense of it.'

'Well, the USPD were the Spartacists, and the Stewards are just shop stewards who support the revolution. But you're right, it is a terrible mess.'

'And we're meeting Spartacists.'

'Yes. These are important people, Ingrid. They're changing Germany. Karl Liebknecht might be there. Rosa Luxemburg was let out of Breslau yesterday. She may already be here. These people matter.'

'Didn't Liebknecht announce a new socialist republic yesterday? I'm surprised he has time to write newspaper articles.'

'That's very glib of you, Ingrid,' Hannah said. 'The *Red Flag* is the mouthpiece of the movement.'

As the cab crossed the railway line at Kolonnestraße, Ingrid saw that the houses were smaller in this part of town. She wondered if it had been a gradual change, or whether the towering blocks of Charlottenburg had slowly shrunk, and if they travelled further they would wither away to nothing.

They drove for some time down a long straight road, with young trees and stunted lamps, even fewer lit than in her own street. Hannah knocked on the window frame with her fist and the horses stuttered to a halt.

Hannah climbed out, gave the driver a mark and said, 'You'll have double if you're still here when we come out.'

The driver took the coin and secreted it beneath his large woollen cloak. 'As you wish, Fräulein,' he said, the cloak forming a passive black mountain with his head on top, steam rolling from his nostrils like cigar smoke.

'This way,' Hannah said.

The door to the block was open and, as they passed the caretaker's rooms, Ingrid saw that the door was ajar and the space behind black. She followed Hannah into the courtyard, filled with odd dark shapes and the smell of iron and earth, and into the back building, straight down into the cellar, where the shape of a door was picked out in a line of lamplight.

Hannah knocked. She was answered by a single tap. She knocked again in a series of stops and starts and the door was opened by a young pimpled man with a large brown moustache.

'Comrade Mandelbaum!' he said. 'A pleasure.'

'Königsberg,' Hannah said. From her jacket, she produced a small buff envelope, soft and wrinkled from use and covered in stamps and postmarks. 'Mama sent me with this. It's notes about the Stinnes–Legien meeting. Apparently it couldn't wait.'

'It could not,' he said, taking it off her and ripping it open. 'Max!' he shouted, holding the notes in the air, 'Stinnes–Legien – it's from Comrade Mandelbaum.' A tall man with round pince-nez held his hands out for it and Königsberg threw it to him. 'You've made Max very happy,' he said to Hannah. Max ignored them and read the notes feverishly, emitting intermittent gasps of contempt.

'One tries one's best,' said Hannah. 'This is Ingrid Hoffmann, by the way, a close friend of mine. She's a *Red Flag* devotee – she's read every copy!'

236

'Pleased to make your acquaintance,' Königsberg said, laughing. 'Well, you're very welcome. We're on the final proof for tomorrow, so we won't be wonderful company, I'm afraid. Come in and drink a schnapps though. You'll have a long ride home.'

He moved aside and welcomed them into the basement room. It was wide with a low ceiling, and left and right were dark arches that emitted a damp mouldy breath. Three lamps were hung about the room on iron hooks thick with white paint and in the centre was a wide table covered in candles and paper: printed sheets in piles, curling strips tangled together like hair, rectangles of single printed words snipped out and scattered, as if they had been shaken out of a book. Around the room were five or six other people, all poring over texts with such concentration that they didn't notice Ingrid and Hannah's entrance at all.

With a squeak and a low pop, Königsberg uncorked a tall bottle of Mirabellengeist with his ink-stained fingers, took a swig and offered the bottle to Hannah, who was pulling off her gloves. 'We have an illustrious visitor,' he said, wiping his moustache with the back of his hand and nodding into the corner of the room.

There, reading a large sheet of printed paper, was a small stout woman clad in a blouse and thick woollen skirt belted high on her waist. Her face was flat with a long nose and small round eyes, like a barn owl's.

She looked up, then came over to the group, offering the sheet to Königsberg and saying, 'I've changed my mind – let's say "great" instead of "glorious" – it's all too swamped in glory.'

She looked up at Hannah and smiled. 'You're Magda Mandelbaum's daughter. You were barely a girl when I last saw you,' she said, with a slight Polish accent. She kissed Hannah on the cheek.

'Ingrid, this is Rosa Luxemburg. Frau Luxemburg, Ingrid Hoffmann.'

'It's a pleasure to meet you,' Frau Luxemburg said.

Ingrid knew her name and, in the face of celebrity, blushed appropriately.

'You've been in the women's prison in Breslau, I've heard,' Hannah said. 'I hope it wasn't a terrible ordeal.'

'Good God! The wasted years, that's the horror of it. But we are back and we are at work. Karl is here,' she said, intimating a tired-looking man with small glasses and a moustache checking copy at the table. He held his hand up in greeting, but did not look up. His lips moved as he read.

'When were you released?' Hannah said.

'Yesterday,' Königsberg said with pride.

'Mustn't one recover?' said Ingrid.

Frau Luxemburg laughed. The lamplight flickered in her dark eyes. 'My dear, this is the revolution.'

'Your mother's work in the Moabit meetings is mentioned in this edition, Comrade Mandelbaum,' Königsberg said, and led Hannah over to the table.

Rosa Luxemburg put her hand on Ingrid's shoulder and Ingrid envied the certainty she exuded. Luxemburg turned her head, as if offering her ear to Ingrid's secrets. 'Come quick,' she said.

She took Ingrid's hand and led her out of the room and into the courtyard. 'Do you hear that?'

All Ingrid could hear was a consumptive cough, the distant song of metal wheels on rails and a bird chirruping at the top of the courtyard.

'Are they coming?' Ingrid said.

'No, the bird. Listen!' she said.

Ingrid looked at her, her white smiling face even more owl-like in the dark. 'It's a nightingale, do you hear? But there's another song behind it, further away. It's going gligli-gligligliglick? Do you hear it?'

Ingrid heard the song – gligligliglick – echoing in another courtyard, intermittently drowned by the nightingale's whistling chirrup.

'I first heard it in the Botanic Gardens with Karl and Sophie and we couldn't for the life of us identify it. Then in the prison in Breslau, I was surrounded by them, and do you know what it is?'

'No,' said Ingrid.

'A wryneck. And do you know why it's called a wryneck?'

'No,' said Ingrid.

'Because it twists its head back and forth, snapping it like a snake. Very peculiar behaviour, very unique.'

They stood lit only by the meagre blue light of the night sky and listened to the birds, the nightingale close by and the wryneck far away, and the whole time Frau Luxemburg held on to Ingrid's hand.

'I don't know it,' Ingrid said, afraid that Frau Luxemburg was expecting her to say something. 'I'm not very good with native birds. I grew up in Africa.'

'The most oppressed workers in the world,' Frau Luxemburg said sadly. She let go of Ingrid's hand and when Ingrid turned she was already silhouetted in the bright doorway, all blouse and billowing hair, disappearing into the room.

Ingrid returned to the basement and found them collating the sheets they had read. When Hannah and Ingrid said their goodbyes, Frau Luxemburg and Liebknecht were so deep in conversation that they didn't acknowledge them.

They came out onto the street and the cab was gone.

'I knew it,' Hannah said.

'What'll we do now?' said Ingrid.

'We'll walk to Hauptstraße. There's a little rank by the post office.'

'It's so late,' Ingrid said.

'But wasn't it remarkable meeting her?' Hannah said.

'Yes,' said Ingrid, taking her friend's arm. 'It was very remarkable.'

'I knew you'd be happy you came. She's aged terribly,' Hannah said. 'She looks like an old woman now. Prison is very cruel. Such a tragedy.'

As they walked, they passed a smattering of men in the street, no women. A few of the businesses, closed down when the owners left for the Front, were plastered with signs warning of cholera and typhoid, but also posters advertising war bonds, some ripped, the split faces of the model families fluttering in the biting wind.

'Do you have any heat at home?' Hannah said. 'Trude's a whizz buying it black, the little Kneißl.'

'Mother manages somehow,' Ingrid said. 'It's terrible to think of everyone else going without. I feel ashamed.'

'Yes, we should feel ashamed,' Hannah said seriously. She looked up at the sky and said, 'They'll call this the German Revolution, you know. Five people in a basement.'

'Do you think this is what it was like in 1848?' Ingrid said. 'I'd imagined something more triumphant. Barricades and gunpowder and Hussars – that sort of thing.'

They heard a crack, a sound that ricocheted off the walls ahead. Ingrid looked into the sky. A drunk who had been stumbling forwards a few metres in front of them also stopped.

'Fireworks?' Hannah said.

'When did you last see a firework?'

They walked on, but the drunk didn't move. When they caught up with him and he turned his shaking head towards them, Ingrid saw that he wasn't drunk at all. 'A few pfennigs perhaps, ladies?' he slurred. He was barely twenty and his head wobbled loosely on his neck like a toy. He had a great scar across his right cheek; the tip of his nose was missing and the lobe of one ear.

They pushed on, shaking their heads no, and as they came close to the picture house by Kolonnestraße underground station they heard the sound of shoes pounding on the cobbles and a young man ran across the road in front of them, pursued by a group of Freikorps militiamen.

'Get back!' Hannah said and opened her arms wide, pushing Ingrid against the wall. Ingrid hit her head on the sharp edge of a high stone windowsill and screeched.

The running man turned at her scream and caught her eye. He was very young, a teenager, and his irises were large and black like the eyes of a cow. A shot rang out and he ducked forward, his cap flying off. 'Huh!' Ingrid said, and she narrated the scene in her head as she might tell her mother: he ducked forward and they shot the cap off his head and then he escaped into the underground. But his mouth opened up, wide and red, and she thought he was opening it out in a scream, but it was too wide and too red, and she understood that the bottom of his face had opened up, split by the bullet, and his knees bent and he fell onto his back. The militiamen stopped and the street was silent except for the gutter-like gurgle of the man breathing through the bloodied chaos of his face. Ingrid's heart thumped; she felt it throb on her scalp where her head had hit the wall.

'Good God!' Hannah whispered.

Ingrid became very aware of their breath tumbling out of their mouths like smoke and the sound of the suburban train coming, a deep rumble beneath the ground.

*

The room was dark – Ingrid had shooed Ann-Kathrin away when she had found her in the corridor. Now her mother was at the door to the drawing room saying, 'Ingrid? Is that you? What are you doing?'

'We can go to Buckow,' Ingrid muttered.

'Can you light a lamp?' her mother said. 'Don't mutter cryptic messages to me in the dark – I'm spooked enough as it is, what with Ann-Kathrin padding around all night long. Ingrid?'

Her mother disappeared and she heard the sound of a match being lit and saw the orange light brighten in the doorway. She came into the room with her hand cupped in front of the candle, wearing a nightdress and night jacket. Her hair was down, brushed straight and falling over her shoulders like a girl. She kept her eyes on the candle as she walked into the room. She didn't look up at Ingrid until she was quite close and the light of the candle was dancing on her hands and face. 'Good God, what on earth's happened?'

Ingrid was sobbing, the tears wetting her cheeks and her neck, wetting the wool of her coat, which she was still holding around herself tightly. Her mother put down the candle and took her hand and put another up to her cheek. It was cold and dry and Ingrid leant on it and moaned, 'I'm afraid.'

'Of course you are,' her mother said. 'We all are.'

'We can go to Buckow if you want. If you think it's best.'

242

Frau Hoffmann pulled Ingrid in, so that her face was in her mother's thick hair, which smelt of rosewater and cotton from the fresh nightdress beneath. 'Come come,' her mother said. 'Come come. We don't need to talk about Buckow now. We don't need to talk about it at all.'

She hummed, some familiar lullaby and Ingrid was afraid that she would sing. She didn't sing. She just rocked and hummed and Ingrid thought of Frau Luxemburg, the birds and the woman's dry hand in hers.

Haus am See,
near Buckow, Brandenburg

— November 1918 —

'Look,' Ingrid's mother said, 'with the leaves falling, you can see the house and the lake from here. How bare it looks.'

Ingrid turned, having kept her eyes on the blankets covering her legs for as long as she was able. She saw the roof of the house, the thick tiles russet with rain, and the hooded windows along the top floor. They turned down the driveway, which sloped around the back of the house, descending steeply, and the motorcar rocked and shuddered as it rode the potholed ground. Ingrid, transfixed, saw the little lawn at the front and then the lake behind, its moss-green surface dull with rain. The trees surrounding the lake were bare, a charcoal mist of branches in the canopy, narrowing to the sodden umber trunks, speckled with pale yellow leaves.

The car stopped suddenly and Ingrid touched the driver's seat in front of her.

The engine was running; the driver nodded oddly.

'Are we meant to get out here?' her father said.

The driver looked at him embarrassed. 'Yes, sir, the path

becomes too rugged and the car won't get back up to the road. Von Ketz will send someone any minute – he'll have spotted us.'

'In Berlin, a Baron has the honour of hearing his proper form of address,' her mother said.

'In Berlin, madam, if you'll excuse me saying, as in Brandenburg, we are all the same before the law now,' the driver said.

Her father held up a hand to hush his wife. Frau Hoffmann's eyes narrowed as she weighed up her response, then fell back in her seat.

A tall, crooked man with a limp appeared by the house and waved slowly, his big white hand paddling the air. He disappeared and emerged seconds later wearing an oilskin coat, carrying two large umbrellas. He kept his head pulled down, protecting himself from the rain, which, with his limp, made it impossible to judge how old he was. Ingrid thought of Otto before the war, shuddering with energy. But all of the servants must have gone now, leaving only the oldest, barely able to climb a slope.

'It's so close in here,' Herr Hoffmann said, and opened the passenger door and then the door by his wife – perhaps a comment on the driver's lack of appropriate servility. But Ingrid's father had misjudged the sluggishness of the man's progress and waited, his head held high, as the rain made a slick sheet of his grey hair, dripped from his nose and soaked into his coat. The car filled with the smell of wet wool, mixing with that of the forest, the mud beneath his feet, the trees, the soaking undergrowth at the edge of the lake.

'Hello!' her father called out to the man, but too early, so that he stopped and shouted, 'Yes?', expecting, Ingrid imagined, that her father was giving him a warning.

'I was saying hello!' her father shouted back.

She couldn't make out the man's expression through the rain-soaked windscreen.

The driver bowed his head in embarrassment.

The lame man restarted his progress towards them and Ingrid looked again at the blankets about her legs until she heard the lopsided, squelching gait close at hand and the avian shuddering of the umbrella going up.

'Come along then,' her father said, and Ingrid stepped from the car. She gripped her father's sodden arm and tried to stop her skirts sweeping the wet ground as she climbed out.

'Your luggage?' she heard the man saying. His voice was friendly, but hoarse.

'It's being brought from the station in a trap. A Herr Rüdiger.'

'Yes, he'll do. Not like this blackguard,' the man said, laughing, rapping the motorcar's bonnet with his closed fist. But the tone was friendly and the driver gave him a little wave. How jovial they all are here in the country, Ingrid thought.

They moved away from the car at last, and heard the crunching of the gear lever and the car reversing slowly back up to the road with a high whine.

As they came around to the front of the house Ingrid felt, hopefully, that the sight of it might evoke Margarete's spirit, that she might be here in some form, but no, it was just the wet front of a building. The shrubs around the steps had been removed, bar one sturdy euphorbia, its bright yellow leaves a disconcerting splash of colour. Most of the green shutters were rolled down, the paint peeling, slats missing. The plaster had turned brown and was striated with vertical grey smears. A few tiles had slipped on the chateau-like gable windows; one had completely dropped from the perpendicular sides around the top balcony, revealing a sliver of wood, soaked liver-brown. She didn't sense Margarete at all. She was gone.

Ingrid recognised the cracks in the steps as they went up into the hall and, though colder and damper, she recalled the smell of the house, an indescribably domestic fragrance that cut through her. 'Oh!' she cried out, to shout over the feeling. 'How soaked I am.'

'Don't get ill now, Ingrid,' her mother said, as if it might have been her intention. 'Herr Baron,' she said, 'might we go straight up and change? We are so wet and I think I hear the trap coming.'

Ingrid stared at the invalid open-mouthed. Yes, the man was von Ketz. But quite changed. As tall, but diminished. Pale, almost translucent. He had shaved off his moustache and she saw that the bow of his lip was pointed and that his mouth curled up at the sides, even when he wasn't smiling. But he was smiling at her now, blinking benevolently. 'It is lovely to see you again,' Ingrid said, as if she had known all along. 'And we're so grateful.' Don't you dare cry, she said to herself, though he must have seen the line of wetness build at the edge of her eyelids and her trying to blink it away.

'Let me take you up,' he said, 'let me take something.' He picked up her vanity case. 'I'll show you where you'll be sleeping.'

He went up in front of them, holding on to the banister and rocking to get his bad leg up each step. The smell of wet sourness built as they climbed higher. The carpet had been stripped away on the stairs, so that their shoes clattered as if they were crossing a wooden bridge together. And like a bridge, the wood was dusty and unvarnished. 'It can be icy here in the winter,' her sister had said to her. 'The cold seems to leach out of the walls.'

Her father followed von Ketz and then her mother. Was it broken, the leg? Was it wooden? It bent at the knee, but perhaps wooden legs did that. She found the sight of it so strange that it made the house and their presence in it unbearable. She didn't know how she would spend the next minutes here, let alone a night, a week, a month, until what? Until the revolution was over? They had barely spoken about it, and now they were in this cripple's house. How awful. She wiped tears away with the sleeve of her blouse, before the stairs curved round to the landing, before he would turn, rocking around in that terrible, swinging gait, and see her crying, because of his leg, because of how sad this house was and how absent her sister was, or indeed any sign of life.

'It's all much as it was,' she heard him call. 'We're low on servants of course, but Renate is still here. We obviously took a big hit on the boys, I'm sad to say, and haven't been able to replace them at all, really. Riemann comes to help out with meals and some of the lighter gardening around the house, but we can't keep him on full-time.'

His voice had changed. It was harder and more clipped, trained, she supposed, to bark cohorts of men into a spray of machine-gun bullets.

They stopped by a door. Her father looked at von Ketz, his face passive and strange; her mother was staring at the worn varnish where a runner had been, her eyes wide, her mouth shut tight, her skin ashy. They looked like a senti-mental tableau – a moral painting: 'No family untouched'.

248

Von Ketz said, 'You'll hear that a lot round here, I'm afraid. In these small communities, you notice it more.' He opened the door. 'This is where you are, Herr and Frau Hoffmann.'

The room had been theirs at the wedding. The beds were dark wood, with tall, plain head- and footboards, the nightstands the same dark, bare design. The ornate gilt mirror above the dresser and the tightly stuffed bench and chair, covered with a heavy pattern of intertwined German camomile, did not match the curved simplicity elsewhere. 'His mother had an art nouveau phase,' Margarete had said to her at the same spot five years earlier, 'but not quite enough money to pull it off.'

There was a large dark square on the parquet floor. 'It's an extra job to beat out the rugs, so we put them away at the beginning of the war,' von Ketz said. 'Riemann was going to bring yours down but ...' He trailed off. This room also smelt sour, though he had opened the window, which added a cool earthy note. The windowsill was speckled with raindrops.

'The Baroness, your mother?' Frau Hoffmann asked uncertainly.

'Mama's about, but she's not well, if I'm honest with you. That is, chronically so. You might see her, but perhaps not now. She won't recognise you, I suspect.'

'No of course not,' her mother said, as if that was quite correct.

'She was very fond of my cousin, Christian, and after all that she retreated. You met him at the wedding. Then she had a stroke, we think.'

'How tragic,' her mother said. 'Did Christian ...?'

'Yes,' he said.

They all looked in at the room. Her mother said, 'I must get my salts: the journey's given me the most terrible heartburn,' and she stepped in with Herr Hoffmann and shut the door.

Ingrid was alone with von Ketz. She imagined berating her mother about it, but heard her response – 'Ingrid, you've known him since you were a child. Don't be so trying.' Perhaps that was right.

He began his slow progress down the hall. She looked at the wallpaper – a pretty pattern of stems and small flowers, more delicate than much of the decoration in the house. She remembered it as a background to her sister, her hair brushed out and golden around her shoulders; it was hot, she was wearing a blouse or a nightdress, and she was leaning against the wall filling Ingrid with gossip and worries. Now the joins of the paper were parting like lips. There were prints, a pair of botanical paintings – bearded irises – and many of German Southwest Africa, but none that evoked the heat of it for her, the feeling of the dust under her feet, the sight of a storm rolling apocalyptically across the veld towards them.

'And you'll be in here, Fräulein Ingrid,' he said.

She saw, relieved, that it was not the room she had shared with Margarete, but the one at the end of the landing. The wallpaper was pale green, the bedspread also. The floor was rugless here too, but in the small chamber with its single bed it lent the room an austere feel – a place in which a poet might sleep. The effect was intensified by a little Biedermeier dressing table and chair, and a matching mirror, outlined with a simple, narrow line of inlaid brass. Was it big enough to serve as a desk? she wondered. She thought often of that crowded café in Charlottenburg, the patronising faces, the assumption that a collection of women's poems was of minor importance, because of her inability to select and translate them, because of her inability to convey what had moved her in another language. She tried to justify the trip to Buckow as a chance to translate anew, to select new poems, to become better. What else could she do? Before they had left Berlin, she had feverishly copied poem after poem by hand in the great domed reading room of what her mother still referred to as the 'Royal Library', filling the bottom drawer of her trunk with them, emptying out the fancier stockings and undergarments that Ann-Kathrin had packed for her at her mother's behest.

'It's delightful,' Ingrid heard herself saying to von Ketz. The window was open, the simplicity of the room, its greenness, complemented the earthiness of the wet outdoors, and she longed for von Ketz to leave her alone in it so that she might begin work.

'I hope it will do,' he said.

Feeling the warmth of his breath near her neck, she was driven to the bed, where she touched the counterpane and then the smooth polish of the narrow little table.

'It'll be lovely,' she said turning to him.

He was smiling at her crookedly. 'It must have been very frightening in Berlin. Your father said in his last letter that things had deteriorated; that you yourself had witnessed something terrible.'

'Oh that,' Ingrid said. 'I wish he hadn't said. But it was rather ... ' the man's head hit the cobbles with a dull wet thud like a dropped melon and she no longer knew what was memory and what imagination. 'It was unpleasant,' she managed.

'Well, I'm sorry for that,' he said. He thought hard about

something, looked up at the window. 'The Kaiser's abdicated. That is to say, he signed the official instrument. It was in the paper this morning.'

'Oh!' said Ingrid, unsurprised. It had been announced at the beginning of the month, but still the thought of the battered old man signing, his mouth set and his eyes furious, filled her with a lightness, as if the whole nation had been cut adrift and was floating out into the sea.

'I thought I'd let your parents read it, rather than bother them with it now. We get the *Allgemeine*.'

'Of course,' she said.

'Your parents wrote that you were quite taken by it all. You have a Spartacist friend, they said.'

'Hannah? I don't know if she'd call herself that, but she moves in those circles. They're very impressive people. When you talk to them about how they see the world, it is hard not to agree with much of it. Besides, Luxemburg and Liebknecht won't push for a complete change until they have the backing of the majority of Germans. That's what they told me, at least,' she lied, thrilling at the sense that, in this new world, she knew someone more important than he did.

'So you support them over the new government, even though they're socialists too?'

'I don't support the militias the government are using. I saw them shoot someone in the street.'

'Good God,' von Ketz said. 'So you really are a revolutionary.'

'We're all revolutionaries now,' said Ingrid.

Von Ketz smiled.

What had changed about his face? In her mind's eye, she placed his moustache back beneath his nose, but that didn't fix it. Despite his height, he appeared slight and strange.

She thought of pallid things, of gruel, of silt, of molten candle wax and moths, of aspic and milk. He looked at the floor embarrassed and she willed him to explain himself. But, without looking up at her again, he was gone from the doorway.

*

Ingrid kept her travelling clothes on, but changed into a dry jacket. When the luggage was brought up from the trap, she found the copied-out English and French poems, intending to set to work immediately, but they lay strewn across the bed and she sat at the open window pushing about the drops of rain on the sill with her finger.

She stared out over the corner of forest and lake that the view afforded her. A light flashed as the sun broke through a window of blue in the cloud, shining on the wet ground below where the lake path began, muddied and pocked with glittering puddles. On the window frame, then the wall, and finally the ceiling, the reflected light shimmered, a pattern of waving lines that made her feel as if she were underwater. She imagined the whole house flooded, pushing the window open and swimming out into clear sea, and the lake below her just a pit in the ground, surrounded by trees, and she could see everything that lay at the bottom – the beaver, trunks and sticks and any number of secrets, floating up into the water above.

She heard boots whipped by wet grass and then crunching onto sand and gravel, and from around the house came a figure dressed in black. It was a man, in a black coat and trousers and a narrow-brimmed, black hat. The wet wind pulled back and he grabbed his head to hold the hat on, and in turning he caught sight of her. She sat up. He lifted his hat, revealing his bald head and a spot of black and grey hair above his forehead that sparked, not a memory, but the feeling of one, the emotion of recognition.

She made her way out into the corridor. It was very still in the house. She walked as quietly as she could to the staircase, down the stairs and out of the front doors. The rattle of them opening – glass, painted wood, loose iron fittings and brass – was as familiar as a lullaby.

She recalled stepping out of the house with Margarete before the wedding, when the air smelt of cut grass and Ingrid's throat and nose itched with oak pollen. They were going to walk into town and Margarete had said, 'Well, this is my lot after all. A lake and a house and a "von". Do you think Mummy will love me now I've done as I'm told?' Ingrid had looked at her, afraid and sad, but then realised that the window to the guest-room was open above them and that she had only said it to annoy their mother.

Ingrid took a few steps onto the little lawn in front of the house and looked up the path to where the man with the spot of hair had been, but he was gone. She went after the memory, trying to tie down who he was, but every time she made a grab at it it slipped from her fingers and eluded her. The connection was warm, but she was sure that she knew him from another place, perhaps the wedding, perhaps Berlin.

She dropped it, hoping that it would come to her, and turned to the lake, where the green water was buffeted matt by the wind. Often, since the visit to Buckow had been agreed, Ingrid would stop in the middle of her work, stare at the drawing-room wall in Windscheidstraße and think about the little red house in the woods – a place she had run from four years earlier because of a steaming coffee pot. If she had been less afraid then she might have discovered there something to illuminate what had happened to her sister, saving herself years of doubt.

Ingrid turned left and passed the estate cottages. They were dark, with the same wooden blinds and shutters, painted olive-green; she couldn't tell if there were faces behind in the darkness, in the rooms, looking out at her, recognising her, perhaps, from before. The path broke into a meadow, and she longed for the enclosure of the woods at the other side, when she would be by the water and away from the house.

A bird called out – the peacock was still alive! – mournful and dipping through the wet trunks and over the water. She stopped and looked for it, but had no idea where the sound had come from. It called again, but she saw nothing.

'Fräulein Ingrid – I thought you were resting.'

She was at the edge of the wood, the glassy water to her right, the bank of russet leaves and black wood to her left, the muddy path in front of her, empty. When she turned, von Ketz had appeared on the path like a figure from a fairytale, dressed in a long wool coat and wearing a green shooting cap, with a bright pheasant's tail-feather poked into the band.

'Like some magical forester appearing from nowhere,' she said.

'I didn't mean to give you another fright,' he said

It had been stupid to try and say something clever and she was embarrassed. 'I didn't hear you coming.'

'Would you like me to leave you alone?' he said.

'You don't have to,' she said, disappointed that her trip to the cottage had been thwarted.

He turned. She came up beside him and was aware of the

changed rhythm of his gait: pat-pat, pat-pat, pat-pat it went; two quick steps followed by a slow lifting and placing of the injured leg.

'I suppose it must all feel very different,' he said. 'Shocking, perhaps?'

'That's not what it feels like, no. It is different, but somehow it feels as if I always knew it was going to feel this way. In the end.'

His brow drew up into soft ridges and she had a pang of recognition of von Ketz before, as if she was catching a part of his face beneath the sharp edge of a mask. 'Yes,' he said, 'that's right.'

They passed the path to the little red-brick house and she said, quite casually, 'Who lives down there?'

'At the cottage?' he replied. 'It's for guests. Horvath stays there if he's with us for long stretches.'

'Can we look?'

Von Ketz frowned. 'The forester was there this morning. We should leave it in case he started a fire. He's funny about his fires.'

'Funny about his fires?' Ingrid said.

Von Ketz shrugged the challenge off.

She watched the path come and go, taking in a deep breath through her nose to try and pick up any trace of smoke. There was none. 'He's alive then? Your friend Horvath,' she said, reconciling herself to returning to the cottage later. 'I am glad.'

'Yes,' he said, as if he was unsure. 'He's alive.'

So it probably was Horvath in the cottage. Had Horvath left his coffee at von Ketz's behest to embrace him in the woods? Did von Ketz remember she had seen him there? Were they queers, like Rosenbaum?

'There's not a bald man staying there? Dark hair. Wearing black,' Ingrid said.

'A bald man?'

'I saw him from my window when we arrived.'

'Oh him,' von Ketz said. 'That was just someone travelling through Buckow begging for food from the cellar. They know we have stores.'

'How funny,' Ingrid said. 'He didn't look like a beggar. And I was sure I recognised him.'

'Riemann's constantly fending them off.' He pointed at a row of short, sharply tapering trunks at the water's edge, like stout pencils. 'Look, we still have our good Herr Beaver.'

'He hasn't noticed that anything's changed,' Ingrid said.

'I keep meaning to put a trap out,' von Ketz said, 'He's been here since we came back from Africa, and I've never done it. If it was a hunting dog in the veld, I'd've just shot it, but here ... I've never got used to it really. It's always so cold and wet. Even when it's warm the air seems damp to me. And in Belgium ... '

'I have no sense of it.'

He looked at her, dazed from being knocked out of his recollection. 'No sense of what?'

'What it might have been like. At the Front. I never thought about it being wet.' She'd seen the French and Belgian trenches in grainy newspaper sketches, the soldiers shivering as the guns went off, but she'd imagined it was dry, like a burrow, but of course that made no sense – that they were huddled together, protected as the bullets flew overhead, safe.

'Oh, yes,' von Ketz said. 'In the trench itself, you were often up to your knees in water.'

She wanted to say something to soothe him, but all she

could think to say was, 'At least you'd seen something of war in Africa, I suppose.'

This only made him look sadder though. His pace slowed and he stared blankly at the path. 'In Africa if you shot the Negroes in the veld, they disappeared beneath the thorn bushes. If they were injured you heard some cries, or screams from the women – the women came to the battles too, you know, and stood in a great line howling as we fought. Well, if they were injured you heard their cries, but it was gibberish – screams and clicks and all sorts. But in Belgium if you'd got one – a Tommy – then they would scream out for their mothers, and of course you understood it. When the shelling had stopped you wouldn't believe how quiet it was, except one of them crying for his mother and then one of ours crying for his. Like birds answering one another. So when I think about Africa, about those Hereros and Nama ... Well, now I wonder if they all weren't that scared. And of course they were.'

'Yes,' said Ingrid, feeling as if a tear had been made in a grey fabric and on the other side there was a bright white emptiness, both hot and cold, and quite terrifying. Her face ached and she felt dizzy, picturing Herero boys in the desert and the German boys on their backs in the Belgian mud, thinking of the childish fuzz on their chins and faces, of the dirt under their nails. It would be nice to believe that their passing might be like an angel holding them, touching their smooth cheeks. But she didn't believe in angels, she believed that they sank into blackness, weeping and lonely.

He was a priest. The man with the dot of hair on his head. Where had she met him? Not at the wedding, perhaps in Berlin, definitely inside, in a room.

'And what about you?' von Ketz asked.

'What about me?'

'Your mother wrote that you were working for the government.'

'Oh, yes, but I shouldn't . . . ' She thought of Wilhelm II sitting in some garden in Holland, alone on a damp bench, the water seeping into his breeches. 'I suppose I can say – the Kaiser won't mind now. I translated.'

'Yes, you used to do poems, didn't you? What were you translating for Willy?'

'Oh, anything,' she said, hearing the low clamour of the translation room at the Ministry, smelling the ink and hearing the scratch of the paper, the chatter of telegrams and the muttering of the clerks, and feeling a pain that she could only describe as homesickness. 'Official orders, notes, newspaper articles, propaganda. All sorts. They gave us a mix of everything so that we couldn't put anything together or get too much anti-war stuff, I suppose.'

'But you left?'

'They fired most of us once the war was over – there was no money. And what would we do?'

'A shame for you though, I imagine you were good at it, that you enjoyed it. Do you miss it? The work?'

She blushed, because no one had asked her before. 'Yes, I always miss translating.'

'We have some French and English books in my study – the ones I rescued from Mother. If you need some practice or just something to do until you can go back to Berlin, do go up and try your hand. I'd love to hear a bit. You should do some poetry.'

'I might,' said Ingrid. 'Do you have any Baudelaire? That's who I've been working on recently.'

'Oh, not in the library,' he said, stopping. 'No, I . . . I have read him, but it was a favourite of Horvath's. He could quote the whole of *Les Fleurs du mal*. Remarkable really, but I . . .' he looked about him on the ground as if he was searching for something.

'I thought he . . . ?'

'Yes, he did survive. I meant to say *is*. He was in Gaza, which was . . . That was at the start of the war, and then he was in Flanders. Anyway, he doesn't read any more. I must get back to the house,' von Ketz said, setting off quickly. 'A new family is moving in to one of the cottages.'

Ingrid ran to keep up, thinking about the little Hungarian stumbling out of the bushes four years earlier and the same man alone and afraid in the heat of the Palestinian desert, and the picture made her so sad that she said unthinkingly, 'What about the estate workers that were in the cottages?' But before the sentence was out, she realised what the answer would be. She looked across the lake at the dark little windows and the olive green shutters. 'Of course, they all went,' she said.

'Yes,' von Ketz said. 'I told them to.'

'Otto too,' she said.

'Yes, all of Riemann's boys died in the same month, more or less.'

They were silent until they reached the small meadow in which the house sat. The sky, striped only lightly with a few wispy clouds, filled the flush puddles with blue. Realising that she could think of no other way of linking the conversation back to it naturally, Ingrid said, 'Of course, I think of Margarete here.'

'Of course,' he said.

She thought of all the young faces from the wedding

party, and saw that there was nothing remarkable or tragic about death in youth. Margarete was only an anomaly among their number because she had gone first.

'I wonder . . . ' she said.

'Yes.'

'You have an attic. I got it into my head that she had been in the attic before she disappeared.'

'The attic?' von Ketz said. 'I don't think so.' He looked baffled. 'Why should she have done that?'

'What's in there?'

'Some things Mother brought back from Africa. Things of my grandfather's: dusty objects and drawings.'

'Can I see it?'

Von Ketz shrugged. 'If you want.'

'Renate told me once one reached it through the study, but that one needs a key.'

'I'll get it for you,' he said, but seemed confused and saddened by the whole conversation.

'Do you think of her at all?' Ingrid said.

'Good God,' von Ketz said. 'Of course. Why would you think otherwise?'

'Because no one talks about her any more. She faded away and disappeared and no one says a word about her any more.'

'Yes, we must talk about her,' he said. But Ingrid waited, her stomach in knots, as they passed through the meadow and reached the house, and he said nothing more about her.

He climbed the steps to the house and opened the door. It shuddered and rattled out. 'Here we are then,' he said, pausing with his hand on the frame, 'the survivors.'

*

Their return drew her mother down and she fussed about the empty ground floor until she had established that the old Baroness really was senile after her stroke and never left her room and that von Ketz was not strict enough with her nurse, and with Renate and Riemann. She called for Renate in a sharp, disapproving tone. She arrived, with lines around her eyes, her hair thinner, the shape of her skull more prominent, so that, though still young, one could imagine exactly how she would look as a bonneted old lady. Frau Hoffmann sat to give her instructions, Renate remained standing, and with that her mother laid down the foundations of her regency.

Lunch had been organised, according to Renate, for 'sometime after the Baron returned from his walk', which her mother refined to one-thirty, to be the allotted time daily, unless otherwise specified. Von Ketz had asked the old forester to bring rabbit from the estate and the cook had made it into a creamed goulash and served it with potatoes. Ingrid watched her mother sample each element of the dish in turn – the grey watery sauce, the chewy slivers of rabbit meat, the black onions. She was barely able to suppress a smile when she pushed her fork down on a translucent salt-potato and heard the crunch of uncooked flesh and the silver striking the plate.

By the evening, she had organised the programme for the next day. Table linen had been found and she asked von Ketz whether he wanted breakfast any earlier than nine. His stuttering reply made Ingrid suspect that he had been used to taking it later and probably alone. Her mother's questions to the Baron, to Renate, continued to couch her own expectations in their formulation: 'What kind of brown bread do you have at breakfast?' 'Do you prefer to do a round of the

lake as your postprandial, or a walk up to Buckow and back?'
'Do you take the larger linens to the washhouse yourself at
the end of the week or do they collect them?'

It was only when her mother had settled into the drawing room, the stove filling the air with the smell of burning
tinder, a foxed copy of *Der Nachsommer* from the library in
her lap, that Ingrid was able to excuse herself on the pretence of a headache and the need for some fresh air. Her
mother waved her away distractedly, because Renate had
let the coal scuttle sit on the rug, newly laid out, and she
was explaining how to take the dust out without having to
remove the whole rug and beat it again.

The door rattled, Ingrid's boots crunched on the frost-
damaged stone of the steps, and she was back on the lawn,
her heart beating hard at the thought of the little red house
and what she might find there alone, without von Ketz's
ghostly company.

'Ingrid, dear, where are you going?' It was her father. He
was standing on the lawn, looking out over the lake. An
orange spot glowed in the dusk and he said, 'The Baron has
cigarettes – little Belgian things. Taste like something swept
off the floor, but one must try new things, eh?'

She kissed his cheek and said, 'Hello, Papa,' then tried to
walk on.

'Where are you going, Ingrid dear?'

'I was going to walk round the lake.'

'Didn't you walk round the lake this morning? You keep
going at the thing like a rat in a bucket.'

'Where else is there to walk?'

He shrugged. 'There must be paths through the woods.
You could go up to Oberbarnim.'

'It's too far,' Ingrid said.

His hand was in his pocket. He looked up at the sky and squinted, dragged hard on the cigarette and flicked it away with his middle finger. It hissed in the wet grass. 'I'll come with you then. What's your direction?'

Defeated for the second time, she gestured towards the workers' cottages.

'Righto,' he said.

The smell of the earth was strong in the dusk, the cold scent of black mud and dark water. She was disappointed not to be alone, but the presence of her father also calmed her. Because he was to be relied on, because, whether or not he was mistaken, he appeared to be sure of every decision he made. Often, if she didn't think too hard about it, his conviction was completely reassuring.

'Now, what are we really looking for?'

'Nothing Papa,' she said.

'Mm,' he said. 'You're not going to swim again?'

'No, of course not,' she said, quiet and embarrassed.

'Out with it then.'

The languor of the smoky autumn air freed her and she felt her body relax, knew that there was nothing that she could really reveal to her father that was so terrible. That's what the dusk, the sharp cold air, the smell of burning wood said: tell him.

'There's a cottage,' she said. 'I want to go and look at it.'

'The little red one?'

'That's it – how do you know?'

'The Baron said you were down that way this morning. What's your interest?'

'There might be something there. A clue.'

'To what?'

'I don't know,' she said.

Her father took in a deep breath and said, 'Ingrid, I see what is happening with you here. I knew it would be difficult for you; Lord! I remember what happened last time. But, my darling, we must remember Margarete fondly here, even if it was her home for only a short time. We should have come back more often, normalised life here for you. We must remember Margarete, but not be . . . ' he searched for the word, 'haunted by her. That is the circle you must break. It is not the same as being sad that she is gone, or paying respect to her memory. That is what I do. That is what your mother does. Do you see the difference?'

She pictured his shaking hand, her mother worrying the horn buttons that she had unpicked from Margarete's coat and sewn onto her own.

'Von Ketz seems haunted as well,' he went on. 'Perhaps by the war – he has every reason to be, poor man. We have lost, but we are still alive and we must carry on. We must always be strong and try to find the best in even the darkest times. Otherwise it's all for naught.'

Ingrid didn't answer him and he didn't go on, though she could feel the energy in him, the thrill of his explanation, which she knew he thought good, but had already been overridden in her by the low anxiety that she felt as they approached the path and she was finally able to make her way down to the little red-brick house.

'Who lives here then?' he said. 'Rather sweet.'

'Von Ketz said Herr Horvath used to stay here sometimes. It's empty otherwise.' And then she lied: 'He said we could take a look around, if it's open.'

She knocked at the door. There was no answer. She tried the handle – it was unlocked. The room was dark. It had a bitter smell, of stale coffee and tallow.

She heard a crunch, like a foot on gravel, and the room glowed. Her father had lit a match and, shielding it with his hand, lit a candle stub on the empty table.

They wandered about the ground floor. It was furnished as it had been when she had seen it before the war. At the back of the house in the small kitchen the dripping tap had painted a long green finger on the porcelain of the sink. The seating area was still there, but there was no French novel and there were no horse chestnuts on the windowsill.

Upstairs they found a bedroom, the bed stripped to the mattress, from which a few black and gold horse-hairs emerged, shifting in an imperceptible breeze, like the feelers of an insect. There were paintings here too, three stacks of them leant against the wall. In the dim light she could make out heavy shapes, rolling down one side of the canvas and bursting up the other; the smell of the linseed and turpentine still clung to them. 'Are they von Ketz's, do you think? I can't imagine him buying modern paintings. Maybe Horvath painted them.' She had pictured him painting the most childish clichés of pictures – landscapes, portraits and horses – but of course he was a modern painter and these were the sort of pictures modern painters made now.

'Very ugly,' her father said, not really looking at them. He went to the little window and peered out. She followed his gaze and saw the glitter of the lake between the trees. 'Pretty spot.'

'Yes,' she said, suffused with disappointment. Because there was nothing in the cottage, not even a bureau that might conceal papers or a row of books filled with cryptic inscriptions. It was just a bare little house, empty and cold. What could Margarete possibly have left that would still be here? How could anything have survived the intervening years, the war?

Ingrid joined her father at the window. She looked at the view, then turned back to the room and let out a surprised, 'Huh!'

'What is it?' he said.

'It's very deserted,' she said.

'Seems to be.'

'But there's no dust.'

Her father ran his fingers along the window frame. 'There's a bit here.' He showed her the grey mark on his finger.

'Yes, but it's not dusty like a house that no one's been in for years. Then again, it doesn't look like you could live here: there are no sheets, no plates. It's more like someone's removed everything.'

'Perhaps they have,' Herr Hoffmann said. 'Perhaps Horvath was staying here before we arrived, and von Ketz cleared it out. I know Riemann's up in the village now, but he might have been here before.'

'Wouldn't the Baron have said?'

'Oh Ingrid,' said her father. 'Don't turn this into another of your mysteries.'

She rested her forehead on the window frame and stared down at the grass, purple in the twilight. There was wind in the trees outside and it blew a low note in the stove flue. Perhaps he was right.

'What about the revolution?' she said.

'I beg your pardon?' said her father.

'You said that we must try and find the best in things. But the revolution – surely you're not happy about that. I know you're not.'

'No,' he said. 'I'm not happy about it. But there are opportunities nonetheless.'

'Such as?'

He shrugged. 'People have needs. I have some factories out in Silesia for instance, some paper factories. A great bureaucracy, Kaiser or not, needs paper, and what they're making in the city is worthless. I bought some land in Spandau, near the prison. That might be needed – they'll be arresting each other soon enough. There is always a way, even if it is tight now; I'd have put us all in a hotel for these next weeks if I could have afforded it.'

Ingrid frowned. 'You bought land near the prison?'

'What's that tone, Ingrid?' he said, standing up straighter, his chest out, the guttering candle filling his eye sockets and mouth with black shadow, making his face look skeletal.

'It's benefiting from misery,' Ingrid said.

'It's creating something positive from something negative. If the prison expands, the prison expands. Someone will make the profit on it. If it doesn't, there are the paper factories. If those don't come good, I have some workshops in Kiel. The prison is a long shot, anyway – if it doesn't expand it's a loss, and we go elsewhere.'

'What about Southwest? Was that a good thing too?'

'That's a perfect example,' he said. 'The government needed what I'd bought – the wells at the farm and the land around Swakopmund and a few other bits at Lüderitz Bay. They didn't leave me much choice, what with the Uprising, but we were well compensated there. You just need to spread your risk and try, if you can, to foresee what people want. If you were a man I'd have been able to share all this with you – I'm sure it's a bore.'

'You sold it? The land in Southwest? I thought it had been seized.'

'Of course I sold it,' he said. 'What would have been the point of Southwest if I hadn't sold it?'

'When?'

'When we left. That's why we left.'

'I thought we left because of the Uprising.'

'Yes, this is the point, my love. The Uprising was a terrible thing, but there was an opportunity. There is always an opportunity.'

'And what opportunity did Margarete disappearing afford us? A countryside refuge and a title in the family without any of the expense of the upkeep, I suppose.'

'You cruel little thing,' her father said. 'Do not underestimate how devastating it is for a father to lose his child.'

Ingrid swung her head away, leant on the windowsill and began to cry. 'Oh, I'm sorry. I miss her,' she said.

'Don't be a silly, now,' he said.

'Was it wrong to come here?' she said. 'To the house?'

'No,' he said, and lifted her up so that he could embrace her. 'But let's leave her here, eh?'

She held on to him, smelt the paternal smell in the hair at his ears and the cologne that clung to his stiff collar and remembered with perfect clarity that the man with the dot of hair on his head was Father Schäfer, a priest she had met in Southwest Africa before a dance. She had talked to him in the hallway of the guesthouse in Lüderitz Bay and now he was in Buckow.

*

The next morning was a Saturday and the weather clement enough that Ingrid felt able to make the journey into Buckow on foot, leaving a note for her mother reading simply, 'Walking. Back for lunch.' Her mother was already awake – she could hear her voice in the kitchen – so Ingrid placed the note soundlessly on the hallway table and slipped out.

The dying leaves on the roadside poplars clattered together in a wind that blustered across the ploughed fields, picking up their brown scent – wind that blew great clouds across the sky, flashing sun on the road in bursts. The sound of the wind about her ears was loud and when she entered the forested road into town, the warmth of her wind-blown cheeks and the shelter of the great pines made her feel calm and able.

She found the vicarage easily – an imposing square building covered in greying plaster, with an unpainted wooden door opening straight onto the street. She rang the bell and was met by a young housekeeper, who took her card in to Father Ingelmann.

'Fräulein Hoffmann!' came his voice. 'Come through.'

The girl ushered her into a parlour with one window onto the street, letting in a shaft of sunlight filled with spinning dust. The room was big and square, with a wall of books and a great dining table, covered in hooks, chopped wine corks, wire and bright threads. Behind the table was Father Ingelmann wearing half-moon glasses, sitting at a small clamp tying red thread around a colourful bundle of wax and cotton about the size of a pea.

'What a delightful surprise. I had heard you were at the von Ketzes',' Ingelmann said, coming around the table and shaking her hand. 'Do sit.'

She unpinned her black felt hat, placed it on a side table and sat on an upholstered bench beside the unlit stove. The room was cold; Ingrid could feel a thick draught of air swimming across the tattered veneer of the parquet floor.

'What lovely threads,' Ingrid said.

'Rather nice, aren't they?' said Ingelmann.

'What are you making?'

'Fishing flies.'

'Oh, I see. I've never seen them being made. Is there good fishing in Buckow?'

'It's poor here at the lake, but if you go downstream there are a few nice spots. You don't have a personal interest, do you, Fräulein Hoffmann?'

'Not at all,' Ingrid said, laughing.

Alongside the clamp were a set of tools and a little tin of paraffin wax laid out on a sheet of newspaper. She saw a sheet from the *Red Flag*. 'Are you socialist too, Father?' Ingrid said.

'I beg your pardon?'

'The paper,' she said, pointing.

'Oh,' he said. 'No. I try to read anything I can get my hands on. I try to understand everything from all sides if I can. Do you read it?'

'I was there at its birth.'

'Really?' said the vicar. 'Am I to understand that you are a committed Spartacist, Fräulein Hoffmann?'

Ingrid smiled. 'No, I wouldn't say that. But I met the Spartacists through a friend.'

'I hear that Rosa Luxemburg is an impressive character. She writes very well.'

'She is. Though we only talked for a few minutes and it was about birds.'

'Really?' he said. 'Remarkable times.'

'How do you think it will all turn out?'

'That's in God's hands,' Ingelmann said. 'Though I think without a militia of its own, the Spartacists are in trouble. Luxemburg writes of the importance of a majority supporting a socialist state and that, as a Christian, seems sensible to me, though they'll never do it. In the depths we must navigate in the coming years, the solace of Christ will be much needed. My sense is that her colleagues in Berlin know this and my colleagues there tell me there is much agitating for revolution. When that happens our friend Rosa Luxemburg will be in great danger, as will they all.'

'I hope it doesn't come to that,' said Ingrid.

'Indeed. But, Fräulein Hoffmann, you're not here to talk about socialism, are you?'

'No,' Ingrid said. 'I came to ask if you knew whether a Father Schäfer was in Buckow. I met him in Southwest and I have a notion he might be in town. I'd very much like to meet him again.'

Father Ingelmann went back around the table and picked up a little pair of gold scissors shaped like a stork with a bladed beak. He cut a thread off the fly he was tying and blew the remnant into the air, where it travelled alone, before hitting the shaft of sunlight and being subsumed in a golden cloud of skin, pollen and dirt.

'A Father Schäfer?' Ingelmann said.

'Yes,' Ingrid said. 'He must be a friend of yours. He wrote to Papa from Southwest Africa before the war. You mentioned it when we last met.'

'When we last met?'

'Yes, at the church in Oberbarnim. A few weeks after Margarete disappeared.'

'Your dear sister,' Father Ingelmann said. 'She might have brought so much joy to our little community, I often think.'

'Indeed,' Ingrid said. 'But Father Schäfer, you do know him?'

'Yes.'

'Do you know where he is now?'

Ingelmann looked thoughtfully at his scissors.

Ingrid said, 'He is nearby; he was at the house yesterday.'

Ingelmann's expression changed: his eyes met hers and his lips pursed. 'He should leave the Baron alone. I've told him that.'

'Is he in Buckow?'

'Yes,' Ingelmann said. 'But he was deeply affected by South-west. He hasn't been able to find a parish since his return.'

'Where might I find him?'

'What would you like to speak to him about?'

'I knew him in Southwest. I'd like to speak to him about Southwest.'

'He's barely coherent, Fräulein Hoffmann.'

'Nevertheless.'

'You are persistent, I see.'

'Persistence isn't a sin, Father.'

'But it's also not a virtue.' The vicar threw down the scissors. 'I'm afraid I haven't seen him in weeks. He may have been taking leave of the Baron. I don't know. I am really no use to you. It was a joy to see you, Fräulein Hoffmann, and I do hope to see you in Oberbarnim on Sunday.'

'Yes, Father,' Ingrid said.

She walked onto the street, where the showers of the previous day had dried to a few shallow puddles and dark smudges in the dirt of the road. A motor car and then a cart passed, a group of women from the laundry stood in the autumn sunshine massaging their aching joints. A child pushed a younger sibling along the pavement in a pram as big as she was. It appeared as if the war had barely touched the town, if one ignored the lack of men older than sixteen and younger than fifty.

She made her way to the bakery and asked after Father

Schäfer. They didn't know him, but mentioned that he must have lunched at Giesler's if he had spent more than a day in town. There an elderly waitress said she knew him, though he hadn't been in for days. A vicar would stay at the Havel guesthouse if he stayed anywhere, so she might try there. She did and he wasn't, but she was directed to the Meiers' guesthouse at the far end of town, and was there told that Father Schäfer was out for the day, but that she could leave him a note. She wrote:

Dear Father Schäfer,

My name is Ingrid Hoffmann and I am staying at the von Ketz residence for a brief period. I believe I made your acquaintance at Lüderitz Bay in Southwest Africa and I would be delighted if you would allow me to call on you in the coming days so that we might reacquaint ourselves.

I remain, your humble servant,
Ingrid Hoffmann

Haus am See,
near Buckow, Brandenburg

— November 1918 —

Ingrid watched her mother sewing by the fire in the drawing room. The flames were pale in the early afternoon sun and her needle jumped out of the black fabric, flashing white, then was swallowed back down again out of sight. There was a new enthusiasm to her work and since they had sat there the outline of a wild rose had already been traced and the petals of a second were forming.

Her father was smoking one of von Ketz's cigarettes and reading Ingrid's copy of the *Red Flag*, harrumphing pleasurably every minute or two and saying, '"Karl Liebknecht in a powerful oration ..." Did you hear that, Hedwig? "A powerful oration".' And her mother tipped her head, shrugged her shoulders and said, 'Johannes, my love, if you will read that rubbish.'

'Did you also read that the Servant Laws have been lifted?' Ingrid said, snatching the paper off him. 'That there's going to be an eight-hour day for workers by January. Or that Preuß has just announced women's suffrage in the next election, so you'll finally be able to have a say in how this country's run?'

'Why would I want a say in how the country's run?' Frau Hoffmann said. 'I'm glad to be saved the trouble. Besides, your father and I are in agreement on all things political. That's how it is in marriage, little one. And do you know what I also read in the *Allgemeine*? That this Rosa Luxemburg who writes in your seditious rag is calling for all-out revolution. We'll all be Bolsheviks before Christmas, if she had her way.'

'If you'd read anything she's written,' Ingrid said, 'you'd see that she was arguing for revolution by democratic will and you would see how critical she has been of the Bolsheviks for the way they've handled their revolution in Russia.'

'She's a dumpy thing,' Frau Hoffmann said.

'She's remarkable,' said Ingrid. 'I've met her.'

'You met her?'

'I did actually.'

Her parents looked at her with amused disbelief.

'I did meet her,' said Ingrid. 'She knows Hannah's mother. I met her before we came to Buckow.'

'What did you talk about?' her mother said, a smile still on her lips.

'The revolution.'

'So this is your work?' Frau Hoffmann said, holding up the paper.

'Good Lord!' said Herr Hoffmann. 'Have you been agitating, Ingrid? Are we to understand that you have fomented this whole revolution?'

'This is all terribly amusing,' Ingrid said as her parents chuckled. 'You won't be so amused when we really do live in a socialist state.'

'Don't think it'd be the utopia you believe it to be,' Frau Hoffmann said.

Herr Hoffmann picked up the *Allgemeine* and Frau Hoffmann went back to her sewing. Her thread had knotted and she snapped it off with a hard pull and a sneer of frustration. 'What do they say about the rationing?' she asked.

'Rationing rampant; still no food,' her father intoned.

'They're all starving,' Ingrid muttered.

'Read something else,' her mother said. 'Something different.'

'Here's something for you, Hedwig – a group of demobbed soldiers stole a boat at Krumme-Lanke lake, sailed into the middle, where it capsized and they all drowned. Imagine! Surviving the war and then drowning in that puddle. They must have wanted to do it – suicide pact or the like. What do you say to that?'

'What do I say to that?' her mother said, dropping her sewing things into her lap. 'A horrible thing to read! The worst thing! I don't understand you sometimes, Johannes. Twenty-five years, and sometimes I don't understand you at all.'

Her father's face collapsed into embarrassed concern and he said, 'Quite right Hedwigchen, quite right.'

Her mother shook her head and rethreaded her needle swiftly. She went at the circle of fabric vigorously for twenty or thirty stitches and her father leafed through the rest of the paper in silence. Ingrid fingered the spine of the book she had been reading and thought about the paintings in the little red house, the ugly shapes of them in the flickering candlelight.

They heard the horn of a motorcar.

'Oh, it's our communist friend, eh? The driver!' her father bellowed, laughing.

'Who's he brought?' said Ingrid, imagining the house slowly filling up with the city's quaking middle classes.

277

'No one. Von Ketz had to go to Berlin on some business,' her mother said.

'If it's so dangerous, how come he can go back?'

'Ingrid,' her mother said, 'you agreed to this stay. I'm sure I don't need to remind you that you saw someone killed in the streets.'

She saw his head open up, heard the wet slap of his blood on the cobbles.

'It's also Thursday, when the plane comes over from Hamburg. He can't bear it,' Ingrid said. She had seen von Ketz crouching in the hallway as it hummed overhead. He was pale and trembling and, ashamed for him, she had turned and left.

Her mother put down her embroidery. 'Ingrid, the man's just come back from war. Thank God you never had any brothers to bestow your boundless sympathy on.'

Ingrid, shamed, pushed herself out of her chair and said, 'I'm going up to the study.'

'You're always in his study, Ingrid,' her mother said. 'What are you doing up there? It can't just be letters to Hannah.'

'Translations,' Ingrid said.

'You know,' her mother said, 'I don't see why you couldn't get any of those poems published. They're wonderful. Though of course who's publishing anything but political diatribes now? They're beautiful aren't they, Johannes? Ingrid's poems.'

'They are dear. Wonderful.'

Ingrid watched them carefully, her mother picking at a knot with her fingernails, her father squinting at the paper.

'I did give them to someone. A publisher,' she said, a thrill of insurrection crackling through her.

Her father's eyes rolled up and fixed her over the lenses

of his glasses. Her mother dropped her sewing into her lap again and sighed dramatically. 'Why on earth would you keep something like that to yourself, Ingrid? You are so dull – this secrecy.'

'It felt too important and I . . . I thought you might not approve.'

'Why shouldn't we approve?' her mother said, shaking her head in a show of exasperation as she went back to her work. Ingrid was disappointed that her poems had been denuded of the romance of the censure she had so often rehearsed in her head. 'Of course you can't use your real name. Johannes – she can't use her real name. You don't want notoriety do you, dear?' said her mother, dropping the sewing again. 'Don't tell me it's already being published under your name. Don't tell me that, Ingrid.'

'No, of course not,' Ingrid said. 'They didn't want it.'

'Didn't want it!' her mother shrieked. 'Why shouldn't they want it?'

'Too many women poets.'

'Well, how tedious of them, dear.'

'Very,' her father said. 'You won't make any money out of it,' he added.

With a measure of disappointment, but a lighter heart, she said, 'I might go and work on them now.'

Her mother squinted at the clock, curling her lip as she focused. 'We're eating in an hour.'

'Do you want to take your paper?' said her father.

'No, you can laugh about our crumbling society without the jokey whispers.'

'Drama, Ingrid!' her mother called in a familiar singsong. 'We don't always need drama!'

Ingrid fled up the stairs, to the study. When she passed

the door to her room she stopped, opened it and stared at the little desk and her correspondence there. She wanted to see Hannah. She should write to her, she thought, but looked at the letter she had received from her the day before, full of news about the soldiers' uprising, quotes from Luxemburg and Liebknecht, snippets from Zetkin, amusing stories and little sketches, and she thought of her own lethargic replies. She thought of the bare little red cottage, stripped of any sense of meaning, and the formless paintings. There would be no resolution, not ever.

She heard singing. She stepped into the hall and saw that there was a door open near the end of the corridor. She approached gingerly. The thin reedy voice sang: '*Oh, the meadows, Oh, the meadows, And the highlands, Of spring.*' It stopped and, closer now, Ingrid could hear a feverish scratching, as if the singer had forged the melody and was trying to capture it on paper.

'Are you there?'

'Yes,' Ingrid answered automatically. 'It's Fräulein Hoffmann.'

'Margarete?' came the voice.

'No, Ingrid. Her sister.'

Ingrid stared at a framed print at the end of the corridor; a large aquatint of Bismarck and the German princes pledging allegiance to the Kaiser. She took a step back, believing that she might be able to escape, but the voice said, 'Yes, yes. Let me have a look at you then.'

Ingrid went to the door. Baroness von Ketz, even more shrunk than she remembered her, was sitting in a high-backed wooden chair, her stick-like arms laid out straight along the rests and her feet up on a low footstool, covered in bright Berlin wool-work. Her eyes were large and damp and her mouth was pulled down on one side, revealing a dewlap of wet pink lip. The room was wide and neat, filled with delicate furniture and sunlight, barely hampered by the long white curtains, as thin as silk, the folds rolling down them and opening up, like waves, in front of the open windows.

'So you're back,' the Baroness said in a drunken slur.

'Yes,' said Ingrid. 'But only briefly, until things quieten down in Berlin.'

'What things?' she said, shaking her head in patronising disbelief. 'What things?'

Ingrid knew that she mustn't cause her undue worry, so said, 'Personal things.'

The Baroness nodded grimly. 'The girl in the lake.'

The breeze curled a curve in the curtain behind her that fell open, revealing a flash of greenery from the slope behind the house.

'Yes,' said Ingrid.

'I see her,' the Baroness said.

'Do you?' Ingrid said.

The Baroness closed her eyes and pushed her head against the back of her chair. Tears were seeping out from her eyelids.

'Oh yes, the poor girl,' the Baroness said. Her voice quavered. 'No, I didn't want that for you. I am sad that you are still under their thrall. They love you, I'm sure, but they suffocate you. You must see it.'

'Who?' Ingrid said.

'Your parents, dear.'

Ingrid felt heat prickle up her back, over her neck and into her ears. 'They aren't perfect, but they—'

'They keep you. They groan like dogs. They take your letters – I've seen them. They groan at night. They'll never let you go.' And then, as if it was Ingrid who had been speaking, she waved her stiff claw and said, 'Never mind them, dear. Never mind them.'

She let out a hollow gasp and her eyes deadened.

'Baroness von Ketz?' Ingrid said, but she didn't move. Ingrid took a few steps into the room. It smelt of vinegar and carbolic soap, of sickness and death. 'Baroness von Ketz?' she said again, and touched the woman's arm. The skin felt cold. But Ingrid saw that the Baroness's eyes were open again and watching her. Her lips moved, but Ingrid couldn't hear what she was saying. She put her ear closer.

'I kept the *kirrn*. The club. It's in the attic.'

'Yes,' said Ingrid, feigning understanding, and moved away to call for the nurse, but the Baroness grabbed at her, catching her necklace with a rigid finger, and pulled her face towards her own. Ingrid dipped, clutching at the chain that burned into her bare neck, trying to stop it breaking. 'I saw him murdered,' she said. 'My husband. A great *kirrn* club down on his head – split him like a melon. I always thought he was made of stone and leather. But beneath the club, he was as soft as fruit. I kept it,' she said, 'I keep it in the attic for when he returns.'

'Is everything all right?'

The finger released her chain. The Baroness slumped. There was a nurse at the door whom Ingrid had seen often descending the path to the house, but had never spoken to. She was tall and broad and held a tray filled with small brown medicine bottles.

'Yes,' Ingrid said afraid. 'I was just passing on the way to the Baron's study.' She went to the door and pushed past the woman.

'Do you need to get into the attic?'

Ingrid thought that she must learn to talk to servants now, she must talk to them like the Baroness would, like her mother would, and she said, 'Who are you to question me like that?'

The nurse went grey. 'I beg your pardon, Fräulein Hoffmann,' she said quietly. 'It's just that I've just been up there to collect some medicines.' She lifted up the tray. 'I wanted to mention that I had Riemann unlock it, but he'll be up any moment to shut it up again. I didn't want you to get locked up there, though of course it doesn't make any sense that you'd want to go up. I do apologise.'

'Oh,' Ingrid said, her mouth dry. 'Thank you. No, I'll be working.'

The nurse nodded numbly and took the tray into the Baroness's room.

Ingrid ran to the study. She grabbed at the handle and paused, closing her eyes, trying to force her embarrassment away. It was no good. She hated this countryside and this house. Yes, they will level it. The revolution will succeed, and this house will become a school for girls or a hospital for invalids and the Baroness will be just another patient among the workers and servants that were once her own.

She turned the handle and was delivered into a warm fug of polished wood and leather-bound books. She closed the door behind her. The room was heavy with the residual heat from a large tiled oven in one corner, stoked that morning. A clock was ticking, a pretty wall clock between the two windows – all brass, porcelain, turned wood and dimpled glass – its pendulum licking back and forth at a merry pace, filling the room with buoyant good humour.

She looked at the desk and behind it a line drawn on the wall, which was papered above the dado rail and panelled and painted beneath. The door to the attic. She couldn't let Riemann find her up there or risk getting locked in – it would be too terrible. This wasn't the opportunity. And anyway, she thought, what could she possibly find there that might ease the stone in her stomach and the terrible lightness in her heart? Would she be happier knowing that Margarete, Hans or Nora were definitely dead? She supposed not and so tried to damp her curiosity.

There was an open book on the desk. She went round and sat down in front of it. She saw that von Ketz had worked that morning, because the pile of papers next to the letter rack had been reordered. But he had moved her work back into the centre of the table, the Barrett Browning sonnets were opened at the page she had abandoned the day before, the inkwell was filled, the pen clean and ready. She read the last lines of her translation:

> *. . . to the upper world, and so I am already between evil*
> *and good, ready to testify:*
> *that love – as strong as death – can redeem.*

Here at this desk, in the warmth of the oven, in the autumnal afternoon light from the window, she might forget about the revolution, the Baroness's stiff hand, the *kirrn* club crushing the old Baron's head. She wished that the room was hers, that she had the key, that she owned the house. She wished that the sky would darken and that, in a few hours, there would be a tap at the door and she would open it to find a tray laid with her supper. Then she would read until she was sleepy and slip to bed, where someone would be waiting for her in the dark, someone who would bury his face in her neck and push her book to the floor.

She looked back at the English poem, then at her translation. She didn't like 'upper world'. She put a dotted line beneath and cycled through other options: 'world above', 'the world above us', 'the upper ...' she thought, 'the upper ...', but it was 'upper' that was wrong. 'Overworld.' 'Overworld' she thought. But that wasn't even a word, was it? She had said it too many times to know.

A door closed in the corridor outside, its slam echoing, and behind her came a soft knock. She turned. The door to the attic had cracked open a few millimetres. She put her pen down and leant back in the chair. Would it be terrible to be caught there? What could Riemann do? And if she heard him, she could scream, couldn't she? It wouldn't be so terrible. She stood and went to the window and looked at the sun in the yellow-orange leaves of the lime tree. A bell rang in the belly of the house. It was irresistible.

She walked around von Ketz's desk and, gripping the centimetre of open door with her fingernails above the black spot of the keyhole, she pulled it open.

A small enclosed staircase was revealed, covered in threadbare mauve carpet, twisting up into the room above. There was a museum-like smell of camphor and ancient things. There was sunlight. She put her foot on the first step and heard a crack of dry floorboards. She waited, listened for movement in the corridor and, when she heard none, mounted the step and made her way up into the cold stuffy air.

She found herself in a large room beneath the roof, with a sloping ceiling, punctured by little round windows, like portholes, along both sides. Light streamed in from those that faced south, towards the lake; those on the other side were filled with cold November shadow.

Except for the windows, the room was empty, the floorboards bare and dusty, but at each side, away from the staircase, there were further doors. She first tried what she believed to be the wrong door, the one that she couldn't have seen when she returned to the house that night at the wedding, but it was locked. She put her ear to the wood and listened, as if she might be able to judge how full the room was on the other side, but she heard nothing except the blood in her ears, the creaking of her cartilage and the brush of her skin.

Afraid that the second door was also destined to disappoint her, she pulled down on the door handle and shoved it forward. It flew open, cracked against its hinges and then, with a shudder, bounced back towards her, almost shutting again.

She pushed it again more gently and looked inside. This room was surrounded by dark wooden plan chests, a metre deep and a metre high, filled with long shallow drawers. Along the surfaces were bundles of papers, cloth- and leather-bound books in neat piles, stacks of glass jars, wooden boxes, some varnished, others raw, and metal instruments – pincers and pins and scalpels. The smell was of wood, but also mothballs and carbolic, and ancient sheets of yellowing paper.

On the curved windowsills, on top of boxes and pinned to the sloping walls were objects she recognised from Southwest Africa: the leather strings Hereros used to hang their clubs and leather pouches from their bodies, but which here were bundled into nests like dried noodles; a branch of acacia, grey and twisting, creating a crown of thorns; and on the wall a Herero *kirrn*. She wondered if the matt patches on its glossy tip were raw wood or human traces and heard the crack of skull, a dull thud on the veld, and pulled herself away from it, to safer things: the papers, the jars, the books.

On the edges of the books were dates and tribal names; others were numbered and lettered with an obscure code – 'REP94.23.3', 'APG76.441.0'; another said simply 'Baron and Baroness Emil von Ketz' and then the date of Margarete's wedding. Ingrid pulled it from the middle of the pile, and opened it, stung to find pictures of her sister, in her wedding dress, standing in the archway of the red church at Oberbarnim, von Ketz, tall and young as he then was, Margarete almost smiling, her lovely teeth visible.

'There you are,' Ingrid said, and touched the matt paper, appalled by how little the feel of her sister's image gave back to her. 'It is all so dead with you gone and I don't feel there's any use for me in the world without you.'

Feeling the sting of tears, she turned the pages and found more images of them, one with her parents, and Ingrid herself at the side of the group, her chin held in the air in a pose she remembered believing was becoming, but which in fact made her look arch and cold. Who are you? thought Ingrid, looking at her own sepia face. How clever you thought you were and how little you knew about anything.

She turned to the back of the book where a collection of other photographs and papers had been loosely gathered. There was a picture of Margarete before the wedding that she hadn't seen before, on the jetty at the lake edge; she already seemed faded. There was a small photograph of the von Ketzes' farmhouse in Africa, another of von Ketz as a baby, wrapped in a long lace-covered dress, with the name of the only photo studio in Okahandja in an elegant brown script below. There were pictures of other children, surely von Ketz's siblings – plump babies and infants with straw-blond hair and short von Ketz brows. And a face that she hadn't seen for years: Hans Ziegler, their houseboy in Southwest.

Her lips parted and she let out a short sigh, like a withheld sob. Hans was standing straight, wearing a smart wing collar tight and high around his neck, and a jacket and watch chain. Ingrid had never imagined she would see his face again – his high arching brow, the freckles across his nose and cheeks, his little ears, his teeth that always appeared to be too large for his mouth and in the picture were parting his earnest lips. She put her fingers to his face and said his name out loud. 'Hans.'

There was something dissonant about the picture though. She had not seen him in those clothes before, though he might have been lent them by the studio. His face was thinner, the sockets of his eyes deeper. The shudder of the camera gave him an oddly aged appearance, despite the fact that it must have been taken before they had met him.

She would keep it for herself. She slipped the picture into the opening of her blouse and looked down to see if it was visible. She felt a thrill at the idea of passing down the corridor, the edges of the stolen picture scratching at her camisole.

'Fräulein Hoffmann?'

Ingrid froze.

She turned around. There stood a man, quite small, with glasses containing two flat opaque lenses, as black as polished jet. His fingers reached out for the door frame, trembling self-consciously until they touched the painted wood, which, once found, they gripped with alacrity. He pulled himself into the room, the black lenses pointing in her direction, like giant blank pupils.

'Did I frighten you?' the little man said.

'Yes,' she said, moving backwards until she felt her skirt pushing against the cabinet.

'You're moving away from me.'

She must get past him. She must push him over, tumble him to the ground and run down the stairs back into the house.

'*Ou avons-nous parlé en français avant?* Fräulein Hoffmann?' he said, switching to German again. 'I can sense how frightened you are. You must not be – it's only me. Leo Horvath.'

Horvath. The friend who might have been her husband, but was now a caricature of a blind man, with his dark glasses and his hands and feet shuffling closer and closer to her.

'Of course!' Ingrid cried, the tone of her voice manic. 'Here you are! I had no idea.'

This loud exclamation finally stopped his progress. 'It was going to be a surprise – I was going to be at the dinner table tonight. But here *you* are,' he said.

'Yes, the Baron had said that there were some photos up here,' she said, but she hadn't needed to lie and now would be caught out. How stupid she became in this house. How much she would have preferred to have stayed in Berlin and risked the crowds, the barricades and the bullets. She thought about the boy's blood, creeping down the channels between the cobbles, the feel of Hannah pulling at her coat, pulling her away, the Freikorps surrounding the body, their triumphant shouts. She thought of von Ketz in Belgium and wondered who she would be if she had seen it over and over, again and again; men falling, blood gushing into the mud and the water.

'Are you here for a visit? Are you no longer in … ?' Austria-Hungary? She didn't even know what to call his country any more. At least there was still some semblance of Germany.

'I've been in Berlin, actually. But now I'm here until things calm down. Emil insisted.' He smiled. He was staring just past her head. 'So we're all waifs and strays here.'

Ingrid nodded. She wanted to leave. She feared that the heat of her skin, her sweat, was spoiling the photograph of Hans, wiping away his likeness.

'I think the Baron used to have a Negro's head up here.'

'A head?' Ingrid said.

'Yes, Emil's grandfather was an amateur anthropologist. Rather gruesome. It must have been very hard coming back, I imagine,' Horvath said, his mouth still smiling, but speaking with sadness and empathy.

It was all too much and Ingrid choked out a sob, dropped to her knees, covered her face and wept. She heard the clicking of Horvath's knees as he knelt beside her. His hand was on her arm and his voice was close. 'Oh, you poor thing. No one's noticed, have they? No one's noticed at all.'

'No,' she said shaking her head, 'I see her everywhere.'

'Of course you do,' he said. 'Of course you do.'

*

Back in her room, the picture hidden in her writing slope, Ingrid sat on her bed saturated with despair, fed by the image of the severed head, Horvath's lenses like dead pupils, Margarete in her dress and her own, young, expressionless face. She couldn't shake the feeling as she washed and changed for dinner, not until she was walking down the corridor, when it became gloom, thinking about Father

290

Ingelmann's prevarications and the coming awkwardness of that evening's meal. As she descended the stairs, though, she heard laughter from the dining room.

When she entered, Horvath was holding on to the back of his chair grinning. Her mother was saying, 'Of course, Ingrid couldn't believe her luck.' She threw her arm out in Ingrid's direction and said, 'Dearest, we heard you had quite a fright in the attic.'

Ingrid blushed and said, 'I was just surprised,' embarrassed also that she had been somewhere she shouldn't have been.

'Now tell me, dear Herr Horvath,' her mother said, turning back to him, 'Was it gas?'

'Mother!' Ingrid muttered.

'Oh, it's quite all right,' Horvath said, and Ingrid was doubly shamed that her mother's question had not been badly received. 'People are always so polite with me now, as if I were a child – it's unbearable. Yes, it was the gas, and I'm afraid it was from our side. It's all about the direction of the wind you see, but it came back on us.'

'Dear God!' her mother exclaimed.

'My lungs have almost recovered,' Horvath said. 'Others were in a worse state.'

'And what will you do now?' Herr Hoffmann said.

'Oh, yes, you were a painter,' said Frau Hoffmann.

Ingrid was stung again. He was a painter; he had lost everything and she had backed away from him in disgust.

'Yes,' he said. 'No more pictures for me.'

How could one possibly respond to such a statement? She watched her mother and father. They remained thoughtful.

Von Ketz arrived and Horvath's face brightened as he heard his awkward steps. 'Baron!' he said.

'You have found the Hoffmanns,' von Ketz said.

'Yes, yes,' said Horvath. Von Ketz went to him and put his arm round his shoulder. 'Look at us,' Horvath said. 'Quite a pair of boys about town, eh?'

Frau and Herr Hoffmann laughed loudly. But Ingrid couldn't laugh, because it was terrible, and she pretended to have forgotten something, and ran back up to her room. Sitting in the dark, loss broke over her like a wave and she fell onto her bed and wept into the pillow. When a little of the blackness lifted, she was able to turn onto her side and with shuddering gasps recalled her sister laughing and the vast affection of her clinging embraces and her awful teasing and how she trembled with life. She wanted to comfort her. She tried to picture her in heaven, but she knew that she was somewhere cold, dark and alone, that no one could reach her, not ever.

*

Ingrid began to build a routine in Buckow. Always hopeful for good news from Berlin, she would read the *Allgemeine* from her father, and then the *Red Flag*, which Riemann bought for her second-hand from a socialist friend who worked at Schloss Flemming. The first time he had brought it to her, she had said how sorry she was to hear about Otto and his boys. He left without responding and she thought she had offended him, but he came back the next day with the paper and a pear from his garden. 'It's the last of the crop,' he said. 'These don't store well, so they need eating up.' She was on the terrace with a blanket over her legs and she ate the pear, which was soft and sweet, and read Rosa Luxemburg's piece in the *Red Flag*, thinking of her wide face in the dark and hearing the songbirds in the courtyard.

If the weather was fine, she took a turn around the lake, even if it was raining, and then sat with her parents in front of the drawing-room stove. Horvath was often in his room, doing something he described as work, but Ingrid knew to be the slow adaptation to his new life in the dark. She passed his bedroom when Renate was cleaning and, pausing as if to adjust a button come undone on the back of her tailor-made, she saw a great book of Braille and a line of brown bottles. She watched Renate with barely restrained disgust pick up a swab, dropped in error, the cotton stained yellow.

During the evenings spent in the drawing room, von Ketz could not be pressed into telling stories about Southwest Africa, despite her mother's attempts, but he could be encouraged to talk about it generally in geographical or cultural terms. This took the form of a sort of game that her mother called 'African Walking' that involved each of them in turn describing journeys, sometimes just around buildings or towns they all knew, and describing each element in detail. Frau Hoffmann was least interested in her turn, and most rapt with von Ketz describing the journey to and from their own farm. 'And what did it look like from the rise?' she would say, and, 'Oh, we called that tree the Jew's hat,' and, 'Yes, that was beautiful – if only someone could describe that particular heat, that particular smell.' She would drink Veltliner from the cellar, to which she would add a little Fachingen water – very little. The best of these evenings ended with her staring contentedly out of the black window, her middle finger touching her jaw, the worst with her in quiet tears and Herr Hoffmann saying, 'Oh come now, Schätzchen, we mustn't get maudlin.' He would stroke the back of her hand, and Frau Hoffmann would cry until Horvath, von Ketz and finally Ingrid slipped away to their rooms.

Ingrid was able to translate in the afternoon, once von Ketz was done with his correspondence, and this brought her brief but great joy. Von Ketz was a careless smoker and left cigarettes, pipes and tobacco on the desk that she had to clear away before she could start work. She would pick up the pipes and smell them as she read through her draft from the previous day. Once, curious, she sucked at the ivory spout, filling her mouth with the brown trace of burnt tobacco.

A week later she found an ivory stem on the floor by the chair, and placed it in her pocket. With this in her possession, it was only a matter of days before she had a bowl and was hoarding tobacco, taking it in amber tufts whenever she had the opportunity and storing it in an old peppermint tin in her vanity case. She carried the stuffed pipe in her pocket and smoked it out of the window before she started writing, dipping back inside if she heard someone on the path below. She found the smoke biting and harsh at first, but the sense of gifting herself something was irresistible. Soon the pipe accompanied her on her walks, her pockets became studded with stray golden threads and the pipe's smoke became the reassuring scent of her solitude.

If he was done setting traps with the forester, shooting or visiting estate cottages, von Ketz knocked on the door of the study in the afternoon and asked if she wanted coffee, if Riemann had sourced enough that day to make a pot. If not they drank thin, dusty East Frisian tea from a rationed caddy that had been found in the cellar and which her mother kept locked in her room. He was always keen to hear what she had written, but she couldn't bear the sound of her own voice, and so gave him the sheets to read aloud. Soon she copied out the work from the day for just this purpose, excited to hear how it sounded in his mouth.

This ritual continued undisturbed for almost two weeks, until a letter arrived from Berlin. Riemann brought it up to her while she wrote and she put her pen down to receive it. Ingrid turned it over and read the sender's address on the back of the envelope: A v. Galen, 14 Wörther Platz, Berlin. She tried to imagine Frau von Galen writing to her; or perhaps she would find some amanuensis's signature at the bottom of a standard reply. She couldn't bear to find out.

She looked at the poem she had been working on, then back at the envelope. This lasted for some hours as she tried to work, and she produced two lines of translation, one of which she crossed out. Then, with unthinking haste, she tore the letter open and read it three times over, going too fast each time and only catching snatches of the words, until her heart had calmed enough to let her take each sentence in.

Dear Fräulein Hoffmann,

I received a collection of translated poems from Herr Necker-Weiß with a recommendation. I read them with great interest and am impressed with the quality of the individual pieces. I question how they hang together as a collection in themselves, but would be willing to discuss this with you, should you be able to find the time to visit me in Berlin in these strange and dangerous times. Perhaps we might find a route to publication together, though I can make you no guarantees on this front. The work must be all on your side and it isn't always possible to pull such things off.

I remain, with best wishes, your
Agatha von Galen

She felt a brittle joy at the possibility of something beyond Buckow, beyond the war and Berlin. It did not have to be life-changing, just a thin finger of light reaching out to somewhere beyond herself, connecting with the world. Something greater than Buckow and Berlin, than childhood memories of the veld, a black houseboy speaking French and English, and a dead sister.

There was a tap at the door. Her cheeks were burning and she felt as if she was glowing red. 'Fräulein Ingrid?' The side of von Ketz's head appeared around the door. 'Do you have time for a bit of reading now?'

'Yes, come in,' she said, pushing the letter back into her pocket as von Ketz opened the door with his foot and brought in the coffee things. The smell calmed her and, although she had tried to compose herself, von Ketz said, 'Is everything all right?'

'Yes, of course,' Ingrid said.

'Good,' he said, and poured for them both. 'What have we got today?'

She stood up from the desk and, having nothing to show him, dug around in her papers until she found a sonnet that she had worked on unsatisfactorily more than a year ago, but which was copied out neatly and would serve as a substitute for an imagined afternoon's work. 'Shakespeare,' she said.

'The Tiecks be blown, eh?' he said.

'You can't translate enough Shakespeare.'

'So it seems,' he said, sitting in his wingback chair and taking the poem from her. She sat down opposite him and stroked the fabric of the red chair, where the silk had softened and split into separate fibres, revealing the grubby white cotton beneath. Von Ketz crossed his legs and read:

'Tired of all this, I ache for death's rest, And see the desert like a vagrant born . . . '

What would he think of her little book when it was published? she wondered, watching his lips moving, his eyes glancing at her between the lines. She pictured von Ketz in the stifling dance hall in Lüderitz Bay. That von Ketz would have picked up the book, frowned at it, the lines on his short forehead deep even then, and he would have tossed it down and said, 'Well done you, eh?' Full of fraternal affability, but not feigning any interest in the work itself. Certainly not sitting in front of her reading the poems to her out loud.

'*. . . Weary of this, I wish I were gone, But in death I leave my love alone.*' Von Ketz let the sheet fall to his lap. 'It's lovely.'

'I've forced all the rhymes,' Ingrid said.

'The rhymes are good,' he said, taking the anger to be directed at her work.

'Beaten and weakened?'

'Well, nothing rhymes with weakened,' he said, frowning down at it. 'Beacon? Hardly though. Deacon? I suppose that won't help.'

Ingrid laughed. 'And strength through lame direction. Deacon,' she said and they both laughed.

'Yes,' von Ketz said giggling. 'It improves everything, doesn't it? In the beginning, when God created the universe, the earth was formless and desolate. Deacon.'

They laughed again and searched for another line, but the joke eluded them and they sat content and smiling, the air smelling of stale coffee, wood polish and tobacco. Ingrid let her eyes wander along the rows of books behind him, over the shapes in the rug, finding birds and lizards and little

Arabs in the geometric forms. He was as good as he could be. He would do fine.

Von Ketz lit one of his cigarettes and sucked at it, the tobacco cracking. His hands were very beautiful. She wondered if he had killed anyone with them. She wondered if he had touched other women with them since Margarete had died. Or other men. The smoke reached her and she was riveted by her appetite for it.

The clock chimed out a quarter past the hour. They sat in silence and it made her happy that they did so without embarrassment. If she were his wife she would be suggesting changes to the house, she supposed, and apologising about her parents. She would be generous to his friends, saying that she would move Horvath into a better room. He would question whether she had the right to decide – teasingly, in a way that had become habit. She would encourage him to eat more, walk more. She would hold him at night, look down at his weak body in the blue light, but then he would stiffen. Above the sheets she held the great weight of his head, her face in his hair telling him he was home; and beneath he was tugging her nightdress up, his long fingers climbing up her thighs. She saw her sister's pleading face, put her hands together in her lap and searched around for something to say, to change him back to the von Ketz that she had grown comfortable with in the past weeks: a pale, sexless brother. 'What was it like in Africa, do you think?' she said.

'When?' said von Ketz.

'During the war.'

'Oh, I think pretty tame compared with the Uprising.'

'But the British have it now. Maybe there are some Englishmen on our farm right now. Can you imagine?'

'I can't, actually. The whole thing was bought by a

Dutchman straight away. Your father is very canny with those sort of things.'

'Is he still there, the Dutchman?' Ingrid said.

'Why shouldn't he be?'

'Because of the Uprising. Papa said he sold it to the government, but later.'

'Oh,' von Ketz said. 'I mean, it wasn't straight away. It was after the Uprising. And maybe it was the government. I can't remember.'

'But what was left of it? Didn't they burn down your house as well?'

'The land was left of course. I don't know what happened to the house we lived in. They would have done well to burn that down.' Von Ketz topped up his coffee. 'Does it make you sad to know the British are there?'

'I don't know,' Ingrid said. 'I'm not sure it felt like ours, in the end.'

'I think your sister never got over leaving.'

'Do you think?' Ingrid said, surprised at this assertion. 'I always thought she hated it when we were there. But perhaps it was her home. Perhaps it didn't matter that she found it hard.'

'Maybe she thought marrying me would bring it closer, somehow. Africa, I mean.'

'That's unfair,' she said, pleased that he had spoken about her. She worried again that she had misunderstood everything; that he had always loved Margarete and that it was she who had disappointed him. 'Did you love her? Did you always love her?' Her impertinence made her shudder.

He didn't move. Was he going to pretend that she hadn't said it?

'She was remarkable,' he said.

Ingrid felt as if she couldn't breathe. She wanted to get up and leave, but it was impossible after a comment like that.

'You're looking forward to getting back to Berlin, I imagine,' von Ketz said, the tone a little colder.

'That's right,' Ingrid said, though also thinking that sharing the study in Berlin there with her father was not the same as having even a few hours completely to herself here. They had become completely precious.

Von Ketz looked a little put out and said, 'You're not scared of the revolution?'

Ingrid shook her head. 'People's desire for status,' she said 'That only brings misery. And war.'

'Is it better to desire money?'

'Is that what replaces it?'

'Human beings like a hierarchy – they'll build it from something, if it's not class, then it will be wealth.'

'Perhaps,' she said, 'I hope not. If the rules are right, and everyone has the opportunities, that's a fair start. It's really not that radical – I'm not at all radical, I'm not a Spartacist, like Hannah. But you have to believe that these hierarchies have been bad for us. It's common sense.'

Von Ketz smiled and drew on his cigarette. 'Common sense,' he said.

Ingrid sat up in her chair. 'Whoever's in power is going to eradicate the aristocracy you know. Politically, I mean.'

'Yes,' von Ketz said. 'I imagined they would.'

'You're not afraid?'

'Afraid is the wrong word. I don't agree with it, but I'm ready for it. I understand that paternalism has suffered a blow, that the Junker has become a figure of hate, that that way isn't acceptable at *this* moment. People will want it back again, though, or something like it. They always have. Think of Caesar.'

'Yes, that worked out well,' she said.

He chuckled. A shifting cloud filled the room with warm light. The tick of the clock was louder. 'And what's your place in this new world?' he said.

Ingrid shrugged. 'I don't know. Not anyone's wife, I suppose. I would like to work again; without war, work is hard to find.' She felt a wave of nostalgia about the Ministry, the back of Hannah's head as she scribbled, Herr Rabe's constant dry cough.

'You don't think you'll marry?'

'No, I don't imagine so. Not because I don't want to, but whom am I going to marry? There's no one left. Mine will be a generation of spinsters. By the forties, Europe's going to be full of us.'

'And that's a good thing?'

'Perhaps,' Ingrid said. 'I hope so. Maybe we'll change things.'

'You're a great optimist, Ingrid Hoffmann,' von Ketz said, laughing.

She couldn't be, she thought. An optimist couldn't possibly be this sad.

There was a knock at the door.

'Come in!' von Ketz said, his smile erased.

It was Riemann. 'A card has been dropped off by hand for Fräulein Hoffmann,' he said.

'I'm awfully popular today,' Ingrid said, afraid that it was a second note from von Galen recalling her previous offer. Ingrid took the card, marked with the address of Meier's guesthouse. It said:

Fräulein Hoffmann,

I can see you at your earliest convenience. You may come for me at Meier's this afternoon.

Yours sincerely,
Father Schäfer

'Is it news from Berlin?' Von Ketz said.

'Hannah,' Ingrid said. 'My friend. You'll excuse me.'

*

The Meiers' guesthouse in Buckow was family-run. The leaching of men to the war meant that the daughters now carried bags and drove the trap to the station. When they weren't at work, they sat about in a small parlour opposite the guest sitting room, slumped in their chairs and gossiping with the egg-eyed stare that marked out Frau Meier and all of her kin. The maid that saw to the guests' needs and greeted Ingrid at the door was an old maiden aunt, thin, with swollen hands mutilated by arthritis.

'Oh. Hoffmann. Yes,' she said and gestured to the guest sitting room with rigid fingers. The room led on to a conservatory overlooking the lake. There, between two potted ferns, looking out over the water with his hands in his pockets, stood Father Schäfer. He turned as she entered. The dot of hair was still above his forehead, though it was greyer, and his eyes were still ice blue. But his skin had been aged prematurely by the Southern African sun; it was heavily wrinkled and looked thin and waxy, jaundiced almost, covered in liver spots.

'Fräulein Hoffmann, take a seat,' he said, and she smelt

the staleness behind his thin yellow teeth, like old library books. He had aged thirty years in ten.

She sat and said, 'It is remarkable to find you in Buckow, Father.'

'Yes,' he said. 'I must say your letter surprised me. Father Ingelmann had just paid a call to ban me from ever darkening von Ketz's door again and it was made quite clear that it would be highly inadvisable for me to stay in Buckow any longer. I had heard that the Hoffmans had arrived from Berlin and had hoped I might have got some answers that had eluded the Baron, but I appeared to have been wrong. I was planning to leave tonight, in fact. After months of searching, Father Ingelmann has quite suddenly found me a position in a veterans' hospital near Nuremberg. Remarkable timing.'

He sat down and crossed his legs, adjusted the cloth of his trousers then drew a deep breath, as if preparing himself for bad news. 'I had quite given up hope of any sensible answer about my little quest. So tell me, Fräulein Hoffmann: where is our man?'

'Our man?' Ingrid said. 'Which man?'

Father Schäfer laughed, then nodded. 'I see.' He put his two index fingers together and touched them to his mouth. 'I have to say, I think it's appalling that they've sent you, Fräulein, to play their final hand.'

'Father Schäfer, really. There's been a misunderstanding. I'm not here about any man.'

'Why are you here then?' he said, with apparent boredom.

'I saw you at Baron von Ketz's house on that first day. From the window. And I last saw you in Southwest Africa almost ten years ago – it was such an impossible coincidence.'

303

'You're right, it is no coincidence, but even if you thought it was, it hardly explains why you needed to see me so urgently.'

'I wanted to hear what you had to say. Everyone's being so cagey about you, trying to pretend you don't exist. Even Father Ingelmann. And now you say it's no coincidence you're here.'

'And yet *you're* saying your visit today has nothing to do with Hans Ziegler.'

Ingrid was completely muddled by the priest's labyrinthine conversation. 'The man you're looking for is Hans Ziegler?' she said.

'So you do know what I'm talking about,' Father Schäfer said, excited, leaning forward in his chair as if he was winning an argument in court.

'I know who Hans Ziegler is. He was our houseboy in Southwest Africa. But how do you know who he is?'

'I know because you told me about him when we met at the guesthouse in Lüderitz.'

Ingrid shook her head. 'I don't understand how ... Why does that mean you're in Buckow looking for him?'

'I found him. Once you were gone, I found him in the concentration camp on Shark Island. I wrote to your father to say I'd found him, and when he tried to deny any knowledge of what had happened, I sent him back to Germany, to claim what was rightfully his.'

Ingrid's mind was swimming. 'Hello!' she called. 'Can I have some service? Hello!' She fell back into her chair and gripped her head as if it hurt.

The old maid appeared in the archway, and looked at Ingrid distastefully. 'Fräulein?'

'Bring me cognac or schnapps.'

'If you're are ill, Fräulein, I can . . . '

'Bring it,' Ingrid repeated. 'Anything.' The woman sucked at her dentures and left the room.

Ingrid looked at the bloodshot whites of Father Schäfer's eyes. He didn't blink.

'I am not here at the behest of my father or Baron von Ketz,' Ingrid said.

'I see that now,' Schäfer said.

'If you are willing, I would like you to start from the beginning. Let me be clear, I understood that Hans was last seen near our farm during the Uprising, but never made it to Okahandja. But you're saying you found him in Lüderitz? On Shark Island?'

The old waitress arrived with a glass of clear schnapps and put it on the side-table. Father Schäfer watched her, waited for her to go, then turned to Ingrid and said, 'Yes, I was ministering at the concentration camp at Shark Island. It was a ghastly, inhumane place. Many didn't speak German, but many who did were Christians, and I was able to give them a little succour.

'There was one inmate who caught my attention, though, because he was a half-caste. I noticed also that he was a favourite target of the camp guards, because he appealed to them sporadically with stories of his aristocratic heritage. He was mad, they thought, or at least deluded. I began talking to this man and realised quickly that he spoke not only German, but also a range of Bantoid dialects, as well as French and English. Quite remarkable. He was in a terrible state of course, as they all were, shackled like slaves, stinking, starving. I asked him his name, and he said: Hans Ziegler.'

Ingrid's eyes filled with tears.

'Of course I didn't make the connection straight away. But then he told me his story: that he had been betrayed by his employer or his brother, he wasn't sure which, and that the soldiers who arrested him and the authorities at the camp wouldn't believe, or didn't care to believe, that he was half-white, had never fought in the Uprising and had no place being in a camp for Herero warriors. It was then that I remembered your search for your houseboy. I went back to the guesthouse and found out your name. That's when I knew that he was telling the truth.

'It took some weeks to get him out, but I was able to find enough paperwork about the Hoffmanns, the von Ketzes and the farm to prove he was no fighter and eventually the authorities were bored enough of my pestering to hand him over to me. He was very unwell of course: skin and bones.'

Father Schäfer slowed for this revelation, fixed her gaze to make sure that it elicited the hoped-for response. It did. Ingrid laid her hands flat to her face and let out a sob. Father Schäfer's fervour was satisfied; cooled, he waited for her to quieten.

'I'm sorry, Father. I didn't know any of this. I didn't even know he had a brother,' Ingrid said, wiping her eyes.

'But you're living with him,' Father Schäfer said. 'Hans is the son of the old Baron. Emil von Ketz is his brother.'

Ingrid felt light, as if she was dissolving in the bright air of the conservatory.

'Oh, you can't be surprised, Fräulein Hoffmann. Even a virtuous young lady like you. Southwest Africa is full of the mongrel progeny of German sinners. Few of them turn out as well as Herr Ziegler. And that was only because the Baron adored him – the other children died and Emil von Ketz was a terrible disappointment to him, apparently. I've never managed to spend more than the briefest of seconds in his company, despite my best efforts, but by all accounts he's rather a wet fish.'

'That's unfair,' Ingrid said, though the priest had upended everything and she didn't know what was the right thing to say and what not. Perhaps it wasn't true. It couldn't be. 'Is that why you're here?' Ingrid said. 'You think Hans is living with Baron von Ketz? How would he have got here?'

'I sent him here over four years ago.'

'Why?'

'Hans Ziegler had been grossly wronged, since the day that the elder Baron von Ketz begat him by raping a Christian woman.'

Nora's face flashed in front of Ingrid's eyes.

'He has a claim on that family,' Schäfer continued, 'through his blood, through what is owed to him. I've spent my life ministering to these people, seeing the degradations they are forced into by people that are meant to be their betters. And here I was with someone who had every right to redress those wrongs done to him. Herr Ziegler knew of course where the family seat was, so I wrote to von Ketz. I got no reply, so I wrote to Father Ingelmann, who I knew from the seminary in Barmen, and got your father's address. I wrote to him and finally word arrived from the old country. Do you know what he said, your father?'

Ingrid shook her head.

'That Herr Ziegler was a liar. That he was no son of the Baron's, but that he could be provided for financially as a "previous retainer of the family Hoffmann". Can you imagine, Fräulein? This man had been born in sin, yet honoured his father and mother, worked tirelessly for your family for next to no recompense and distracted warring Herero warriors as you were fleeing to the safety of Okahandja – men who had killed his own father. For that, he was locked up. I found him, appealed to your father, and all he could offer was money.'

Father Schäfer took out a handkerchief from his sleeve and put it to his mouth as if nauseated.

'What did Hans say?' Ingrid said.

'About what?'

'Did he not want the money?'

'Good Lord, Fräulein Hoffmann! Have you been completely deaf to the story I've told you? There was no chance he was going to be paid off; I made sure he held firm on that. He is a man of far stronger moral fibre than your father or his own brother. No, I raised my own money and I sent him back. He was elated by the idea.'

'You sent Hans to Germany?'

'That's right.'

'When?'

'He set off at the beginning of 1914, before the war.'

'And then?'

'He disappeared.'

'You never heard from him again?'

'No, never.'

'Perhaps he just disappeared with the money.'

'Fräulein Hoffmann, do you despise Herr Ziegler?'

'Not at all!' Ingrid said. 'He was my friend.'

'Then why do you keep casting aspersions on his character? He is not the sinner in this narrative.'

Father Schäfer shook his head with frustration. Ingrid, shaken intermittently by dry sobs, took a shuddering breath and then a gulp of schnapps. 'You must have heard,' she said, 'that my sister disappeared.'

'Yes,' he said. 'I heard.'

'It was in the summer of 1914.'

'What are you suggesting, Fräulein?'

'I'm not suggesting anything,' said Ingrid. 'But it can't be a coincidence, can it?'

Father Schäfer touched his handkerchief thoughtfully to his chin. 'From what I understand from Herr Ziegler, your sister was not altogether enthusiastic about having her marriage arranged with someone she never loved. Perhaps, like Herr Ziegler, she didn't play along with what your father and the new Baron von Ketz wanted. And she, like him, disappeared.'

'What on earth are you implying?' said Ingrid.

'I'm simply observing that two people who opposed your father and Emil von Ketz disappeared. I would like to find out what happened to one of them; you, I assume, are more interested in the other.'

Ingrid finished the schnapps and stood. 'Father Schäfer, I must speak to my father. But your suggestion that he or even Baron von Ketz are somehow dangerous people – there you are quite wrong,' she said, tears breaking her speech again. 'I will get the truth from him. When you have reached your hospital in Nuremberg, send word to me and I will tell you what I've found out. Hans was very important to me, and your story, even if half true, makes me miserable. But if he has come to any harm, it won't have been at my father's hand, I can promise you that.'

Father Schäfer looked unconvinced by her speech.

'You can't think he's at the house or here in Buckow,' she said.

'No. I assume he must be in Berlin,' Father Schäfer said. 'If you're an African and you're hiding or being hidden, you can't very well move about unnoticed in a provincial Prussian town like this. I've asked around and found out nothing from anyone of any use.'

'They never saw a black man here?'

'Oh they've seen plenty of black men. A group from a living museum in Berlin visited Buckow before the war, and for a week the town was full of Africans. There are many colourful stories about them, but ask them to identify an individual African and they're blind to it. Hans is half white, but show them a photograph of him and they'll give you any number of stories about Negroes in grass skirts with stretched lips and red skin, sure that it's the same man. Ridiculous little backwater.'

'It was for the wedding – the Baroness organised it,' Ingrid said. 'A little group of them played at the wedding. I'm sure that's what they were talking about.'

'What a strange idea,' said Father Schäfer.

'Perhaps,' she replied. 'The guests enjoyed it. And strange or not, if you were an African man, it might have been the first opportunity you had to visit a small German town unnoticed.'

'What a deceitful little web,' Father Schäfer said, standing abruptly and offering Ingrid his stiff hand. She shook it. 'Now the Spirit speaketh expressly,' he said, 'that in the latter times some shall depart from the faith, giving heed to seducing spirits, and doctrines of devils.'

'Speaking lies in hypocrisy; having their conscience seared with a hot iron,' Ingrid went on.

The priest raised his eyebrows. 'You had a missionary in Southwest?'

'No,' Ingrid said. 'Nora, Hans's mother, read the Bible to us every night.'

She went to the door.

'Did you know Herr Ziegler's mother well?' the priest said.

She turned back to him. 'Yes,' she said.

'She was there at the fighting in Waterberg, you know, with Samuel Maherero, no less – the rebel leader. The Herero women take part, calling to the field. Stirring stuff. Hans told me that she was a very proud Herero woman, and a great Christian, despite her suffering. Do you know much about the Battle of Waterberg?'

'I know that we won,' Ingrid said uncertainly.

'Hard to say won. It was barely a victory at all. General von Trotha's line collapsed and the Herero were able to escape through it. They took all their cattle with them, their wives and children too. It wasn't decisive at all.'

'It ended the war, didn't it?'

'That's right. Because the Herero escaped into the Omaheke Desert. Von Trotha had had enough of Hereros by that point and ordered that all of them, armed or not, should be shot on the spot. Of course the Hereros retreated, so shooting them was difficult. Instead von Trotha's men just closed the line and walked the lot of them into the desert, the men, the women, the children and their cattle. They cut off each water hole and pushed on until they collapsed one by one. Very efficient, all told. You know, they found skeletons fifteen metres deep in the desert, where men had desperately dug for water, but of course found none.'

Ingrid wiped tears from her face. 'I thought Samuel Maherero escaped,' she said.

'That's right. He made it across the desert into British territory, can you imagine? About a thousand of them got there. Of course by the end of the war, that was a good chunk of the Herero. Von Trotha wiped out over three-quarters of them. Now, Fräulein Hoffmann, that's a decisive victory,' he said.

*

Her heart thumping, she ran into the drawing room still in her coat with gritty mud crunching beneath her outdoor boots. Instead of her parents, she found Horvath sitting in an armchair near the stove. She couldn't tell if he was asleep or not; his chin rested on one hand and the black lenses of his glasses stared at her.

'Fräulein Ingrid?' he said.

'Yes,' she said. 'I was looking for my father.'

Horvath smiled. 'He's in the basement with Emil. They're choosing wine for dinner.'

'Thank you,' she said.

'Are you quite well, my dear?' he said. 'You sound very alarmed.'

'Don't worry about me,' Ingrid said.

'We all do,' said Horvath.

She should have responded warmly, but could think of nothing but Hans in the camp, his clothes hanging from his bones. She left the room with a nod that Horvath couldn't see and headed straight for the kitchen, where a door led onto a brick staircase descending into the damp of the cellar. It was dark, but her eyes quickly adjusted and a faint lamplight picked out the steps as she made her way down and the door closed behind her.

She could hear men's voices, the bass reverberating around the vaults. She walked towards the light and found them in front of a wall of wine bottles in terracotta tubes, stacked up between brick pillars. Herr Hoffmann was holding a bottle of wine, thick with dust, and von Ketz the lamp, the flickering glow making them look like apostles in a mannerist painting.

'Papa,' she said.

'Good God, Ingrid!' Herr Hoffmann said, grabbing at his chest. 'You scared the life out of me!'

'You caught us at the wine red-handed,' von Ketz said.

'I need to talk to you,' Ingrid said.

'Must it be now?' Herr Hoffmann said jovially.

'It's about Hans Ziegler.'

Her father's smile faded. 'All right,' he said.

'Should I go?' said von Ketz, looking at Herr Hoffmann.

'No, you can stay,' Ingrid said.

'Are you unwell?' von Ketz said.

'I'm well,' she said. 'But I talked to a Father Schäfer.'

Von Ketz took a few steps back until he was pressed up against the wall of bottles.

'Oh?' her father said. 'I had understood that Father Schäfer was leaving Buckow.'

'He said that Hans Ziegler is the Baron's brother.' She looked up at von Ketz's face. The lamplight made deep black lines of his frown. She looked at her father. His chin was raised, one hand was on his hip, the other still holding the wine bottle as if he were about to throw it.

'Is it true?' Ingrid said.

'He said he was,' von Ketz said.

'But how could one possibly tell?' said her father.

'I'm sure Nora could tell,' Ingrid said. Both men stared at their feet. 'Schäfer said that he found Hans. That he had been put into the concentration camp on Shark Island. Did you put him there?'

'He got caught up in the Uprising,' said Herr Hoffmann.

'You sold our farm straight away to some Dutchman, according to Baron von Ketz here. I bet his father wasn't even killed by Herero warriors, was he? I bet if I wrote to the Colonial Office I'd find out that the Uprising hadn't come anywhere near the farm when he died.'

Von Ketz's face became sadder. He looked at Herr Hoffmann.

'No, the Baron wasn't killed by Herero warriors,' Herr Hoffman said.

'Who killed him then?'

'Hans did.'

Ingrid shook her head. 'That's preposterous. You just said he might be his son.'

'My father certainly treated him like a son,' von Ketz said bitterly.

'And he treated him as badly as a son,' said her father. 'Hans knew that he would never have any rights to the farm, to a family like ours. Hans was a very frustrated person, Ingrid, though he was a good man, in his way.'

'Why would he murder his own father if he was such a good man?'

'Ingrid, we have kept this from you for a reason. It is a bad thing and I would not underestimate what solace there is to be found in ignorance.'

'I don't want to be ignorant any more!' Ingrid shouted. 'I don't want you choosing what I know and what I don't!'

Through the shimmering film of tears, she watched her father, waiting for him to shout back at her, but he didn't. Calmly he said, 'We let your sister stay at the von Ketzes' in Southwest Africa; you might remember. It was the day before we left the farm. The Uprising had begun, but you're right, it hadn't reached Luisenhof Farm. Nevertheless, Hans knew it would be there soon and had planned to use it as a cover to kill the Baron. Emil, who was of course the Baron's legitimate son, was almost eighteen and Hans realised that he would receive everything. He was furious, Ingrid. He knew that, however much he learnt, however many books he read, he would always be a country kaffir.'

'The tragedy of the educated Negro,' von Ketz said.

'When I arrived,' her father went on, 'the Baron was already dead. Hans told us his story about the Uprising, but of course Margarete had seen everything. You can guess what effect that had on her.'

Margarete had seen Hans club the Baron to death and had never told Ingrid.

'The Baron was a monster,' she said. It must have fed Margarete's hysteria, helped drive her over the balcony, helped drive her into the lake. 'Oh God,' Ingrid said, for Margarete.

'The Baron was a very troubled man. He was also cruel, I know that. So does von Ketz. That's why we didn't report Hans, but he was a murderer, Ingrid. We couldn't take him back to Germany with us. Can you imagine how your sister would have felt after what she had seen him do?'

'So what did you do? Why was he in a concentration camp?'

'We didn't do anything. We left him there, that was all. We didn't know what had happened to him until Father Schäfer's letter.'

Ingrid shook her head. 'But ... But who burnt down our house?'

'The farmworkers,' Herr Hoffmann said. 'I asked them. We were leaving for good and we wanted to keep up the Uprising story as much as Hans did. We couldn't live with that sort of scandal. We let them burn the house down and we brought you back here, Ingrid, where you were safe. Where we could all get on with our lives.'

'What life?' Ingrid screamed, and pulled a bottle from the wall, flinging it to the ground. It smashed, spraying onto her face and across the floor, filling the air with the scent of red wine. 'I thought they were going to kill us, but you'd organised it all! I waited for Hans to come back, but you knew he was as good as dead. I thought my sister was insane, but you knew that she had seen terrible things and you made sure she didn't tell me. Your horrible endless lies have ruined her life! My life!' she said, flinging another bottle across the room, and then another.

Her father grabbed hold of her wrists and held them in front of her like a gaoler. She pulled away, the wine sloshed across the sodden floor, the broken glass scratching and chinking. 'Why couldn't you just trust me, like I trusted you?' she said, her wrists aching and her tears dried up.

'I'm sorry, Ingrid. But the truth had ruined your sister and we couldn't bear it if it ruined you.'

'Did he come back for her? Is that where she went?'

'He never made it to Buckow, Ingrid. He just wanted more money than I'd offered him in Africa and he thought if he came here he could get it. Schäfer had pushed him and pushed him. He was so angry. But he did drive Margarete away, I'm sure of that. She learnt that he was in Germany and she was terrified. I did everything I could to make her feel safe, to get to Hans before he found us. And I did. I met him in Berlin and he was handsomely paid off and we never heard from him again.'

'Then why did she have to die?'

'I don't know,' her father said. 'Maybe she needed to

disappear. Maybe she's somewhere better, in this world or the next. You don't know what resources I've put into trying to find out what happened to her, Ingrid. The pain. I couldn't make her feel safe, neither could von Ketz. We live with that every day. But you're safe, Ingrid. You're always safe with us.'

'There's no safety in deception,' she said, and left them in the cellar, the scent of wine heavy in her skirt.

PART FIVE

— Understanding —

Berlin

— December 1918 —

Unwilling to share anything with her parents, Ingrid planned her trip to Berlin to meet Frau von Galen alone. But in her planning, her mind kept wandering back to Hans and to the possibility that, if he had been trapped in Germany by the war, he might conceivably still be in Berlin. However unsound her father's account of Hans's return might be, she knew that his arrival had led to Margarete's disappearance.

She had to focus on her translations, she continued to tell herself, but all of her reasoning did not quell her desire to find Hans. In a moment of despondency, she had written to Hannah asking her to find out whether the living museum was still resident at Berlin Zoo, in the hope that the small Ovambo group might be a link back to Hans. Then she wrote again asking her to ignore the request, which was foolish, but this letter she never quite posted.

Ingrid walked into town with a travel bag and bought her ticket, leaving a day earlier for her meeting with von Galen than she needed to. She had decided not to tell her parents about the trip at all, knowing that her mother would protest.

She left a note on the breakfast table starting with the sentence: 'Do not worry; I am safe.'

The train curved, cutting through the smooth white fields, and Ingrid touched the hair at her temples. The intermittent shocks of elation at the thought of meeting von Galen were continually overwhelmed by Hans and Margarete, whose faces and voices broke over her translations like the sea over a dyke. She saw her sister sunk in the dark water of the lake and Hans clubbing Baron von Ketz to death on the dusty ground of the African veld. She reminded herself again that she would not find Hans in Berlin; at best she might meet someone who had met him. And, she reasoned, even if she was led to the door of his room, what relief would it bring her?

She heard raised voices in the corridor and a tearful woman's remonstrations. The train shuddered and accelerated. Steam filled her window and then was gone. The moon was already visible, a huge pale disc, hanging prophetically in the blue sky. She covered it up with her thumb, wondering if it had an aureole, like the sun – it did not – and when she took her thumb away it looked unreal to her, a painted stage-set prop.

There was another disheartened cry from the corridor and a man appeared at the door to her carriage, his eyes searching the empty seats, then finding her. He pulled the door open and said, 'Comfortable up here?'

'Yes,' she said, uncertainly.

'Yes, it looks pretty comfortable to me.' He dropped down onto the seat in front of her. She saw two other men pass the corridor window and there followed another cry of incredulity. 'Pretty comfortable in first class,' he said. She started to understand what was happening. In the next carriage

322

the men's voices became heated and there came a series of thuds. 'People should be able to sit where they want.'

She frowned. 'What is it you want me to do exactly?'

The question confused him and he touched his cheek in an awkward, childish gesture. 'We don't think there should be classes – in society or in trains.'

A ticket inspector ran past the window and the shouting abated briefly and then rose.

'That seems sensible enough,' she said. 'Not much of a motto though.'

'It is sensible.'

'And what do you want me to do?' she repeated.

'Well, if you're not a capitalist or an aristocrat then you shouldn't be in a separate carriage.'

'You want me to sit in a different carriage, then?' she said.

The man thought about this for a second, then said, 'Yes.'

The door opened and the ticket inspector bellowed, 'Get out of here, this minute!'

'There shouldn't be any classes,' shouted the man, springing to his feet. The train pitched and he fell onto Ingrid, bristling with apologies, as the ticket inspector tried to keep his balance, while grabbing at the man's jacket. Ingrid got her hand onto his chest and pushed him back slowly, the train straightening, helping her lever him forward. She stood.

'Fräulein, please take a seat,' the ticket inspector said.

'No, thank you,' said Ingrid, and picked up her travelling bag, the horn handles clattering together, before being silenced by the grip of her gloved hands.

She pushed past the intruder and the inspector, made her way out into the corridor and walked unsteadily alongside the compartments, from which other first-class passengers peered out from the gloom, their faces colourless and afraid.

There was another barrage of angry words and she heard footsteps coming from behind her. Looking at the windows reflective in the dusk, she saw that it was the man from her carriage, finally sent packing. She supposed, from his strut, that he was trying to look to his comrades as if he was escorting her out.

She passed through second class, women with children standing on their laps to look out of the window, a few men reading papers, elderly ladies with their bags held tightly on their legs watching her with curious disdain.

Finally, to the awkward laughter of her escort, she opened the door into third class, receiving a blast of icy wind and deafening noise as she crossed from one door to the other and entered the packed carriage.

The occupants – groups of demobbed soldiers, a nun, thin mothers with their babies, two sailors, a row of men with their backs to the wall holding cards and passing a hip-flask between them – stared up at her blankly.

'There won't be any classes – on trains or in society,' the man called from behind her.

There was a muted cheer from a few of the soldiers, but most of the passengers looked back down at their babies, their drink, their hands or their cards. A young man in a demob suit gave up his place on the wooden bench for her.

She sat down and looked over at the window, milky with condensation. Her travelling bag on her lap felt comforting and she understood why the old women in second class took up the position so readily. I won't be afraid, she thought, and this affirmation calmed her. She looked over at the man, who was crouching by the door, smoking a cigarette that he held between thumb and forefinger like a needle. It was warmer in third class and she would have told him so, but it might have dampened the triumph for them both.

*

Ingrid rang the bell to the family apartment in Windscheid-straße. She heard a window open above her and then bang shut. When she took a step back and stared up, the windows were black. She rang the bell again, but there was no answer. She should have forewarned Ann-Kathrin that she was coming, but she had been afraid that the news would get back to her parents before she had left Buckow. She tried the bell for Ann-Kathrin's rooms in the side building of their block. Again no one came, and finally she reached Herr Schwarz, the caretaker, a large friendly man with eye-laps so large that his wire-frame glasses rested on them. He nodded to her through the door and unlocked it.

'Fräulein Hoffmann! I am surprised. Are you in Berlin alone?'

'Yes,' Ingrid said. 'But just for a night. Ann-Kathrin was meant to meet me,' she lied, 'but I'm quite sure it's no fault of hers. The letter must have gone missing.'

'Well, barely a thing comes through now, Fräulein. The government militias have gone wild. They shot twenty-five people at Stettiner Bahnhof today, if you can believe it. It's been a mess since November, but at least it's not been bloody until now.'

'Have you all been safe here?' she said, as he locked the door behind her.

'Oh, yes, quite safe. One wonders how it'll come off, of course, but in Charlottenburg one is out of the worst of it, I suppose.'

She followed him upstairs. 'Do you need a key?' he asked.

'Not if Ann-Kathrin comes back tonight.'

'She was certainly here today, so I'm sure she's just out on errands. I'll leave a note for her to say you're back for the evening. She'll come right up.'

He let her into the apartment and she clicked on the electric lights. She put down her bag in the empty hall, where pale rectangles on the wall revealed where pictures, now in storage, had hung. She looked into the drawing room. It was filled with the sheeted shapes of their furniture.

She had brought her stolen pipe, which she lit and smoked as she wandered into the in-between room. Some of the pictures had been left on the walls. The bigger ones were also covered in sheets, but there was one small picture, a watercolour of an ivy-clad garden gate, that was uncovered. She smiled at the thought of Ann-Kathrin keeping one favourite picture on show to decorate her intermittent cleaning.

In her father's office, she rested her pipe in his ashtray and felt around on the highest reachable shelf for the key to his desk. She searched through stationery, ink pots, metal nibs, ribbons and letters, opened and unopened, but there was no sign of anything mentioning Hans Ziegler. All of the correspondence kept in his desk drawers were sentimental things written by herself and Margarete, love letters from her mother and postcards from places they had visited on their journey to and from Southwest Africa.

She locked up and, in search of schnapps to get the chill out of her, she walked through to the dining room, and was there struck by something amiss. The air was different, warmer and drier, and there was a pleasant smell of something baked. She turned the light on and found the room just as desolate as the others, their long dining table under its white sheet, like a sarcophagus.

She felt a pleasant warmth on her cheek. She looked at the oven in the corner of the room, a blue-and-white monolith over two metres high, and she put her hands on the glossy Dutch tiles. They were hot. She opened the oven door; it had been swept out, but it released a hot dusty breath. She reached in, tapped the pipe out and secreted it in her jacket pocket. 'Ann-Kathrin? Hello?'

She went through into the back of the apartment where the kitchens were. 'Hello?' she called.

She turned the light on in the kitchen. The good smell filled the room and there on the back of the stove sat a dark loaf of bread. She touched the range. It was still warm and she took the hook and lifted off the hot plate. There in the bowels of the oven orange embers glowed.

'Fräulein Hoffmann!'

Ingrid shrieked and dropped the hook and hotplate.

Ann-Kathrin, in the doorway, screamed in response.

'Good God! Ann-Kathrin, you scared the life out of me.'

'And you out of me, Fräulein Hoffmann!' Indeed, Ann-Kathrin looked terrible: thin, pale and trembling.

'My dear Ann-Kathrin, I'm terribly sorry. Don't be frightened. We're not back; it's only me. I did write, but it mustn't have come.'

This didn't calm Ann-Kathrin, who said, 'But you can't stay here, it's quite impossible. It's all closed up. We must telephone Buckow and ask what's to be done.'

'But I don't need a thing, I really don't. And look, you're already using the stoves.'

Ann-Kathrin seemed to take this personally, saying, 'I haven't been taking advantage, Fräulein Hoffmann. We've had terrible problems with the range in our rooms and Herr

327

Hoffmann begged me to use this one while you were all away.'

'Of course! I didn't mean it as an affront. I just meant it was quite warm enough for me to rough it in my old room.'

'The bedrooms are freezing.'

'They can't be that bad,' said Ingrid, going for the door. 'I'm far hardier than you think.'

'No, Fräulein Hoffmann,' Ann-Kathrin said, barring her way. 'They're quite unsuitable and your father would never forgive me if I let you sleep in a shut-up apartment.'

Ingrid realised, with embarrassment, that Ann-Kathrin was likely sleeping in their rooms herself. 'I see,' she said.

'I'm sorry miss, but you must understand. If I'd heard earlier . . . '

Ingrid pushed past her and said, 'Then let me phone Fräulein Mandelbaum. I've obviously disturbed you.'

'Yes, Fräulein, it would be sensible if you were able to stay with someone else. That would be the wisest option, really. For your health.'

'Yes, don't lay it on with a trowel, Ann-Kathrin. I'll be gone the moment I can.'

She marched through to her father's study, Ann-Kathrin at her heels like a jilted lover, and picked up the phone. 'Monbijou 465, please,' she said. She was connected and the Mandelbaums' servant, Trude, answered.

'Trude, it's Fräulein Hoffmann. May I speak with Fräulein Hannah?'

'Of course, madam,' came the answer and a few seconds later Hannah's voice.

'Oh, thank God you're there, Hannah. It turns out I can't stay at Windscheidstraße.'

'Of course not, you silly thing. I bet the servants are livid.'

'They are rather.' To add to the pathos for Ann-Kathrin's sake, she added, 'I'm having the most terrible day – I was beset by revolutionaries on the train, and now don't even have a bed to sleep in.'

'Ghastly, Ingrid! Take a cab immediately. Trude will pay for it when you arrive, don't think of trying.'

'I'm terribly sorry. I'll be there in half an hour or so.'

'Quite right,' Hannah said.

Ingrid put the receiver back on its hook.

'It's all arranged,' Ingrid said.

'It really is for the best, Fräulein,' said Ann-Kathrin miserably, and Ingrid felt ashamed for being bad-tempered with her. She walked past her, through the dining room, and stopped by the little uncovered picture. Ann-Kathrin was in the doorway, holding onto the frame, trembling.

As a peace offering, Ingrid said, 'It's a lovely picture, this one. It was my and Margarete's favourite. We used to make all sorts of stories up about what we might find behind the little gate. I'm glad you like it too.'

'Yes, madam,' Ann-Kathrin said. 'I do.'

Ingrid picked up her case and left the apartment. When she got onto the street she looked up at the window and saw Ann-Kathrin. Ingrid hailed a cab, but couldn't shake off the sense of Ann-Kathrin watching her until she was over the Spree and into Berlin proper.

*

The Droschke driver had to take a detour around the Tiergarten. As they turned up Friedrichstraße, she rubbed the condensation from the window and watched the soldiers and sailors who peppered the walkways in front of the shop fronts with small squares of card and wood scrawled with pleas for food and money, some blind, others missing arms and legs. Shops were still open, but the shelves were bare and the proprietors, fat with layers of clothes in their unheated stores, looked anaemic and stricken.

Ingrid disembarked on the corner of the small park outside Monbijou Palace. Hannah had already appeared at the grand entrance to her block and was pushing a plump maid down the steps with a purse in her hand. 'Ingrid, darling, isn't this marvellous? What a delight,' she said, embracing her and covering her cold cheeks with kisses. She dragged Ingrid to the first floor of her building, taking her straight through the hall and into the drawing room, shouting, 'We only have Trude at the moment, so we have to hang up our own things,' and disappearing with their coats.

Ingrid, dazed, took in the room around her. The warmth made her face sting. She pulled her blouse away from her skin, lest she should sweat into it before she had met the rest of Hannah's family. She had been to the apartment many times before, but was always picking Hannah up and had never ventured into their living room.

She was struck by a long, framed lithograph of people wearing Polish dress drinking and dancing around a bar manned by a Jewish barkeeper and accompanied by a Jewish fiddler. There were also etchings of Italy, a watercolour, a painting of a man and a woman with Hebrew writing in stained gold letters beneath. On the floor, on tables and dressers, lay wonderfully incongruous objects: a sitar, an art nouveau nymph, Moroccan blankets over the furniture trailing feathery tassels, a simple menorah, an ugly novelty ashtray in the shape of an open hand. And there were two oil paintings quite unlike anything that Ingrid had seen before: blocks of colour laid on top of one another, exploding from the centre of the picture, and flying across the surface.

'Fräulein Hoffmann,' said a woman's voice. 'You're very welcome.'

She turned to find Hannah's mother standing in the doorway. Her black hair, tied back into a large bun, was streaked with three thick strips of white. Her face was harder than her daughter's, but there was something of Hannah's jovial wickedness in her eyes. She gave the impression, in her smile, that there was a shared joke between them, something unmentionably funny that they were keeping to themselves.

'Come in then,' she called into the hallway. As she gave Ingrid her hand, a young man with thick black hair and a neat beard appeared by her side.

'You remember Saul,' Frau Mandelbaum said.

'It is good to see you again,' Ingrid said. She had seen him last before the war, when he was still an anxious youth, escaping past her in the hallway with his books. He had grown into a slim, tall man. His face was pleasant at rest, but lovely when he smiled, giving off a different kind of warmth to his sister – something reassuring, where Hannah's was passionate.

'You've been well, I hope,' Saul said, and flushed red.

Frau Mandelbaum touched his cheek. 'Just back from the Front. It's terrifying what's happening in their name. You must get out of the city again as soon as you can, dear. We would if we could, but there's so much to be done. Saul can escort you back on the train – I heard there was some ugliness on your way down.'

'Discretion, Mother!' Hannah said, coming into the room and throwing her gloves off into a brass Indian rice tray.

'Must you repeat everything I tell you so soon after you hear it?'

'Dear, don't try to be precious because you've got a friend to visit.'

'Mother!' Hannah said, falling onto the sofa with affected disdain, but, like her brother, also flushing red at the slightest hint of embarrassment.

'I'm going to pay a call on Trude – she will no doubt be doing something unwise with the trout. Ingrid, don't let Hannah badger you – but you know her well enough to fight your corner, I'm sure,' she said and was gone.

'Sit, sit,' said Hannah.

Ingrid did as she was told and Saul took a seat in a modern chair. The legs of it curved into the seat and then behind him, creating the back, in one organic piece, as if it had grown up from the carpet. He crossed his legs.

'Did you want to contribute?' Hannah said to him.

'I was thinking before I spoke,' Saul said.

'How terribly mature of you,' said Hannah. 'And what was it you were thinking?'

Saul paused to adjust his watch chain, then said, 'I was simply going to wish Fräulein Hoffmann all the best for her meeting with Frau von Galen.' He looked Ingrid in the eye for a second and added, 'She is an influential woman.'

'Well,' said Hannah, performing the sign of the cross the wrong way round. 'Saul has blessed your visit, Ingrid. You may sleep happy tonight.'

Saul brushed the teasing away with one hand. He turned to a side table and picked up a wedding invitation on top of a pile of correspondence and pretended to read it. Ingrid wondered who was marrying in the middle of a revolution. Or were there many girls greeting their returning heroes, wanting or having to be married quickly? Perhaps they were two a penny in Berlin; the Hoffmanns didn't have enough friends to know.

'I'm sorry about my letter, about the Ovambo group at Berlin Zoo,' Ingrid said. 'I almost wrote to retract it.'

'Ingrid, don't be ridiculous,' said Hannah. 'Of course you want to know what happened to him. It's all so tragic. I wrote you the most marvellous letter back full of exclamation marks. You'll get it when you return to the sticks.'

'Did you go to Berlin Zoo? Is the living museum still there?'

'Before we get to all that, dearest, might I ask if it's not best that the whole thing is left alone? I don't want to bat you back when you feel you've been struggling against the tide all along, but you did say this African might have killed someone.'

'In Africa,' said Ingrid. 'Under very specific circumstances. And that's only what my father told me; it might just be another of his lies. Hannah, I know I should leave it be, but I would go mad thinking that Hans might have been in Buckow when Margarete disappeared, but that I never knew for sure.'

'She was unwell, Ingrid. She'd been unwell for years.'

'Yes, I know, but she was well at the wedding. I know it might be wishful thinking, but I was there for all of those nervous attacks and she wasn't in that state. But if something had set it off, had driven her to ... to do whatever she did. Well, I want to know what that was. If I can find it out, I have to.'

Hannah tapped her foot on the floor as she considered what Ingrid had said. 'OK,' she said. 'I did find out about the living museum at Berlin Zoo and it was closed when the war started.'

'Yes,' said Ingrid, smiling but despairing. 'I expected that, of course.'

'But then I found the manager.'

'How?' said Ingrid, brightening.

'He still works with the zoo, but now does lizards. Can you imagine? I dug him out in the reptile house, and interrogated the poor man surrounded by little scaly creatures.'

'You didn't!'

'Of course, darling. You said it was important.'

'I did,' said Ingrid, holding her friend's hand. 'What did he say?'

'He didn't know anything about this Hans Ziegler of yours, and didn't remember any other Africans other than his Africans, so I asked if I could talk to them. Of course nearly all of them either went back to Africa or were from British colonies, so fought for them. One lucky chap made it back to the Congo and then we sank him on Lake Tanganyika. A few stayed though.'

'In Berlin?'

'Yes. He'd got back in touch with them before the end of the war about a new show, but nothing came of it. The women were married and wouldn't have anything more to do with him. There was a man too, but he has apparently become an upstanding Berliner and works on the trams as a conductor. The idea of sitting about in the cold banging drums in front of Germans didn't appeal any more, apparently.'

'Does he know where he is now?'

'No, I'm afraid he didn't,' said Hannah. 'But I do.'

'How?' said Ingrid.

'Oh, I just rode the trams until I spotted him. He's called Herr Winzer. Berlin is hardly replete with African tram conductors. It was glorious fun. I've seen the whole of Berlin – the strangest corners.'

'You must have been at it all week!'

'Three or four days.'

'Hannah, it's unbelievable.'

'I was quietly impressed with myself. It was a hoot. I felt like I was in one of those terrible Edgar Wallace novels. And I hardly have anything else to entertain myself with since Herr Rabe ejected us from the ministry.'

'Did you talk to Herr Winter?'

'Winzer. With a "z". No, I thought you should do that. What have I got to say to him? He's on the number fifty-two tomorrow from midday. We'll need to catch it at Alexanderplatz. Luxemburg and Liebknecht have published the new Spartacus League programme – I'm handing it out with Mother in the morning, so we could meet at two. We mustn't be riding the trams after dark. That would give even me the willies.'

'Oh Hannah,' Ingrid said and embraced her friend.

'Now, don't be soppy, Ingrid. That won't do at all.'

Ingrid fell back on the deep sofa. 'It'll be just before my meeting with von Galen.'

'Then let's do it the day after that.'

'No,' Ingrid said, 'I can't wait any more. I just want to know if it's a dead end and, if it is, get on with my life.' She looked at Hannah and smiled. 'Have you seen her? Frau Luxemburg? I read everything I can get my hands on.'

'Oh yes. I don't know how she has the energy. Did you read her article in the *Red Flag* last week about disarming the homecoming troops?'

'Yes,' said Ingrid. 'That was brave.'

'Wasn't it?'

'I say,' Saul piped up again, 'might one ask what you two are up to? I don't think you should be going into town at all at the moment. And what's this about an African killer?'

Hannah sighed and said, 'Saul, can't you reintegrate into polite society in silence?'

'Does she joke with you like this all the time too?' Saul said.

'She does tell a lot of jokes,' said Ingrid.

'Oh Saul,' Hannah said. 'Don't be dull.'

He sprang up from his chair and stood with his hands behind his back in front of the white canvases bursting with coloured shapes. Ingrid waited for him to say something, but he didn't; he just stood in front of the paintings, his head down. Hannah shrugged and hung her hand over the arm of the sofa, and they listened to the sounds of clattering crockery in the kitchen and a motorcar driving by in the street outside.

*

Ingrid and Hannah ran across Alexanderplatz to Dircksenstraße. 'Quickly!' Hannah shouted. Hannah got there first and put one foot on the step of the tram and cried, 'My foot's stuck!'

Ingrid saw the conductor moving towards the back of the tram. Just before he came to Hannah's aid, she climbed in and pulled Ingrid up behind her. 'It's free! What a relief!' she cried.

They paid the conductor and found a seat. Ingrid watched him walking down the little passage of the tram, turning the handle of his ticket machine and dropping coins into his leather wallet. Intermittently, she looked out of the window or said a word to Hannah, so that he didn't notice her watching him, but when she glanced at the other passengers on the tram, she saw that they were openly staring at him as he worked. The children asked their mothers, 'Why are his palms pink?' or said, 'He's like coal.' Even when the questions were put to him directly – a skinny boy asking, 'Why are you so black?' – he didn't respond, just cranked the handle of his ticket machine and said, 'Thank you.'

'Should we just say something?' Ingrid said.

'We should wait until it's empty,' Hannah said. 'The line doesn't end far out – I'm quite the expert now. We can catch him before we jump back on the returning tram.'

Ingrid thought about Saul in front of the modern paintings in Hannah's drawing room. 'What will your brother do now the war is over?' she said.

'My brother! Have you got eyes for Saul?'

'For God's sake!' said Ingrid. 'I was just trying to show an interest.'

'Oh, sisters-in-law!' she squealed. 'What a thought. Mother's a terrible liberal, you know. As long as I marry a good Ashkenazi Mensch, it would be a dream for them. One with a mixed marriage, one with a Jew; they'd be the envy of Oranienburgerstraße.'

'I'm sorry I asked.'

Hannah cackled. 'Well, he does nothing at the moment. My uncle – mother's brother – has the store in Spandau. He'll get him in there somehow.'

'He owns Mandelbaum's, the department store?'

'That's the one.'

'Doesn't that mean your mother's brother has the same surname as your father?'

Hannah laughed. 'They're not related. Honestly. Of course, we're all a bit more related than your lot, I'm sure.

Though I suspect there are plenty of Müllers that marry other Müllers.'

'My lot?'

'You gentiles. And especially with your family's ascendancy into the upper echelons in Buckow – you'll be spreading those hardy mongrel traits among all the inbreds.'

'Upper echelons? What do you mean by that? That we're social climbers?'

Hannah's smile dissipated a little, but the shape of it still clung to her lips. 'No, I meant ... It was a joke.'

'Well, there's barely any family left since Margarete died.'

'Sorry, Ingrid,' Hannah said, but Ingrid found the tone more cross than regretful. 'I thought we were joking.'

'Your brother's right – everything's a joke with you.'

Hannah, her smile completely faded, sat back in her seat and turned to the windows opposite.

This was the worst thing she could have done, because Ingrid expected a final cutting retort, as her mother would have thrown her, but Hannah just looked upset. Miserable and unsure of what she would even say to the conductor, Ingrid sat dumbly as the tram emptied. It pulled up to the final stop, and the last passenger, an elderly woman, climbed down to the street. The conductor stood at the open door, busying himself with his wallet, waiting for them to leave.

'Excuse me, are you Herr Winzer?' Ingrid said.

His eyes flicked up and he froze.

'My name is Ingrid Hoffmann – I was wondering if you could help me.'

He didn't move.

'I'm searching for someone, an old friend, from Southwest.'

'Fräulein,' he said, with a light African accent, 'I don't know anything about Southwest.'

'Are you not Ovambo?' she said, recalling the tribe from the wedding and hoping to ingratiate herself with her anthropological knowledge of Africa.

'What's an Ovamba?' he said.

'Ovambo. It's a tribe,' she said, then repeated, 'Southwest.'

He raised his chin and said, 'I live in Berlin, Fräulein. And I was born in what was German *East* Africa.'

Ingrid looked at Hannah, willing her to say, 'Let's just leave.' Instead, she said, 'Nevertheless, we're looking for an African man. There can't be that many of you chaps in Berlin. He's called ... What's he called again, Ingrid?'

'Hans Ziegler. You were in Buckow before the war, performing for a wedding as a group of Ovambo. It was the same time as Herr Ziegler was in that area, we think. We wondered if you'd seen him.'

'I don't know any Hans Ziegler.'

'We could make it worth your while,' Hannah said.

Ingrid tried to catch her eye. They were losing him and now Hannah was trying to bribe him.

'I don't know any Hans Ziegler,' he said, looking over at the driver. 'I've never been to Buckow.'

'We know you were there,' said Hannah.

They felt the tram rock as the driver climbed out of the cab at the front. 'I can't speak to you here,' he said.

'Why not?'

'I'll lose my job if I'm seen speaking to women who've been riding around in the tram all morning. They'll think something is up.'

'Where can we talk to you?'

'You can come to my apartment in Neukölln this

afternoon if you wish,' he said dismissively, climbing out of the tram himself and holding the barrier chain in his hand, ready to close off the entrance.

'Yes, that's fine,' Hannah said hopping down. 'Where?'

The man looked put out. 'Ratiborstraße 55.' He watched their faces to see if the address would put them off, then added, 'It's down by the Landwehr Canal. A side street.'

'Yes, very good,' Hannah said. 'We'll come.'

*

They walked down from the raised U-Bahn station, surrounded by shivering young men, who joined the crowds below. Men huddled together, divided by professions they had until recently held: soldier, sailor, factory worker. The crowds were dotted with the crackling coughs of the Blitzkatarrh survivors, struck down by the waves of flu that had washed over the city as the exhausted troops filled every empty bed and bedroom floor in Berlin. The steam of their breath rolled up into the December sky in clouds, and they appeared to Ingrid like horses, the same restless stillness, the same dense energy; a feeling that one of them could kick out suddenly and kill you; that if one startled it would spread through them and they would move en masse, vast and wild.

On the street, Hannah moved closer, and despite their briefly shared enmity, Ingrid took her arm as they walked down the side of the canal, in the direction of Görlitzer Bahnhof. The water of the canal was dark and slimy, the raggedy plants growing on its banks absorbing its blackness where they touched the poisonous water. Canal boats were arrayed along one side, a jagged mess of vessels and oil cloth, crawling with men hammering at wood and skinny dogs nervously sniffing around the decks.

They turned into Ratiborstraße. There were few crowds of men here, but many more children; groups of them huddled together in doorways, others screaming along the broken cobbles in shorts, their thin legs pounding the road. One little girl held a cat possessively to her chest; the animal was quite still, its legs stretched out in front of it, its head cocked in tired resignation. A boy had climbed a bare plane tree, knocking the remnants of snow from its branches, but his friends had wandered off and he called down to them plaintively for their attention and help.

They found Herr Winzer's name by the main door to the block and, asking the little girl with the cat, were met with a blank hostile stare, until Hannah said, 'The black man, dear,' which was rewarded with a pointed finger and the instruction, 'Back-building, fourth floor.'

They passed through two courtyards that smelt of animal dung; in the second they discovered the source: a row of empty stalls, the final one containing a grey-looking sow. As they passed it, and Hannah held her handkerchief to her nose, it squealed and shifted, making the iron sheets of its tight enclosure shudder, the sound rattling up the high walls and windows around them, rising to meet the sound of pneumonic coughs and a baby's screams.

The door to the apartment was opened by a frightened-looking black girl, not much younger than Hannah and Ingrid.

'My name's Fräulein Hoffmann,' Ingrid said, out of breath from the climb. 'I've come to see your father, Herr Winzer?'

The girl said, 'Yes, one moment.' She paused, unsure of herself, and then, her eyes flicking over to the door of the apartment opposite, said, 'You had better come in.'

They shuffled into the narrow corridor, which smelt of

cheap cooking fat, fried potatoes and onions. Herr Winzer stood in a doorway at the other end of the corridor. Changed out of his uniform, he was wearing a brown woollen suit, white shirt and a tie – a thin black strip dropping from his high collar. He let them pass him into a little reception room, modestly furnished, with a large brown oven that gave no heat, four wooden chairs and an oleograph of Jesus fishing on the Sea of Galilee.

'Please, take a seat. We are not used to visitors,' he said. 'I would offer you something but . . . '

'Oh don't worry, we'll have a dram at home. Gosh you're jolly high up,' Hannah said, peering down into the grubby courtyard.

'We don't have any alcohol at all in this house,' he said emphatically.

Hannah and Ingrid nodded. He gestured to the chairs and they sat.

'Thank you for seeing us,' Ingrid said.

'As I said, I think it's unlikely I can be of any help to you.'

'But you were in Buckow,' Ingrid said.

'I don't have anything to do with that *show* any more,' the man said.

'Of course,' said Ingrid. 'We found it ghastly too. I grew up in Africa.'

Herr Winzer met this information with blank indifference.

'When you were there in Buckow,' she said, 'I believe that this friend, Hans Ziegler, was there. I think it's possible that he used your presence there as a cover and that he might have made contact with my sister.'

'There were no other Africans in Buckow,' Herr Winzer said. 'Who was he?'

'A friend, as I said. He was our houseboy in Southwest.'

'British now,' said the man.

'Yes. He speaks English as well – or did.'

'Did he fight?'

'I don't know. I just know he was sent here before the war, but then he disappeared. He must have come through Berlin. I have a picture,' she said, which she produced from a pocket in her coat and held out to him. He took it. Hannah looked down at it too.

'Can I keep this?' Herr Winzer said.

'No,' said Ingrid and held out her hand. He returned it and she pushed it into her coat pocket, in between the leaves of her poems.

'Fräulein . . . ?'

'Hoffmann.'

'I really don't think I can help you. I'm very sorry. I may have been in Buckow, I was in many places, and I don't remember much about them. But I'm sure I would have remembered an African.'

'Aren't there any societies for African people in Berlin?' Hannah said.

Herr Winzer laughed. 'Really, Fräulein, I am as likely to be surprised to see a black face in the street here as you are.'

'Of course,' she said. 'But perhaps in your church, or . . . If it's a black church?'

'We are Mennonites. My church is not a black church. And they have closed them all down anyhow.'

'Closed down the churches?' Hannah said.

'Mennonites are pacifists.' He sat up straighter in his chair. 'We refuse to fight. In any wars.'

'Of course,' Ingrid said.

What was there really to discover? What would she do if she found Hans? Whatever her sister might have seen or

343

understood, she had decided to die, she had left her. What could Hans say that would change that?

'Ingrid?'

It was Hannah. She was standing, so was Herr Winzer.

Ingrid stood too and said, 'Herr Winzer, it's my sister, you see. She disappeared and, it's not that I believe that Herr Ziegler had anything to do with that, but he tried to get in touch with my father at that time and then disappeared. And it can't be a coincidence that my sister went missing at that exact moment. Not that he did anything to her, just that, I ... Perhaps he said something to her.' Hannah took her arm and tugged at her. 'My sister is ... was very impulsive. Or perhaps it was some sort of – I don't want to say revenge, but Papa owned land in Southwest, and perhaps ... Or perhaps the emotion of seeing him was too much, and she ... and she ...'

Herr Winzer blinked nervously. The trees in the court-yard rattled, releasing a flock of pigeons. 'She might have killed herself?' Herr Winzer said.

Ingrid nodded.

'She had tried before,' he said.

Ingrid nodded.

'My wife took her own life,' Herr Winzer said. 'Left me alone with my little girl. She tried many times and then one day during the war, while I was in Belgium carrying stretchers and could do nothing to stop her, she succeeded. She left me with my girl and now we will not see her in heaven.' He moved as if he was going to take Ingrid's hand, but stopped himself. He looked down at her fingers. 'There is no mystery in suicide, Fräulein Hoffmann, if that is what your search is about. No more than the mystery of death, the terror, in any of us. But some of us can stand it – the only real mystery is that we are able.'

Herr Winzer touched his tie-pin, then the studs on his collar.

'Come on,' Hannah said softly, pulling at Ingrid's arm. 'Come on Ingrid. Let's go.'

'I'm sorry,' Ingrid said. 'I am sorry.'

They walked back along the corridor. Through the glass in the kitchen door Ingrid caught sight of the girl again, waiting by the stove with her hands crossed in front of her and her head down, as if in prayer.

At the door Herr Winzer said, 'There is a woman, a Frau Weintraub, who came here from Rhodesia. She ran a boarding house near Hasenheide that was open to black people – there are very few who take us in. I can ask her if she knows anything about a Hans Ziegler.'

'Oh, thank you,' said Ingrid, but muted now. 'Let me leave you a card.' She took a thin pencil from her pocket and wrote the address of the house in Buckow on the back of one of her cards. 'This is where I'm staying at the moment. If you did hear anything, or . . . anything.'

'Of course,' he said.

As Ingrid descended the stairs, Hannah gripped her hand. Ingrid stopped. She scrunched up her eyes tightly and tears dropped onto the dusty painted wood of the floor. She felt Hannah's head on her shoulder and her arm round her waist. 'You've done your best, Ingrid,' she said.

Ingrid shook her head. 'I haven't done my best. I haven't at all.'

*

After much argument, Ingrid went to Frau von Galen's alone, distressed and fearing the return of the numbing despair that had taken hold of her after Margarete's disappearance.

Von Galen lived in a building on Wörther Platz, in an area of grand houses built during the seventies or eighties, whose residents still had the means to pay servants to clean the glass on their front doors. As she rounded one corner of the square, a housemaid stretched up gripping a grey rag, hacking back and forth, the stained underarm of her white blouse pressed to the pane below.

In the square there were children, the boys in short trousers despite the cold, screaming; their blue-mottled legs skipped around the tired men and women scattered on benches. The wooden slats were stained black from the previous night's rain, which had melted the snow. Their coats will get wet, Ingrid thought, but, as a gust of wind pulled a flurry of the plane trees' last yellow leaves from their speckled branches, she saw a common resignation in the stoic faces, as if the creeping seep of water up through their trousers, their skirts and their underskirts did not concern them any more.

At number fourteen, Ingrid found von Galen's name among the field of brass buttons and, knowing that any delay would suck the resolve from her, stabbed at the bell with her thumb.

The hall beyond the great glazed doors was empty. The white light shone onto the tiles on the floor: a cream and orange chequerboard bound in black. She heard hard boots rapidly striking the steps of the staircase. A middle-aged woman with long grey hair, loosely pinned, stepped into the hallway and stopped still. She stared at Ingrid through the pitted glass and threw a corner of her shawl over her shoulder. Was this von Galen, Ingrid thought, or the woman's servant?

The woman unlocked the door and pulled it open. It

shuddered and scraped, and she shouted, 'It's you, is it? Ingrid Hoffmann?'

'Yes,' said Ingrid.

'I beg your pardon?' said the woman, turning her ear towards her and pushing her grey hair behind it.

'Yes,' said Ingrid, 'I'm Ingrid Hoffmann.'

'You'd better come in then,' the woman said. 'I'm Frau von Galen.'

Ingrid walked in and Frau von Galen shoved the door shut, making Ingrid jump.

'Thank you for inviting me, Frau von Galen, I'm—'

'You look terribly unwell, my girl, like you've just been rescued from a fire,' von Galen said.

'Pardon?'

Von Galen walked on past her and turned left up the wide staircase. Ingrid followed, her legs aching as she tried to keep up with her rapid ascent. 'Like you've been pulled from the sea barely alive. You're horribly pale,' said von Galen, her voice echoing against the cold painted walls.

'No, I just—'

'We're first floor, so you won't have to come far in those boots,' she said.

Ingrid looked down at her plain black boots and then at von Galen's, which, other than being a little shorter at the heel, looked almost identical.

Von Galen entered first and held the door open, raising her arm to guide Ingrid in. The apartment opened straight onto a long room-sized hall with a balcony at one end. The white light fell on an ornate Turkish rug, red at the edges, but worn to a dirty pink in the centre. The walls were covered in pictures: etchings of the Lorelei and the Rhine Valley, daguerreotypes of men with great white whiskers in heavy Gründerzeit clothes, black shining pools of oil paint in gilt frames with bouquets and women's hands and faces emerging from the dark. There was a round table at one end of the runner, as if marking its end point, and on the table a brass sculpture of a woman: Daphne, her arms outstretched, the fingers turning into branches. At least Ingrid supposed it was her, because she only saw the branching fingers, the table being covered with piles of books in various faded shades: yellow, blue, forest green.

'Come this way,' von Galen said, and led Ingrid into a warm sitting room. Ingrid could hear the glass-like splitting of the burning coal behind the door of a huge tiled stove that reached up to the ceiling, decorated with pineapples and topped with green-glazed pineapple leaves splaying out overhead.

There was a divan covered with scratchy Arabian blankets, and an armchair pulled up to a side table containing a coffee pot, with steam curling up from its spout, and there, beside a sugar bowl, lay Ingrid's manuscript. 'So here we are, Fräulein Hoffmann,' von Galen said, circling the little table and dropping onto the divan. 'You will have coffee,' she said, pouring two cups. 'It's chicory – I'm not the sort of woman who hoards luxuries that could be better used elsewhere. There's no milk, of course. There's nothing in this city at the moment except returning soldiers, and half of them don't look like they're going to survive the winter, certainly not this influenza.' She pushed the cup intended for Ingrid towards the armchair she was meant to sit in. 'But there's always poetry.'

Frau von Galen, half reclining, put her finger to her temple. Her hands were studded with antique-looking rings. Her dress was simple, but new, the cut modern. The shawl was very old, but also very fine, intricately woven with Alpine flowers picked out in reedy gold thread.

'Throw your coat anywhere,' Frau von Galen said. 'We do not stand on ceremony here, dear. We don't have the servants for it. I've one girl left – Waltraud – but she is beset with consumption most of the year, so we get by as best we can. I'm sure it's the same for your people.'

'Yes,' Ingrid murmured, taking off her gloves and coat, unpinning her hat. She laid them as requested on a low leather ottoman, pushing the pin through the mauve ribbon around the brim, and then sat in the armchair allotted her and clasped her hands together. Her palms were sweating.

'Thank you for taking the time and—'

'Don't thank me,' Frau von Galen said. 'I publish. You have something to sell me – we are like two businessmen, you and I.'

Ingrid smiled, unable to come up with a response to this that sounded either witty or sensible, her thoughts interrupted by Herr Winzer, his daughter, his dead wife. The smile seemed to disappoint von Galen; she offered Ingrid a slow blink, keeping her eyes closed for a second too long, enduring.

When she opened them, she said, 'Tell me about the collection.'

Ingrid looked away from her, at the wall opposite, moving her wet palms against each other. She was distracted by a stuffed owl, frozen as it pounced on a mouse whose dusty little tail bent in a dramatic curve. She felt her lips formed to make a sound, but the owl stared down at her and she had already forgotten the question. 'Collection' she did remember, though, and said, hot with embarrassment, 'The poems are mostly by women.'

'Yes, I have read them, Fräulein Hoffmann. But tell me what your intention was.'

Ingrid shifted in her seat. She looked down at the table, but the owl remained a white speckled presence in her peripheral vision. The coffee smelt pleasant enough, but she couldn't possibly drink it; couldn't possibly reach out and pick it up and put it to her lips. The distance seemed unfathomable. 'Intention' she had said. 'My intention was ... My intention was ... There was no intention.'

Frau von Galen let out two hard laughs, 'Ha ha.'

Ingrid laughed too, her body flushed and she relaxed. Von Galen's look was one of patronising approval, that Ingrid was finally dropping her affectations.

'There was no intention,' Ingrid went on. 'There are a lot of poems by women, because I was looking for good things to translate that hadn't been translated before, and a lot of those were written by women. There's no point to it, other than that they were poems I liked.'

'You see no thread?'

'Yes, but not an intentional one.'

'Never mind intentional,' said Frau von Galen. 'There is a thread, isn't there?'

'Yes,' Ingrid said, sounding like a schoolgirl and realising that von Galen probably wished her to sound like an adult. Ingrid sifted through the poems in her head, seeing patterns, repeated tones and shapes. 'The lives of women and ...'

Frau von Galen nodded. 'The minutiae of women's lives. Women taken seriously, taken as the subject of poetry. That seems to be the case for many of them, certainly.'

'Yes,' said Ingrid, realising that she was leaning back in the armchair. Thrilled at being talked to this way, but

350

feeling, at the same time, that, despite righting her ship, she might be capsized at any moment. 'The landscape of being a woman. Love, of course, but also friendship, the room, the rooms we live in.'

'Yes, that's good,' said Frau von Galen. The compliment was thrilling. 'The rooms of a woman's life, like an emotional landscape. That's good. I want you to think about that. In terms of a book. Because these are not right yet – they don't hang together yet, and there's an uncomfortable seam of literalness in the translation at points, which needs excising. Avoided mostly, but it raises its head, especially when you're dealing with too many French verbs all together.'

Ingrid winced at the criticism, was brought down by 'not right yet' and the weary sense of more work that she might not be able to accomplish. But she remained mesmerised by the words she repeated back to Frau von Galen: 'A book?'

'Yes, I want you to think about this as a proper collection. One that's publishable. It doesn't need much – some cuts, perhaps one or two new poems, some of this exactness knocked out. When can you get it done by?'

'Get what done by?'

'The changes. How long will it take to have a proper manuscript pulled together? I should like a foreword – nothing elaborate. Just something that suggests a way in. I don't want anything didactic, d'you hear?'

Ingrid nodded.

'So?'

Ingrid thought about her hour or two at von Ketz's desk. If they were to stay in Buckow and she were able to keep a clear head, she might manage to repair things slowly. Two weeks to a poem. A month to do each new one, because there would be holes as she edited. She would have to work out a way of getting to libraries with French and English books. The foreword would take her a few weeks. And there would be editing. 'Perhaps a year,' Ingrid said.

'A year!' Frau von Galen said. 'What a thought! Good God, girl! How long are you working each day?'

'Three or four hours,' she lied.

'Are you married?'

'No – I live with my parents. In Buckow, at the moment, but normally in Charlottenburg.'

'That's no good,' von Galen said. 'That's no good at all. You must come here I suppose. There's room, though you won't be waited on, I can promise you that. This heat is only because you're a visitor – I'm swaddled like the Christ child most of the time.'

'Come here?'

'Yes, you must come here and finish the book. Your parents can spare you for a few months. I shall write to them.'

'But I would have to—'

'You have something more important to do? More important than this?'

'Can I—?'

'Think about it if you must, but I'll need an answer within a week. I'll send the letter to you today to give to your parents and if you don't receive it within that time – it is all chaos here – then you must send a telegram. I would rather avoid travelling out. It is dangerous to be too long on the streets.'

'Of course,' said Ingrid. She had received the offer she wanted, or some form of it, and felt as if she had been flayed.

'Which one do you like best?' said Frau von Galen.

'Brontë,' said Ingrid, unable to dissemble.

'Yes, that's good, isn't it? And which one did he like?'

'Who?'

Frau von Galen lifted her chin up as if she were going to nod, but she didn't nod. 'You gave this to a man to read – for his approval.'

'Necker-Weiß?'

'Vain child.'

'Yes,' said Ingrid, her face burning. That was exactly what she was – a girl, desperate to be approved of, by that man, by this woman, but unable to bear it when she got it.

'And that ridiculous waxed moustache,' said Frau von Galen. In the seconds it took Ingrid to realise that Necker-Weiß was the vain child and to feel great shame at having apparently approved this judgement so readily, von Galen said, 'Well? Which one did Necker-Weiß like best?'

'He liked Eliot best. But he thought she was a man.'

Von Galen laughed. 'Go on then,' she said. 'Read it to me.'

Ingrid pushed herself up unsteadily and held out her hand to take the manuscript. Frau von Galen remained immobile. 'You don't know it by heart?'

Ingrid nodded. She rubbed her wet hands on her skirt and said:

'The sky is cloudy, yellowed by smoke.
The view: those houses opposite
Cutting the sky with one long line of wall
Like solid fog: far as the eye can reach
Monotony of surface and of form
Without a break to hang a guess upon.
No bird can make a shadow as it flies—'

'Can it not?

'I beg your pardon?'

'Can a bird make no shadow as it flies?'

'I . . .' said Ingrid. 'I don't know, but . . ..'

'Well, it's not bad I suppose – masculine, but domestic – good forms. You've caught it well – that "reach" is more of a "stretch" in the original, but "reach" is good, perhaps "reach" is better,' she said, offering the word in English. 'I always find her a bit provincial, but that's of course the point. I understand her, even if I don't like her, and that's important. That's vital.'

'I think provincial is unfair. She wrote about the provinces, but there's nothing provincial about the depth. The intellectual depth.'

Frau von Galen smiled. 'Perhaps I've underestimated her.'

'Perhaps,' said Ingrid weakly, amazed both at the forcefulness of her opinion and at von Galen's thoughtful acceptance of it.

'Forget Necker-Weiß and his kind. Is that clear? Forget him. Write for yourself. I don't mean narcissistically, I mean imagine yourself as the reader – informed, intelligent, sensual.' Ingrid shrank at the word.

Frau von Galen took in a deep breath and released it slowly, a sigh, her index finger still attached to her temple as if she was pointing at herself. 'What's this block this afternoon? What's this misery, this confusion? I don't see it in your writing, but you're deeply distracted, and it'll be no good to you. A man? You haven't even drunk your coffee. This is hard to get; even the fake stuff. Who is it? You're in Berlin for something else.'

'My sister,' said Ingrid, her bottom lip trembling, but managing to hold back the tears.

Frau von Galen, apparently unmoved, drank Ingrid's coffee. 'Well, it's been a pleasure, Fräulein Hoffmann. You must publish under your own name,' she said, standing. 'I wish you well with whatever you are searching for. Let it be dealt with when you come back to me, mind.'

Returning to Buckow, Ingrid sat dazed on her third-class bench. Her mind moved between von Galen and the book, her sister and Hans, making each scenario appear unreal, like two separate dreams. If she were able to forget her sister and Hans, able to go back to Buckow and accept that there were mysteries which might explain their fate, but about which she had the strength to remain ignorant, then that would be her triumph. She would return to von Galen. But when she thought about Margarete's face, about the feel of Hans's hand on her back guiding her out to her lesson, she knew she would keep digging at the secrets, whatever they destroyed.

Haus am See,
Buckow, Brandenburg

— January 1919 —

Cold and anxiety kept Ingrid half awake throughout the night, but it was the sound of a shot echoing in the woods that woke her fully, and she pulled the blankets over her head to try and warm her nose and ears, where it smelt of old goose down and her stale breath. She heard the door rattle.

'Yes?' she said, muffled by the counterpane, rubbing the sleep out from her eyelashes.

'It's Renate, miss,' came the voice. 'We haven't enough coal to do your stove here, but there's a roaring one in the drawing room, and your mother is taking her breakfast there. She said I might mention it.'

'Yes, thank you, Renate.'

Renate didn't move away at once, but paused behind the door, as if listening for movement. Ingrid stretched so that the springs of her mattress rang out and heard, in response, the sound of Renate's boots dissipating on the corridor floor.

She rolled onto her side and looked at the cream leather

suitcase hidden beneath her desk. She would send a telegram to her mother from Berlin. The note from her last trip
had been taken badly and her mother was searching Ingrid
out every hour with a banal question or request. Ingrid
would write: 'With v Galen. Don't worry. Sending letter
tomorrow.' Of course, she had no money for this telegram.
She would have to steal the marks from her father.

Ingrid reached out from her bed and lifted the heavy
curtain. The window was translucent, filled with sparkling
swirls, iced onto the inside of the pane. Experimentally
she blew a cone of breath into the cold air and it rolled out
straight, like cigar smoke. She didn't believe that running
away would cause her parents to abandon her. Anyhow,
it wasn't really running away, because she was twenty-
eight, she was old. Yet she wasn't sure if the risk – however
small – was worth the gain, because no book of poetry, however lovingly published, would really offer her a new life,
unsupported.

Every other route she had explored, though, was impossible. Christmas had come and she had watched her mother,
von Ketz and Horvath laughing behind the shimmering
heat of the dinner-table candles. Ingrid had chewed the
thin Lebkuchen as she lit the candles on the tree, had
stared at the brown pebble in the church at Oberbarnim at
midnight mass, had sneaked into the garden with her pipe
and sat shivering in the woods smoking and watching the
wrens and the blackbirds working over the dead leaves for
insects. Hiding out in Kassel, the socialist Chancellor Ebert
had ordered the shakily controlled paramilitary Freikorps to
fire on the sailors stationed in Berlin City Palace, the same
sailors that had begun the revolution that Ebert now led.
Seventy had died and Ebert had shut down the *Red Flag*.

Now only able to glean her information from the *Allgemeine*, Ingrid read that Rosa Luxemburg and Karl Liebknecht had disbanded the Spartacists to found the Communist Party of Germany as 1918 turned into 1919. Even in this new forum, Luxemburg's calls to delay direct action until the communists had the majority support of the German people were overruled and the party demanded mass strikes. The tightrope walker's pole was dropping from side to side in ever more extreme swings and Ingrid felt that they were all about to fall off.

She had let the new year come and go, poured molten lead sizzling into a bowl of water and listened to her mother reading out the meaning of the fish-shaped gobbet it produced. She had watched her father light an old rocket, found in the cellar, that smoked and popped on the ground, exploding loudly in red sparks, making Horvath scream and giving von Ketz the shakes for the rest of the evening. But the spirit of Christmas and the clean slate of the new year changed nothing. The house was still filled with the ghosts of Hans and Margarete and the lies of her family, the sense of the nation collapsing in on itself. She knew that work that mattered was being offered by Frau von Galen. And if it came to naught? She wouldn't think about it. She had thought about it all too much. She must act.

She fell briefly back to sleep and was woken again by what could only be her mother's sharp tap tap tap on the door. She waited for it to spring open, but the corridor was silent. She roused herself, put her feet on the dark parquet, cold as marble, pulled the door handle, her throat open to emit a groan of despair, but her mother wasn't there. She peered out; the corridor, blue in the morning light, was empty.

*

Breakfast was laid out on a sideboard for them, in accordance with Frau Hoffmann's instructions, though the meagre offering looked sad on the great porcelain dishes her mother favoured. Ingrid knew – because she had heard it whispered conspiratorially behind the scullery window – that the servants' food was included to give the impression of abundance. This did not curb her mother's appetite, who dropped slices of black bread onto her plate significantly, but for Ingrid it took all the joy out of the meal, and she did with as little as she was able, trying but always failing to read in Renate's face whether the effort was appreciated. Of course it didn't matter any more – she might never see Renate or the house again.

'Why do you always eat like a bird now?' her mother said.

'She worries about her figure, I shouldn't wonder,' said her father, draining his coffee cup in two gulps and refilling it.

'I don't!' Ingrid said. 'I just don't have an appetite. And there are people starving in Berlin.' She mustn't sulk. She must leave them with a happy memory of her.

'That's hardly relevant, Ingrid – people are always starving. You're a handsome girl – you mustn't try to be thin and pretty,' her mother said. 'A good eater is a wonderful thing.'

Ingrid looked over her mother's shoulder, so as not to encourage the conversation further. Above the sideboard was a picture of the Kaiser and one of the Kaiserin in separate gilt ovals mounted on the wall. Soon there would be no need for these icons, and they would become as meaningless and decorative as watercolours of flowers.

A silence descended on the room. She looked at her

359

mother's face; her mouth was ajar. The Baroness was standing in the doorway with her wet lop-sided smile. She turned her head slowly, eyeing each of them in turn.

'Breakfast,' she slurred and stumbled forward.

Von Ketz leapt from his seat and gripped her arm. 'Mother, where's your nurse?'

Tears spilled from the Baroness's watery red lids. Her head swung as if it had been cut loose from a rope and she looked at Ingrid. One half of her mouth smiled. She held out her hand.

'What have you got there?' Ingrid heard her mother saying, but as Frau Hoffmann approached, the Baroness's face darkened and she lifted her shoulder, like a child shielding a secret from prying adult fingers.

'For her,' she said hoarsely and looked at Ingrid again.

She was holding a letter. Ingrid moved towards her, slowly, as if she were a wild animal, and took the letter, tugging it loose from her stiff fingers. Ingrid's name and the address of the house was written in a tight sepia script, self-consciously beautiful. The Baroness collapsed like a dropped puppet. Von Ketz caught her and steered her out of the room, muttering warm words under his breath.

Her mother was close; Ingrid walked over to the portraits of the Kaiser and Kaiserin, so that there was a little space between them. She heard her mother sit.

'Poor soul,' Horvath said.

'Indeed, indeed,' her mother said. 'What did she give you, Ingrid?'

'A letter,' said Ingrid.

'Is it postmarked?'

'Yes.'

'Then she must have picked it up from the letter tray

before Renate brought it through. Lord, she must have been wandering around for hours. We must talk to that nurse. Who's it from dear?' Her mother, holding a slice of bread, turned and held on to the back of the dining chair. The blood sausage fell from her bread and hit her plate with a plop. 'Who might it be from?'

Her father came to the sideboard, taking an apple. He looked over her shoulder. 'The hand of a lover, I'd say.'

'Is it, Ingrid?' her mother said seriously, putting the bread down and moving her chair, so that she could turn around properly.

Ingrid didn't answer. She turned the letter over and read a familiar Berlin address on the back of it. It took her a few moments to connect 'Ratiborstraße' with the darkness and poverty of Herr Winzer's street, courtyard and apartment.

'How's the apple?' her mother said to her father. 'Some great mind decided to have the kitchen's hot-water pipe run through the cellar and I'm worried they're spoiling down there.'

He cut a slice from it and bit into it. 'A bit floury,' he said.

Her mother threw up her arms and turned back to the table. 'A bit floury! You see!' she said.

'I'm going into the drawing room,' Ingrid said.

'Yes, yes, do read your letter in private!' her mother said.

'No, it's just I'm cold,' Ingrid muttered, and left the room.

*

In the plump comfort of the chair nearest the stove, usually colonised by her mother, Ingrid read:

Dear Fräulein Hoffmann,

I was both disturbed and somewhat dubious about your visit and whether I might at all be able to help you find your Herr Ziegler. Nevertheless, I did promise you that I would talk to Frau Weintraub, and a promise made before any man or woman is a promise made before God.

The name meant nothing to Frau Weintraub, but I took the liberty of giving her your card, so that she might contact you directly should she recall any detail that might help your cause. It was this card that gave her pause on account of your current address in Buckow.

Frau Weintraub had a guest before the war whom she remembered, because he spoke English – he claimed to be from Rhodesia and gave his name as Mr Courtman. He paid for his lodgings in advance. When, at the end of that month, he had not returned, she found in his room a note stating that, in the event of his not returning, she should send a letter addressed to him at First Floor, 65 Hauptstraße, Buckow, Brandenburg.

I am quite sure that you will not find Herr Ziegler or your sister there after all these years, but the Buckow address might be of help for further enquiries you may wish to make unaided.

Frau Weintraub assisted me after learning of the tragedy of your plight and through a personal connection to myself. She has no desire to excite the interest of the law, especially in these strange and lawless times, and hopes that this information may be given in exchange for complete confidence on your side. I have vouched for you, Fräulein Hoffmann, and I hope you will not disappoint me.

If these details are of any use to you, please do not try to
recompense me – I have no need of charity. And, now that I
have aided you, I would ask you to refrain from contacting
me again. I hope you will take this in the spirit in which
it is intended – as the request of a servant of God who
disdains, as he must, earthly comforts, especially those born
of intrigue.
  I remain your faithful servant, in God,
    Thaddeus Winzer

Mr Courtman must be Hans, Ingrid thought. And if he was,
he had come here to Buckow before Margarete disappeared.

Ingrid looked at the closed door of the drawing room. She
heard the coals in the stove shifting with a light, dry tinkle.

What had he told her or done to her?

A little of her old sorrow and loss was replaced with anger.
Had he come for Margarete? Why her and not Ingrid? She
recalled Hans's smile, his lips breaking to show his teeth,
the crow blackness of the hair at his temples.

She thought about showing the letter to her parents, but
then realised that her father's revelations in the cellar were
still lies. Hans had been here; her father had said he hadn't.
She memorised the address on Hauptstraße in Buckow,
opened the stove and threw the letter inside. It flamed
brightly and she shut it away.

The door opened. It was her mother.

'Ingrid dear, you do look miserable.'

Ingrid stayed by the stove, touching the tiles where they
were almost unbearably hot. Her mother came and took her
shoulders, turned her around and held her, stroking the back
of her bare neck with the tips of her fingers.

'What was your letter about?'

'It was Hannah.'

'The hand looked so odd.'

'Perhaps Trude sent it for her; they make that poor woman do everything for them.' Ingrid hoped the note of casual disdain might cover her dishonesty.

'Mmm,' her mother said, meaning, 'Yes, that's feasible.'

Ingrid relaxed into her mother's embrace.

'We all know that being here is hardest on you, dear,' her mother said, and kissed at her temples. 'Make the best of it, eh?'

Ingrid nodded and felt her mother's matronly breasts crushed against her own.

*

Ingrid, unwilling to ask von Ketz or her father if she might take the sleigh into town, claimed simply that she needed fresh air. Her mother protested and then forced her into her own mink, which was warmer than Ingrid's fox, and forbade her from doing anything more strenuous than a turn around the lake. 'You are by no means to clamber onto that ice,' her mother said. 'It melts from the bottom up, you know, and you can't tell how thin it is until you're under it.'

Ingrid escaped and made her way up the steep driveway, gripping an old theatre ticket that she had found in the coat pocket, the paper softening beneath her nervous fingers. The coat smelt of her mother's old evening scent, Voilette de Madame, that she had abandoned during the war for patriotic reasons.

The road through the woods to the open fields had not been driven that day, and the snow, though not deep, was crisp and white and squeaked beneath her feet. The sky was the same white, a glaring sheet through the stiff black branches of the bare elms. There was no wind in the fields and the road to Buckow was silent. She heard only her breathing, the swish swish of her skirt and the creak of her boots. She couldn't tell whether the pressure around her throat and beneath her eyes was the cold, the strain of walking or the fear of what she would find at 65 Hauptstraße in Buckow.

At Griepensee the wind scattered snow across the iced-over lake towards Haus Wilhelmshoehe, where two distant figures, a woman and a child, skated backwards, swinging side to side like drunks. Houses proliferated, their plaster dirty and unpainted since the beginning of the war, and beneath them the streets' cobbles were hidden under fresh snow. Without grit to spread, the ice on the road peeped out, as smooth and blue as a glacier.

On the high street, a few pink-faced people shuffled past. She heard the barking of dogs and, on Buckowsee lake, the ice grating at the hulls of the boats not placed into dry docks that autumn. Had they been forgotten and would now be crushed? A childhood in the veld and an adolescence in Berlin had left her devoid of the slightest notion of maritime lore. Perhaps there were no longer enough men to bring them in. The war – that was always the answer now.

The butcher called out: 'Blood sausage, liver sausage, Kaiser aspic!' The baker stood behind the window of his shop, squinting at the blank sky, rubbing his belly with his snowy hands, a sparse display of small loaves on the shelves behind him. A woman with a lapdog passed her, the animal trying to keep its body above the snow with a proud high trot, leaping like a rabbit where the snow was too deep.

She counted up the odd numbers on the left-hand side of the road: 59, 61, 63. She looked up and ahead the sign of a haberdasher's swung towards her, creaking. 65.

The butcher called out again: 'Blood sausage, liver sausage, boar! Pâté, Bouletten, Kaiser's aspic!'

She approached the shop gingerly, her mouth dry. It had a large window, filled with pinned sheets of green wool and red cotton, and a dressmaker's mannequin, wearing a simple cream blouse and a long grey skirt. There was a plump woman behind the counter, and an elderly lady sitting on a chair at the front of the shop, who fixed her at once with a questioning stare, making Ingrid push the door open sooner than she would have wished, so as not to appear to be lingering.

A bell rang. The old woman scowled, but the woman behind the counter smiled. Her neatly tied hair was greying and she wore a white blouse with great starched sleeves that bloomed out at the top before tightening around her forearms, to advertise, perhaps, the extraordinary limits of the work that the wares in the shop might service. The woman said, 'Just looking, madam?'

'No,' Ingrid said, but then was at a loss to say what she was doing there.

A flutter of recognition lit up the woman's face and she said, 'Oh, but you're the younger Fräulein Hoffmann. Am I right?'

'Yes,' said Ingrid.

'Of course,' she said. 'I recognise you from the Baron's wedding.'

'Who's this?' came a hoarse cry.

The old woman was leaning forward, her eyes small and black and alight with the white of the snow outside. Her yellowing grey hair was plaited and pinned to her head, and her chin was soft with pale whiskers that darkened around the corner of her mouth, like the moustache of a walrus.

'This is Fräulein Hoffmann,' the shopkeeper said loudly. 'The sister of the Baroness.'

'She's very young.'

'No, the sister of the young Baroness,' the shopkeeper said, blushing.

'Oh, yes,' she said, sitting back in her chair. 'Very sad,' she muttered. 'A tragedy.'

'Are you visiting the von Ketzes then, miss?' the shopkeeper said. 'If I may ask.'

'Yes, we're staying for a little while, while things quieten down in Berlin,' Ingrid said, though her voice sounded removed, as if she was repeating lines she'd learned by rote.

'Quite right,' said the woman. 'Not much happens here in Buckow, thank the Lord. Though we did lose a lot of our boys in the war, there's no question about that. And food's scarce, of course, not to mention coal.'

'We lost our boys,' the old woman echoed.

Ingrid nodded. Embarrassed by a growing silence, she stared down at the counter, at some green shot silk. 'It will sound like an odd question, perhaps,' Ingrid said, 'But did a Herr Ziegler ever work here?'

'No, miss.'

'Or a Herr Courtman.'

'The black man, miss?'

Ingrid felt her heart begin to thud in her chest, but didn't look up from the silk. 'Yes, the black man.'

'He never worked here, miss. Good Lord, a nigger selling plush and crêpe de Chine! The very thought! But he did stay. He came for the wedding, from Southwest. I would say he was quite a sight in a town like this, but the place was full of 'em back then, because of some surprise the Baroness had laid on with Africans and drums and the like.'

'That the nigger?' the old woman said, squinting.

Ingrid touched the silk. The sweat on her fingers left marks on it and she withdrew them. 'Where did he stay?' she said.

'In the room at the top of the stairs, miss.'

'And what happened to him?'

'Well, miss, he was just here for the wedding, as I said. When he left, I can't rightly say. It was after your sister disappeared I suppose, but we're not a hotel, so it wasn't such a surprise. Your father organised it all. I suppose the guest-houses didn't want to take him, though I must say he was quite the most educated man. Quite the silver tongue, he had. We got a little correspondence for him afterwards, and I just left it up there in the room, but otherwise we haven't seen hide nor hair of him since.'

'You haven't been up there since then?' Ingrid said, picturing, with hammering heart, a revelation scrawled on the wall, Hans emaciated from years leading a secret life over the haberdasher's in Buckow.

'We have, miss, but only because your father took most of the furniture from the room and then said we might use it again.'

The bell above the shop door clattered. A young woman in a rabbit-lined hat entered, the change in air causing the soft hairs on it to dance and then still as the door closed.

'Frau Braun!' the shopkeeper said. 'I'll be with you in one moment.' Then to Ingrid, 'Do go up yourself if you like – you've quite a right to.' She opened a stiff little drawer and, after some sifting, took out an iron key. 'Good luck with it,' she said. 'Mind your skirts – you'll come down in a state, I'm afraid, even if you try not to touch anything.'

Ingrid thanked her and walked around the back of the

counter, catching sight of the chaos of paper, string, rusted scissors, pencils, chipped paint and rushed repairs. She passed through the back door and was met by the smell of black bread proving, which she saw on the passage floor in cloth-lined baskets. She mounted the staircase, and the painted wooden steps cracked as she climbed up to a dusty landing, where she found a badly fitting door with a large gap beneath, from which escaped white winter light. Ingrid tried the key. The lock clunked open.

The room was filled with leftovers from the shop: a basket of thin cotton offcuts; a roll of stained and unfashionable curtain material; wooden crates stamped with pre-war dates, some open, revealing wax-paper packets of buttons, needles, ribbons.

On the windowsill lay two letters addressed to Herr Courtman. She opened them feverishly. Both were from Frau Weintraub, requesting that he return to pick up his final things. Disillusioned, she looked about her at the spotty black stains where mildew had got under the wallpaper; at two crates containing a miscellany of domestic items: a few creased napkins and floor-cloths, a baked-dough figure of St Martin smoking a pipe, books, cups without saucers, a spinning top, a dented tin coffee pot.

She peered down to the bottom of each crate, and at the very bottom of one she saw a familiar corner of embroidery. She reached and pulled out the Baroness's phoenix night-dress case that she had given her sister in Africa. It had been repaired – the grey silk trimmed and stitched where it had been torn. She touched the silk. It was rough with dust.

She opened it and looked inside. It was full of letters. All were addressed to Margarete and were from before the war when she had stayed in Buckow. Most were from Ingrid.

But there was one envelope written in Hans Ziegler's hand. The glue of the envelope was brittle and yellow and cracked when she opened it, dusting her fingers with amber. The writing inside was nervous and scratchy, dotted with little sprays of ink and awkward blotches where the quill of the pen had bent. It read:

My dear Margarete,
*   I am in Buckow. I am coming for you.*
*   Your obedient servant,*
Hans Ziegler

Ingrid's face curled into an ugly mask and she shuddered out a few dry sobs, which she managed to choke down, to stop them turning into a flood. She felt around with outstretched fingers, as if blindfolded, until she found a crate stuffed with brown woollen blankets, where she sat holding on to the splintered edge, letting it dig painfully into her hand.

Hans was alive, or had been. He had been near her. Why had he written to Margarete first? She was appalled at her fleeting narcissism. She saw her sister letting the letter drop from her hands, running to the far edge of the lake as he chased her, throwing herself into the water, as he fled. Yes, that is what Margarete would have done when she found the note and knew he was coming.

Her family, her history, seemed to her in that moment monstrous, a great snake, eating itself to sate its desperate appetite. We have destroyed ourselves, she thought, unable to make any sense of the violence and misery that led to this point, to her in this room with this letter. Her discovery was no end though; she was just a spectator watching as the great wheel spun, ceaselessly moving, but never forwards.

*

When Ingrid returned to the shop, the customer with the rabbit hat had left. The shopkeeper had lit the gas lamps, and Ingrid realised that she must have been in the upstairs room for some time, because it was already getting dark. Ingrid held the nightdress case to her chest.

'Why, it must bring back a lot of memories,' the woman said, looking at Ingrid's aching eyes. Her gaze switched to the nightdress case.

'And what's that you found up there?' she said holding her hand out. 'Is it a piece of ours?'

'No,' Ingrid said, gripping it to her. 'It's my sister's night-dress case.'

'What on earth was it doing up there, I wonder,' the woman said. 'Perhaps it came up with the things the Baron brought up from the little red house last month.'

Ingrid's head ached, feeling that every sentence brought new confusion, a sense that she had misunderstood everything.

'What little red house?'

'The little red house on the estate, miss. There had been guests there since the start of the war, but they've moved on, I believe, a few weeks back. The Baron had all of the things brought up that they'd left behind.'

'Why did he bring them here? And why was my sister's nightdress case there?'

'The case, I can't account for, miss, but they were your father's guests, as I understood it. He certainly paid their repair bills here. And the room upstairs is his to use as he wishes, of course.'

'Why is it his to use?' Ingrid said.

371

The shopkeeper looked confused. 'It's always belonged to the house.'

'The house?'

'To your house, miss.'

'The Baron owns this shop?' Ingrid said.

'Well, yes, miss, it ... ' The woman looked nervous as if she was unsure whether she'd said the right thing. 'It was sold with the Baron's house. To your father when you were all out in Africa.'

Ingrid felt drunk. It spread from her head down into her shoulders and arms, down to her feet, and she swayed dizzily. 'I didn't realise,' Ingrid said. 'That is,' she said, because the woman looked distressed, 'I didn't realise about the shop as well.'

'Yes, of course, miss,' the woman said, relieved. 'In fact next door he had bought even before the big house. Isn't that right, Frau Lorenz?'

The old woman nodded. 'Bought the lot up. He's a merry chap, Herr Hoffmann. That's what they say around here, at least. Daughter went missing.'

'Yes,' the shopkeeper said. 'This is his other daughter, Frau Lorenz. This is Fräulein Hoffmann.'

The woman sat back again in her chair. She moved her jaw as if she was chewing something. 'Oh, he's an important man round these parts,' she said. 'This one he bought before the war, certainly. The bakery only last month, and of course the Baron's house, though he lets the von Ketzes stay, which is why he's popular. Land in Africa it was, I believe – or was it diamonds?'

'Frau Lorenz,' the woman said. 'This is Fräulein Hoffmann.'

The old woman ignored her. 'His daughter was married to the Baron, but drowned, poor thing. Well, I say, it's nice that they might stay. What with all that's happening in Berlin and the like, we won't have any Barons or Counts or Princes at all, so it's nice they'll still have a home. I suppose many won't. He's a popular one is Herr Hoffmann; cares about Buckow. Father Ingelmann likes him very much – that I know.'

'I must go,' Ingrid said, putting the key back down on the counter. 'Thank you,' she added. 'For your time.'

'Miss, the Baron just passed in the sleigh a few minutes ago. Perhaps he didn't know you were here.'

'Yes, thank you,' Ingrid said again and left, filled with horror at the idea of having to make the journey back to the house with von Ketz. She needed time to fathom what she had read and heard, time to plan her response and, inevitably, her escape.

Von Ketz's sleigh stood across the street and Riemann sat motionless in the driver's seat; she thought she could get past him without him seeing her if she pulled up the collar of her coat. The fur tickled her face and she pushed forward, slipping by.

What was she to do? Panic rose in her, she felt dizzy. She would have to escape to Frau von Galen and never come back. She would have no money. Perhaps Hannah could help her for a while. Perhaps she could become a governess.

She heard the soft clump clump, clump clump of horses' hooves on snow.

'Fräulein Ingrid!' came von Ketz's voice as the sleigh pulled up beside her.

Ingrid stopped.

'Baron von Ketz!' she said, as if surprised.

He was dressed in a fur-lined woollen coat and a grey fur hat. His hand reached out for her and Riemann dismounted and came round the sleigh to help her up. He greeted her with a nod.

'I wanted to walk,' Ingrid said, desperately.

'Fräulein Ingrid,' said von Ketz with jovial disapproval. 'You walked all the way here in the cold. You'll freeze!'

'I would really rather . . .'

'Come, come,' he said.

She climbed up; she had no strength left to fight him. His grip and the power of his thin arm made her think of ship rope. He changed sides so that he was facing her and she settled in, Riemann tucking the furs around her. Perhaps this was better. It would be over quicker.

The sleigh jerked and the horses pulled away. They picked up speed as the Buckowsee lake road climbed. She didn't look at von Ketz, but could smell the wool of his coat and an unfamiliar woody cologne. The huge iced-over lake lay indigo beyond the road, fading to black, the valley either side marked out by the twinkling lights of houses and the castle at the highest point. 'Who lives there?' she wondered, but said nothing. She wished she was looking out of one of those bright windows at the sleigh making its way along the lake path, thinking how glad she would be not to be in the cold, to come from a normal bourgeois family that worried about their sons returning from the Front, about savings and servants and the price of dried fruit.

Soon out of town, the only sound was the horses' soft tread and the hiss of the sleigh sliding over the snow. The sleigh's lamps shrank her field of vision down to the snow, Riemann's back, and von Ketz in front of her, forcing her to catch sight of his face.

'Did you get what you needed?' he asked.

'Pardon?' said Ingrid.

'In town.'

'Oh,' she said. 'Yes.'

He nodded. They heard an owl calling from the woods. He brushed his upper lip with his forefinger.

'You must be quite bored here in Buckow,' he said. 'So used to the city.'

Ingrid stared at the snow beneath them, lit a gentle yellow by the lamp near her face, creaking on its hook. 'You've been very kind, letting us stay,' she said, playing along.

'Your father said you might be in town, because you had been out walking for a while, so I thought I might come and find you. I hoped to talk to you.'

Of course, he must know too; he had cleared out Margarete's old things from the little red house, so that Ingrid wouldn't find any clues about Hans's visit. Now he'd been sent to keep her quiet. Her father's fingers crept everywhere, secretly buying up property, secretly making money out of anyone and anything, inured to her suffering, inured to anyone's suffering. What a joke it must all be for them, with only her out of the picture.

'I don't think I can bear talking,' she said. And because he seemed so distressed at this response, she added automatically, 'I'm very tired.'

'Yes,' he said and shifted in his seat, grabbed the side of the sleigh, rubbed his chin, his gestures becoming quicker and more fraught.

'What is it, Herr Baron?'

He put his hands together and said, 'I ... ' Then he was sitting forward and he had taken her hand. 'Fräulein Ingrid. Ingrid. I feel that we have got along well these past weeks. I've very much enjoyed our afternoons together. You write so beautifully – your translations – and ... Although the

375

thought when it first came to me seemed rather ghoulish, it seems more natural the more I think about it ... '

'What does?'

'That we ... that you, might ... That *you* might consider becoming the Baroness von Ketz.'

The sleigh hit ice and slid for a second, before regaining its course. Ingrid pulled her hand away and gripped the side, afraid that she would be flung out, but also wanting it; wanting to be flung from the sleigh, rolling through the snowy fields and burrowing down, away from von Ketz, away from the world.

'No, that's impossible!' she cried.

Von Ketz fell back. She was appalled to see his face white with genuine shock. What could he have expected?

'I didn't mean—'

'No,' she said, 'I ... It's a terrible moment to ask and I ... It's Hans. He was here and Papa did terrible things in Africa. And there was a letter. That she read – Margarete. Then she killed herself.' She started to shake. 'Because of Hans, I think. But really, because of Papa.'

'What are you talking about, Fräulein Ingrid?'

But how could she explain? She inhaled a few icy sniffs that crackled in her nose.

'What letter?' he said.

'From Hans.'

'He wrote you a letter?'

'No, he wrote to Margarete. He's been staying at the little red house hasn't he? But you sent him away when we came here last autumn. That's right isn't it? He drove Margarete to suicide to get his revenge on us and you let him stay on the estate, so that he didn't kill you, like he killed your father. Is that what happened?'

'Ingrid, that doesn't make any sense.'

'But he was here, wasn't he? At the house?'

'No, I ... Possibly, but ... '

'What do you mean, possibly?'

He looked out at the dark, and then at her lap. 'He came here. He wanted ... restitution. There was nothing we could offer him.'

'You said he never made it here. You said you found him in Berlin.'

'Your father said that.'

'And you just stood there in silence,' she shouted. 'As is your way.'

He met her eyes. 'It's not for me to tell him what to say to his own daughter.'

'Or in his own house.'

Von Ketz's mouth shrank and he sat in silence like a rebuked child.

Ingrid pulled at the fur blanket. Her face ached with the cold and as they left the woods the wind picked up and ice crystals, sparkling in the lamplight, curled around in feathery clouds and stung her cheeks. How dare he be angry? How dare he play the injured party? 'They put Hans in a camp, you know, they put all the Africans in camps; those that they hadn't already pushed into the desert to die of thirst. Nora too. You wiped them all out, like vermin.'

Von Ketz looked at her. 'You ... ' He gripped his shoulder as if protecting a wound. 'You don't know anything about war. Imagine dying thirsty when you're up to your waist in filthy water, when you haven't been dry in months, when your hands or your feet have been shot to stumps and there's gas creeping down into the shell hole you're lying in. Imagine that.' He looked away from her, injured. 'A shot

377

in the head in the desert, falling to your knees and drying out in the sun, that's hardly a death. They didn't know how lucky they had it.'

She looked away from him, over the great flat fields, smears of blue in the night, and the wind battered the sleigh and made her eyes run. She took out her pipe, which she had stuffed in her pocket, and lit it with a match, sheltering the bowl with her cupped hand. Having only smoked in secret and thus nearly always outdoors, it was a task at which she had become highly proficient.

'What are you doing?' von Ketz said.

'Smoking a pipe,' said Ingrid.

'Why?' he said.

'What a meaningless question.'

'Is that one of my pipes? Did you steal it?' he said.

'No.'

Ingrid expected the sleigh to stop at the top of the drive, leaving them to walk the rest of the way to the house; it was here that she planned to tell von Ketz that she was going straight to the station and returning to Berlin. As much as she wanted to demand explanations from her parents, really she was desperate to get back to Berlin, to get back to Hannah and her poems. She had no more taste for lies.

To her surprise Riemann turned the sleigh skilfully and the horses broke into a canter as gravity pulled it down the steep drive to the house. The horses rounded the corner, leather, rope and iron rattling and creaking as the bridle and reins tightened, the horses gnashed at the bit and the sleigh came to a halt. The horses shook their heads, steam streaming from their nostrils, ice frozen to the whiskers on their noses.

Riemann dismounted and stood ready to receive Ingrid.

378

His eyes were dropped low in embarrassment and he held out his hand stiffly. She looked up at the house. Out of economy, only the lamps of the ground-floor back rooms were lit and visible through the glazed main doors. The rest of the house was a great dark frame around the broken light inside.

'I have to go to Berlin,' she said. 'Baron, would you ask someone to fetch the beige case in my room.'

'Go to Berlin?'

'Yes, it's all arranged,' she said. 'I'll meet Fräulein Mandelbaum there.'

'There are protests, people striking. Haven't you been reading the papers? You can't wait at the station for a train that won't come.'

'I have some options,' Ingrid said. 'It's all been arranged.'

She looked down at her gloved hands.

'If this has something to do with . . . '

She looked at him and said, 'Oh Emil, it has nothing to do with you. It's about Margarete, don't you see? It all is. I have to get back. Please let me go. I can't face my parents – not now. I need to find Hans. Don't stop me and don't mention what's happened. Do this one thing for me, if I ever really did mean anything to you.'

'Shall I fetch Renate, sir?' Riemann said.

'No, Riemann – let me go.'

Von Ketz stepped down into the snow and the sleigh rocked. Riemann went and stood by the horses, so that only the misshapen silhouette of his fur hat was visible behind the corner lamp near the horses' rumps. The door to the house cracked as von Ketz entered, and Ingrid turned away to the lake.

The snow-powdered ice glowed in the dark. The forest around formed a black collar reaching up high and then breaking as it merged with the night sky and the stars. There was a little wind, a whistling around her ears.

She drank in the smoke from her pipe and thought of Hans intoning Coleridge in his own translation:

> 'Day in, day out, day in, day out,
> We stuck. No breath, no motion;
> Shiftless as a painted ship,
> Upon a painted ocean.'

She had copied out the lines from memory a week before, in the warmth, in von Ketz's study. But she would never enter his study again; it was the end of her old life. She thought of her mother and felt tears rising again, but she must have known something too and so she would have to forget them all, at least for a while.

There was still time, she supposed, to climb out of the sleigh, to pass von Ketz and her parents, mutter that she was sick, tired, confused, and all she would have to suffer would be the barely hidden pleasure in her mother's voice that her warnings about the trip to Buckow were well founded. She would be able to slip into bed, sleep, forget her sister, forget Hans. She could even find von Ketz and agree to his proposal. Then every day she could go into the study and sit down at the desk and translate. She could invent a pseud-onym and tackle major works, perhaps. It could be her side of the bargain – marriage for a study and two hours a day of comfortable silence. And an enforced amnesia about how her family had got there and what it had cost. There would be no better offer. But she heard the crack of the lash on the quay in Lüderitz, smelt death in her nostrils and heard the high human screams, she saw her father in the cellar lying to her, saw Margarete fleeing into the water of the lake, and she knew she could never go inside again.

'I will be sad to see you go, miss, if I may say.' It was Riemann. He was looking up at her, a thin figure in fur cap and navy greatcoat.

'Did you know about any of this, Riemann?' she said.

'Some,' he said. 'Ignorance isn't the worst thing though, miss. There are sadder things. Much sadder.'

'I don't know how you can still stand to work for him.'

'He's a good enough man,' Riemann said. 'Besides, everyone else is gone.'

The door opened. She turned and saw her father silhouetted in the warm light of the house. Of course von Ketz had betrayed her.

Herr Hoffmann didn't call her name, but made his way briskly towards the sleigh, as if he were trotting out to take a telegram from a messenger. He wasn't wearing a coat – he expected that what he had to say to her would get her into the house before he became cold.

She looked forward stoically and listened to his approach. Her face was very cold and the cold was creeping up through the floor of the sleigh, into her boots, making her toes hurt.

'That'll be all, Riemann,' she heard him say.

'The horses, sir . . . '

'That'll be all,' her father repeated and she heard Riemann patting one of the horses and the soft crunch of his feet disappearing across the meadow and around the side of the house.

'Are you smoking a pipe?' her father said. 'Is that a joke?'

'If it were, it wouldn't be a very funny one,' she said.

Her father gripped the sleigh. It creaked on its suspension.

'Ingrid,' he said. His tone was disarmingly tender and Ingrid turned back to the lake, so as not to be moved by it. 'I'm sure the proposal was a surprise. You mustn't be embarrassed. It was badly thought through, especially done here in Buckow. But he's a good man, the Baron.'

The branches in the wood moved, tickling each other, trunks creaking like ships.

She turned to him. The light from the sleigh lamps lit his face, small and eager, still childlike. It made his hair blond again and caught the blue of his eyes.

'I went to the seamstress in town,' Ingrid said. 'I saw the room where Hans stayed.' Her hands were shaking beneath the fur blanket. 'But of course you know that because you own it. Because you own all of this.'

Her father looked down at the snow, his hands still holding on to the sides of the sleigh, so that he looked for a moment like a thief in the stocks. 'There's nothing there, Ingrid. It's a storeroom,' he said eventually, the sleigh and the snow damping his voice, making it sound close and domestic.

'Nothing there because you stripped it out after Hans came to expose you. That's why Margarete threw herself into the lake.'

Her father seemed to comprehend something; his body relaxed and he stood up straight. 'Expose what, exactly?' he said.

'What you did in Africa. How you made your money. What you did to him. It destroyed her. It killed her.'

'Ingrid, you know as well as anyone that Southwest Africa was a brutal place. The rules were different there.'

'And yet you made money out of it.'

'It was a war!' her father said, so loudly that she jumped.

'They were trying to kill us. I'm sure the British army was full of decent chaps, but we didn't try to get to know every one of them while they were throwing grenades at us in Flanders.'

'We didn't exterminate the British.'

'I didn't exterminate anyone. I was doing my job. I didn't imprison anyone; I didn't kill anyone. I was just trying to get a railway built, trying to sell some land, trying to give you and your sister a life. If I hadn't, we would be living on a farm and tomorrow morning at five you, your mother and your sister would be heading out in the bitter cold to dig cabbages from the frozen ground.'

'But he did come here to Buckow? And Margarete did see him?'

Her father looked over her lap to the lake. 'Yes,' he said. 'He came here. He got to her, somehow. We tried to protect her.'

'Did he stay at the little red house?'

'What are you talking about?'

'Von Ketz took boxes from the little red house to the seamstress's after we arrived here. Then when I went there with you, it had been cleaned out. The same with the attic. Someone was staying at the little red house. And when I went through the boxes from the cottage I found some of Margarete's things.'

'We've been keeping things in that cottage for years. I don't know where every one of your sister's belongings ended up. Did you see Hans there? Did you? And by the way, he is not a man who deserves your sympathy, Ingrid. He killed his own father.'

'The Baron hung Hereros off his trees like paper lanterns. You know he did. He was a monster.'

'Hans deserted you too.'

'He came back.'

'Not for you.'

Ingrid looked down at the fur blanket. Tears welled up in her eyes. If he had come for her it could have all been different. She would have run away with him; Margarete might have lived.

'Ingrid, come inside.'

'I won't,' she said.

'We can talk about it all.'

'We?' she said and laughed. 'Who else knows? Mother probably. The Baron of course. Perhaps Renate knows? It seems Riemann does. Perhaps you all know and you've all been laughing at me, lining me up to take Margarete's place, because she had the good sense to end it. Because how could she live with herself once she knew what you'd done?'

'I did nothing!' her father shouted.

The wind left the trees, changed direction, moved beneath the sleigh and threw dusty, sparkling snow up around them.

'Your sister brought everything on herself. She left us. She left you. And I won't let her poison you.'

Finally he had started to shiver. Ingrid turned away; she couldn't bear to look at him.

'She left you,' he said again. 'Hans left you. Do you know who hasn't left? Me and your mother. We're still here. We're not perfect and we haven't made perfect decisions, but we did try to make something of ourselves and to keep our family together. To make sure you and your sister didn't have the lives that we had. That you were happy.'

'And hasn't that worked out well for you,' Ingrid said. 'One dead and one about to leave. For good.'

After she had uttered it she heard how stinging it was and waited for his fierce retort. But it didn't come. 'Ingrid,' he said, tender again. 'You were always the good one. Come inside. You belong here; she doesn't.'

He reached out to her and she pulled away, he lunged for her wrist. She scrambled out from under the blanket, over the opposite side of the sleigh. The pipe fell from her hand and the burning tobacco hissed in the snow. The sound of her father coming round the sleigh panicked her and she ran across the meadow, down the broken wooden steps, onto the jetty. She turned and saw his small figure scrabbling down after her, and so kept running, launching herself onto the lake, where she hit the thick white sheet and her feet went from under her, her momentum spinning her whole body round, sliding flat across the ice, coming to rest face down.

She heard her father's feet on the jetty and pushed herself upright. He paused at the edge and then jumped down after her, hitting the ice and slipping immediately too, his feet kicking before he fell with an ugly thump and a bitter cry. The wind blew ice crystals against her face like sand and filled her ears with a soft high whistle.

She heard her mother coming. Her father pushed himself up into a sitting position. Ingrid got to her knees, planning to run across the lake, to where her sister had plunged in, and then disappear into the woods, to find her way to Berlin alone. But what was the point? she thought, looking at her father with his head in his hands, a little man collapsed on the ice. She believed him; she believed that he really had done his best. But how could she live with the things that had been done to buy this lake, this crumbling title and this marriage? She must forget them.

She heard her mother's feet on the steps.

'Come back in,' her father whispered. 'Please Ingrid. Think of your mother.'

But she was as tainted as he was and, as she arrived at the jetty and let out a scream at the sight of them on the ice, Ingrid shouted out, into the darkness, 'I won't think of her. I don't want to see her. I can't.'

'Oh, Ingrid,' her mother called down pitifully, 'You don't have to see her and you mustn't. If she cared for us, if she had cared for you, she wouldn't have run away with him. Oh, how we wanted to save you the burden of it, but let her still be dead to you. We will carry it together. We will speak of her as we have always done, as if she had died that night in the lake.'

A wave of tiny shivers ran up one side of Ingrid's body. She was struck dumb. The trees creaked and clattered. Beneath her knees the cold of the ice had begun to permeate her legs. She could make out her father's eyes in the dark, white in the meagre light of the winter evening.

'Hedwig,' he said, and her mother, realising her mistake, took in a quick breath and was silent.

'Where is she?' Ingrid said.

Neither of her parents answered. Only her mother, whispering through tears, said, 'Oh Ingrid.'

'Where is she?' Ingrid shouted.

'She left us!' cried her father. He was on his knees. Her mother, in silhouette, held her hands to her chest, like a wife at the quay watching her husband's ship departing.

'I could have got her back,' Ingrid said.

'You think I didn't try to get her back?' her father choked out. He was crying. She had mistaken the cracking of his voice as anger, but he was crying like a child, a shuddering, whining sob.

'What did you do with her?' Ingrid said, tears freezing on her face, her mother's quiet wail filling the air from the jetty.

'I did everything for her and she wanted to ruin us.'

'You know where she is? You've seen her?'

He cried and cried like an injured child and moaned into his hands, 'She would have taken you with her too. She said she'd take you away too.'

She heard feet hitting the ice. Her mother had jumped down. She threw herself over Herr Hoffmann, saying, 'Oh Johannes, shush now. Come Johannes, be quiet now,' and with horror Ingrid heard the rhythm of habit in her voice. The scene had been acted out behind closed doors many times and tonight was only the first time she had witnessed their despair.

Her mother held out her hand to Ingrid in the dark, but Ingrid didn't go to them. Instead she shouted through her tears, 'Tell me where she is!'

'No, I won't.' His horrible sobbing was muffled by the fur of his wife's coat. 'No, I'll never tell you.'

He sobbed on, but she already knew. She knew exactly where her sister was.

Windscheidstraße 53, Charlottenburg

— January 1919 —

Ingrid made her way clumsily over the road. It had become a grey ice crust, with deep grooves, like tramlines, where the coaches and automobiles rode, strewn with hunks of filthy ice that had cracked off and been thrown up by horses' hooves and the wheels of cars. Snow softened the pavement opposite and her gait righted as she approached the door to the Hoffmanns' apartment in Windscheidstraße.

She rang the bell and waited, staring at the beige tiles on the floor, that grew up the walls and blossomed into art nouveau peacock feathers at shoulder height. She could still run away. She could still run back to Buckow, run to Hannah, run to von Galen and lock herself away with her work.

At the far end of the large hallway, a door opened and the dark face of Ann-Kathrin peeped out, blinking. Ingrid lifted up her hand to identify herself. She dipped away again and then reappeared holding the hand of a black-haired toddler, who walked alongside her, staring nervously at Ingrid through the glass.

Ann-Kathrin lifted the child up and came to the closed door, covering the child's face with her hand. Through the glass she said, 'Fräulein Ingrid, I'm afraid you can't come in. Everyone here is sick – Flanders fever. It's terribly contagious.' The child cocked his head to look at her.

'I'm here to see Margarete and Herr Ziegler,' Ingrid said.

Ann-Kathrin's face turned white and, without another word, she disappeared up the front staircase. Ingrid heard the boy's muffled request to be allowed to walk by himself, but it was refused, and his sad cry echoed in the stairwell, dissipating as they climbed higher.

Ingrid waited. Her hands grew cold and she pushed them into the pockets of her fur coat. She might have brought a muff, but such practical concerns had felt idiotic. She was very aware of her body, pressure in her chest, her stomach, in her throat, behind her eyes.

She heard a crack, like gunshot. The fighting and the strikes meant that her journey from Buckow had been long and broken, the station unmanned, the first train never arriving, the second arriving but travelling one stop before forcing them to disembark. She spent the night trying to sleep on a station floor, with beggars and injured soldiers.

When she finally arrived in Berlin, the whole city had been dark, strange and dangerous. There were people missing where there should be people: on the streets, on trams and buses, in coaches and cars. And in groups where they shouldn't have been: blooming out of doorways, clubs and bars normally closed during daylight. Nervous groups of Freikorps militias stood at intersections with rifles, nervous workers and demobbed soldiers waited in the shadows of shop awnings, the windows behind broken or boarded up.

She heard feet on the stairs. She didn't look up until the footsteps stopped and the building was filled with silence.

Then she looked.

Margarete was standing in the hallway.

Ingrid's teeth chattered.

As a child she had been harried by a wasp, put a glass over it and found it dead the next day. Her sister appeared to her like this wasp: exactly the same in form but imperceptibly smaller, darker.

Margarete smiled nervously and held on to the wall, as if the hallway between them were a pool that needed to be swum across. She was older, her hair fell out of its loose pinning in pale locks, the colour of old paper. Her dress was pale too – it might have been white, like her wedding dress, but it was too dark in the hallway to tell for sure. Her sister's wrists were bare. Her ankles were bare. Ingrid put her fingers against the glass of the front door. It moved, the latch knocking loosely against the keep. Margarete walked forward.

Ingrid stepped back and gripped her chest. Her whole body shook, but her sister came inexorably, came at her like a ghost in a dream.

Ingrid's boot creaked in the snow of the pavement. The white winter sky became reflected in the rippled glass, obscuring Margarete's approach.

She appeared, resolved into a smiling face. Ingrid felt a stultifying panic, as if Margarete's touch might kill her. The door opened, and Margarete reached out to her. She moved forward and was holding her hand, small and dry as it had always been.

'Little Fly,' Margarete whispered, and Ingrid was in her arms, barely able to walk, but walking somehow, through the

Margarete looked at the child and Hans took her other hand, encouraging her to go on, so that she was strung between them, a link in a dance. Ingrid looked at his hand over Margarete's and in the waxing and waning of emotion, in the coming and going of numbness and pain, she was stabbed with jealousy. Don't touch her, she felt, but buried it by crying out again, 'Why did you leave me?'

'I had to get away. Hans found me.'

Ingrid waited, but Margarete was finished, as if that were explanation enough. Ingrid wanted to measure her words, to elicit clear answers from Margarete, but only managed to string the mysteries together with increasing volume: 'Why did you marry von Ketz? Why did you marry him and then disappear? I saw you with him, under him. I thought you were dead and you let me think you were dead. And you've been hiding for all these years? At the red house? And then here? Why didn't you write to me? I mourned you! I grieved for you!'

'It's Papa. It's him. Mama and von Ketz of course, but it's Papa who kept us in the little red house in Buckow during the war.'

'As prisoners?'

'No. They still love me, despite everything; you know how sentimental Mama and Papa are.'

'Then why did you stay there?'

Hans looked at Margarete, waiting to see how much she was prepared to say. But there would be no more secrets now, Ingrid thought. She would have it all out.

'Father Schäfer found Hans in the camp on Shark Island. He was taken there after we'd left. When he heard Hans's story, he paid for his journey back to Germany, so that he could come for me.'

'But Schäfer thought it was a moral victory,' Ingrid said. 'He thought Hans was returning to avenge wrongs, to claim his birthright. He's still searching for him now.'

'That was never possible. Not alone,' Hans said.

His voice, completely familiar, reverberated in her ears. Its closeness shocked her. She didn't look at him, but said, 'So you tricked a man of God.'

'Ingrid!' said Margarete.

'I'm sorry,' Ingrid said, still not looking at his face. 'I just meant … It doesn't matter. So you needed Margarete to get the money off Papa? And then,' she said, looking at their intertwined hands, 'you fell in love.'

'No, I came for Margarete,' Hans said. 'She was the only reason.'

'We were always in love, Little Fly,' said Margarete.

'Always?' Ingrid whispered. She looked at Hans for the first time, looked at his face, which showed the trace of the last ten years in a few deeper lines on his forehead, tobacco stains on his teeth, but who was still as beautiful as she remembered him. She wanted him to lean across the table, pull her head towards his, with his fingers in her hair, and then she thought of her sister and the child and was disgusted at herself. 'When? When did you fall in love?' said Ingrid, and the volume and shaking of her head caused Margarete and Hans to look at her as if she were mad.

'At the farm in Southwest,' said Margarete.

'When at the farm?' Ingrid said, trying to control her voice.

'Every week he rode me over to the von Ketzes' house. We talked. We … ' she shrugged, able to think of no better explanation, 'fell in love. It was all very innocent, back then.'

Ingrid had believed that she had been about to uncover

a great conspiracy, but it was just a love story. And it wasn't hers. 'Hans came that Christmas. When you got well again. Before the wedding.'

'That's right,' said Margarete. 'He found us in Berlin. He watched the house and waited until there was no one else from the family in the apartment but me. He waited for two weeks for the opportunity, then he hand-delivered a letter.'

'I was terrified she wouldn't receive it.'

'But I did, Little Fly. He told me he had come for me and it was all I could do not to run out of the house and embrace him on the street.'

'Why didn't you? Why didn't you just run away then?'

'With what?' said Hans.

'We had nothing,' Margarete said. 'We had nowhere to go, Hans would have found it impossible to work in Germany.'

'You could have worked on the tram,' said Ingrid.

'What are you talking about, Ingrid? Are you angry at us?'

'How could I be?' Ingrid said. 'I'm sorry. Go on.'

'The only option was going back to Africa, to Southwest. But we needed security.'

'Money,' said Ingrid.

'Yes,' said Margarete. 'We needed Papa to support us.'

'Is that why you were suddenly so keen to marry von Ketz?'

'Yes, though I wasn't the only one. It was everything that Mama and Papa had worked towards. I knew that if I married him, if I became the Baroness von Ketz, that they would have their title and I would have my freedom, in a funny way.'

'How clever of you. But why did you have to leave at the wedding? Why couldn't you have said goodbye to me? Surely a week wouldn't have mattered?'

Margarete looked down at the table, and answered like a suspect to an interrogator. 'It all just happened far quicker than we thought. For the plan to work, we had to be able to say that the marriage was consummated, so that von Ketz didn't just have it annulled straight away. And we had to prove that immediately. We didn't want to take any chances.'

'How could you ... ?' She turned to Hans. 'If you are in love with her, how could you let her?'

'It was Hans you saw,' Margarete said. 'And I'm still terribly sorry about it. Hans called von Ketz pretending to be from a nearby house. He said there was a problem with one of the estate workers: a pregnancy, so that it sounded scandalous enough for him not to talk to anyone about it straight away. Then the idea was to get Renate to discover me with Hans, but dressed like von Ketz. They're the same build. They're brothers, Little Fly.'

'I know,' Ingrid said.

'You've worked it all out, you clever thing. I knew you would.' Margarete smiled bashfully. 'But then you came up. And I felt terrible for you. It worked for us, in a funny way, because it was doubly confirmed and Renate couldn't deny she'd seen something. We knew we could force von Ketz to attest to it too, once we had told him what was happening. We had to tell him straight away, so that he wouldn't come up with his own account. Then it was all in motion and we couldn't stop it. We had to disappear that night.'

Ingrid swapped von Ketz for Hans in her image of Margarete on her wedding night. She felt sick at the thought and wanted to pull away from her sister, but couldn't bear the idea of upsetting her so much that she would stop the conversation, when there was so much that still didn't make any sense.

'How did Hans get to you in Buckow?'

'He arrived at the same time as the living museum.'

'You'd organised it,' Ingrid said, realising the shrewdness of it.

'Yes,' said Margarete.

'Everyone at the wedding said the Baroness had.'

'I was the Baroness by then.'

Ingrid laughed a little. How useful her foolishness had been to them.

'And you wanted to go straight to Africa?'

'Yes,' said Margarete. 'We didn't want much – enough land to sustain ourselves somewhere out in the veld, where a white woman and an African could live. That's all we wanted. If they agreed to everything, I would just disappear, which wasn't so unimaginable, given the history of my nerves. Mama and Papa would still have their title to go with everything Papa had bought up and wouldn't want von Ketz divorcing me after the fact. They've covered up too many secrets for that.'

'And what about me?' said Ingrid.

'I wanted to tell you everything, but Papa said he would cut us off if I said a word.'

Ingrid heard the child march his lead soldiers across the floorboards, puffing out a muted drum beat.

'And von Ketz? How did you force him to agree to your plan? He can't have wanted to be married to a runaway, to never be able to marry again. Didn't he deserve anything? Didn't he love you?' Ingrid said, feeling a rising urge to defend him.

Hans smiled coldly and Margarete let out a hard little laugh. 'He never loved me,' Margarete said sweetly, as if Ingrid were a stupid child. 'He's a sissy, Little Fly. You must have guessed it. He's in love with that little Hungarian painter.'

'He's his wife,' Hans said.

This seemed cruel. 'Horvath,' Ingrid said. 'He's blind now.'

'Yes, we used to see him stumbling about the estate,' said Margarete.

Anyone can be cruel, Ingrid supposed, even the most damaged.

'Did Papa know?'

'Of course Papa knew! Everyone knew. That was why the Baron hated him. That family was ruined; the Baron had ruined them. The von Ketzes are a joke and went to Africa because they had nothing here but an old house that was falling to pieces, and they would have come back with nothing if it hadn't been for Papa. Von Ketz made a show of being put out about it all on the wedding night, but he didn't fight it, because for him it was the perfect solution too. A marriage which he didn't have to maintain or consummate and a reason never to marry again.'

'He wanted to marry me,' Ingrid said.

'Huh!' Margarete said. 'That would have been clever, if he'd pulled it off. But you said no, of course.'

'Yes,' Ingrid said. She sat back in the hard kitchen chair, letting her hand slide out from beneath Margarete's. 'When did you decide to pretend you'd killed yourself?'

'That wasn't the intention. Not quite. But Papa said it was the only way to stop the police trying to find me.'

'And all this happened in the house that night? All this bargaining?'

'In the attic. Then they kept us up there, until the house was empty again and we could go to Hamburg with our tickets to Africa.'

'Why didn't you go?'

'The war started. They stopped the passenger ships and soon the British were all over Southwest. We had to come back and wait for it to be over. We thought the war was only going to be a few months. Mama and Papa were so desperate to keep us away from you that they hid us in Buckow. They were sure they'd lose you too if you found us. We weren't allowed in the house, so they banished us to the little red cottage, where only a few people would know we were.'

It must have been lovely after all of that struggle, locked away to make a family. 'I found your pyjama case at the seamstress's with my letters,' she said to Margarete. 'Papa had cleared it out of the little cottage.'

'We had to leave everything behind.'

'You kept a few things,' Ingrid said, nodding to the cases.

'I don't need letters to remember you, Ingrid.'

Ingrid had kept everything of Margarete's; she hadn't let her parents throw away a thing. 'Were you in the little cottage when I came to Buckow at the start of the war?'

'Yes. Father was terrified you'd find us. He was so angry you'd come.'

'Were you there when I was in the cottage?'

'Yes,' said Margarete. 'But we'd promised.'

'You could have come down. You could have given me a sign. If I'd known you were alive, I'd have kept the secret. I'd have done anything,' Ingrid said.

Margarete looked at Hans for support. They looked at each other with such tenderness; it must have been a halcyon time, trapped in their little Arcadia as the world outside crumbled. Ingrid was gripped with envy. She heard a distant crackle of gunfire. 'They're dissolving the aristocracy. Von Ketz is going to lose his title,' she said. 'So are you.'

'It still means something,' said Margarete. 'To be a Baroness, even if it's just in name.'

'Does it?' Ingrid said. 'I don't think it means anything any more, if it ever did.'

'Our place in society is everything to Papa. The title won't stop being important to him. And it's not just the title, but also the terrible things that happened in Africa. If people knew, it would bring the whole family down. It wouldn't matter if Papa didn't care about it, but he cares more than anything.'

Ingrid ran this scenario through her head. 'What terrible things? What Papa did there, what Hans did to the Baron, that is . . . It isn't . . . ' How could she say without also saying that what Hans had endured would not be scandalous to any German? That, in their eyes, what he had experienced was an abstract question of native rights, and nothing to do with human beings. How could she say that even his murdering his own father would be seen as somehow in his nature and would only bring the Hoffmanns more pity, not derision?

'What do you think Hans did to the Baron?' Margarete said.

'Killed him,' said Ingrid.

Margarete and Hans became still. Ingrid was afraid they were going to drive her from the apartment.

Margarete, stiff and monotone like a clairvoyant channelling the dead, said, 'Hans didn't kill the Baron. I did.'

Ingrid's mouth dropped open. 'Why?' she managed, in a hoarse whisper.

Margarete continued in her dead tone. 'Papa sent me to the von Ketzes' every week. You remember. They would have done anything to cement themselves to that family. We had money before the von Ketzes, but no status. The marriage – it was everything to Papa and Mama. Every week, while the Baroness and Emil sat in the parlour, the Baron took me upstairs and ...' she blinked, trying to find the appropriate phrase, '... touched me. Every week. Then the Baron asked if he could have me stay the night. Papa agreed.'

'Oh Margarete,' Ingrid said. 'He can't have known.'

'He knew he was a bad man. He knew I didn't want to go there. I couldn't tell him why, I ... I didn't understand it. I couldn't tell anyone.' There was a shudder behind the mask, a physical attempt to damp something down. 'I don't think the Baron knew about Hans and me. And I had never told Hans what the Baron had been doing. But he knew him well enough to know what danger I was in, when he heard that I had been asked to stay at the von Ketzes' house and realised that the Baron had come to collect me in person.

'Hans was too late to ...' She shook her head, refusing the memory. 'He banged on the door when he arrived, because the Baron had locked it. The Baron woke in a rage and went out with his gun. There was a terrible fight, screaming, and I ran downstairs. I was wild. Hans was on the ground and the Baron was beating him with the butt of his gun. I went back into the house and the first thing I saw was the table full of bottles. I grabbed one. Then I hit him over the head with it. It didn't even break. He fell down like he'd been shot. I was scared that he was going to get up again. So I kept hitting him with the bottle. Then Hans pulled me off him, but he was already dead.'

Margarete's eyes were dry now, but Ingrid's were full of tears. 'Did the Baroness know?' she said. 'Emil?'

'They never left their rooms. That's all I know.'

Margarete turned to Hans like a puppet, and he took the

dead voice from her lips. 'Your father arrived and I told him what had happened. He was very afraid; everything was lost. But we already knew from our farmhands that the Uprising had started further south and if our progress to Okahandja was slow enough, we could pretend the farm had been attacked. It was his idea. So I dragged the Baron out in front of the house and I beat his head in with a *kirrn* so that no one would know what had really happened. I would have done anything to keep Margarete safe.'

They sat at the table. The child played. Ingrid wept. A child shouted in the stairwell; a voice replied in the courtyard.

Margarete stood. 'I need to make something for Manfred.' She put her hand on Ingrid's shoulder as she passed. Hans and Ingrid watched her go.

Hans opened his mouth, but stopped. Her heart jumped at the thought that it might be something personal, something that would rescue at least him for her, but what could that possibly be?

'What about Pina?' she said.

Hans frowned. 'Who?'

'Pina. Our dog.'

'Oh,' he said. 'Your father killed her, to make the story about the Uprising more believable.'

Ingrid closed her eyes and thought of the dog's beautiful brown eyes – a tragedy of a scale that she was able to comprehend, if only briefly.

'Was it by the thorn bush, near the stone at the front of the house?'

Hans shrugged. 'Perhaps.'

She nodded and wiped at her cheeks with flat palms. She should sit with him silently. But she found the silence so oppressive. 'What did Papa say?'

Hans frowned. 'When?'

'When you confronted him in Buckow.'

Hans held up his hands to express the plainness of his answer. 'He was angry.'

Yes, even if he was ashamed he would have been angry. Then the memory of Father Schäfer's description of the camp seized her. Then she recalled her father's laughter and was released again.

'Do you think he felt anything else?' Hans said. She hadn't quite caught his tone. Anger? Sarcasm? She tried to answer plainly, aware as well that she wanted to push at the burden, to try and lighten it for her father, whose kind eyes she saw, and gentle hands she felt touching her head as she read.

'He must have felt guilt,' Ingrid said.

Hans reached into his jacket pocket and took out what looked like a thin brass coin, with two holes punched through the top, the German imperial crest and a five-digit number: 17645. He placed it on the table as if placing a bet.

'What is it?' said Ingrid.

'It is a passmark. This is my second one; I was given it when they released me from the camp. The government decided to hand them out to those Africans who were allowed to move about the country. When the Uprising came, that also meant those Africans whose lives meant something. When the call came to wipe out all Herero, armed or not, warrior or not, then such numbers became important. When you are being attacked by white men who do not see the difference between Nama, Herero, Ovambo, who do not even see the difference between Negro and half-caste, such marks become vital.

'Your father said he would meet me and my mother in Okahandja. We agreed to stay behind and burn down the farmhouse, make sure that the scene was set for the arrival of the authorities, so that they would believe the Baron's death was just another atrocity perpetrated by black men. But before he went he stole my original passmark and my mother's. Then he sent the authorities. My mother escaped to Waterberg. Of course she fought after that betrayal – what else could she do?

'Me they found in the burnt-out ruins of the house, my face beaten, a white man bludgeoned to death in the next-door farm. When I told them my story and they searched me, they found no passmark to prove that my story was true. I was officially nothing. My mother, they drove into the desert after the battle, men like von Ketz. He might have even seen her there. They drove her into the desert and now she is another body in the Omaheke. You found your sister, but I will never find my mother.'

Ingrid tried to imagine her father pocketing Hans and Nora's passes, knowing that he was sentencing them to death. She searched for his goodness, recalled him meeting Hans, her father's easy way with him, his warmth. 'My father approved of you terribly. I'm sure he feels guilty. I'm sure he didn't mean for you to end up in a camp.'

Hans laughed a little, a puff of air. 'Approved of me?' he said. 'How enlightened of him. I told the authorities who I was of course, so they asked your father to come and identify me. He came to the jail in Okahandja. He said he'd never seen me in his life.'

Ingrid looked up at Hans's face. It was high and stony. His eyes were wet. He was enduring still, enduring her inability to comprehend, enduring her pity.

She felt as if she was holding his story away from her, as if she were trying to decide whether she was able to take it all in and feel it. Surely that would kill her. Surely her only salvation was to never feel it, to never try and understand it, but then he made a noise like he had choked, and she realised he was trying not to cry. She felt ice-cold and empty, and knew that something had broken in her, that it had been broken for ever.

The clanking of the range roused her. Hans wiped away his tears and his face looked very clear now, very quiet.

'Did you know I loved you?' Ingrid said, desperate. There it was in the world. She had set it afloat and pushed it out, never to come back.

Hans shrank. He looked at the table top and said, 'Fräulein Ingrid, you were a child in Africa.'

'I still loved you.' His gaze remained fixed on the table. 'But you were in love with Margarete, even then. Certainly when you saw her in Buckow. Because she's beautiful. And you're only a man, after all.'

He breathed slowly and regularly; he was furious. 'You know,' he said, 'Margarete was the only person who ever talked to me like a person.'

'Margarete?' Ingrid said. 'She was a little bigot in Africa. I was the one who talked to you like a person. I'm talking to you like a person now. I never stopped thinking about you. Never.'

'Me as a person? Or me as an archetype?'

'An archetype?' Ingrid said. 'Don't talk to me like a teacher – you're not my teacher any more.'

'What do I love?' he said.

'Poetry,' she said triumphant. 'Language.'

'And what do I hate?' he said.

'What are you talking about?'

'What do I hate? In the world.'

'My father? The Hoffmanns? Me, I suppose,' Ingrid said. They heard Margarete returning from the kitchen.

'What do I hate?' Hans said to Margarete, lightening the tone of his voice, as if he were sharing the end of a joke.

'What do you hate?' said Margarete, confused, carrying a plate and wiping her fingers carelessly on her skirt. 'The damp here, the snow when it gets dirty, marzipan, the sea.' She frowned. 'Why?'

Hans's eyes met Ingrid's, and she dropped hers. 'No one hates the sea,' she muttered, her cheeks burning with shame.

Margarete sat down and put the plate on the table, containing a slice of grey rye bread, a smear of butter and a boiled egg. She touched Hans's hand and his fingers curled around hers.

'So now you know everything,' Margarete said.

Ingrid nodded. She felt as if the world beyond the room had become very silent.

'And?' Margarete said.

Ingrid let her head shake gently back and forth. There was nothing to say. Her tears had dried up.

Her sister let go of Hans and peeled the egg. She tapped it on the plate, then rolled it about in the flat of her palm. Ingrid had never seen her opening an egg like this. Where had she learned it? What had happened to her in these past years? Margarete peeled the egg in a curling strip, the membrane holding it together like the skin of an orange.

Ingrid had heard everything and felt she understood nothing.

She looked about the room, looked again at the pile of luggage with only the top case open.

'Are we in Buckow so that you can be here?'

'Yes,' Margarete said, throwing the last of the shell onto the plate. 'We're just here for a short time, though. That's why Papa only let us open up a few rooms.' She sat back in her chair with the glossy white egg balanced on her fingertips. She looked afraid.

'Where will you go?'

'Come here,' Margarete said to Manfred. The boy smiled and climbed onto her lap. She pulled open the white of the egg and gave him the powdery yolk. He laughed and bit into it. She ate some of the white herself and said, 'Back to Africa. They've reopened a route, now the war's over. There's no life here for us.'

The room landed, the furniture returned to its place on the floor, the light became normal light, her clothes settled on her body, her body on the chair. Of course, she thought, looking at the little tableau in front of her. They are leaving again.

Ingrid stood. 'Well,' she said, 'I suppose I have to get back.'

'Get back where?' Margarete said.

'To Hannah's tonight. Then back to Buckow.'

Hans looked down at the table. He has understood, Ingrid thought. Margarete looked appalled though, and said, 'But how can you go back to them now, after everything you know?'

'What else can I do?'

She went to Margarete, bent down and kissed her cheek. She touched Manfred on the head. She nodded to Hans. He moved his chair and stood. She could not smell clove oil now, only the lightest sense of his sweat, the German pomade in his hair.

407

She took her coat and walked out of the room. Margarete cried out, there was some fussing, some moving of furniture, and Manfred sobbed. Ingrid opened the door and left the apartment, she descended the first flight of stairs, as Margarete's feet pounded the floorboards. Then her voice came, echoing against the hard cold walls of the staircase. 'And after all this, you're just going to leave? That's it?'

'What can I do, Margarete? I can't lose you again, not again,' she said, crying and gripping her chest.

Margarete ran down to her and grabbed her and they fell to their knees in the icy stairwell. There they wept until Margarete fell away from her on the floor, and Ingrid, barely able to walk, wailed and descended the stairs, leaving her sister to Hans and to Africa.

She passed through the hall and onto the road, where the snow was still bright white in the coming dusk. She walked snivelling down the street, empty of traffic, down to Alt-Moabit. She crossed the bridge, over the Spree where grubby plates of ice clinked together like wine glasses, and headed to Monbijoustraße, where she could see the onion dome of the synagogue, its golden crown still shining in the dying light of the day.

*

The door opened and Trude looked out at Ingrid warily. The candlelight threw a strip of yellow over the grey-blue ice on the steps, a centimetre thick because there was no spare salt to throw on it. Trude squinted. 'Fräulein Ingrid,' she said, surprised. 'Oh do come in. Hannah will be delighted, I'm sure. Mind the ice, dear. Mind the ice.'

'I don't want to trouble anyone,' Ingrid said miserably. 'It's just I can't stay at our apartment. I can wait here, on the step.'

'Dear Lord! You'll catch your death out here, miss. Come in, come in. There's a great strike, in case the news hadn't reached you out in Buckow. They're up in arms and we're all terribly worried,' she said, guiding her through the door and into the warmth of the hallway, that smelt of good domestic things: beeswax, cologne water and white vinegar. How nice that she knows who I am, thought Ingrid. How nice that she knows about Buckow.

Trude gave her a few vigorous rubs on her arms and said disapprovingly, 'I'll fetch Fräulein Hannah, but you must go straight to the drawing room and warm yourself at the stove. You're really impossibly cold.'

Ingrid let herself be guided forward by the woman, passing through the hallway into the drawing room where, startled on the sofa, Saul sat, yellowish and thin beneath liberal layers of wool blanket. Ingrid was stung with embarrassment, but too overwhelmed to change her course, and let Trude place her by the ornate stove, that gave off a beautiful rolling heat.

'No, Herr Mandelbaum,' she said. 'Don't get up. It's only Fräulein Hoffmann, standing at the door like a wastrel or I don't know what. No, you can't stand, my dear,' she said, pushing him back down into his seat. 'Herr Mandelbaum's had the Flanders fever, miss – was struck down quite sudden, but is now recovering, thank the Lord. So we're all very pleased. But now Frau Mandelbaum's quite ill. It's been going through the city like a plague, I tell you.' She pulled at Saul's blankets. 'Their cousin Levi, poor lad, succumbed last year, and it seems it's raising its head again, as if we haven't all suffered enough. He was a strange boy though, so I can't say anyone's mourned so terribly much.'

'Trude!' Saul managed.

But the exclamation caused him to break into a crackling cough, that left him speechless for long enough for Trude to continue, 'You mustn't strain yourself, my dear. Just make sure Fräulein Hoffmann doesn't go anywhere, and I'll see if I can't find out where your sister is.'

Saul, his cough still coming in fits, looked up angrily as Trude left, but was unable to say anything further. He lay back in the armchair, took a sip of water and breathed slowly until he was able to manage, with genuine concern, 'Are you quite all right, Fräulein Hoffmann?' And then with a deep breath, 'You don't look well.'

Ingrid stared at Saul. He looked up at her with genuine compassion, his hair very black on his unshaven chin, against his pallid face. She stood clinging to herself in her fur coat. A puff of air forced its way out of her nose. Then another and she started to laugh. Saul looked briefly confused and then laughed as well, coughing and laughing in turn, until feet on the stairs forced them to calm themselves, and their laughter came only in fits, leaving tears on their cheeks.

'Good God! Ingrid dear, what an earth are you doing here?'

Ingrid looked up and opened her mouth, but what could she say? Hannah slowed and said, 'Did no one take your coat?'

'I'm so cold,' Ingrid managed, though her voice had become quiet and rasping, as if she were also sick.

'Well, the heat of the stove won't get through that thing,' she said, attacking the hooks and eyes of the fur coat and pulling it off her, throwing it onto the rug with a harrumph, like an animal shot dead mid-leap. Ingrid gripped herself and Hannah unpinned her hat.

'There,' Hannah said, tossing Ingrid's hat down on top of the coat. 'Let me pour you some cognac.'

Hannah went to the decanter and looked back up at Ingrid as she poured. Ingrid felt the heat of the stove working its way through the thick cotton of her jacket, then her blouse, then her chemise, finally reaching her skin.

'Well, you'd better tell us what's happened. Don't mind Saul,' Hannah said, pre-empting Ingrid's concern. But she wasn't concerned about Saul. She felt as if she was drifting out into the middle of a great lake, without any sense of where the bank lay.

'Margarete's alive,' Ingrid said.

Hannah stopped pouring. Her face turned as pale as her brother's. She attempted to respond to this statement a few times, then looked down at the crystal stopper in her hand, as if she might divine the answer there. 'Where?' she said.

'In Berlin.'

'Good God!'

'Your sister who died?' Ingrid heard. It was Saul. She turned to him. He looked at her with such frank concern that she looked away at once and stared down at the circles and diamonds of intertwining white flowers on the blue rug. She traced a circle with the toe of her shoe until she was able to say, 'She's not dead. She's here in Berlin. She's going back to Africa, though, so I've had to leave her again.'

She moved the toe around the square, then back to the circle, touched each little green flower, and related the story of the last few days, of the letter from Herr Winzer, of the little red house, her father on the ice of the lake, her journey to Berlin and the meeting with her sister and Hans, and finally her journey here to the Mandelbaums' drawing room.

When she looked up Hannah was still standing at the open decanter, the stopper still in her hand. 'Ingrid, it's unbelievable,' she said. She looked at her brother.

'It beggars belief,' he said.

'It's all so gothic,' Hannah said, but not with her usual pointed irony; it was a statement of fact.

She continued to pour two glasses of cognac as if she had only been interrupted for a second, and then went to the divan and threw out her hand, inviting Ingrid to sit next to her.

Ingrid did so. Her mind was full of images of Africa, of sand and stone, of camps filled with dying men and women, of her sister beating the Baron to death with a bottle.

Ingrid took a gulp of cognac and let it burn in her as she looked down at the patterned rug in the hope that moronically following its trailing flora would free her mind, but knowing that nothing would free it now.

'Has it been terrible here?' she asked, still staring at the floor.

'Oh Ingrid, don't let's talk about here.'

'But I can't bear to think about it any more. Tell me what it's been like here. Is it all collapsing around us? Will there be anything left?'

Hannah paused thoughtfully. 'Well, you've heard about Eichhorn, the chief of police, I suppose?'

Ingrid shook her head. 'Tell me,' she said. 'Anything. Please.'

'Well, after the massacre of the sailors at the Palace, things were already very bad. And the only person who refused to fire on the sailors was Eichhorn, which, naturally, the Chancellor saw as treason. So Ebert's fired him. Of course the communists have risen up against Ebert and the government, against the republic. But they can't win it, Ingrid. If Mother weren't struck down with this flu, I would be worried for her life on that account, because of her associations. I'm terribly worried about Liebknecht and Luxemburg. I'm worried about all of them. There's not enough communists to win against Ebert and the militias. The communists are all out on the streets. Perhaps they'll have a chance if the numbers are there, but I don't see—'

'Shall we go?' Ingrid said.

Hannah's face shimmered. 'And do what?'

'March with them.'

'Fräulein Hoffmann!' Saul said. 'They killed seventy people at the Palace. On Christmas Eve.'

'Shall we go?' Ingrid said again.

'The militias are vicious,' Hannah said.

'We can't just let it happen,' Ingrid said. 'We could do something, instead of sitting here like everyone else, waiting in our drawing rooms. We could be out there in it. What else have we got? There's nothing else left.'

Hannah turned her head, as if she had heard something. She sat like this thoughtfully for what felt to Ingrid like an interminable length of time. Then she stood and went into the hall. She came back wearing her coat. 'Quick then,' she said.

Ingrid picked her things up from the floor.

'Hannah! Will you stop!' Saul said.

'Goodbye, dear,' she said and kissed her brother's forehead. 'We'll be quite all right. Don't you dare tell Mother – she's in a bad enough way as it is.'

'Hannah!' Saul cried again, but they were already on the steps, hand in hand.

It was so cold that Ingrid's face hurt and the exposed parts of her gloved hand were numb, even though it was held tight in Hannah's. They didn't dare look at each other, but pushed on past Monbijou Palace, to Hackescher Markt. It was so empty that Ingrid became afraid that they would find no one, that everything that the newspapers had reported was a lie, that there was no revolution, no strike, that there had been no war.

'Ingrid,' Hannah said. They saw men running beneath the railway bridge that led to Zirkus Busch. Ingrid thought she heard the high hush of a train on metal tracks, but realised it was the gathered cries of a crowd. Men and a spattering of women appeared around them as they crossed the bridge onto Museum Island, and there they found, in the darkness of the winter afternoon, the crowd, surging between the freezing stone columns of Schinkel's pseudo-Roman Forum, past the domes of the cathedral and then the palace, the colossal public statues beset with men, like swarming bees, men hanging from the outstretched arms of Kaisers and muses, swinging red flags, placards jumping above the plain of people like the sails of ships, the smell of bodies, of gunpowder, of hungry mouths, shouting, screaming, the sound of gunshots and fireworks, and Hannah and Ingrid holding hands, screaming, throwing their fists into the air, surging forward with the crowd, until they were the crowd, until they were part of the body flooding Unter den Linden like a river, streaming down to the Reichstag, to the centre of Berlin.

PART SIX

— Swimming —

Born-am-Darß, Mecklenburg-Western Pomerania

— June 1924 —

The meeting was in a thatched house, with a cool terra-cotta hallway connecting the front and back doors, and a large drawing room filled with chairs gathered from neighbouring homes. The owner of the house, Frau Zawadzki, a plump grey-haired woman, stood at the back of the room near the small low windows, misted white by the bright sunlight. A bumblebee was caught at the glass, buzzing in deep bursts. The house smelt of lingering breakfast coffee, bread and cut grass. Exhausted from a night awake with the baby, Ingrid had wanted to pass Frau Zawadzki when she arrived, walk straight through to the back garden and fall asleep in the shade of a sycamore tree. Instead she helped lay out the literature and waited anxiously for people to arrive.

Slowly the room filled and Frau Zawadzki signalled that they should begin.

The audience listened attentively. Only one woman in the front row seemed uninterested, concerned instead with something stuck beneath her nail; a click-click-clicking that

Ingrid had to grind her teeth to endure. The other women sat still, sometimes nodded in agreement, sometimes frowned and blinked when the points that Ingrid and Hannah made were more socialist than they were used to.

In their first meetings, the audience had tired when just one of them spoke. Now they spoke together, standing, Hannah beginning, making the audience laugh, Ingrid following, Hannah breaking in, Ingrid finishing, as she did now. 'In the first Federal Election,' she said, 'the first time that women were allowed any kind of active role in politics, women represented nine per cent of the Reichstag. This has dropped, ladies, to just six per cent in the last election, a drop reflected in our own German Democratic Party. We are enfranchised and we are fifty per cent of the German Reich; that six per cent must become fifty. The Reichstag is better with us in it. It is more balanced, it is fairer.'

Ingrid nodded to signal that she had finished speaking, pleased with this last rhetorical flourish. The women clapped politely.

They waited for questions, a pile of membership enquiry forms beside them, but no one came forward. As the room cleared, the women nodded pleasantly, not quite meeting their eyes. An elderly lady approached them, dressed in a blue artist's smock. 'Are you the poet?' she said to Ingrid.

Ingrid smiled. 'No, I'm not a poet.'

'Are you not Ingrid Hoffmann?'

'Mandelbaum now,' Ingrid said.

'But this is yours, isn't it?'

Ingrid saw that she was holding her book. The cover was blue, the slim serif letters silver; Frau von Galen rejected the masculine ugliness of German Gothic script. It read: *Echoes: 50 Women's Poems*. Only inside did it reveal that the poems were English and French and that they had been 'Selected and translated by Ingrid Hoffmann'.

While still recovering from a gash above her eye, sustained during the march in Berlin when the police had charged the crowd, Ingrid had called on Frau von Galen. Under her patronage the laborious process of putting the book together had begun, with Ingrid working in Hannah's father's old study, a few months after Frau Mandelbaum had died, leaving Hannah and Saul orphans and the house quiet and filled with sadness. She had finished the book in June 1919, on the first day that they had been able to leave the windows open all day long, only closing them when the sky darkened and the rooms started to fill with moths and bright green lacewings. Sweating with mental effort in the candlelight, she had been elated.

'My goodness,' said Ingrid, astounded to see the little cloth-bound book in a stranger's hands. 'I'm just the translator. But how wonderful that you have it.'

'Well, I liked it very much,' the woman said, and quoted a line to her, *'Can the flower of friendship wither years, and then revive anew? No, though the soil is wet with tears, How fragrant it once grew.'*

'Why, you've learned it off by heart!' Ingrid said, filled with both joy and embarrassment, neither of which she could bear in public.

She turned to Hannah, who said, 'Oh Ingrid! Finally! A devotee!'

And the woman laughed pleasantly. 'Are you working on something new?'

'I am. I'd always wanted to translate *Aurora Leigh* – it's long of course. And there's been a lot of work for the Party,' she said, indicating the untouched forms on the table, 'but it's coming on slowly.'

'And she's become a mother,' Hannah added.

Ingrid nodded and smiled. 'Yes, I've also had a baby.'

The woman held up the book and said, 'Well, I loved it. I can't wait to read what you're working on now.' She gave her a visiting card. 'Please let me know when you've written more.'

'I will,' Ingrid said, and the woman left them to thank Frau Zawadzki, the village's only German Democrat, for her hospitality.

*

Hannah and Ingrid walked back to the cottage that they were renting for a few weeks that summer. The trees along the side of the road were filled with blackbirds in song.

'What are you thinking about?' Hannah asked.

'Rosa,' said Ingrid.

'What about her?'

'She has become rather a benchmark,' Ingrid said, 'whenever we do anything political. I think of her and then ...'

'Ask yourself whether it's all futile?'

Ingrid laughed. 'Yes.'

When the uprising turned violent, Rosa had gone into hiding with Karl Liebknecht. They were found and friends saw them arrested by Captain Pabst's men. Hannah and Ingrid knew the outcome would be grim. Still, Ingrid's blood ran cold when she saw their grainy pictures side-by-side, like the Kaiser and Kaiserin, on the front of the newspapers. They had been questioned, tortured and beaten. Karl Liebknecht was taken to the Tiergarten and shot. Ingrid imagined his body bleeding on the frozen path, the grey branches above him reaching up into the sky. Rosa was knocked to the floor with a rifle butt in the room they had interrogated her in and shot in the head. Liebknecht was delivered, nameless, to a morgue, Rosa thrown into the Landswehr Canal. The body emerged four months later.

Ingrid cycled through these thoughts; they brought her no relief, but felt necessary.

She took out the key to the cottage – it was dark-grey metal, the length of her hand – but when they approached the door was already open and her daughter Sybille was sitting on the doorstep, her feet pounding the grass. Saul came out of the door and scooped the child up and she screamed and cackled and then sat happily in her father's arms, until Ingrid was close, then she tipped over and clung to her, scrambled on to her.

Saul leaned forward as Sybille was passed over, and kissed Ingrid on the mouth, his hand on her waist. She was tired, but she felt full up and happy. He smiled at her and said, 'Were they terribly impressed?'

'We won them over! Every last one of them!' Hannah shouted, her voice echoing around the bare walls of the cottage as she passed inside. 'I'm getting my swimming things and we're going to the beach.'

Sybille held tight to Ingrid's hair, burbled and kissed her cheek wetly.

'How was it?' Saul whispered.

'Fine,' she said quietly. 'I don't think we converted the masses.'

*

The path from the cottage to the sea led them through the wood. The beech, oak and Scots pine were still, as was the deep carpet of ferns, and the air was filled with sweetness. Sybille wouldn't walk, so Ingrid carried her in her arms and

Sybille threw herself backwards, so that, upside down, she could look at her father and her aunt. For a few minutes she was thrilled by the echo that her screams made, and cried out, a piercing bird-like cry, that filled the woods, until Ingrid was able to hush her.

The sound made Ingrid think of the peacock in Buckow and von Ketz, her parents and Margarete, finally Hans. She counted back the years and realised that Manfred must be ten. It wasn't a disturbing thought, because her picture of him at that age was so abstract. What was strange was the thought of Margarete at thirty-five, the mother of a ten-year-old. And then what? But, with relief, she realised that she need not solve that puzzle now; that Margarete, Hans and Manfred would live on without her in Africa, would manage; that since the wedding they had survived perfectly well without her. In fact, almost everyone in the world survived perfectly well without her, and finally the thought did not terrify her.

They heard the sea. The trees around them shrank and leant back, away from the salty air and into the forest. The path widened and the ground softened, sand spilling through a gap in the grassy dunes. The sand led them to the beach, studded only with a few bathers and a number of open Strandkorb seats, their salt-worn candy stripes hidden behind their high wicker backs.

The moment Sybille saw the sea, she whined for it, twisting in Ingrid's arms. They had put on their bathing suits beneath their clothes, and Ingrid waited for Saul to remove his shoes and socks, shirt and trousers, before handing her to him. She watched him make his way down the beach with her, holding her hand as she walked, Saul always more patient than she was able to be. The sun lit up the red bands of his bathing suit and the whiteness of his skin and the blackness of the hair on his head, beneath his arms and down his legs. Thank God for Saul, she thought.

Hannah and Ingrid also changed into their bathing things, but, finding a Strandkorb empty, they paid the beach warden twenty pfennigs and sat side by side in the padded chair, their bare legs touching.

Ingrid took an envelope from her bag and squinted at it.

'Are you going to read it?' Hannah said.

'Yes,' she said. 'I think I must.'

Hannah squinted up at the sky, then looked towards Saul. She sat forward and pulled her swimming cap on, buttoning it up under the chin. 'I might go and swim straight away, you know. It is rather warm, after all.'

'Oh,' Ingrid said. 'You don't have to.'

'Let me,' she said, and left Ingrid to her letter alone.

She picked it open and took out the blue sheets, covered in the familiar looping script of her mother.

Dearest Ingrid,

The briefest note to say how happy we were to see you at Windscheidstraße. We were sad again not to meet your husband, but we will take the scraps that are thrown us and I hope that time will continue to heal. You looked so well, dearest Ingrid, and you really are still your father's joy, so please don't keep away from us if you can bear it.

Baron von Ketz (I know what you'll say, you little socialist, but what else am I meant to call him now? Herr von Ketz? It sounds too ridiculous) was very ill with the Flanders fever this spring and it turned into pneumonia, but he has survived it, by the grace of God.

What troubles that man has had and still how generous he is. Horvath remains a delight and, while I don't mean it as any judgement of your life since we last saw you, I can't help thinking that he is a wonderful 'son' of sorts to have around. He is such a comfort to von Ketz.

I read your book of poems; if we were on better terms I should have scolded you terribly for not telling me about it. Gottlieb, that good friend of Fräulein von Torgelow, mentioned it at the most exquisitely boring dinner. I was embarrassed, I must admit, because they don't know about our troubles, but the point is that I found it wonderful. I particularly loved the Brontë poems – I knew her novels as a girl – yes your mother isn't such a dullard – and you have captured her essence exactly. You were always a talent, dearest Ingrid. We never pretended otherwise.

My indigestion has achieved brave new heights. Dr Ammann says he's never seen the like, and worries for my voice.

Your darling father is well, though, I need not repeat, he misses you. Be kind to him. Be kind to us and forgiving. We have always tried our best, even when it might seem that we haven't. We have all done so much wrong, every one of us, but so often it is in pursuit of something else that seems right. As your precious one grows, you will see this yourself, no doubt.

We will be in Königsberg for a month in September, because your father has some business there – to think, we will now have to travel through 'Poland' to get there. I will send you a forwarding address for us for that time, which is not – as I know you will be thinking – because you have to write to us, but just in case there was an emergency or you suddenly did write to us at Windscheidstraße and you didn't get an answer. I couldn't bear the idea that you might be waiting thinking it was we who were angry with you.

So my dear Ingrid, I hope your little family is well. We long to meet the little one. We long to.

With love my darling one,
    Mama and Papa

P.S. Child in Africa had typhus. Now recovered.

Ingrid was unsure if this hurried last sentence referred to Margarete or to Manfred. She pictured them both sick on the farm in Africa, but then drove the image from her mind and looked back out at the sea. Hannah's head was far out, a black speck in the royal blue of the deep water. Was she going out or coming back?

She watched Saul throw Sybille into the air. She remembered the feel of his cold wet skin beneath his swimming costume after he had peeled it off the day before, his mouth tasting of sea salt and his neck at her mouth smelling of sweet sea air.

Hannah's head had grown and her pale shoulders appeared from the water. She ran back up the beach, shouting out some joke to Saul, who laughed drily at it, as he swung his daughter around by the arms, a trail of sparkling water like shattered glass whipping off her legs in a curve.

Hannah was suddenly by Ingrid, water dripping onto the white sand, making little brown platelets in it. 'Come and lie with me while I dry out,' she said.

Ingrid followed her and lay down beside her. The heat of the sun was tempered by a warm breeze. Ingrid thought about the previous evening, the sound of Saul and Hannah chatting downstairs while she was given her two hours at the desk, which was now just referred to as 'Ingrid's Two'. In the holiday cottage they were renting it was at a little desk in the room that Hannah slept in. Ingrid worked by the window, smoking her pipe, until it was too dark to see, then she closed the window and lit a candle and was accompanied for the last half-hour by her own reflection in the black glass.

Her favourite moment was just before her handwriting became illegible in the dark, when the paper, her body, the garden outside and the lagoon beyond were painted in a muted palette of cornflower blue and indigo. She thought about Hans and the phrase repeated automatically, *Commejedesendey flovesimpossible jenemesontiploogiday parlesaler.* She breathed in the scent of the mock orange blossom around the window and was filled with joy and saddened by her inability to hold on to that joy, saddened that she was even thinking about that joy, rather than just experiencing it.

'What was that poem that that woman quoted to you?' Hannah said.

Ingrid opened her eyes and blinked at Hannah's face, the trees and the sand behind her, which the sun, pink through Ingrid's eyelids, had temporarily washed all the colour from. 'It was Emily Brontë. "Come Walk with Me".'

Hannah, shading her eyes with her hand, said, 'Go on then.'

'What?' Ingrid said.

'Say it for me.'

'Oh good God, no!' Ingrid said, closing her eyes and putting her head back down on the sand.

'Such false modesty!' Hannah cried, so loudly that Saul shouted, 'What?' from the water's edge.

'Your wife's being unduly modest!' Hannah shouted back.

'Yes, she does that!'

Ingrid laughed. She put her hands on her stomach where the black wool of her swimming costume had become pleasantly warm in the sunshine.

'Now come on Ingrid. Make this moment a bit more contemplative. You must know it off by heart. Don't be shy Ingrid, dearest – I want to be impressed. I want to feel like I only love the most impressive people.'

Ingrid smiled. *'Come, walk with me—'*

'Wonderful!' Hannah cried, and dropped her head back to the sand, closing her eyes.

Ingrid laughed again.

'Start again, start again,' Hannah said, 'I've ruined it.'

Ingrid began again.

> *'Come, walk with me.*
> *Only you can see*
> *to bless my soul now –*
> *Once we made love on a winter night,*
> *wandered through the snow;*
> *Can we not rekindle that old delight?*
> *The clouds rush by black and wild*
> *Spraying shade across mountain cliffs,*
> *As they did long ago,*
> *And at the horizon they rest at last,*
> *Piled in looming masses,*
> *And moonbeams flare and fly so fast*
> *We scarcely see their flashes.*

'Come, walk with me, come walk with me;
Once our number grew,
But death beats us back like the sea
And sunshine steals the dew –
Death plucked at us one by one and we
are left, the only two;
Now my love conquers just your shores,
they have no anchor but for yours –

'"Don't tell me that it may not be
that human love is true.
Can the flower of friendship wither years
and then revive anew?
No, though the soil is wet with tears,
How fragrant it once grew
The living sap once gone
Will never flow again
And more sure than that living dread
The narrow coffin of deadly
Time splits the hearts of men."'

They listened to Sybille screaming and splashing in the water, the sound of Saul roaring at her.

'Ever cheery,' Hannah said, and poked Ingrid's bare leg.

Ingrid laughed. 'Poetry's not for optimists.'

Hannah laughed back, but the expected retort didn't come. She took Ingrid's hand. 'Let's never go back,' she said.

'Where to?'

But Hannah didn't answer. She just let her head roll back on the sand and became very still as if she had fallen asleep. Ingrid sighed. 'I always want to go back,' she said, turning

428

from Hannah and covering her eyes with the crook of her elbow. 'But not today.' Saul called her name, called for her to come down to the sea and, distantly, half obscured by the yaps of gulls, a cord struck a metal flagpole, ringing out to them on the beach like a bell.

Further Reading

Although I remain unconvinced that novelists should publish extensive bibliographies for historical works that are explicitly fictional, I do wish to both credit a few books that were hugely helpful to me in my research and suggest some further reading, both fictional and nonfictional, that I could recommend should the subjects covered have sparked an interest.

My sense of Berlin directly after the war was hugely influenced by Alfred Döblin's *A People Betrayed*, of which there is a wonderful translation by John E. Woods that is sadly out of print, but still available in libraries. The research of my book also happily coincided with an excellent exhibition at the German Historical Museum entitled *Der Erste Weltkrieg: 1914–1918*. Sadly, the accompanying book (*Der Erste Weltkrieg in 100 Objekten*) doesn't mirror the exhibition exactly, and isn't published in English, but does give an engaging visual overview of the First World War from the German perspective. Hardly an obscure recommendation, but if it is new to you, I would highly recommend

Erich Maria Remarque's novel of German soldiers in the First World War, *All Quiet on the Western Front* (the original German title of which translates less poetically, but much more bitingly, as *In the West, Nothing New*). It remains so readable, and is filled with human warmth, even as it's describing the most atrocious horrors.

For a general understanding of the German Revolution of 1918, I can recommend Stefan Berger's *Inventing the Nation*, about the roots of German national identity, and Mary Fulbrook's *A History of Germany 1918–2008: A Divided Nation*, an excellent overview. There are a number of biographies specifically on Rosa Luxemburg, but I was most moved by her letters, which have been published as *The Letters of Rosa Luxemburg*; many letters are also available online.

There are sadly relatively few book-length titles, either in German or English, that cover the Uprising and subsequent genocide of the Herero and Nama peoples in what is now Namibia. This is in part because the atrocities appear to some, perhaps, as a footnote to the greater genocide enacted by the German state four decades later. More importantly, the chilling truth about a genocide successfully carried out, especially one on a people with little written culture, is that it erases history and culture with it. Nevertheless, Jon M. Bridgman's *The Revolt of the Hereros* seems to me a very good summary of the terrible events that form the backdrop to this book. It is a balanced and readable account, carefully researched while remaining very aware of the impossibilities of relating the full story when half of the players were exterminated. As fiction goes, again the field is sparse, but I am always happy to recommend Uwe Timm, whose novel *Morenga* is available in English in an award-winning translation by Breon Mitchell.

Acknowledgements

I am overjoyed to be working with Little, Brown again. I thank them for their support and remain particularly indebted to Clare Smith for her boundless encouragement and outstanding editing.

I would like to thank my agent Karolina Sutton at Curtis Brown for her continuing sage advice, support and fine Polish dining experiences. I also want to thank Lucy Morris at Curtis Brown, for her speedy and enthusiastic responses to all my dull questions.

I want to thank all of the early readers of this novel, in particular Christine Garfath and Toby Garfath, and, as ever, my mum, Loraine Fergusson. I would also like to thank the many friends and colleagues who have discussed the book with me, particularly Michael Ammann, who has to put up with my typing, sighing and prevaricating on a daily basis.

I would like to thank the many people who shared their experiences of Namibia with me, particularly Laila Akhlaghi, Edith Baker and Katharina Eva Will. Special thanks go to the Namibian writer Naomi Beukes-Meyer, for her careful reading and feedback on the Namibian section of the book.

In researching this book, I have also been blessed with access to many wonderful libraries. I would particularly like to thank all the lovely staff at the London Library, the Bristol University Library, the Library of the German Historical Institute London and the Berlin State Library for their help and advice.

Biggest thanks and eternal gratitude have to go, as always, to my husband Tom, who has read countless versions of this book, given me invaluable advice along the way and always been there for everything that mattered.